THE BEST PART OF LOVE

AMY D'ORAZIO

Quills & Quartos
PUBLISHING

Dedicated to Allie and Lexi who are far and above the best things to ever happen to me

TABLE OF CONTENTS

PROLOGUE

LONDON, AUGUST 1811

E lizabeth, at the window of her sitting room, was charmed by the scene before her. It was a warm, sunny day with the gardens in full bloom and a small bunny hopping about madly while two sweet little boys—babies, really—squealed, laughed, and futilely tried to catch it. It was a hopeful sort of day, even for someone who had long since given up on hope.

She winced as the smaller of the two boys tried desperately to reach the bunny and instead fell face-first on the stone-paved walk. Ever the stoic, he permitted himself only the slightest of whimpers from the safety of his nursemaid's arms before pushing away and seeking the bunny again. Elizabeth shook her head as she watched him run, worrying he was too small for his age and wondering how he might be tempted into eating more than he presently did.

"Lizzy, my dear, why do you shake your head so?"

Elizabeth turned to her aunt and smiled. "He is so small. Little Edward is destined to be a good bit taller, it would seem. Henry never eats."

Lady Gardiner smiled. "It is the curse we bear as mothers. No matter what we see, there will be something over which to fret. Henry is a fine boy and growing well. He favours you. One could hardly expect any child of yours to be large, not unless you were to marry a man of much larger stature."

The idea of marriage made Elizabeth frown. Before she could reply, Mrs Baynes, her housekeeper, entered. "Lord and Lady Matlock have arrived."

"Oh yes, Lady Matlock said that she and the earl wished to speak to me this week."

"Would you like me to leave?" asked Lady Gardiner.

"No, I cannot think there is anything they will say that you cannot hear, and if Lord Matlock thinks otherwise, he is sure to tell us straightaway. He is ever celebrated for his frankness." She laughed lightly, and her aunt joined her.

"I cannot disagree. Very good, I shall stay."

Elizabeth sent for some tea, and soon the door opened, and the Earl and Countess of Matlock were announced. The needed pleasantries were made, and Lady Matlock moved to the window to observe the two little boys at play.

"Lady Gardiner, where are your elder children?"

"Still at home in the schoolroom, my lady, with their governess." Lady Gardiner smiled and indicated the seat next to hers. The Countess took the offered chair while the earl sat next to Elizabeth on the settee.

When all were settled, Elizabeth gave Lady Matlock an expectant look, and she, in turn, looked at her husband. He cleared his throat awkwardly.

"Elizabeth, you are looking very well—very well, indeed, my dear. I believe it was just your birthday, was it not?"

Elizabeth nodded warily, knowing that, when the earl resorted to overt flattery, it generally meant he wanted something. "Yes, last week."

Lord Matlock chuckled in a determinedly cheerful manner. "Finally of age, dear?"

"I am just twenty."

Lady Matlock shook her head. "Your experience has far outpaced your years."

Elizabeth acknowledged her with the slightest inclination of her head.

There was an awkward silence while the occupants of the room stirred their tea, glanced out the window, or shifted uneasily in their seats. Finally, Lord Matlock spoke.

"I have good news for you. The key persons involved in the...ah... situation, one might say...have been...well, they have been...they are no longer of concern. Some met a different end—with these sorts of people, anything is possible. All are accounted for except the gunman, but he is not important. We believe he did not understand his part but was only doing as told. I doubt he even knows your identity. They will still seek him, of course, but he is not considered a threat to you."

Elizabeth inhaled deeply. "So, that means…"

"You and his lordship are out of danger. You can go on with your life as you knew it."

"My life as I knew it." Elizabeth gave a bitter little laugh. "I am sure I do not even know what that means. My life as I knew it no longer exists. What am I? A country girl? A newly married peer? A young, widowed mother? I cannot say which version is the real one."

"Oh, Lizzy—" Lady Gardiner began, but Lord Matlock continued in a brisk tone that he likely felt would hearten her.

"You will make a new life, I believe, one that encompasses the new with the old. You are Lady Courtenay and have many responsibilities, both to your husband's estates and to his lordship. Of course, his lordship is your first concern."

"Yes, I know." Elizabeth spoke sharply, giving Lord Matlock a severe look.

Lady Matlock laid a quieting hand on her husband's arm with a look that mimicked Elizabeth's. Her words, directed at Elizabeth, were soothing. "You have done so much; no one could fault you, my dear. Lord Matlock would not suggest otherwise."

"Certainly not," the earl agreed. "But it is time to go on."

"Go on?" Elizabeth raised an eyebrow. "What does that mean?"

An awkward pause ensued until Lord Matlock ventured forth. "We have spoken of this before, and as you are aware, your boy requires a father, and the only way he will get one—"

"I am in mourning!" Elizabeth exclaimed, pressing a hand to her bosom. "I lost my husband!"

"Two years ago! I do realise, based on your tender age—"

The settee screeched in protest as Elizabeth leapt to her feet and stood over Lord Matlock, her colour high. "My age has nothing to do with it! I loved Henry, and I shall not defame the memory of my husband."

Lord Matlock was not cowed. He stood, raising his voice over hers. "Lord Courtenay would wish you to live up to the expectation—"

"Lord Courtenay is presently out of doors chasing a bunny!" Elizabeth shouted over him. "He has no expectation of *anything* beyond some biscuits later!"

Lady Gardiner rose hastily, coming to stand with them. She placed one hand on Elizabeth's back. "Let us lay down our arms. I do not wish for Elizabeth to become distraught."

With that, all were recalled to their manners and propriety. Lord Matlock tossed himself into the nearest chair with only a faint grumble indicating he was not truly offended. His wife gave him a reproachful glance, and he looked away, repentant.

Elizabeth was re-seated, blinking back tears. They mean well. They only want what is best for Henry…and for me. Quietly, she said, "Pray forgive me. I find myself a bit melancholy today. The anniversary you know…'tis a rather difficult time."

Lady Matlock leaned forward. "Yes, my dear, but it will get easier. I promise."

Elizabeth nodded.

The countess continued, "Elizabeth, you have done more, and done it better, than any lady could. You do credit to yourself, the Courtenay family, and your own family. So please understand that what I say, I say with only the highest degree of respect."

Elizabeth looked at her warily.

"Your son is a peer, and as such, he must be raised in a certain way —a way with which you are not familiar. There are things he needs, things that a father—the right sort of father—will provide. Guidance, experience, and the wisdom of generations are all necessary for a young man who will one day help shape the future of England."

Elizabeth sighed and turned her face towards the window.

Lord Matlock spoke, his tone calmer than it had been earlier. "It will be to your advantage as well. Surely, you would like more children? You would not wish young Henry to be without brothers and sisters, would you?"

Elizabeth stared sullenly out the window. "The notion of meeting gentlemen with the design of finding a husband is alarming. I was scarcely out when I married, and the society of Meryton is hardly the *haut ton*. I know nothing of identifying suitable gentlemen or turning away the dissipated. Alas, any mistake I should make will have significant consequence, not only for me but for my son."

She turned her head to see the earl and countess exchanging

glances. Lord Matlock slowly put his hand into his pocket and withdrew a paper.

"Your concerns do you credit," he said gently. "Naturally, we should wish to provide every manner of assistance to you—arrange it all for you if you like."

"What is that?" Elizabeth asked suspiciously.

Lady Matlock offered an explanation. "Among the higher circles of society, arrangements between houses are still common. Your next marriage will ideally elevate you and your son, along with any future children. If nothing else, you must ensure the estates and your husband's family name do not diminish. You must do that much for your late husband and for young Lord Courtenay."

"So that page would be…?" Elizabeth raised an eyebrow and fixed her gaze on Lord Matlock.

He shrugged and looked a bit sheepish. "Suitable prospects, if you will. Gentlemen who would be worthy of your consideration and who we believe are amenable to a match."

Elizabeth rolled her eyes. "You wish to broker my next marriage? Broker me?"

"No, no," Lord Matlock said hastily. "Of course not, not at all… unless you would wish us to do so?"

Elizabeth gave a huff of annoyance. In truth, the notion seemed reasonable. Once the necessity of remarriage was acknowledged, it was as sensible a scheme for obtaining a husband as any, particularly because the idea of falling in love again was absurd. She could not fall in love because she was already in love with a dead man's memory. Thus, her object in a future marriage partner was one who was kind, intelligent, and a good father—one with the appropriate standing in society and who did not physically repulse her. The earl and countess were certainly as capable of judging those qualities as she was.

Elizabeth resisted the idea a moment longer, looking back towards the window. She could not see her son but heard his shrieks of laughter, and she imagined him running about on the grass. Did they still seek the bunny, or had they gone on to a new game?

Rising in her seat, she took the paper from Lord Matlock's hand. She unfolded it and began to read. "Lord Reginald Rochford of Oxfordshire, age thirty, never wed. Mr George Allen, heir of Allen Park in Hertfordshire, age forty, widower."

Lady Matlock interjected, "He is forty but a very well-favoured gentleman. You would not think him a moment past his thirtieth year."

Elizabeth gave her a doubtful glance and kept reading. "The Viscount Beauchamp, age three and twenty, never married. The Viscount de Comyn, age eight and twenty, never married. Colonel Richard Fitzwilliam—" She gave Lord Matlock a severe look.

"My son," he admitted. "Recently returned from the Continent and a fine man, but I would not forward him over the others."

"Thank you," Elizabeth spoke drily. She suddenly felt too fatigued to continue reading the remaining twenty or so names on the list. She folded the page, laying it on a small table, then went to the window and looked down on the boys playing in the garden. "I suppose your coming here today should not surprise me. I have seen your impatience growing."

"It is not my impatience," the earl protested. "Rather, it is an urgency born of the growth seen in your son and a new confidence that you are both safe at last."

Elizabeth sighed, unable to disagree. "Is there one you favour? Mind you, I am not agreeing to this; I am only curious."

Lady Matlock replied, "There are several we look upon favourably. Is there something you would wish us to consider in the selection?"

Elizabeth turned back to face the room, squaring her shoulders. "None who are fair. He must be tall, and I prefer dark eyes and curly hair."

Lord Matlock, returned to jovial spirits by having nearly prevailed in his quest for the day, remarked, "Well, if that is not the very opposite of the late Lord Courtenay, I cannot think what is!"

"My point exactly," replied Elizabeth. "I cannot consider anyone who looks even slightly similar to my late husband."

Elizabeth considered a moment further. "I shall not decide this now. What I should like—nay, what I insist upon—is to spend the autumn in Hertfordshire as I have been, as Miss Elizabeth Bennet. I require a few months to accustom myself to the changes about to occur in my life."

"It is settled then. The decree will remain until the first of January." Lord Matlock agreed readily, his prize within grasp.

Lady Matlock spoke, her voice cautious. "Elizabeth, if I may offer a word of advice. This business of finding a marriage partner can be difficult. Lord Courtenay settled an extraordinary fortune on you, particularly as you came to the marriage with nothing. There are few ladies with a fortune as splendid as yours, few with such connexions as yours, and you are young and beautiful as well."

"Thank you."

Lord Matlock added, "I dare say the man you marry will earn some sort of favour from Prinny himself."

Elizabeth nodded, but she did not entirely comprehend their meaning.

The countess continued. "The machinations and arrangements that might arise could be rather ruthless. The gentleman who marries you will have much to gain from the alliance, thus there will be many dishonourable men willing to stop at nothing to obtain you. Even those who are honourable might go to great lengths to have you.

"I say this not to frighten you but merely to caution you. It would be daunting for the most worldly of ladies, but for one of your tender years with no experience among the *ton*, it worries me."

Elizabeth looked down at her teacup. "I understand why this match should be arranged, but I am not yet willing to concede. Allow me the autumn, and we shall see to more in January."

The earl and countess smiled graciously at Elizabeth, and with a few more encouraging remarks, the topic was done. Business now aside, they took tea until Lord Courtenay was deemed ready for his nap. He was brought to his mother for a kiss and some soothing over a skinned knee that had ensued from his determined pursuit of the bunny.

His lordship was an amiable and friendly child, apt to see a friend in every strange face, but Lady Matlock was well known to him, and he toddled towards her readily. The countess exclaimed in delight. She made no secret of her readiness to become a grandmother, though with two bachelor sons, such pleasures were not imminent. She pulled the boy onto her silken lap, cuddling and tickling him. Lord Matlock was equally interested in Henry, showing him a trick involving a handkerchief and a coin and revelling in the little boy's excited laughter.

AFTER A BRIEF VISIT WITH THE YOUNG LORD, THE MATLOCKS departed. As they walked the short distance to their townhouse, Lord Matlock asked, "Might I assume we are of a like mind on this matter?"

His wife gave him a quick nod and smile. "Being that she

expressed her disinclination for another fair-haired husband, our two sons are out of the running, and I so wished to have her in the family."

"Darcy could have no objection to her."

Lady Matlock laughed lightly. "Perhaps not to her, but he will object violently to the notion of our attempting to marry him off."

"Perhaps not." Lord Matlock enjoyed the look of surprise on his wife's countenance. "I do think Darcy at last recognises that his homes would benefit from a mistress and his sister from having a sister. Once he will admit he is in need of a wife, it will fall to us, I assure you."

"You seem quite certain!" Lady Matlock smiled. "He could wish for no better than Elizabeth, though I do wonder what you meant by saying the regent could grant favour to her husband."

The earl paused to nod to some acquaintances as they passed. "I imagine some sort of title—perhaps only honorary, but a title neverthe-less—will be bestowed on the man Elizabeth marries. Gardiner was knighted for his role, and this is far more significant. The gentleman will raise the future Lord Courtenay, and given the circumstances, obeisance to the reigning monarchy will be paramount. What better way to ensure loyalty? Not that the Darcys' loyalty to the Crown can be faulted in any case."

"A title would not matter so much to Darcy as would the distinction for the Darcy name. There is no question Elizabeth brings that and more."

"So, Darcy and Elizabeth…" Lord Matlock smiled at his wife. "It has a very good sound to it, does it not?"

ONE

DERBYSHIRE, 1809

The gentlemen who were gathered at the Matlock estate near Derby represented the most powerful in Parliament as well as the wealthiest in England. They were the cream of society as had been their fathers, grandfathers, and many generations before, and they liked it as such.

The occasion was, ostensibly, to shoot and fish, but all knew they were gathered for one true purpose: to find a solution to the massive problem that had so recently landed in their laps. Failure would have far-reaching consequences, and it could not be considered.

Servants were busily setting out refreshments and drinks in the room as the gentlemen assembled. It was understood that the deliberations would be long, and to adjourn before a solution was found would be impossible. The gentlemen greeted one another and discussed only trivial matters as the servants attended to their tasks. When their duties were finished, Lord Matlock instructed them to leave the room and not return unless summoned. As the last footman departed, the earl engaged the lock on the door.

Lord Liverpool had charge over the proceedings, and Lord Matlock indicated he might begin. Before he could, however, he was preceded by Lord Whitworth, a man of more interest than influence, who was given to nervous effusions.

"A disaster! Why, any manner of doing might come forth, and with the king gone mad—"

Liverpool, celebrated for his sobriety and dedication to restraint, held up his hand. "I understand your anxieties, but let us first discuss what is known before we give way to our fears, shall we?"

With that, Whitmore was silenced, and the discussion could begin.

"As I am certain you are all aware, the Courtenay fortune is extraordinary, and the lands they own are extensive. Upon the Earl of Courtenay's death two years ago, the holdings went to his son Henry Warren. Lord Courtenay succeeded his father's seat in Parliament the same year. His brother, the Honourable Francis Warren, received a generous settlement as well as an estate in Ireland from their mother's people.

"Francis is the younger brother?" Lord Owen enquired.

Liverpool gave what was, for him, a smirk. "Francis is Henry's twin. For ease of discussion, I shall henceforth refer to the two brothers by their Christian names.

"Francis is younger by only an hour, and he was known to be heartily resentful of that fact. Long before the conspiracy was born, it was observed that Francis did not like his brother. Even their school-masters at Eton attested to the rivalry although Henry was less vitu-perative in his expression of it. However, from all that can be determined, it was not until Francis took up with his latest circle of friends that the notion of fratricide moved from vague notion to well-conceived plan."

Owen asked, "Are we certain Mr Francis Warren was behind this? Could the group have acted without his knowledge?"

"Francis hid his actions well," Liverpool replied, "and, naturally, did not fire the gun himself—that was hired out. We have no firm evidence linking him to this as yet, but we shall seek it, either by the word of his co-conspirators or in some sort of written proof."

"Does this group, the radicals, have a name?" asked Lord Moore.

"The group has not a name, a creed, discrete members, nor a clearly defined mission. Their cause may be loosely described as a desire to topple existing class structure. They are against Parliament and those in it, as well as the sovereign and the Prince of Wales. They are devoted to the writings of Thomas Spence and Thomas Paine, and they admire the French and American rebels. They support the Catholics, the abolitionists, even"—Liverpool emitted a dry, short chuckle—"the writings of Mrs Wollstonecraft." The gentlemen laughed.

"The fact they are so ill-defined makes them difficult to follow, and observation has thus been limited to a few key persons of interest. As the group had few resources, and did little besides vent their spleens, they were generally disregarded.

"Their object in approaching Francis was money. The coffers of the Courtenays, as we are all aware, are sufficient to support any number of radical uprisings. Mr Francis Warren is a man with little sense and an excess of vanity, matched only by his pride. In exchange for his financial contribution, he was promised a position of honour and authority within the new order that the group would establish.

"And how did the group plan to establish this new order?" Liverpool moved to a table, unfolding some documents upon it. The men gathered closely around him. "In the usual manner of rebels, a number of assassinations were planned, including my own and several of you in this room. Family homes would be destroyed, and attempts would be made on the lives of our sovereign and his male heirs—the Prince of Wales first and foremost."

A grave silence ensued; it was sobering to see one's name on a list composed by assassins.

Liverpool continued, "Killing Lord Courtenay was the first order of business, and it was achieved. Francis Warren would be the next Earl of Courtenay and in control of the family fortune but for one thing…"

"Which is?" Owen asked.

Liverpool allowed a scant smile to breach his sombre mien. "The plans were in motion when Francis learned his brother was betrothed. Henry further confounded him by marrying within a week of his brother's hearing the news.

"The conspirators advanced their timing, hoping to beat the inevitable, but they have failed. I learned a few days ago that Henry's young widow is with child. If the child is male, it will be he who inherits and not Mr Francis Warren."

A short and heated discussion followed as this information was acknowledged, disputed, accepted, and placed within the context of the various rumours and hearsay to which the other men were privy. When the group was settled, rational conversation began.

Liverpool continued to hold sway. "Matlock, have you any insight into the matter of Lord Courtenay's marriage?"

Lord Matlock was quiet throughout the proceedings. An intelligent man, he was noted for his ability to remain silent unless he had something of worth to offer. When he did speak, he was listened to with respect. The elder Earl of Courtenay, father of the more recently deceased earl, had been one of his dearest friends, dating from their days as schoolboys. Therefore, he could boast a greater understanding of the family than the others in the room as well as a more personal interest in upholding the Courtenay family name and keeping it unsullied by accusations of disloyalty and treason.

Lord Matlock cleared his throat. "Henry Warren was of age when his father passed; I believe he and his brother were thirty this year. Although I am his godfather, he neither required nor sought my counsel when he set his mind towards marriage. I learned of his rather precipitous wedding in the tattle sheets, as did you all."

Whitmore was first to react, his voice quivering with nervousness. "She is a country nobody! How are we to know she is not part of the plot? Perhaps she used some sort of arts to lure him. She might spend the Courtenay fortune supporting these radicals, or she might raise her son to do so."

"Lady Courtenay was formerly Miss Elizabeth Bennet, and she brings with her an entirely different set of concerns," Lord Matlock admitted. "She is the daughter of a gentleman of little consequence whose estate is in Hertfordshire near the small village of Meryton and not ten miles off the Great North road.

"Meryton and its neighbourhood are rather rustic. Mr Bennet is one of the more prominent landholders, and his estate brings in only about two thousand a year. Mr Bennet's family has been on the land for above a century, but many of the other families in the area are either recently risen from trade or mere farmers. There are four and twenty families of note within the environs of Meryton, but they are all unknown among the *ton*.

"Concerns that Lady Courtenay—or perhaps her father—is sympathetic to the cause of her brother-in-law's radical friends have not yet been laid to rest. Mrs Bennet is descended from tradespeople; therefore, it is possible the Bennets were sympathetic to a change in the order, although there has been no indication of seditious activities."

"How did such a girl ensnare Lord Courtenay? How would she manage to meet him?" Lord Moore asked, amazed. Having recently seen three of his daughters through their first Seasons and into the marriage state, he could deem the process nothing short of arduous.

"We do not know," Liverpool admitted. He paused, taking a drink from his glass. "However, I must say, Lady Courtenay is full young. She had only recently come out into country society, and she had not been among London society at all until she married. So as unlikely as it was for her to meet Henry, it was even more unlikely that she would have met Francis, or any member of his cohort, prior to her marriage. I suspect we shall find she had no part in the plot, but we still must learn what we can about her."

"However, we must also protect her," Lord Matlock added. "As Lord Courtenay's widow, she now controls the Courtenay lands and fortune for the benefit of the possible heir apparent. Mr Francis Warren and his colleagues are aware of that, and they might attempt any number of plots to prevail in their objective. They might persuade her, they might coerce her, or they might simply kill her to achieve their goals. A man who would stoop to killing his brother could have no scruple in ridding himself of the inconvenience of a widow and unborn child."

Lord Matlock paused to allow them all to consider his words.

"Efforts to apprehend the key traitors must be given the highest priority. We must also do all we can to retain Lady Courtenay within our control until her lying in, both to protect her and to watch her, ensuring she does not sympathise or collude with the radicals."

Much discussion ensued with debate on the ideal means of achieving both goals. In the end, it was decided that a special group comprised of selected military men of valour would be placed on this mission to eradicate the conspirators. These men would be overseen by a few members of Parliament who would direct the efforts on behalf of the whole. Lord Matlock would serve as the intermediary between Parliament, the military, and Lady Courtenay.

For young Lady Courtenay, a remote place in the country would be found where she might give birth to her child in safety and secrecy. A companion and suitable protectors would accompany her. Once the sex of her babe was known, along with the bent of her loyalties, further plans would be laid.

WITH A CRY, ELIZABETH PUSHED HERSELF INTO A SEATED POSITION AND looked about wildly until her breathing gradually slowed. She rubbed her face, her hands growing wet from the tears that were present since the day the devastating news had arrived, even as more flowed down her cheeks. She cried so much these days, it was hardly any effort; the tears leaked without ceasing.

On the other side of the bed, Jane struggled sleepily into an upright position. "Lizzy, what is it? Did you have a dream?"

Giving her eyes one last wipe, Elizabeth lay back on the pillows. "I suppose I did though, mercifully, I do not recall it."

Jane pulled her sister into her arms and stroked her hair as she always had since girlhood. "You will be well again, I promise."

"I do not know whether I want to be well again. My grief is an odd comfort. It makes him still feel real. The day I begin to recover is the day he slips away from me."

"He will always be a part of you," Jane disagreed gently. "Always in your heart. You also have your child to consider—a part of Henry that will go on."

"I hope it is a boy." A ghost of a smile crossed Elizabeth's face. "And I pray he favours his father in every way. Is that absurd? I want to recreate my Henry in my son."

"It is not unexpected. But your child will be Henry, and you as well."

Just then, Elizabeth felt a small thud deep within her, proclaiming her child was awake and desirous of attention. "Jane, place your hands on me. The baby either agrees with me or is incensed by such notions."

Jane placed her hands on Elizabeth's abdomen and remained thus for several minutes, but the baby was still too small. Although Elizabeth could feel it, it was not yet ready to be known to others. Jane eventually took her hands away. "Will you sleep now, dearest?"

"I shall, though I beg your pardon in advance should my cries waken you again."

"I shall not mind. 'Tis what I am here for: to provide you whatever comfort I am able."

Elizabeth soon fell into a restless sleep as Jane lay awake, thinking of all that had transpired in the past months.

Elizabeth had gone to Bath in the winter with her Aunt and Uncle Gardiner. Their aunt had suffered the loss of two pregnancies, leaving her weak, pale, and uncertain whether more children would be possible. A midwife had urged her to take the waters in Bath, confident they would restore her health and her ability to bear more children. The Gardiners had two daughters but yearned for a son who would one day inherit Mr Gardiner's substantial business interests.

Jane had been shocked when, no more than a month after their departure, an express arrived saying Elizabeth was engaged to be married to a wealthy earl. Mrs Bennet immediately became enraged that she had not permitted her brother and his wife to take Jane to Bath as well, but Jane could only delight in her sister's good fortune.

Mrs Bennet had ceased her fretting when her sister, Mrs Philips, observed that Elizabeth marrying well could only be to the advantage of the other girls, and Jane was now certain to be married to a marquis or a duke. (Mrs Philips did, after all, know well how her sister could best be soothed.) It was shortly thereafter that all were off to Towton Hall in London where Elizabeth was married to Lord Courtenay by special licence—the very home in which Jane now rested beside her sister in the mistress's bedchamber.

The happy couple—for they were truly happy—had gone off to Italy for the summer, a holiday cut short by the announcement that Elizabeth believed she was increasing. Lord Courtenay was delighted by the news, and he wished to bring his bride back to England at once, not taking any chances on the health and safety of his wife and heir.

Nearly as soon as they were back on English soil, Henry's brother, Francis, a gentleman Elizabeth had met only at her wedding, requested Henry's presence at their ancestral estate in Lancashire to deal with some matters that had arisen in his absence. Her husband discouraged Elizabeth from accompanying him as, by this time, she was ill nearly every morning and frequently required an afternoon nap.

Henry had departed on what was usually a four-day journey, resolved he would make it in three. Within five days, Elizabeth had an express from Francis saying her husband had failed to appear at Warrington Castle. Shortly thereafter, another express informed her that Henry's ransacked carriage had been located within ten miles of Crewe in the parish of Coppenhall. Several days later, a third express notified her that the bodies of Henry, his coachman, and his valet had been found.

Jane would be eternally grateful that her late brother had insisted she and Aunt Gardiner stay with Elizabeth in his absence, for Elizabeth was nearly maddened with grief over the loss of her husband. It was made worse by the fact that she could not see him. By the time she knew of his death, more than a week had elapsed, and due to the heat of summer, a quick burial was required. Mr Gardiner stepped in, assisting Elizabeth and corresponding with Mr Francis Warren, who oversaw all the details of having his brother laid to rest in the family plot at Warrington Castle.

With a sigh, Jane turned, seeking a more comfortable position in which to find sleep. Something about the entire matter troubled her exceedingly. She wondered whether knowing what had occurred caused her to recall Mr Francis Warren with suspicion. She had known him only briefly, yet she had witnessed Francis looking at Henry several times with pure malice in his eyes.

"WHAT A PERFECTLY DREADFUL NOTION," LADY MATLOCK DECLARED.

Lord Matlock was surprised. "We need to protect both her and the babe."

"So you will put her in prison? I hear Newgate is rather secure. Shall we ask her to have her child there?"

The earl looked at his wife with his mouth open.

Lady Matlock continued to speak. "A confinement is a very delicate time for a lady, and in this case, the lady is scarcely more than a girl, a few years older than Georgiana. Would you have someone send our niece off to the country for the birth of a child, alone save for some hulking soldier to watch over her? No. She requires another lady, someone experienced in such matters."

"A companion could—"

Lady Matlock made a sound of disgust. "Not some hired lady! She needs family, someone who is a comfort to her. Her mother, perhaps? To send the poor thing to the country alone when she grieves for her husband is utter cruelty. I am surprised you would support such a thing, James."

Lord Matlock kept to himself the fact that he had conceived the scheme. "We shall refine the plan a bit. I shall see what I can do."

A day later, the solution was in hand.

Lady Matlock accompanied her husband to Towton Hall, the London town home of the Courtenays, where she made the acquaintance of the young lady of whom she had heard much. Given the sensitivity of the matter, it was decided a lady's hand might be needed, and the countess was glad to be of use.

Observation of mere seconds convinced her of the lady's genuine grief over her loss, and Lady Matlock soon concluded that, unless the girl was a remarkably skilled actress, she could have had nothing to do with the assassination of her husband. The poor dear was nearly in a stupor of sorrow as she listened silently to the arrangements that had been made for her.

Since the investigation had led to the happy news that Mrs Gardiner, Lady Courtenay's aunt and the wife of a tradesman, was also increasing, it had been decided that Lady Courtenay and Mrs Gardiner would be sent to the country for the birth of their children. From there, if Lady Courtenay gave birth to a daughter, she would return to town—or wherever she wished to go—to remain under the close protection of men of the Home Guards while Mr Francis Warren and his band of traitors were pursued. The earldom of Courtenay would then be no more, assuming the traitors met their just end.

If, however, Lady Courtenay delivered a male child, he would be the next earl and require the highest level of protection. To hide him from his uncle and any others who sought to corrupt or kill him, it would be reported that Mrs Gardiner had given birth to twins who would reside in Cheapside while their cousin, young Miss Elizabeth Bennet, returned to Hertfordshire, having assisted her aunt through her confinement.

Upon leaving Towton Hall, Lady Matlock voiced her concerns for this plan as well.

"Surely, you do not think Lady Courtenay will be able to pass herself off as a maiden in Hertfordshire among friends and relations who have known her since she was a babe! They all knew of her marriage, did they not? It is more than six months since then."

"They do know, of course," Lord Matlock admitted. "Villages of that size cannot help but induce intimacy among its inhabitants. Furthermore, my understanding is that her mother, Mrs Bennet, was rather proud of Lady Courtenay's elevation to the peerage and spoke of it often.

"Naturally, the best way to manage it would be simply to hide her away in Scotland or somewhere remote. However, given her youth and inexperience as a mother, such a scheme would be too cruel and unjust. So a plan has been formed that will, in essence, hide her in plain sight. We shall depend upon the good citizens of Hertfordshire—who, by all reports, uniformly esteem her—to aid us in this cause.

"Parliament will pass a decree mandating the concealment of her identity. Neither Elizabeth nor any of her acquaintance will be permitted to so much as mention the Courtenay name. To speak of any connexion of that family to her will be considered treasonous as it could endanger both Elizabeth and the young earl, and it will be dealt with accordingly.

"The people of Hertfordshire are her friends and relations. They would surely not wish to place her in danger. The insignificance of these people—they do not, by and large, go to London, nor do they see many strangers—is to our benefit. They are far enough from the London road that there is no cause for outsiders to travel through the town. It is not a perfect plan, but it is the best we can do, short of causing further pain to Lady Courtenay and the child."

Lady Matlock sighed dubiously. "What of these Gardiners? They live near Cheapside! Hardly an area of town suitable for the rearing of a young earl."

"We have looked into the Gardiners and see nothing objectionable in their doings. Their home is fine, and the family is prosperous and well mannered. It will surely be no more than a few months, and the earl will be a babe in a nursery. It cannot matter whether that nursery is in Cheapside or Carlton House.

"Furthermore," the earl explained, "anyone seeking out what remains of the Courtenay family will be looking for a mother and her son. In separating them, we disguise their identities. A young boy in an undistinguished area of town will be more easily overlooked, as will a young, unmarried lady living in the country."

"And once all the instigators have been dealt with? Will she resume her life as a dowager countess or remain as Miss Elizabeth Bennet?"

"This is where you will come in, my dear." Lord Matlock smiled at his wife. "If Lady Courtenay successfully delivers an heir, it will be paramount to see her married—and married well—to a gentleman of consequence from a good family with unquestioned loyalty to the monarchy. To have such extensive property and large fortune in the hands of some young country girl of whom nothing is known is not ideal. Such a girl could perhaps be persuaded by rogues or reprobates to raise her son to espouse a revolutionary creed. She is at loose ends now and will require the guidance of the right sort of husband to maintain the Courtenay name properly."

The earl sighed and shook his head. "These widows one sees about town… If there can be a greater argument for the fact that a lady requires a gentleman's hand to keep her steady, I know not what it might be. These widows can be nigh unto wanton if the reports I hear at my club are true."

Lady Matlock rolled her eyes. "Might I mention that if you are hearing these stories at your club, the gentlemen speaking them are equally guilty of poor behaviour?"

Lord Matlock chuckled. "Just so. In any case, Lady Courtenay will require a husband post-haste for the benefit of her son, assistance with the lands and fortune over which she has control, and to keep her in hand. She is only eighteen, as you have so noted."

"Have I been distinguished as a matchmaker for her?"

The earl nodded. "Only the best, my dear, can be entrusted with so important a mission."

In February 1810, Elizabeth reached the end of her confinement, delivering to her late husband and the Crown, a new Earl of Courtenay. He was named after his father, Henry George Goderich Warren.

It was rather fortunate for the scheme to conceal him that his "twin," Edward Thomas Gardiner, was not only born within a fortnight of young Henry but was also fair-haired and slight. Based on the looks of them, the notion of the two boys being twins was believable.

They were much alike in temperament as well; both babies were genial, content, and inclined to enjoy a good sleep, even in their earliest days. Edward was Mrs Gardiner's third child, and she assured Elizabeth that such complacent babies were far above the common way, indeed exceptional. Many a happy day was spent doing no more than cooing over the precious boys, tickling their bellies, grasping their little hands, and kissing their soft cheeks.

In the middle of April, Elizabeth returned to Hertfordshire under the re-assumed identity of Miss Elizabeth Bennet. With her went three men, ostensibly footmen, but in truth, former soldiers adept with gun, blade, and fist who would protect her night and day. A similar group would be in service at the Gardiner residence to protect the earl.

Elizabeth fought violently against the idea of a separation; however, she soon came to realise it was in little Henry's best interests. Parting from him was the most difficult thing she had ever done although she knew the Gardiners would care for him as their own child. She reminded herself hourly that she left her son in London for his own safety—that their disguise was made more persuasive by their separation. She spent a great deal of time weeping: longing for both of her Henrys, and wishing she might understand how she could go on with her life. The only thing that could console her was the notion that she suffered for her son's future felicity.

In May, her father invited her into his study for a brief conference. She appeared with her usual reddened eyes and listless countenance. For a moment, father and daughter sat together in silence. Mr Bennet was first to speak, clearing his throat and choosing his words carefully.

"It is astonishing to think this began only a little more than a year ago, is it not?"

Elizabeth nodded, looking not at Mr Bennet but at her hands gripping the handkerchief in her lap.

"I would say the course of the year is well beyond anything any of us might have imagined."

Elizabeth gave a weary laugh. "Very much so."

Mr Bennet took her hand. "Your mother and I sympathise with your predicament, my dear. We can never truly know what you suffer, but we do wish we might do anything in our power to ease your distress."

"Thank you, Papa."

"I am speaking to you today because I am concerned. You have always been my courageous, brave girl, and I would say you need that courage more now than ever. You are grieved and rightly so; however, for your son—and for your husband's memory and family name—you must pull out of this. No more weeping, no more sadness. You must be the Elizabeth Bennet you were, not her grief-stricken shell."

Elizabeth sighed. "I know, but it is so difficult."

"Difficult or not, I must remind you of your duty to be seen as a happy young lady. You cannot appear to be grieving, else you risk putting yourself and your son in danger. Furthermore, you have not been made for poor spirits. You are a joyous creature, and you rob yourself of your own felicity by carrying on in this way." Mr Bennet's tone implied he would brook no opposition.

"You are right. Tomorrow, you will see a new me or, rather, the old me become new." She gave her father a wan smile.

He smiled encouragingly in return. "You are a wonderful, brave girl, and I am exceedingly proud of you, as I know your husband would be too. Go along now, and I shall look forward to a smiling face at breakfast tomorrow."

It was not so easy to pull herself from the depression of losing her husband, but Elizabeth did it. By the time it was autumn again—one year past the hated event—she could nearly always appear similar to her old self. She was perhaps not quite so vivacious or inclined towards giving her opinion. She spoke less and listened more than in the past, but in general, she thought she gave a good show.

Her mother, having long proclaimed Elizabeth to be her least favourite child, now gave her a marked deference that was almost comical. Still, Elizabeth took advantage of this deference to institute some changes for the betterment of her sisters. She insisted on having masters brought in to tutor the ladies into an acceptable level of accomplishment in music, dancing, drawing, and languages. Kitty and Lydia were put into the hands of a governess who would remain until Elizabeth and Jane were both married. Whenever her mother protested, Elizabeth reminded her of the ways of higher society, and Mrs Bennet said no more. The neighbours found, with the absence of the generally unruly Miss Kitty and Miss Lydia, that the society of the Bennets was far more agreeable.

Elizabeth's days settled into a pattern of long walks, reading, visiting neighbours, and the like. She was fortunate that her husband's estates employed excellent stewards to manage the holdings; however, there were still matters for her consideration, and these were brought to her attention through a complicated arrangement of clandestine letter writing and communication through Lord Matlock, who had been appointed as an intermediary of sorts. She grew to have a great deal of esteem for Lord and Lady Matlock. Even though she realised they would never have condescended to know her had she not married Henry, they were kind and helpful to her now.

She visited her son at the Gardiners' home on rare visits to town, being careful not to show preference for him over her cousins in the event she was observed. The short time with him was treasured, and she mourned when she was forced to return to Hertfordshire.

In the spring of 1811, some happy news came from the disaster: Mr Gardiner would receive a ceremonial knighthood. The precise reasons behind it were not published abroad; it was simply said that he had served the Crown in an official and confidential capacity. It was an honour Mr Gardiner felt he scarcely deserved, though he received it with great gratitude. Elizabeth could not risk being present for the occasion but sent her sincere well wishes to her uncle and aunt.

By that summer, Elizabeth despaired that the matter would ever reach its resolution. Mr Francis Warren remained at large, as did the man who had done the actual shooting. Lord Matlock indicated on his last visit that they believed they were close to apprehending her errant brother-in-law. But such had been said to her many times previously; thus, she could scarcely believe it. However, she knew that, once Francis was captured, her time of respite would end, and so, in some odd way, she did not mind his continued status as a fugitive.

TWO

LONDON, SUMMER 1811

Fitzwilliam Darcy was sitting in his study with his cousin and dear friend, Colonel Richard Fitzwilliam, with whom he shared guardianship of his young sister, when they heard a firm rap on the door. The gentlemen were awaiting this interview with dread and anticipating the outcome before it had even occurred.

"Come in, please," Darcy called out, and the door opened, admitting Mrs Shopes.

Darcy had hired Mrs Shopes the previous month to serve as companion to his fifteen-year-old sister, Georgiana. Mrs Shopes was a solid, practical sort of woman and the widow of a general in the army. She had found the military lifestyle much to her liking and had often accompanied her husband in his travels, relishing the encampments and austerity most of all.

Darcy offered Mrs Shopes a friendly smile and assisted her to a seat while Fitzwilliam offered to pour her some tea. She declined both the chair and the tea. "I shall be brief, Mr Darcy. With all due respect, I feel it my duty to tell you that I shall not continue in your employ in two weeks' time."

Mrs Shopes, having heard of the attitude and behaviour of Miss Georgiana Darcy from past governesses, would only agree to a six-week term of employment within Darcy's household. At the time, he had been so desperate to have someone for Georgiana that he agreed, but he now wished that he had required a longer tenure.

"I regret to hear that." Darcy kept his voice amiable and pleasant with none of the authoritative manner he usually showed to his servants. "If this is in regards to the other night, I want to assure you that neither Colonel Fitzwilliam nor I hold you in any manner accountable for Miss Darcy's actions."

"I would not see that you reasonably could, being that I was at my sister's in Middlesex that night."

"Of course not, no," Darcy agreed hastily.

"I believe what Mr Darcy means to say is that one month is a very short time. However, I have witnessed a marked improvement in Miss Darcy's behaviour during that time, which, I can only suppose, will continue to increase," Colonel Fitzwilliam added, eager to placate the lady.

Mrs Shopes sighed. "Good sirs, please believe me when I say, if I thought that to be true in any way, I would be glad to stay. As it is, I cannot see that Miss Darcy and I shall do anything more than argue violently. I shall become her gaoler, and that is not a position to which I aspire."

Darcy realised he must acquiesce, and Mrs Shopes left with a spring in her step that he had not seen in the month she had resided in his house. As the door closed behind her, he looked at his cousin, who tossed back the remains of his brandy before speaking. "Was she the third one?"

"Yes," Darcy replied succinctly. "I cannot think how we might find another, not when Georgiana's antics have clearly begun to precede her. However, even if we do hire someone, the matter of retaining her is a different issue altogether."

"Georgiana knows very well that these people are in her employ. She does not afford them the respect they deserve because she views them as servants."

Darcy's difficulties with Georgiana had begun to emerge the previous year when his sweet little sister suddenly and alarmingly began to take on the appearance of a woman. Until that time, she had been complaisant and obedient, if somewhat timid.

He had been her guardian since their father's death, when she was a girl of ten and he a young gentleman of only two and twenty. She was always appreciative of all he did for her and rewarded his efforts with honour and respect as well as an almost embarrassing adoration. So it had been until the spring of 1810 when Georgiana turned fourteen.

It began with frighteningly rapid changes in her figure that outpaced many of her friends and left her with the appearance of a much older girl. His aunt took him aside and told him that, when a young girl's figure is formed at such an early age, many times she develops either excessive shyness or excessive coquettishness. Darcy had anticipated the former but got the latter, much to his surprise and dismay.

Suddenly, sweet, shy Georgiana was behaving as if she were some near-spinster of five and twenty, desperate for a husband. Every time they walked together in the park, she drew the notice of various gentleman who observed her appreciatively and then looked at him either enviously or challengingly, sometimes both. Georgiana, against all expectation, cultivated the attention and had grown more silly and disobedient, despite all efforts to the contrary.

Darcy rose to pour a bit of brandy into his coffee and returned to his seat. "There is always such a fine line with companions: to encourage Georgiana to give them the respect they deserve while, at the same time, admonishing her to recall her place. It is a delicate balance and one I fear she does not see."

"My mother or Lady Catherine would be more than happy to assist you."

Darcy grimaced. "No. I refused them when she was younger, and I do not wish to give her over now because it has become challenging."

"That leaves only one option," Fitzwilliam pronounced, looking at his cousin with a devilish grin. "You must marry. At least a wife cannot resign her post, and they would be equal; therefore, Georgiana would be more inclined to follow her guidance."

"Do not plague me so; I have heard quite enough of it from your parents." Darcy rubbed his temples. "I do need to marry. Perhaps I should permit their influence over it."

The teasing look left Fitzwilliam's eyes. "You would allow them to arrange your union? Darcy, I am surprised to hear you say it."

Darcy removed his hands from his head and picked up his cup, staring into it. "I must have now reached the age where I see the bene-fits of marriage outweigh the drawbacks. I trust your parents; they would not choose poorly."

He laid down his cup rather sharply. The liquid splashed onto the saucer, but he did not notice. "Georgiana needs more than a paid companion who might hie off at the slightest notice. Each and every day, I fear what might come next. An assignation? An attempt on her virtue? An elopement?"

Fitzwilliam seemed dubious. "Georgiana would benefit from your taking a wife, but would you? Georgiana is already fifteen. In a few years, she will be married and gone, but the wife will remain. Do you not think your own needs should take precedence in this matter?"

Darcy shrugged. "I know my duty, and I trust your parents will not match me with someone I would detest."

He slowly tapped his fingers against the arm of his chair. "If you were to ask me in this moment whether there was a lady to whom I would wish to be married, I would have to say no. But I know I tend to be withdrawn at parties and balls where I might meet someone. There could be any number of ladies I might find agreeable had I the opportunity to know them.

"Alas, I am rarely afforded such an opportunity because, the moment I give a lady above the slightest bit of notice, I have raised her expectations, and our names are put together in the tattle sheets. So I must go along, giving only a nodding acquaintance, and hope to find true love. How can it possibly be done in such a way? I have been out in society for a long time now. I have tried it my own way and have come up empty-handed. What harm could there be in changing tactics?"

Colonel Fitzwilliam's tone was still marked by doubt. "Let us hope those do not become famous last words."

IN THE LATE SUMMER OF 1811, THERE WAS AN ITEM OF GOSSIP IN circulation amongst the inhabitants of Meryton that was the cause for great excitement.

"Have you heard, Mrs Bennet? I have just learned from Mrs Long that Netherfield Park is let at last! Do you want to know by whom?" Lady Lucas was nearly breathless with excitement.

Mrs Bennet smiled indulgently at her neighbour. "You want to tell me, and I have no objection to hearing it."

"Well then, my dear! It was taken by a single young man of large fortune from the North, who came down in a chaise and four just last Monday to see the place. He was there but half an hour before he agreed to the terms. What a fine thing for all the girls of the county! Indeed, you must know I am thinking of his marrying one of them. It would surprise me greatly if your beautiful Jane did not catch his eye," Lady Lucas proclaimed with a knowing smile.

"I do not like to boast of my own child, but Jane's beauty is admired by all. So you must tell me the particulars of this young man's situation. How much a year does he have? Where is his family's home?"

At this prompting, Lady Lucas happily settled into a complete reporting of all the particulars, of which Mrs Bennet heard only two pertinent points: trade and five thousand a year.

She sniffed discreetly but disapprovingly. The elevation of her second daughter to the peerage had resulted in a like elevation of Mrs Bennet's hopes and expectations for her other daughters.

This Mr Bingley might do very well for most of the young ladies of this county, but for the sisters of a countess, I think not. Surely, if Lizzy could manage to catch a wealthy earl, no less than a duke will do for Jane!

Of course, she said none of this but graciously replied, "We have so many lovely young ladies in this village, Lady Lucas; perhaps one of them will be so fortunate as to draw the attentions of this Mr Bingley. Your Charlotte was looking well in her blue muslin at the last assembly, and young Maria has grown into quite the beauty."

Lady Lucas smiled hopefully, heartened by her friend's flattery, and she soon departed, intent on discussing with Charlotte some more elegant hairstyles.

Later that night, Mr and Mrs Bennet enjoyed time together before the fireplace in the sitting room that adjoined their two chambers.

"Mrs Bennet, I suppose you have heard about the new neighbours we are expecting at Michaelmas? I am sorely disappointed in the good ladies of Meryton if you have not," he teased.

"Yes, I heard. I am certain the young man will make a welcome addition to the neighbourhood." Mrs Bennet spoke disinterestedly, her attention engaged on selecting a new thread for the handkerchief she was embroidering.

"Am I correct in assuming that I should be among the first to visit Netherfield and make Mr Bingley's acquaintance?"

Mrs Bennet appeared to be absorbed in her needlework. "If you would like. I have no objection to your visiting Mr Bingley. 'Tis the proper etiquette, to be sure."

Mr Bennet stared at her for a moment, his brow furrowed. A young, unmarried man worth five thousand a year had come into the neighbourhood, and his wife seemed unaffected. "Mrs Bennet, is something wrong?"

"Not at all. Why do you ask?"

"I think it curious that this eligible young man should come into the neighbourhood and you would not wish for him to become immediately betrothed to one of our five daughters."

"I suppose that is his design in settling here? To marry one of our daughters?" Mrs Bennet looked teasingly at her husband.

"His design—Oh, what nonsense you speak! No, no, but he may very well take a liking to one of them."

"I pray he would not."

"Indeed?" Mr Bennet was now thoroughly perplexed. Was it not still his wife's ambition to see her daughters married to wealthy men? When had this change come about?

"A fortune from trade? I suppose the size of the fortune itself is respectable enough, but Lizzy is of the first circles now. She will return to London in a few months, and then think of the rich and titled gentlemen with whom she will acquaint her sisters! No, Mr Bingley and his five thousand a year from trade can be no more than a pleasant diversion. Our daughters will marry dukes and earls or, at the very least, extremely rich landowners."

Mr Bennet frowned. He could not like such sentiments. Nevertheless, he knew his wife: once her mind was set to something, neither reason nor sense would dissuade her. Sighing, he picked up his paper and hoped young Bingley would take a liking to Maria Lucas for his own sake.

DARCY RELUCTANTLY ACCEPTED AN INVITATION TO DINE AT HIS UNCLE'S house, suspecting he was being summoned for advisement—or perhaps even admonishment—pertaining to Georgiana. His uncle could have nothing to say that Darcy had not already thought, but nevertheless, he knew he must give him his due.

When the ladies withdrew from dinner, Darcy watched his uncle lean forward and draw a deep breath, and he knew the time had come.

"I am loath to tell you how I think you should be raising your sister."

"Then, pray, do not," Darcy replied firmly. "I assure you, I hear from my aunt daily on the subject."

"You have been an excellent and diligent guardian. We simply feel there are things about a girl at such an age that a bachelor cannot apprehend."

"Once the right sort of companion has been secured—"

"No, no." Lord Matlock shook his head vehemently. "It will not do, and in any case, the good candidates have all gone running."

Darcy took a drink of his port. "Georgiana's reputation as a difficult and spirited young lady precedes her." He rose, laid his napkin on the table, and walked to the window. "How has this happened? She was once such a pleasant young girl, so demure and sweet. This bold defiance is entirely unexpected."

The earl poured another glass of port and swirled it in his glass. In a tone that implied the idea had just occurred to him, he said, "What if you were to take a wife? Someone to guide her is certainly just what she needs."

Darcy rolled his eyes. "I wondered how long it would take you to say it."

"Do you disagree?"

"I cannot." Darcy returned to his chair with a sigh. "A wife would be of great benefit to Georgiana, as well as to myself."

"At least you are relieved of the urgings of Lady Catherine to take her daughter as your wife."

Darcy leaned back. "I am happy for my cousin Anne and hope she will find great felicity with Mr Maddox. As for myself…" He sank into his thoughts.

"Yes?"

Drumming his fingers against the table, Darcy considered how much to confide. "I know I must marry a lady of excellent fortune and good connexions to credit my station."

He stopped for a moment, causing his uncle to prompt, "However?"

"I should like someone who is interesting and witty—someone I enjoy spending time with and not merely to fulfil my duty and bed occasionally to produce an heir. To marry any of the ladies of my acquaintance would be to consign myself to this infernal loneliness I always feel. The only difference is that I would still be alone but with someone else in the room."

His uncle showed a surprisingly compassionate countenance. "Why are you lonely? You have us, and you know we love you as a son."

"I thank you, but alas, it is not the same."

Darcy raised himself up a moment later, not wishing to seem glum. "I have much in my life for which to be thankful, and I am. However, I wish to marry in a manner that does not condemn me to eternal wistfulness."

"Is there someone who holds your fancy?"

"My efforts have been directed towards avoiding attachments, not forming one," he admitted.

"Would you like our assistance?"

Darcy pressed his lips together tightly as he considered what he would say next. "I am not quite ready to turn my future over to you."

Lord Matlock protested immediately, "We understand your needs and have only—"

"It says nothing to my trust in you. I am not quite ready yet to commit to it. I am for Hertfordshire soon. Bingley let a house there and wants me to look at it. When I return, we may revisit the topic."

"Hertfordshire, eh?" Lord Matlock raised an eyebrow at his nephew, bringing his glass to his lips to hide a faint smile. "Well, perhaps you will meet someone of interest there."

"In Hertfordshire? I think not!" Darcy laughed. "The society there is nothing short of savage. Nevertheless, the estate, should it prove all it is reported to be, will be suitable for Bingley. I shall accompany him to be certain he does not find himself purchasing a crumbling castle with poorly drained fields or falling in love with some farmer's daughter. Do not worry: I shall not return with an attachment for myself."

Lord Matlock only shrugged and smiled.

THREE

HERTFORDSHIRE, OCTOBER 1811

There is little I dread more than this wretched assembly save my return to London society this winter.

However, as she had months to prepare herself for the latter and only hours to become ready for the former, the former took precedence in Elizabeth's mind. Already, she could feel her anxiety mounting, and as she sat looking in the glass above her vanity, she gave herself a bracing scold.

"Your son needs a father, and you need a husband. You will not find one by reading in your library or wandering the fields of Hertfordshire! If you cannot do this, then you might as well resign yourself to an arranged match. If you wish to find a husband on your own, you must go out, you must dance, and you must enchant. This assembly will be an ideal place to practise those arts. At least for this night, you will be among friends you have known your entire life—surely, a dance or two is not impossible."

Not for the first time, she keenly felt how she despised those who had taken her darling husband from her. Never had she thought she would again be single, alone, and sitting among the young maidens of society, all them seeking a "good match" such as it was.

How could anyone possibly be a suitable match for her? Henry had been everything that was desirable, amiable, loving, kind, and intelligent! No one could ever hope to match him.

For a moment, she allowed herself to become lost in bittersweet recollection.

We were in Italy, strolling the streets of Florence and seeing sights such as I never could have imagined only months prior. Henry delighted in my wonder, and he matched my eagerness to see and do all that could be seen and done. The Italians are much less reserved in expressions of feeling and emotion than the English, and thus did Henry and I feel quite at ease walking hand in hand on the street, indulging in a kiss whenever we wished, and giving all appearance of the young lovers we were.

Henry made a rather bawdy comment to me—he did delight in shocking me—but my maidenly sensibilities had waned dramatically over the days in Italy, and so I did not blush but returned a rather bawdy comment of my own.

He swept me off my feet in delight, laughing loudly and twirling me around in a close embrace, proclaiming, "Lizzy, I shall love and adore you until the day I die!" We quickly turned on our heels, intent on returning to the carriage and the house, both of us eager to make our bawdy remarks a reality.

Lost in her memory, Elizabeth spoke aloud. "…love and adore you until the day I die? That day certainly came far sooner than either of us could have ever foreseen in even the very worst of our dreams." With a start, she recalled herself to the present and saw the tears in her eyes.

"This is not helping!" Elizabeth informed her reflection. I must not be caught in melancholy right before this assembly. I must ready myself, I must go, and I must dance. Surely, this first time out will be the worst.

MERYTON SOCIETY HAD ARRIVED EN MASSE TO THE ASSEMBLY. THE townsfolk were always eager for a gathering of this sort, but on this occasion, there were two additions to the party that raised interest even further.

The first was the appearance of Miss Elizabeth, who had rarely been seen in society for the past two years. Miss Elizabeth was always well regarded, and although the townspeople did not speak of it, they were all saddened by what had happened to her. Moreover, hidden or not, she was one of their own who had become an exalted personage, the only countess many of them had ever seen, much less known. All were eager to spend time in her presence. Elizabeth placed a determined smile on her face, resolved to appear happy as she greeted each one.

The second and still more enlivening event was the appearance of the new occupants of Netherfield Park. Those who had already been introduced looked forward to becoming more intimate, and those without an introduction hoped to be so gratified.

By the buzz throughout the hall, Elizabeth supposed that Mr Bingley and his party had already arrived, and so they had. She saw them standing by the refreshment table, assuming rightly that the blond man wearing a blue coat and an expression of eager enthusiasm on his countenance was Mr Bingley himself.

Miss Charlotte Lucas, a dear friend of the Bennet girls, removed herself from her group and came over to see Elizabeth and Jane. She smiled encouragingly at Elizabeth as she greeted the sisters. "Dear Eliza, how well you look this night."

"Shall I make it through without causing any embarrassment?" Elizabeth laughed weakly.

"Of course you will," Charlotte spoke soothingly. "You will have a dance or two; it will be just like old times."

Elizabeth gave a little doubtful shrug, then looked away, her friend's kind solicitude bringing her emotions a little too close to the surface for comfort.

Charlotte decided to change the topic. "Have you met the Netherfield party?" On their negative reply, she identified them all.

One of the gentlemen, a Mr Hurst, she reported to be married to Bingley's elder sister, Louisa, a small and rather plain woman who had evidently wished to compensate for her rather colourless demeanour by an excess of jewellery and ornaments. The younger of the two sisters was identified as Miss Caroline Bingley, who was pretty enough and dressed fashionably, if a bit ostentatiously for a simple country assembly.

"And the taller gentleman? Do you know him?" Jane enquired.

"He is Mr Fitzwilliam Darcy of Derbyshire, and one of Mr Bingley's oldest and dearest friends. He comes from an old and respected family, and"—she lowered her voice—"worth ten thousand a year, maybe more."

Even before Charlotte's report of Mr Darcy, Elizabeth had begun to look at him, a queer fluttery feeling arising in her chest for reasons she could not quite understand. He was undeniably handsome, tall with a fine, muscular figure and regal bearing. He had thick, dark, curly hair, and his dress was impeccable. Not a dandy, but his clothing was fashionable and well made.

Very handsome indeed. The thought made her both intrigued and ashamed, as though she betrayed her husband's memory. Her shame was not enough to stop her, however, and she looked at him again, searching her mind to recall whether his name had been on Lord Matlock's list.

He had little interest in dancing, choosing instead to walk about the room looking unhappy. *You and I are both not pleased with the evening. What makes you so unhappy to be here? Then again, you might wonder the same of me.*

Mrs Bennet joined them at the same time, as did Charlotte's father, Sir William Lucas.

"Mr Bingley has requested an introduction." Sir William glanced questioningly at Elizabeth. "If you would be so obliging?"

Elizabeth replied, "We would be honoured," at the same time her mother said, "If we must. They are to be our neighbours after all." Elizabeth elbowed her.

Mr Darcy did not accompany his friend to be introduced, giving Elizabeth the first indication that he considered himself above this society. Mr Bingley proved amiable and kind, and he immediately solicited Jane for a dance. One glance at her sister's blushing face told Elizabeth how pleased Jane was with his request, and she smothered a smile.

As Jane went off with Mr Bingley, Elizabeth wandered through the hall, greeting her friends and relations with great pleasure. She had just received a cup of punch from young Mr Goulding when her mother immediately beckoned her back to her side.

"Lizzy? Lizzy! Come here this instant, child!" Mrs Bennet hissed loudly. Elizabeth joined her quickly. "Speak to Jane, and make sure she knows she is not to encourage this Bingley person."

"Mama, he seems a very amiable gentleman, and Jane is having a nice time dancing with him."

"Oh, for pity's sake! I suppose you would well like to see her settle for some tradesman, but I assure you, it will not do. 'Tis best to stop it now before it goes any further."

"Mama, lower your voice. Mr Bingley or his party might hear you." Elizabeth flushed.

"I do not care a bit if they do! Best they know now their pretensions will be discouraged in this quarter."

"Yes, Mama, I shall speak to her when their dance is ended." By this time, Elizabeth would have agreed to nearly anything to get her mother to stop her offensive speech. She attempted to move away, but her mother grabbed her arm.

"If you should happen to dance with Mr Bingley, forward Charlotte Lucas to him. She is a good girl, and at her age and being so plain, she will not mind being married to a tradesman."

Elizabeth gasped at the coarseness. "Mama!" Glancing around in mortification, she noticed that both Charlotte and Miss Bingley were nearby. Closing her eyes, she silently prayed for a moment that they had not heard her mother, though it seemed unlikely.

At the end of their set, Mr Bingley escorted Jane to Elizabeth and excused himself. When he had gone, Jane allowed her smile to droop, looking at her sister in concern as the two ladies found some seats. "Lizzy, are you well?"

"I am well enough. I know I have not danced, but I feel mostly at ease, which is more than I might say of our mother. Mama is vexed."

Jane frowned at her hands. "Because Mr Bingley is from trade."

Elizabeth nodded.

"Mr Bingley is an agreeable gentleman and has not ever worked."

"I know, and what is more important is that I can see how well you like him." Elizabeth squeezed her sister's hand in sympathy and added, "In London, we need not worry about Mama. Think of that, Jane."

No more could be said as Mr Bingley approached and offered a cup of punch to Jane. Beaming, he asked, "Miss Elizabeth, would you like a drink?" He held out the second cup, which had obviously been intended for himself. Elizabeth declined it immediately.

"Not at all, Mr Bingley, but I do thank you. I believe your exertions on the dance floor rendered you in far greater need of it than I, who spent most of the first sets in a less active manner." She smiled kindly at him, her estimation of his gentlemanly manner still further improved.

"Let us rectify that straightaway! Will you dance the next with me?"

"Oh!" Elizabeth flushed, realising her words sounded like a hint, when in truth, she wished for the precise opposite. *A dance, or two, you promised yourself—no, I simply cannot, not with a man so wholly unknown to me.*

Mr Bingley stood awaiting her answer, and Jane gave Elizabeth a furtive look of encouragement.

Elizabeth forced a determined smile. "It would be my honour, I thank you." Her heart began to pound with anxiety over the notion, accelerating as the music began again, indicating the next set would form.

DANCING HAD ALWAYS BEEN ONE OF ELIZABETH'S FAVOURED activities prior to her marriage, but she had not participated in it since the death of her husband. How strange it was to take the arm of another man, to be close enough to detect the faint whiff of his fragrance and see the spot on his neck where his valet had nicked him while shaving.

She felt exposed walking towards the set of dancers, beset by guilt and imagining poor Henry looking upon her with disappointment, as though she forgot him and their son so that she might be off with other men.

I cannot do this. Her hand, resting lightly on Mr Bingley's coat, trembled with nerves she had not even experienced on her first dance as a young girl. With each step forward, she considered halting their progress and telling Mr Bingley she could not dance, but she would not permit herself such a weakness.

She hoped it would be easier once the dance began, but it was not. How wrong it seemed to permit Mr Bingley to touch her hands—to smile at him and caper about, acting the part of a carefree young maid enjoying a dance with a handsome gentleman. She reproached herself for the silliness of their conversation: casual banter about Hertford-shire, Netherfield, and other subjects of no consequence. Did any of it matter? Her breathing became rapid, far faster than was induced by the dance, and she yearned for it all to end before she did something to humiliate herself, such as cry or scream.

She breathed a sigh of relief when it finally ended. Her gown concealed her shaking knees as she returned to her place where only

Mary remained. Jane had been summoned across the room to her mother, no doubt being chastised for dancing with someone who was not suitable for Mrs Bennet's elevated pretensions.

As she sat there, her anxiety and sadness began to overwhelm her, and she decided she would do no more. She had danced one dance; that was enough on this first time out. It was a relief to remove herself from the crush and find an out-of-the-way spot towards where the matrons sat. As she rested, regaining some semblance of her equanimity, she noted that Mr Bingley again asked Jane to dance. *Two dances! He does like her!*

As she watched the dancers, her eye was occasionally drawn back to Mr Darcy, who was strolling around the room looking uncivil. He had recommended himself to no one; the burgeoning public opinion was that he was a most disagreeable, haughty man. He had not danced with anyone outside of his own party, despite the fact that the ladies far outnumbered the gentlemen at this assembly, and more than one lady sat in want of a partner. *Perhaps I should hope his name is not on Lord Matlock's list.*

He ambled over towards where she sat and paused by a table, contented, it would seem, to be an observer. She was behind him but quite close, and thus it was that she could not have missed nor misheard an exchange that occurred just moments later between Mr Darcy and Mr Bingley.

Mr Bingley had completed his second dance with Jane, and he subsequently made it his object to enliven his increasingly unpopular and taciturn friend.

"Come, Darcy," said he. "I must have you dance. I hate to see you standing about by yourself in this stupid manner. You had much better dance."

"I certainly shall not. You know how I detest it unless I am particularly acquainted with my partner. At such an assembly as this, it would be insupportable. Your sisters are engaged, and there is not another woman in the room whom it would not be a punishment to me to stand up with."

"I would not be so fastidious as you are," cried Bingley, "for a kingdom! Upon my honour, I never met with so many pleasant girls in my life as I have this evening; and there are several of them, you see, uncommonly pretty."

"*You* were dancing with the only handsome girl in the room," said Mr Darcy, looking at the eldest Miss Bennet.

"Oh! She is the most beautiful creature I ever beheld! But there is one of her sisters sitting down just behind you, who is very pretty, and I daresay, very agreeable. Do let me introduce you."

Elizabeth heard this with alarm, not wishing to offend the man by refusing him, especially after Bingley had entreated him so earnestly. *Oh no, no, no. I beg you would not induce him to ask me! I cannot, shall not—not now, not tonight.*

"Which do you mean?" and turning round, Mr Darcy looked for a moment at Elizabeth till, catching her eye, he withdrew his own and coldly said, "She is tolerable but not handsome enough to tempt me, and I am in no humour at present to give consequence to young ladies who are slighted by other men. You had better return to your partner and enjoy her smiles, for you are wasting your time with me."

Elizabeth gasped at his comment. *Of all the incivility! I do not know that I have ever seen such a rude, disagreeable man! Just who does he suppose he is? I would not dance with him if he* did *ask!*

She rose from her seat and, with her own best haughty appearance, swept by Mr Darcy, using only one lifted brow to make him aware that she had heard his rude comment. *Give consequence to me, indeed! Thank you, Mr Fitzwilliam Haughty Darcy, but I already have more consequence than I desire.*

DARCY FOUND THE EVENING INSUFFERABLE. HE HAD LITTLE expectation or wish of forming any acquaintance of importance in this town—Bingley might or might not settle herein; at this point, anything was possible—and thus he did not intend to trouble himself overmuch.

Darcy did not have ease among strangers in the best of circumstances. He was offended by the whispers about his income, his station, and his person that began nearly as soon as he had entered the room, and this further disinclined him to seek introductions. Moreover, he generally found it difficult to make the polite chat that was expected, and he was fully aware of his tendency to give offence. In short, it was always far easier for him to stand apart and remain silent in these gatherings.

To consider meeting a new young lady and being required to find subjects for polite, disinterested conversation, as well as dance with her, was unthinkable. Bingley was absurd to even suggest it. Darcy's intent was to be as disagreeable as possible so Bingley would leave him in peace.

As soon as Bingley left, however, he was struck by remorse, for he realised the young lady in question heard what he had said despite his belief that he had spoken softly. The lady had risen from her seat, and with a half-amused, half-severe look towards him, she went to join a group of young ladies he assumed were her friends. With great spirit, she related something to them, causing a general titter of laughter amid surreptitious glances in his direction.

The worst of it, however, was still to come. As the young lady had brushed by him, her gown lightly caressed the tip of his shoe even as a delicate whiff of her sweet scent filled his senses, and he felt an inexplicable but unbearable pang of longing for her. His heart pounded madly, and at once, he somehow just knew it—she was the one. It was she for whom he was destined, and in her, his happiness would reside.

This young lady, whose name he did not know, exacted her revenge for his graceless utterance in the cruellest way imaginable: she made him fall in love with her.

Fall in love with her! Darcy scoffed at himself even as the thought entered his head. *Take hold of yourself, man!* Love at first sight is the subject of bad poetry—not an actual occurrence, and certainly not an affliction indulged in by intelligent, learned, and rational men!

I must admit, however, that I am feeling very...odd. Am I ill? It must be a fever of sorts, for what else could explain the shivers going up my back and the curious pounding of my heart?

He had, of course, seen many beautiful women before; had not the most handsome ladies of the *ton* shamelessly presented themselves to him for years? When this young woman spoke, she would surely prove herself a simpering, uneducated country miss. *How could I possibly be in love with her? Absurd notion!*

Yet, for some reason, despite these sensible arguments, he could not stop looking at her, longing to touch her and speak to her. He felt connected to her, and above all, he wished he had agreed to dance with her.

He spent the rest of the evening in a state of growing enchantment. He alternately stared at her and tried to persuade himself to stop. Several times, he thought to seek an introduction, but it appeared his opportunity had passed, and another did not arise.

I cannot be in love with someone to whom I have not even spoken. But his heart would not agree with him.

THE DAY AFTER THE ASSEMBLY WAS SPENT AS MOST DAYS WERE AFTER assemblies: in the reliving of them. Charlotte, Maria, and Lady Lucas called at Longbourn early and stayed long. Lady Lucas was pleased that Mrs Bennet made much of Mr Bingley's dance with Charlotte while, at the same time, dismissing entirely the two times he had danced with Jane.

There was also a great deal of conversation the utterly despicable Mr Darcy. To render such an insult against one of their own would have been met with ire no matter who the lady was, but the fact that it had been done to Elizabeth, who had already suffered so very much, made it absolutely unforgivable. Lady Lucas said that Sir William had even gone so far as to suggest excluding the odious man from an impending evening gathering, but Elizabeth intervened hastily and persuaded them otherwise. She had no great fondness for the man, but she liked Mr Bingley and did not wish to see any of his party offended.

A few days following the assembly, Elizabeth awoke early and indulged in a brief walk through the countryside. Upon her return, she heard the sound of Lydia singing quite pleasingly in the music room, and she hastened in to compliment her.

Kitty was at the pianoforte, playing while Lydia sang. By the time Elizabeth arrived, they were nearly half finished, but she enjoyed the rest and clapped her hands with great enthusiasm at the end, nodding in acknowledgment to Miss Avery, their governess and the lady behind their proficiency.

"You girls have come along so well!"

Lydia sighed. "With little to entertain us, what else could we do?"

Elizabeth tried to be sympathetic. "This is what young ladies your age should be doing—bettering themselves to become truly accomplished."

Kitty grumbled a bit. "You and Jane have all of the fun."

"Soon enough, Jane and I shall be boring old married ladies, and it will be you going to balls, parties, and dinners," Elizabeth reassured them, "but in London, where wealthy, handsome gentlemen will admire you for your many talents and sweep you away to some grand estate." Her sisters were duly encouraged and smiled at the thought.

Kitty showed her sister the next piece she and Lydia would learn, and Elizabeth made them happier still by promising each a new bonnet when it had been mastered.

Elizabeth felt Kitty and Lydia suffered the effects of their father's disinterest. Upon entering their teens, they began behaving in a silly and strident manner alarmingly similar to Mrs Bennet. When Elizabeth came into the means to do so, she hired Miss Avery to curtail these growing tendencies and all but forced her father to take an interest in the girls—reading, riding, and playing chess with them, just as he had done with her. She could not yet know whether it was successful, but both girls showed evidence of becoming a credit to the Bennet family one day even if they acted petulant at times. Mr and Mrs Bennet might have thought Elizabeth's edicts a bit high handed, but all Elizabeth needed to do was dangle the notion of improved marital prospects in front of her mother, and her will was done. She felt a bit guilty for doing so, but as it was to the improvement of her sisters, she put that guilt aside.

After leaving her younger sisters, she went into the drawing room where a bit of a disagreement was occurring. Jane was gently insisting, "They are our neighbours, Mama. We must call upon them."

Mrs Bennet frowned, stabbing viciously at a piece of needlework. "Such connexions are unsuitable."

"Unsuitable? How so?" Elizabeth did not hesitate to enter the fray.

"You know why," Mrs Bennet replied with another unbecoming scowl, her needle attacking the fabric with no mercy and no creditable result.

"I have no apprehension in calling on them. I think it would look very odd if we did not."

"A countess calling upon some man in trade? Absurd, utterly absurd! It is not done!"

"I am not known as a countess to them," Elizabeth replied firmly. "Nor do I wish to give away my position. They are neighbours, and furthermore, they are no longer in trade."

"That might be so, but they are not gently bred either!"

"I shall call on the ladies, Mama, and so will you."

Mrs Bennet looked away, grumbling "ladies, indeed" under her breath. She was silent for a few blessed moments while her daughters looked at her unwaveringly. Finally, she said, "I shall get my things."

Although Mrs Bennet had acquiesced, she had not done so cheerfully, and she spent the carriage ride to Netherfield in a stony silence, staring out the window to communicate her disapproval. Had she understood that, for her daughters, this was more of a blessing than a curse, she might have spoken simply to aggravate them, but as it was, she remained silent.

"I AM CERTAIN THEY DO NOT EVEN KNOW THE PROPER ETIQUETTE FOR A morning call," said Caroline Bingley disdainfully from her place at the window.

"They will probably stay all day," agreed Mrs Hurst.

"I can scarcely bear to imagine of what topics they will speak! Surely, fashion, society, anything of interest is unknown to them! What shall we—"

"Caroline!" Mr Bingley looked at both of his sisters severely. "This is country society. If you wish to serve as my hostess, I expect you to behave kindly. And do not think you will be absolved of such things once you are wed. If you marry a gentleman, you will spend time at his estate and be expected to treat his neighbours with respect."

Caroline frowned at her brother, not impressed by his forceful tone. "Some counties, you must own, are far more civilised than others. Derbyshire comes to mind, of course. Everyone in Hertfordshire is a farmer."

"Most in Derbyshire are sheep breeders," Darcy remarked. "Country is not town, no matter what county you reside in."

Caroline flushed at his rebuke, but Darcy barely noted it. He was busy schooling himself to appear calm, assuming he would soon see Miss Elizabeth Bennet, as he now knew she was called.

In the days since the assembly, he had told himself that this silly notion of love at first sight was nothing more than a fleeting thought brought on by his recent feelings of loneliness and worries over Georgiana, as well as his rising determination to marry. As soon as he spoke to her, reality would intrude and dispel these strange ideas that afflicted him.

The room was soon a throng of Hertfordshire's residents except for the Bennets. Darcy felt his head turn, almost against his will, each time the door opened, but it was always in vain. The room filled with the gentry of the area. Young lady after young lady was thrust at him, their smiling fathers or mothers behind them in a most insupportable fashion. Bingley, he saw, received the same treatment but did not appear as vexed by it as he was.

Darcy took to lingering on the periphery of conversations so he would not attract undue notice by any of them and, as such, missed the entry of his heart's desire. He became aware of her only when he heard Miss Bingley greet her, somehow managing to make the name Miss Eliza sound like an epithet. He turned about, feeling his stomach drop into his shoes as a deep flush spread over his entire body and his heart began to pound.

Calm yourself. You do not even know her. Intent on a proper introduction, he moved to where she stood speaking to Miss Bingley, heedless of the fact that Miss Bingley would surely believe he had crossed the room for her benefit.

Miss Bingley preened when he appeared, enjoying having him at her side as though they were greeting guests together. "Miss Elizabeth Bennet, please allow me to introduce you to our esteemed guest, Mr Fitzwilliam Darcy."

Miss Elizabeth offered a proper curtsey, and Darcy bowed. To his shock, rather than court his favour, she turned to leave. He stopped her with the stupidest, most commonplace subject that sprang to his lips. "The weather has been exceptionally fine. Tell me, is it generally so?"

Elizabeth turned back to him, a mischievous gleam in her eyes. "I would say the weather hereabouts is always what I consider to be tolerable. However, I am not so fastidious. To me, many things are tolerable."

Darcy was mortified and felt the flush only recently abated return to his cheeks. At least she was teasing him about it. Heaven only knew that, if she were to walk up and slap him, he would deserve it. But now, she was moving away from him once more.

"A moment, please."

She turned back again.

"I wish to offer an overdue apology."

She raised one eyebrow, looking delightfully saucy. "Why? As we have only just met, I cannot imagine how you might have offended me already. Nor could I think you were the sort of gentleman who went about offending ladies unknown to you."

He smiled despite his embarrassment. Seeing good humour in her eyes, he admitted, "I am not the sort of man who would usually do such a thing, but I am afraid I did so at the assembly."

"Indeed?" Elizabeth was the picture of innocence. "Well, then you must have had good reason to do so. Did I offend you?"

"No," he admitted. "However, it was unkind of me…"

"What was it you said? I wish to be certain, should I accept your apology, that I am accepting it for the correct grievance."

He looked at her and judged by her sparkling eyes and suppressed grin that she remained somewhat amused. "I said you were tolerable but not handsome enough to tempt me, and I was in no mood to give consequence to ladies slighted by other gentlemen."

Elizabeth gasped theatrically and placed her hand on her bosom. "Oh my!"

"I am exceedingly sorry for such an appalling remark and hope I might make amends for any distress it caused you."

"Hmmm…" She continued giving him that teasing look. "May I clarify one thing?"

"Certainly."

"Are you sorry because you did not mean it? Or is it only regrettable because I heard you? Understand, I am not seeking to be flattered; I only wish to be perfectly clear on what it is I am supposed to forgive."

He repressed the beginnings of a chuckle. "It was both entirely untrue and unkind in its utterance. It was based on nothing more than my desire to be rid of Bingley's pestering."

Miss Elizabeth looked over at Mr Bingley, who was making sheep's eyes at her sister and looking in every manner like the happily besotted youth he was. "Mr Bingley is indeed a fearsome, and no doubt dangerous, creature. I can readily apprehend that you might have to employ any means possible to extricate yourself from his evil clutches."

Darcy now permitted himself a broad smile. "He seems harmless enough now, but I assure you, when he sets his mind to something— such as the cause of making me dance—he can be both relentless and ruthless."

She inclined her head. "Very well. I appreciate your candour, and I accept your apology. No amends are needed."

"Thank you, Miss Elizabeth." Darcy frantically cast about in his mind for something else to say that would permit him to continue speaking to her.

"If you will excuse me, sir." With that, she was gone—to Darcy's profound disappointment.

ELIZABETH WALKED AWAY FROM MR DARCY, WONDERING WHAT SORT of impulse had led her to tease him so. It certainly was not his open and welcoming countenance; Mr Darcy was rather serious, even a bit severe. *I must begin by being impertinent; else, I shall soon grow frightened of him.*

Although she held a slight measure of concern for having offended him, it was a fine thing to feel a bit of her old self emerging. Elizabeth could not deny that the events of the years since her brief marriage had left their mark on her. When she had first lost her husband, she had existed within a haze of grief and sorrow. That eventually gave way to anger and then loneliness. All emotions had to be carefully modulated and concealed from the world, enabling her to impersonate a reasonably happy, well-mannered young lady.

While she thought she had met with some success in her disguise, it had dulled her nevertheless. She often felt as if she viewed the world through a warped glass, and of late, it would seem anxiety was her only true feeling. She had pretended to be something she was not for so long a time that she almost forgot how to be herself.

Teasing Mr Darcy made her feel more like her former self. Even though she knew not why he, of all people, would inspire it, she still enjoyed it. Now she knew that the courageous, impertinent, witty, and teasing girl was still within her somewhere. If she could be that girl with such a man as Fitzwilliam Darcy, surely no one in London would intimidate her.

FOUR

In the fortnight following their first two meetings, Darcy did not see Miss Elizabeth, which suited him very well. His interaction with her at Netherfield had inflamed him in a manner he knew was both enticing and dangerous. Being in control of his sensibilities and behaving in a rational manner were of great importance for a gentleman of his station. He could not understand what it was about Miss Elizabeth Bennet that tempted him to act otherwise.

He expected to see her at the various neighbourhood dinners to which the Netherfield party had been invited and thought it very odd when he did not. There were four occasions at which the Bennet family and the Netherfield party were mutual guests, and in each of these instances, Mr and Mrs Bennet, Miss Bennet, and Miss Mary, were in attendance, but Miss Elizabeth was not there.

The fourth occasion was at Rowney Abbey, seat of the Dugdales, an unremarkable family who were best described as mild and inoffensive. They had two vapid daughters—who said little and appeared to think even less—and a dull son of four and twenty. They had forwarded the daughters to both Darcy and Bingley at their first meeting. It was to their credit that they recognised quickly such efforts would be unfruitful and vexing to both men.

As was becoming his habit, Bingley rapidly found Jane Bennet among those gathered and formed a little tête-à-tête with her. Darcy joined them soon thereafter.

"Miss Bennet, how are you this evening?"

"I am quite well, Mr Darcy, and yourself?"

"Very well, I thank you." He paused, sipping his drink and ignoring Bingley's eyes, which were telling him to go away. "I notice Miss Elizabeth does not join us this evening. I hope she is not unwell?"

"She is perfectly well, sir, and I appreciate the enquiry on her behalf." Miss Bennet smiled blandly.

Bingley, bless him, spoke up with far more inquisitiveness than Darcy could permit himself to display. "I wonder that we have not had the pleasure of her company at these past few soirees that we have all attended! I enjoyed meeting her and hoped to further our acquaintance."

Miss Bennet smiled though Darcy noted a distinct look of discomfort. "Lizzy is not always of a mind for an evening out. Her preference is for quieter pursuits at home."

"Indeed?" Bingley laughed, his mind unfettered by any rudeness that might be inferred from further enquiry. "I would not suppose it from some of the tales you have related to me." Turning to his friend, he said, "Darcy, you must hear Miss Bennet's story of the occasion in which her spirited sister had a dance master who was a bit too familiar!"

Miss Bennet was blushing fiercely. Darcy pitied her but could not deny his need to hear more of Miss Elizabeth. "It is true: my sister has always been of a lively, playful sort of disposition, but she also recognises the need for temperance and wisdom. Please, good sirs, do excuse me. My sister Mary needs me to turn pages for her." She curtseyed and departed.

Bingley trailed after her, devoted to keeping her within his reach, while Darcy was left to ponder Miss Elizabeth and the odd duality he had begun to perceive in her nature.

He had observed, at both the assembly and the Bennets' morning call, a great deal of reserve and elegance in her manner, far more than he would expect to see in a girl raised in the country with limited social discourse. At times, there was a timidity in her, a quiet sort of watchfulness, yet on other occasions, he saw a glimpse of a teasing, playful sort of disposition—such as when she had refused to hear his apology and, at the assembly, when she had left after his rude remark and gone to her friends. There was no doubt she had told the story with great animation and good humour as he had seen them all laugh and glance his way.

Why concern yourself with comprehending her character? Knowing more of her can only put you in greater danger. You would do best to know nothing about her because she can never be more than a lady you met briefly in the country.

The Bennet family, as a whole, continued to puzzle him. He had heard their means were rather modest. The estate was entailed and brought in only two thousand a year, yet the daughters had dowries of ten thousand each. Darcy could not think how Mr Bennet had managed it. *Perhaps Mrs Bennet brought a large fortune to the marriage?*

Thinking of that lady brought the oddity of the Bennets even more to mind. Despite roots in trade, and her current status as minor gentry, she conducted herself as the haughtiest of the *haut ton. And now I have the opportunity to dine with her.*

The lady was without restraint in her attempts to verify his income and standing in society. He withstood her questions for as long as he could bear it and with as much circumspection as possible, yet he could not help but confirm some of her beliefs of his grand estate and revered family.

"I have heard, Mr Darcy, that your estate is in Derbyshire."

"It is."

"And your parents have passed? You have my condolences."

"Thank you. My mother passed away twelve years ago, and my father, five."

She clucked sympathetically at him. "Just one sister then?"

He gritted his teeth. "Yes, she is fifteen."

"Raising a girl through that age is a difficult task. You are to be commended for undertaking it."

He gave her a curt nod.

"With such means at your disposal, I suppose you must have a companion for her? Or is she still in school?"

"She has a companion, madam."

"Oh, good. Of course, a companion can never be all a girl of that age needs. She needs a mother, and if she has not, then a sister will do almost as well."

Purposely misunderstanding her, he said, "My sister must content herself with only a brother as there is no one else. We have extended family enough."

She tittered, her ample bosom shaking alarmingly in her low-cut dress. "Mr Darcy, surely you must understand that I meant she should acquire a sister through marriage. My Jane there"—she gestured down the table to where Miss Bennet sat—"is such a lady! And well experienced in the guidance of those younger than she. I do not suppose you know it, but besides Mary and Lizzy, I have two other daughters who remain in the school room."

Darcy chose not to respond.

"I cannot understand why there is this absurd custom whereby we must shut away our younger daughters until their elder sisters marry. Why, my Lydia, with her lively spirits, could make any party that much more agreeable! But so it is, and my Lydia awaits her turn at home."

Darcy had no opinion to offer on Miss Lydia Bennet, having never seen the girl.

"I would advise that you marry as soon as you can, Mr Darcy. It will be to your sister's benefit as much as your own."

Darcy again remained silent, but Mrs Bennet was neither dismayed nor reproached by his reserve. The conversation continued on with Darcy in silent indignation as Mrs Bennet did all she could to alternately urge him to marry and forward Miss Bennet to him. From there, she gossiped about her neighbours, pointing to each in turn and relating bits and pieces about them. The sum total of this discourse was that the Bennets were far and beyond the superior of the country society in which they found themselves, but they did all they could to provide the example of more genteel ways to the neighbourhood. Darcy breathed an enormous sigh of relief when the ladies rose to depart, taking the vulgar Mrs Bennet with them.

Likewise, Mrs Bennet was left with no great opinion of Mr Darcy, and she voiced her vexation loudly to Jane in the ladies withdrawing room. "I would dare you to find a more arrogant and unpleasant man. He had no conversation—quite silent, no doubt censuring us all. I am very disgusted with him. Such pride! If only he knew to whom he spoke!"

SHE IS HERE. A PAINFUL THRILL WENT THROUGH HIS CHEST.

The occasion was a party at Lucas Lodge several days later. Miss

Elizabeth was present with her family and engaged in conversation as he entered the room. He would not join her—he could not so plainly show his admiration—and instead chose to accept a glass of wine and walk over to the window near where she stood.

The conversation, held with the colonel of a regiment newly quartered in Meryton, was one he might have enjoyed. They spoke of travel on the Continent, and Miss Elizabeth admitted to having gone to Italy, which he found surprising. Had Mr Bennet taken his family? Singular.

He lingered, eavesdropping for some time and avoiding those who attempted to draw him into different discussions. He hoped she did not see his purpose; he flattered himself that she did not.

As the dinnertime approached, Darcy was surprised to see Sir William move towards Miss Elizabeth, evidently intent on escorting her into dinner. She quickly whispered something, and he looked fleetingly embarrassed then quickly went to Miss Bingley, extending his arm.

Darcy could not comprehend why Lady Lucas appeared momentarily flustered and made a quick motion to the housekeeper. But he could not concern himself with it overlong as they entered the dining room minutes later and he had the pleasure of being seated next to Miss Elizabeth.

"Miss Elizabeth Bennet," he acknowledged, as he assisted her into her chair.

"Mr Darcy."

They were across the table from Mr and Miss Bingley. To Bingley's dismay, Miss Bennet was seated at the far end of the table, eliminating the possibility of discourse with her, at least during dinner. It was fortunate for the rest of them, however, as Mr Bingley's liveliness and amiability carried the conversation.

With Miss Elizabeth's attention on Bingley, Darcy took advantage of the opportunity to surreptitiously study her. He began by examining her hands, delicate and pale as one rested lightly in her lap, the other curled elegantly around her fork. She had graceful arms, her elbows dimpling sweetly. Her neck was equally graceful though he saw little of it through the mass of dark curls gently bouncing onto it. He had concerned himself rather little with the styles in which ladies wore their hair but thought he much preferred the manner in which Miss Elizabeth wore hers to any he had seen before. It was the particular combination whereby both restraint and profusion were—

"I believe we have caught Mr Darcy wool-gathering." Miss Bingley's voice pierced his musings, and he came to attention at once. He could see by her countenance that she had noted his study of Miss Elizabeth and was displeased by it.

"Darcy is not always such a dull fellow," Bingley laughingly told Miss Elizabeth. "He is lively enough in other places, I assure you."

In a jaded, mean tone, Miss Bingley added, "Generally among those he considers his equals in consequence."

Darcy was mortified and opened his mouth to disavow her implication.

Miss Elizabeth turned and looked at him full on, stopping his words and making his pulse race. She raised one perfectly formed eyebrow, and he saw a teasing light come into her eyes. "Is that so, Mr Darcy? Are we to be denied the full measure of your wit because our consequence lacks dignity?"

"Absolutely not," he protested immediately. "I am not so vile as to refuse to converse with those of a different station or circle in society." He cast a severe, censuring frown at Caroline Bingley, who did not appear to notice him.

"Yet you have been silent. Surely, a man of your sense and education would have much to contribute to the conversation if he so chose."

Darcy was speechless, truly unable to compose a response. He could not admit the truth of his thoughts, which had been focused on his admiration of her. Yet he did not wish her to think him as unbearably haughty and arrogant as she likely would if the conversation stood as it was.

The pause drew long, and Bingley, never one to enjoy silence, decided to speak. "Perhaps it is not disparity in consequence that renders him uneasy but, rather, the society of ladies that induces him to quiet. Darcy is such an eligible marriage prospect that he seeks to avoid notice. I think he fears that, if he should speak too long or in a manner too familiar, a matchmaking mama will take hold of him and force him down the aisle." Bingley laughed at his own wit. "He is so accustomed to avoiding conversation with ladies that, when it is forced upon him in a dinner arrangement, he is discomfited, having had little practice in the drawing room."

Miss Elizabeth joined Bingley in his laughter, peeping up at Darcy when she finished. "Is that true? Has my presence rendered you silent?"

Yes, indeed. "Of course not."

"May I assure you that I harbour no matrimonial design on you whatsoever? You may exercise your wit on us with impunity; you are in no danger from me."

This did raise his interest, and he decided to tease her as she had him. "You are an unusual female, indeed, not to seek a husband."

"I did not say I do not seek a husband; I said I do not seek *you* for a husband." She smiled charmingly as she said it, and he was enraptured. "However, why should that render me so unusual? Did Mr Bingley not just intimate that you do not seek a wife—nay, that you avoid situations in which you might find yourself attached?"

"It is not unusual for a gentleman to delay taking a wife," Darcy opined. "In my experience, however, a lady who does not seek a husband is uncommon."

Miss Elizabeth's eyebrows rose. "Permit me to understand you. In this room are"—she quickly counted—"eight young ladies of a marriageable age who are still maidens. You believe all those ladies wish to marry you? You are very certain of your desirability, sir."

Darcy's mouth opened as he sought the appropriate rejoinder. As he could not contrive a politic means of saying what he thought, he was fortunate that Bingley rescued him by entering the conversation again.

"Darcy is a very good prospect. Few gentlemen have so much to offer a lady: wealth, consequence, and a family name that is nearly as old as England itself."

"Ah." Miss Elizabeth nodded, her eyes sparkling with a good humour that rendered her words inoffensive. "So you think us all so mercenary that we would settle with you for your fortune, never minding the fact that you have remained mute in our presence for the entirety of our acquaintance? What if a lady was the sort to prefer conversation and laughter to jewels and gowns?"

"It is natural and just," Darcy replied with confidence, "that when a lady's future, as well as that of her children, depends on the worth of the man she marries, she will marry a man with as great a fortune and as much consequence as she is able."

At once, the teasing light left her eyes, and it was replaced by a glimmer of sadness though her tone remained confident and light. "That is a dim view of the world. Like most arguments based on prejudice, it is weakened by the fact that an entire population is painted with a brush stained by the characteristics of only a few." She took a sip of her wine, and he saw her hand tremble slightly. "As you are under such suppositions, I cannot deny the sense in remaining silent. Who would wish to draw the attentions of such creatures as you imagine surround you, who seek to entrap you for your fortune and consequence?"

At once, Darcy felt he had offended her though he knew not how. He intended to tease and banter as Bingley did, yet he had caused sadness to come into her eyes. "I would, indeed, be far more inclined towards liveliness if I knew more ladies who valued affection above fortune; however, it is a difficult thing to discern given the strictures of our society as well as my own admittedly great limitations."

She offered him a brief, small smile that did nothing to conceal the hurt in her eyes. Although he had no notion of why she looked so, Darcy felt a great surge of protective impulse well up within him. He frantically thought of what more might be said or in what manner the conversation might be redirected towards that which was light and amiable. Before he could say anything, however, Mr Goulding, who was sitting to Miss Elizabeth's left, drew her attention, and the opportunity was lost.

HATEFUL MAN. WHO IS HE TO IMAGINE THAT EACH OF US IS SO DESIROUS of his hand in marriage? And to look down on us all—we who have been so welcoming, so obliging to him and his friend! A more despicable, rude gentleman I could not find.

Elizabeth was first discomfited and then vexed by the extent to which Mr Darcy stared at her throughout the remainder of the meal. He attempted to disguise his looks, but on occasion—when he surely believed she did not see him—he would stare at her quite intently. She could not think why unless he had heard the rumours about her and sought to confirm her identity. Perhaps he was cataloguing her faults, storing up little witticisms with which to entertain his friends at her expense. The thought angered her, and she decided to reprove him for it.

She made a show of being interested in the conversation away from him for some time. Then, when she knew his attentions were on her in full, she turned to him with no warning and spoke without preamble. "What is it, Mr Darcy?"

He blinked several times as though coming out of a trance, but his voice was as haughty and composed as ever. "I beg your pardon?"

"Your gaze is so severe, I must wonder what about me displeases you. Perhaps there is food on my face? Pray, tell me where the offending morsel lies that I might remove it directly." She gave him a falsely sweet smile.

"I did not intend to stare at you; it must have been mere absence of thought."

She did not believe him for a moment. "Well, I am relieved. I had supposed you to be cataloguing my faults, and I thought you must have found a surfeit of them, indeed, to be at it for such an extended period of time."

Now, he chuckled. "No, there is nothing marring your countenance, I assure you. I have far more profitable claims on my time than to spend it seeking imperfections in such beauty as yours."

Elizabeth's eyes flew wide in surprise at his comment. He had evidently shocked himself too as he flushed and seemed briefly discomposed. He recovered quickly, however, and took a large gulp of his wine.

Elizabeth was baffled by Mr Darcy's compliment, unintended as it seemed, and was relieved when Lady Lucas rose soon thereafter, taking the ladies with her to the drawing room. She nodded to Mr Darcy as she left, glad to escape his confusing manners: so severe and arrogant one moment and so unexpectedly disarming the next.

DARCY WATCHED MISS ELIZABETH QUIT THE ROOM WITH RELIEF, accepted a glass of port from Sir William, and quietly chastised himself for showing his preference so overtly. For whatever offence he might have served in the past, he could not risk having a flirtation now.

You must not raise her hopes. She is not for you. He resolved that he would neither speak to her nor look at her for the rest of the evening.

It was a difficult task. When he entered the drawing room, he heard Miss Lucas request that Miss Elizabeth play and sing, which she did. She was proficient at both activities, conveying not only technical perfection but also depth of emotion. He found himself pleasurably enthralled by her song, but he was then deeply mortified to realise he was watching the rise and fall of her bosom as she sang.

That, in combination with the love ballad she was singing, caused him to slip into a bit of a daydream, imagining her playing the song just for him. What might it be like to be alone with her in the music room at Pemberley as she played such a song? His mind went to the fainting couch in that room, and he imagined carrying her from the bench and laying her down upon the couch.

It was the sudden realisation of his burgeoning desire that pulled him from the scandalous turn his thoughts had taken. He flushed and glanced about, relieved to see that no one appeared to notice. He frowned at himself severely, shocked that he would have such lascivious thoughts of a pure country girl whom he could never claim as his own. *Yet I dally with her, if only in my mind.*

AT THE PIANOFORTE, ELIZABETH STUMBLED THROUGH A PASSAGE, discomfited to see Mr Darcy's stare again focused upon her. When he scowled at her error, she was embarrassed. *Do you think I wish to exhibit? I was compelled to play by my friend, our host's daughter, and nothing more drew me onto this bench. I claim no great talent or accomplishment in music.*

Her ire was further fuelled when, at the end of her song, Mr Darcy rose abruptly and left the room as though he could not bear to hear more. *Hateful man.*

ALONE IN HIS CHAMBER THAT NIGHT, DARCY SERIOUSLY PONDERED HIS growing fascination with Miss Elizabeth Bennet. He realised that his actions were such as to risk raising her expectations—expectations he could not, and would not, fulfil.

The conversation on the carriage ride from Lucas Lodge to Netherfield had centred on that lady's family, and though mostly aimed at Bingley, a few darts lodged in Darcy's conscience as well.

"The nothingness of that family, yet how they perceive themselves! Quite insupportable, do you not agree Mr Darcy?" Miss Bingley was clearly prepared to be merciless on the Bennets.

"Caroline," Bingley warned, "I will not have you saying such things about Miss Bennet's family. She is a beautiful, kind lady who has done you no wrong."

Miss Bingley quickly interjected, "Jane Bennet is a dear, sweet girl, and I anticipate continuing our friendship while we are in Hertfordshire. However, Charles, you surely have no notion of furthering the acquaintance. Sweet as she is, she would be laughed at in London."

"I disagree," Charles replied stubbornly while Darcy looked at him with alarm. Perhaps his friend's infatuation with Miss Bennet had progressed further than any of them had realised. "What I see is that I am a man with a fortune from trade, living at a leased estate, whose position could only be improved by marriage to a gentleman's daughter."

Miss Bingley was nearly apoplectic in her reply. "Marriage? Charles! I forbid you to fall in love with some unimportant country miss! Think of what you do to me! We would not be received!"

Darcy interjected with a quiet, "Charles, she is correct, you know."

His gentle rebuke startled both Bingley and his sister out of their squabble, and the darkened carriage was silent for several long moments.

Darcy continued a few moments later. "Your position, as well as that of your sister, could be materially damaged by marriage to anyone outside of the *ton*. With your fortune, you could unite with someone more prominent, and it would raise the prospects of Miss Bingley and your future children. Marriage to a poor country miss from nowhere will affect not only you but also generations after you. You must consider that in your selection of a bride."

Darcy pondered his words and considered them with regard to Miss Elizabeth. True, his fortune and his heritage made his position in society more solid than Bingley's, so he was less worried about being received or the effect on Georgiana's marriage. In reality, no matter what he did, Georgiana's dowry alone would ensure her more offers than she would ever desire.

No, in Darcy's case, it was not his position that concerned him; it was the possibility for ridicule.

And ridicule him they would if he did marry a penniless country miss with no connexions. The kinder among the *ton* would laugh at him for being taken in by a fortune hunter while those who were taste-less would make lewd comments about a marriage contracted in accordance with his baser desires. The speculation would be rampant that he had been forced to marry her.

He could already see the gentlemen at his club and their repugnant, sly winks and hear their comments about Miss Elizabeth's beauty and comely figure. And for the more brazen, there would be wonderment that he had not simply taken her as his mistress. He had seen it occur before when gentlemen of good standing married actresses, governesses, or any lady from the outside. They generally retained few of their old connexions, received few invitations, and, worst of all, attracted mockery and derision.

Blast! Darcy thought later that night as he struggled to find sleep, tossing violently in the bed. *How is it that I can see her worth and others would not?*

At once, Georgiana's face came into his mind. What would he do if Georgiana announced she wished to make such a poor alliance? A gentleman of modest means—someone like the son of Mr Goulding, perhaps, or that of Sir William Lucas?

I would tell her absolutely not. I would ascribe her desires to youthful misperception or infatuation, and tell her it could not be borne. Yet if I did something of the like, how could I rightly deny her without being a hypocrite?

He spoke aloud in the room to emphasise the point to his own wilful heart. "You must marry in accordance with your station. It cannot be her. It simply cannot. You will put her aside. You will do as you must."

FIVE

As the ladies gathered at breakfast the next day, with Mr Bennet behind his newspaper, Mrs Bennet apparently decided the time had come for some deeply felt chastisement of her eldest daughter.

"Jane, it is unkind of you to allow Mr Bingley to continue his attentions. Consider the other girls in the district for whom he could be a fine match. They have not your connexions, dear, and a wealthy man from trade will do well enough for many of them."

Jane was agape at this astonishing speech, and Elizabeth interceded. "Mama, I believe Mr Bingley is a fine match for Jane, and they seem to like each other very much. I cannot imagine why you are not more pleased with him, but as long as Jane is, nothing else really matters."

"The sister of a countess married to a man in trade? No, indeed, it is not done."

"I care only that Jane should marry and be happy with a man she loves."

"Oh, I see what this is about." Mrs Bennet scowled. "You know as well as I that, if Jane had been with you in Bath, his lordship never would have looked at you. Now, as you are required to go back to London seeking a husband, you want to have your beautiful sister out of the way, and who better than Mr Bingley to take her? I shall not hear of it. He is wholly unsuitable, and you are a very selfish girl!"

Elizabeth was stunned by this ridiculous speech. "My only concern is my sister's felicity in marriage."

"What greater felicity can there be than a wealthy and powerful husband?"

Jane recovered sufficiently to respond. "Mama, I like Mr Bingley very much. He is everything a young man should be: kind and amiable. I care not one bit where his money has come from."

"Nonsense!" Mrs Bennet cried stridently. "You will accompany Lizzy to town for the Season, where you will attend balls and parties and meet so many wonderful gentlemen that you will scarcely be able to choose—gentlemen with titles and fortunes that make Bingley's wealth look like nothing."

Jane protested, "But I do not—"

"I shall hear no more of this! No more Mr Bingley!" Mrs Bennet set her utensils down firmly, stood, and swept indignantly from the room.

Jane cast a troubled glance at Elizabeth, who reached over and patted her hand. "If you fall in love with Mr Bingley and he loves you in return, let nothing stand in your way, not even Mama. Once we are in town, we will see him often, and I will see to it that he has an invitation to any party we attend." She smiled mischievously at her sister. "Perhaps his close friendship with a countess will raise his connexions enough for even Mama."

"Lizzy, I do not wish to embarrass you or do anything improper—"

"My dearest wish for you is a love like the love I had in my marriage, brief as it was. You know that Henry's wealth and title meant nothing to me. What meant everything was his love. Unfortunately, I am left with merely the title and wealth, but although I had his love only briefly, I would not have lived without it for anything."

Tears formed in Elizabeth's eyes, but she blinked them away. "A marriage without love is a grim prospect. Dearest, you must stand up to Mama, whether it is Mr Bingley or any other man most fortunate to earn your affection. Do not give up on it—not for her, not for anyone."

"DEAREST, YOU MUST STAND UP TO MAMA." IT WAS THESE LAST WORDS that came back to haunt Elizabeth two days later as she rode towards Netherfield.

The previous morning, a note had arrived from Caroline Bingley

entreating Jane to dine with her and Mrs Hurst for the gentlemen were
to dine with the officers of Colonel Forster's regiment. When the note
was received as the Bennets were at breakfast, Mrs Bennet had
snatched it from Jane's hand and, after reading it aloud, pronounced,
"What elegant handwriting Miss Bingley has, and how very gracious
of her to invite you to dine. You must be equally gracious in your
refusal."

"Refusal?" Jane said in surprise. "I am pleased to dine with Miss
Bingley and Mrs Hurst this evening."

"Oh, Jane, really! You need not spend your time with these ladies
or their brother. Enjoy a quiet evening at home; you will have little rest
once you get to town. Why, there will be parties and balls and evenings
at Almack's to entertain you almost every night, and in between, the
opera, the theatre, teas, dinner parties—"

Elizabeth interrupted her mother's fantasies. "But for now, we are
in Hertfordshire, and the sisters of a gentleman that Jane esteems wish
to know her better. I think she should go."

Mrs Bennet shot a glare in Elizabeth's direction. "Jane, you will not
go to Netherfield for dinner, and that is the end of it."

Jane stood so abruptly that her chair nearly toppled over. Glaring at
her mother, she stated, "I *will* go to Netherfield tonight for dinner. I am
in love with Mr Bingley, and I shall further this acquaintance with his
sisters because I very much hope that they will one day be *my* sisters!"

The entire breakfast table was shocked into silence by this unprece-
dented display of defiance from Jane, as well as the sentiments she
revealed.

"Very well, but you will not use your father's carriage," remarked
Mrs Bennet with deceptive calm.

Jane, red-faced and shaking with anger, proclaimed, "Then I shall
walk." She fled the room.

So Jane set out on foot, but unfortunately, she was caught in a rainstorm. She arrived at Netherfield wet, muddy, and on the verge of a
fever. Although her dress was quickly taken care of by the house staff,
nothing could be done to avert the fever that rapidly overtook her. This
led to her instalment in one of the guest apartments to the delight of Mr
Bingley and the dismay of Mrs Bennet.

"I do hope you are happy, Lizzy," said Mrs Bennet upon receipt of
the note from Netherfield. "If Jane should die, it will be due to you
encouraging her to pursue Mr Bingley."

"It is just a cold, Mama," Elizabeth protested. "People do not die of trifling colds. However, I do believe I shall go to Netherfield to see how she fares. Neither Mrs Hurst nor Miss Bingley strike me as the sort to nurse an ill guest."

"Go at once. By all means, get her home before this Bingley fellow does something to induce her to marry him."

Elizabeth was truly concerned with the state in which she found her sister. Jane was alarmingly warm and had a sore throat and severe headache. Not surprisingly, neither Miss Bingley nor Mrs Hurst had been particularly solicitous to her, and Elizabeth decided the apothecary was needed directly.

Smoothing Jane's hair, she assured her that she would return shortly and proceeded to the breakfast room, where she assumed she would find her host and hostess to request their assistance. She paused in the hall, not intending to eavesdrop on the conversation occurring therein but overhearing it nevertheless.

"And now we must entertain her sister as well? Dear me, will all the Bennets be set upon us?" Miss Bingley's voice dripped with displeasure at the notion.

Mr Bingley replied, his tone mild, "I think it very kind of Miss Elizabeth to come and see to her sister."

Miss Bingley sniffed. "Such a sight it was when Miss Bennet arrived! Quite shocking—petticoats six inches deep in mud and the lady soaked to the skin! I had no notion country society was so lacking that a lady would walk three miles alone and through a rainstorm."

Mr Bingley replied, "The severity of the storm was unexpected. I am certain Miss Bennet had no warning of it when she set out."

Mrs Hurst argued, "No lady who had any understanding of refined society would have continued through the storm. Once she realised how dreadful she looked, she should have returned home straightaway."

"Mr Darcy," Miss Bingley drawled. "You would surely not want your sister to make such a spectacle."

"No, I would not."

Elizabeth heard their censure and despised them all the more for it. She considered it an excellent time to enter the room and leave them to wonder whether their uncharitable remarks were overheard.

Mr Bingley, the only one who had been charitable, was also the only one to appear guilty on her entry. "Miss Elizabeth! How does Miss Bennet?"

"Very poorly, I fear. Would you be so kind as to summon the apothecary?"

He agreed, and with this, Miss Bingley and Mrs Hurst seemed to glean some notion of what was expected of them. They rose with a sudden sickly sweet concern, exclaiming over dear Jane, and how dreadful it was to be ill, and oh, how she must suffer, and on and on until Elizabeth thought she might be taken ill herself from the nauseating insincerity.

They did as they should, however, and soon the apothecary arrived, and Elizabeth found herself with an invitation to remain at Netherfield.

WHEN MISS ELIZABETH APPEARED FOR DINNER THAT NIGHT, SHE WAS met by an unwelcoming group. Mr Bingley was, of course, all that was kind and solicitous, but once at the table, she was placed too far away from him for his kindness to have any effect. She sat beside Mr Hurst, who was interested in nothing that did not rest on his plate, and across from Mrs Hurst, who divided her attention between her sister and playing with her bracelets.

The dinner passed with merciful swiftness, and immediately afterwards, Elizabeth went to attend to Jane, pleased to find her in a peaceful sleep. Despite wishing she could remain in her own apartment, she had no cause for remaining upstairs. Indeed, she owed it to her host and hostess to join them in the drawing room. Much as she knew she was unwanted, she did not wish to give way to poor manners, for they had done her a kindness in inviting her to stay.

She found the group engaged in various occupations. Mrs Hurst read a small publication, Mr Hurst and Mr Bingley played cards, and Mr Darcy was at a writing desk, with Miss Bingley close by and intent on his actions. She watched the pair with some amusement.

"How delighted Miss Darcy will be to receive such a letter!" Miss Bingley exclaimed.

He made no answer.

"You write uncommonly fast."

"You are mistaken. I write rather slowly."

"How many letters you must have occasion to write in the course of the year! Letters of business too! How odious I should think them!"

"It is fortunate, then, that they fall to my lot instead of yours."

A moment later, she said, "Pray, tell your sister that I long to see her."

"I have already told her so once by your desire."

"I am afraid you do not like your pen. Let me mend it for you. I mend pens remarkably well."

"Thank you, but I always mend my own." Elizabeth hid a small smile at Mr Darcy's evident desire to be left alone and Miss Bingley's wilful ignorance of it.

"How can you contrive to write so even?"

He was silent.

"Tell your sister I am delighted to hear of her improvement on the harp, and pray let her know that I am quite in raptures with her beautiful little design for a table, and I think it infinitely superior to Miss Grantley's."

"Will you give me leave to defer your raptures till I write again? At present I have not room to do them justice."

"Oh, it is of no consequence! I shall see her in January. But do you always write such charming long letters to her, Mr Darcy?"

"They are generally long; but whether always charming, it is not for me to determine."

"It is a rule with me that a person who can write a long letter with ease cannot write ill."

"That will not do for a compliment to Darcy, Caroline," cried her brother, "because he does *not* write with ease. He studies too much for words of four syllables. Do not you, Darcy?"

"My style of writing is very different from yours."

"Oh!" cried Miss Bingley, "Charles writes in the most careless way imaginable. He leaves out half his words and blots the rest."

"My ideas flow so rapidly that I have not time to express them, which means my letters sometimes convey no ideas at all to my correspondents."

"Then they serve no purpose," Darcy proclaimed, "and should be set aside until you possess the time needed to compose an informative missive."

"If I did that," Mr Bingley said with a laugh, "no one would ever receive any correspondence from me."

Elizabeth had become a bit lost in thought during this exchange, recalling a letter she had once received from Henry. In the brief time of their acquaintance and marriage, there had been few letters written. Indeed, from the time they met in Bath until his death, they were scarcely separated, save for the time she returned to Hertfordshire to tell her parents of her intention to marry. Even then, he was hard on her heels and in Hertfordshire only two days later to speak to her father.

In that short time apart, she had received three letters from him. Those letters were now her most prized possessions, but she permitted herself no more than occasional perusal of them. One was written exceedingly ill. It, too, had words that were blotted and blotched, scratched out and underlined, and she had wondered that such an educated man would write something so disordered. However, at the end of it, Henry had written the loveliest words:

> *Pray, forgive my poor excuse for writing. When you are in my thoughts, my darling girl, I can scarcely hold onto my pen, for my hand trembles with the wish to touch you, and my heart pounds so, it threatens to expel me from my seat. All of it speaks to my extraordinary love for you, but alas, it does not make for a neatly written letter. I shall send it anyway, that you might see how great your effect is on me, and also, how we must never be parted again, for my letters are too illegible for us to bear it.*

She glanced over at Mr Bingley, whom she realised was a good-natured soul. No matter the way or the determination with which his friend and sister tried to slight him, he greeted it with good humour, and she found herself wishing to defend him.

"A letter can express many things besides the words that are written. Quickness of opinion, emotion, and the regard of the author are contained in the writing of it, and if those things are conveyed through an unsteady hand, even that may be a compliment to the reader."

She drew the attention of everyone in the room, and all of them stared, having not before seen the inclination of Miss Elizabeth Bennet to voice an unsought—and contrary—opinion.

Mr Darcy was quick to respond. "I cannot think of any better way to compliment my reader than to present to him or her a letter that I have composed carefully enough to make it legible."

"Yet, in your caution, do you not suppress any indication of the true state of your being that carelessness could not constrain?"

"The state of my being, such as I wish it to be known, is made evident in the words I have written."

"A person who chooses his words carefully does so because he wishes to convey a specific message that does not always reflect his true condition. You write to your sister, and perhaps you do not wish her to know that your state is one of disorderly sensibility. Thus you make every effort to write a stately and calm letter."

Mr Darcy wrinkled his brow. "What guardian would wish his ward to know he is filled with riotous emotion?"

Elizabeth smiled. "That is my very point. You write in such a way as to conceal anything you do not wish made known. Mr Bingley's writings, such as they are—and I do beg your pardon, sir, for I have not seen your writing and cannot attest to any blot upon it—are honest."

Miss Bingley seemed anxious that Mr Darcy's attentions were on Miss Elizabeth and he might grow vexed by her impertinence. She stood hastily. "Miss Elizabeth, perhaps you will favour us with some music?"

Elizabeth did not answer straightaway as she found herself locked in one of Mr Darcy's intent gazes. With great deliberation, he raised one eyebrow at her and dipped his pen back into the ink. With an untidy flourish, he added one more line and his signature to the letter. After a moment's consideration, he dipped his pen into the ink once more and flicked a rather generous blot onto the bottom of the page. Elizabeth watched him with amazement.

Gravely, he said, "There you go, Miss Bennet. Do you suppose that my sister will be better able now to discern the truth of my fondness for her?"

Elizabeth sat motionless and mortified, fully comprehending Mr Darcy's rebuke. A flush rose to her cheeks, and she was confused by what, if anything, she should say in reply.

She was saved by Miss Bingley's urging, "Miss Elizabeth, I beg you would play for us."

"Forgive me, Miss Bingley—yes, I would be pleased to play." With great alacrity, she went towards the instrument.

She chose a piece that did not require her to sing as the agitation of her spirits would have prevented it. Even with her hands slightly shaking, she managed to do credit to the piece. She had practised diligently in the past years, and it showed in her exhibition.

Her confusion arose from several things; the first being regret at having provoked Mr Darcy as she had. She saw readily his vexation and felt his reproof was warranted.

Why do I insist on teasing this man? Elizabeth could not comprehend what it was in Mr Darcy that raised this mischievous, impertinent spirit within her. As she had noted on their first official introduction, something in him awakened something in her—the essential part of her that had lain dormant since those dark days in 1809.

Perhaps she was ready to regain that essence of herself, the part of her that, in the past, had always enjoyed a debate and expressed her opinions, too readily in some cases. It was rather a good feeling to return to what once was, even though she had chosen a poor subject on whom to exercise her wit and opinions.

Darcy excused himself for a moment, going to the hall where the post was collected, wanting a moment to gather his composure. He was both exhilarated and frightened by the exchange between them. His little gesture with the ink on his letter was purposeful flirtation. Now he could not decide whether he regretted it or relished it—maybe both.

What was the meaning behind their banter? Did she see through him? Did she know his feelings? Was she saying that his mask was inadequate?

In the same moment that his heart exulted in the thought of it, his reason intervened. This was not good, and if she did suspect that he harboured a tender regard for her, it was so much the worse. Miss Elizabeth remained entirely unsuitable, and if he raised her expectations in any manner, then he was not the honourable gentleman he had been raised to be.

That thought calmed him until he walked back into the drawing room and saw her perched so prettily at the instrument. Willing himself to remain in the moment rather than be lost to some undoubtedly erotic flight of fancy, he sat and listened to her, permitting himself the indulgence of gazing upon her as she exhibited.

After she played, Miss Elizabeth apparently felt she had spent sufficient time in the drawing room to ensure that her obligations to her hostess were fulfilled, and she excused herself for the night. Darcy watched her go with both regret and relief, and then, deciding that he, too, had had enough company for the evening, excused himself.

He ascended the stairs quietly, and as he passed Miss Bennet's chamber, he heard Elizabeth speaking within. His manners urged him to continue down the hall to his own rooms, but his wishes won the battle, and he lingered outside the door, eager to know of what they spoke. Elizabeth was clearly relating the events of the evening to Jane. As he listened guiltily, he convinced himself that he wished to know more of Miss Bennet's feelings for Bingley when, truly, he wanted to hear whether Elizabeth said anything of him.

Miss Bennet mostly murmured inaudibly, but Miss Elizabeth's responses were clear.

"It was a quiet evening. I read, and the others played at whist."

Another murmur.

"By enquiring of the gentlemen, I can only assume you wish to learn more of Mr Hurst, who was both well in looks this evening and managed to remain sober for nearly a quarter of an hour."

Darcy stifled a chuckle that threatened to burst forth.

Elizabeth continued on. "You wish to hear of Mr Darcy, then? No? Well there is only one other, Jane, a blond gentleman, I believe…"

Darcy heard Miss Bennet laugh quietly, and he smiled at Elizabeth's ability to cheer her ill sister. "I will torment you no longer. Yes, the indefatigably amiable Mr Bingley was charming and in good cheer. I believe that, if a tornado were to tear through Netherfield, he would smile approvingly at it. He looked dashing in a blue coat, seemed to have an excellent grasp of the finer points of whist, and finished nearly all of his dinner though I suspect he cares little for fish. What else would you like to know?"

Miss Bennet was now laughing at Elizabeth's summary of the evening and spoke louder. "Oh, Lizzy, you are too much at times. Now you must tell me, was it truly so awful?"

Elizabeth was more sedate in her response. "Miss Bingley clearly wishes me to leave, if not Netherfield then at least the common rooms. Hers is a superficial hospitality at best. I would not have you feel badly on my account; I could not abandon you to them. At any rate, I will exact a payment for this time when I drag you about London with scores and scores of ladies like Miss Bingley disparaging us at every turn!"

Darcy's brow rose. Were the two Bennet girls off for a London Season? Some scheme of Mrs Bennet, no doubt, who was not circumspect in her desperation to secure rich and titled husbands for them.

He moved quietly down the hall towards his chambers as he considered the implication of the Bennets in London. Would they intrude upon his notice? Seek to gain invitations using his name? He briefly imagined Mrs Bennet in town with her vulgarity and pretensions, and he shuddered.

With a brief frown, he realised that, more than ever, he must cease any sort of encouragement of Miss Elizabeth. The connexion would not do—not at all—and it would be best if any familiarity was discouraged now.

SIX

Darcy rose early the next morning, firmly resolved that any and all particular attention paid to Miss Elizabeth Bennet would cease. He would show no partiality or any action, no matter how innocuous, that would reveal his feelings for her. With that in mind, he departed his chambers for the stable, visions of a long, mind-clearing ride through the countryside directing his steps.

Several hours later, he returned: muddied, tired, and possessed of a mind still filled with thoughts of Elizabeth Bennet. As he came around the corner of the stable, he thought he heard her voice. Looking around, he saw her in the side yard, away from the eyes of the stable boys or anyone else passing that way.

He did not recognise the man she was with, but by his dress, he was a servant. Nevertheless, it could not be denied that he was a fine figure of a man. He had a handsome countenance and appeared a bit older, likely near thirty. He was large, nearly as tall as Darcy was but far more heavily muscled, his shoulders and arms straining against his coat. He stood close to her and handed her a letter before whispering something in her ear. She smiled up at him.

Darcy reeled back in disgust even as a lightning bolt of jealous rage shot through him. Such shocking behaviour! In plain sight no less... well, not exactly plain sight, but surely she must know she might be seen. *How foolish to risk not only her own respectability but that of her sisters as well. Stupid, stupid girl!*

He had his gloves in one hand and smacked them smartly against the palm of the other as he strode towards the house, full of self-righteous indignation. *Should I inform Bingley? I cannot abide the thought of her taking advantage of his easy nature to conduct an affair under his roof. Bingley must return her to her father's home straightaway.*

Jealousy and disappointment burned and roiled in his stomach. He longed to confront her and hear her explanation for such wanton behaviour. Perhaps knowing her true character would release him from her enchantments.

He nodded firmly, resolved to speak to her of the matter directly on her return.

AGAINST HER BETTER JUDGMENT, ELIZABETH HAD SENT JERVIS, HER footman/protector, to Longbourn to retrieve her letters from Henry. She had scarcely slept the night before, struggling with her longing to see them again, and had finally given in to her wishes.

Jervis had naturally accompanied her to Netherfield, and Elizabeth had asked Bingley's housekeeper, Mrs Nicholls, to find a place for him. Being a local woman, she knew the truth behind Longbourn's cortege of well-fed footmen. The good lady said nothing of the matter to her master or mistress and quietly placed Jervis where he needed to be within the house. Mrs Nicholls thought Miss Bingley would scarcely notice an extra servant as she had not bothered to know the ones belonging to Netherfield.

Jervis met Elizabeth in a secluded spot by the stables as Elizabeth hoped to avoid questions about him and his task. Giving her the letters, he mentioned, "There is some additional correspondence that awaits you at Longbourn: letters from Mr Stokes." Mr Stokes was the steward of Warrington Castle.

"I shall see to them on my return tomorrow." She smiled up at him, thanking him, and they departed. Jervis dropped behind to shadow her as he usually did.

She made for the house, Henry's letters feeling like a living creature in her hand. She both dreaded and anticipated seeing them again. It was always such a delight to read the letters and imagine, for a time, that she was awaiting Henry's return. The feelings they elicited in her were too pleasurable to deny—the hope, relief, and joy lifting her heart from its usual frozen state.

However, all too rapidly, the delight would be followed by anguish as she was recalled to reality. It was akin to losing him all over again, recalling that he would not come back and she had no hope, no relief, and no joy. With those memories, her poor heart would again become encased in its shell of determined complaisance and hidden grief.

Was it worth the few brief moments of pleasure for the intense melancholy that came after?

"Miss Bennet." She nearly jumped from her skin, having not noticed Mr Darcy in the hall. "I wonder if you would oblige me? I must speak with you on a matter of some delicacy." He gestured towards a small sitting room that was currently unoccupied.

She was so surprised that she followed him into the room without question. He closed the door behind them, causing her to protest, "Mr Darcy, pray leave the door ajar. It would not do to have the servants gossip about our being behind a closed door together."

For some reason her statement caused him to emit a bitter chuckle. "You are concerned over being in a closed room with me?"

She pursed her lips, choosing not to ask about his odd comment. She took a seat while Mr Darcy elected to remain as he was, towering over her.

He frowned down at her. "I observed your actions by the stables. You are fortunate I am the one who saw you; I abhor gossip, and you may depend upon my secrecy on the matter. I do implore you to exercise greater discretion, however. If you have no regard for your own respectability, you must think of your sisters."

"My actions by the stables?" Elizabeth raised her chin and her left eyebrow, returning severity for severity. "I beg your pardon?"

Mr Darcy leaned over her, speaking angrily. "I saw you, Miss Bennet, with a footman."

"And what of it?"

Darcy straightened, folding his hands behind his back. "It is not fitting to behave in such a manner. I am no babe in the woods, Miss Elizabeth, and I do apprehend the meaning of the sight I saw before me."

Rage blossomed within her as comprehension dawned. "Of what do you accuse me, Mr Darcy?"

His words were clipped. "You were alone in a hidden spot with a man unrelated to you. You stood too close to him. You received a letter from him."

Elizabeth felt herself tremble and knew her face must be flushed from the effort required not to slap this presumptuous, hateful man. "And from this you conclude something of a licentious nature?"

She inhaled deeply and rose, not wishing to show any subjection to this odious man and his execrable suggestions. "That man was a footman from my home, whom I dispatched this morning to retrieve a letter from my bedchamber at Longbourn. I met him by the stables because I was returning from a ride as he arrived. It was no more scandalous than sitting in my mother's drawing room and asking him to retrieve a letter for me. As for the letter itself, need I remind you that most servants neither read nor write, so love letters are out of the question."

"You would have me believe—"

She took a step towards him and did her best to appear threatening. "Jervis is my servant and no more than that. I shall thank you to keep your vile suppositions to yourself."

Darcy simply looked at her, his breath coming a bit hard as he stared down at her face. At long last, an embarrassed look came over him. "I beg your pardon, I should not have—"

"No, you should not have. You were quick to judge, and as with most judgments made in haste, yours were greatly in error. Allow me to impress a truth upon you, sir: you do not know me, and this incident should serve as your reminder; things are not always as they seem."

With that, she swept from the room, maintaining great dignity the entire way to her bedchamber. Then she locked the door behind her and had an excellent, and relieving, bout of weeping.

DARCY HASTILY WITHDREW TO THE LIBRARY WHERE HE FELT CERTAIN he would encounter no one. He was utterly mortified, both by his ill-judged and offensive accusations as well as by the wild, irrational jealousy that had incited them.

Not good, not good at all. Miss Elizabeth Bennet was turning him into a blathering idiot, going about making a cake of himself at every turn. He must gain control of his thoughts and feelings at once!

He was deeply ashamed at the manner in which he had insulted her. He realised he should have supposed the man was a servant performing a task for her, or at least considered the possibility before accusing her. After all, in recalling it, they were truly not standing so very close together, nor did they seem to have hid. They were merely in an out-of-the-way place in the yard. He had seen nothing more damning than the man handing her a letter—and, as she had rightly stated, servants generally did not read or write.

He placed his head in his hands, thinking of his embarrassment, and was in that very position when the door was flung open.

"Mr Darcy! There you are, sir!"

A more unwelcome intrusion he could not have imagined: Caroline Bingley in high dudgeon. "Come this instant. We are being set upon by more Bennets!"

"More Bennets?"

"Their carriage is arriving even now. Come with me. I insist."

He dutifully followed Miss Bingley to the drawing room where Bingley also sat. A few moments later, Miss Elizabeth arrived, and much to his dismay, he could clearly see by her reddened eyes that she had recently wept. *Darcy, you are a brute of the lowest order.*

Miss Elizabeth sat with admirable composure. "Miss Bingley, my mother has sent a note indicating she believes Jane must return home though I have told her that Jane remains too ill to be moved."

"We should not think of it!" Bingley cried, even as Miss Bingley replied coolly, "In all likelihood, she has the right of it."

During his brief time in Hertfordshire, Darcy had found himself, in turns, embarrassed, irritated, and wearied by the silly yet conceited Mrs Bennet. The woman was coarse, uneducated, ill mannered, and uncouth, yet she possessed the airs of a duchess, particularly with regard to the marital prospects of her five daughters. All of said daughters were handsome creatures, but they were nevertheless country girls with little fortune and a lack of connexion to superior society. In his estimation, Mrs Bennet's pretensions were anything but realistic.

Mrs Bennet was taken to see Jane, whom she proclaimed to be quite well despite the fever, cough, and sore throat that continued to afflict her. "Dear Jane is very comfortable here; however, a daughter's place is with her mother, so I shall take her home."

"Mama, Jane must remain at Netherfield," Elizabeth protested. "The apothecary has recommended it."

"Apothecary," Mrs Bennet dismissed the man with a wave of her hand. "Jane is well enough, and the ride is short. We shall have her settled at Longbourn in no time."

A polite little argument ensued: Mrs Bennet and Miss Bingley against Elizabeth and Mr Bingley. The former declared Jane well enough to return home, and the latter insisted she was not. Eventually a compromise was struck, with the Bennet ladies to return to Longbourn on the morrow, provided Jane's fever had abated.

Mrs Bennet, having been forced to give way, was disgruntled and took Miss Bingley in her sights, even though the lady had so recently been her ally. "Miss Bingley, it is a very sweet room you have here. I believe Mr Bingley is but leasing Netherfield; is that not so?"

Miss Bingley was also dissatisfied and had the correct sense that Mrs Bennet was disparaging her. Darcy grinned inwardly as Miss Bingley raised her chin, fully prepared to release her own pretensions.

"One cannot be too quick to settle, and although Netherfield is a charming home, we are used to moving in more cultured society and at a time in life when social obligations do increase. The confined and unvarying society of the country—"

"Confined and unvarying? You are quite mistaken. We dine regularly with four and twenty families, estate owners all. I beg your pardon for my forgetfulness, but do tell me: Where is your father's estate?"

Miss Bingley did not respond; Mrs Bennet knew the origin of their fortune. Darcy felt an unmanly urge to giggle at the sight of the two most pompous ladies he knew attempting to outdo one another.

Elizabeth made an attempt to deflect the rising tension in the room by interrupting. "Mama, how is Charlotte Lucas? Has she called at Longbourn since I have been away?"

"Oh, Charlotte—such a solid, dependable girl! She will make someone an excellent wife. Her skills in estate management would be an asset to any man." She paused to beam knowingly at Mr Bingley, who appeared bewildered. "A pity she is so plain, but beauty fades where good heartedness will abide."

"Mama!" Elizabeth gasped, obviously embarrassed by her mother's coarse speech.

Darcy saw her blush and felt ashamed of his previous amusement. Elizabeth clearly did not find her mother's airs acceptable and was mortified by her behaviour—a feeling that he was certain she experienced with regularity.

He again felt in his chest a sense of protectiveness from seeing, as he had before, that certain something fragile about her: the whisper of a shadow that would flit across her face or a brief moment of sadness, always so quickly gone. Did he imagine it? Did he wish it there to justify this odd, fierce sort of desire to be her protector—to care for her and love her as she deserved?

It was just this impulse he yielded to now: the desire to protect and ameliorate her woes. Perhaps it might even make her look more kindly upon him as, at this moment, she certainly thought him horrid. "Miss Lucas seems a genteel, pretty sort of girl, and I have no doubt that the man she weds will be a fortunate one."

Elizabeth looked at him in shock, and Mrs Bennet preened, certain that Darcy's approbation would be all that was needed to secure Bingley's heart for Charlotte Lucas.

Bingley appeared increasingly baffled by the conversation and seemingly unconscious of the air of tension running through the room. Thus, he redirected the conversation to his own favourite sort of discourse: ideas for future amusements. "Mrs Bennet, I find myself much of a mind to hold a ball here at Netherfield. What say you to that?"

Mrs Bennet gave Bingley a supercilious smile. "How kind of you to think of your neighbours in this way, but it is unnecessary. You would not wish to undertake such an event when you are so newly arrived. Your poor sister!—much of the work would fall to her, you know, and if one is not experienced in entertaining at a country estate—"

Caroline sniffed haughtily. "I am quite capable of arranging a simple country dance."

"Truly, you need not burden yourselves. 'Tis such a challenge with so many details and instructions for the servants; otherwise, nothing gets done properly."

"It is not a burden, to be sure, particularly to one who is most capable of instructing her many servants—"

"Servants require close guidance for an event of true elegance and—"

"I am well aware of the requirements for a successful party."

The two traded thinly veiled set downs for a few more minutes, and so it was that Bingley found himself committed to hosting a ball at Netherfield, and Miss Bingley found herself determined to produce an event the likes of which Hertfordshire had never before seen.

AFTER DINNER, THE EVENING BEGAN AS QUIETLY AS THE PREVIOUS ONE had. Most of the party were engaged in the reading of various books or letters or, in the case of Mrs Hurst, the gossip pages from London.

Mr Darcy was engaged in a book, but not so much so, Elizabeth noted, that he would not take any opportunity to stare at her. It was tiring trying to discern what he was about or what he sought to find in her, and so she disregarded him, her mind pressed by weightier concerns.

Her book could not content her. Instead, she found herself continually drawn to memories of her past and anxieties for her future. Her apprehension over going to London had been brought to the fore by Mr Darcy's judgment of her, and seeing her mother behave so spitefully to Miss Bingley had worsened the effect. She did not know whether she could thrive in a place where similar behaviour abounded.

The company of people such as Mr Darcy, the Hursts, and the Bingleys would become familiar to her. She would go to parties with scores of ladies like Miss Bingley and Mrs Hurst and dozens of men like Mr Darcy, and somehow among them, she must find a suitable father for her dear son. She sighed heavily as little Henry's sweet, cherubic face appeared in her mind.

Miss Bingley's strident voice provided contrast to the precious image. "One hundred gowns, Louisa! Have you ever heard of such a thing?"

Mrs Hurst agreed she had not.

"Make no mistake of it, the widow of the Earl of Courtenay is clearly hunting a husband and intends to be at every ball and party until she has one. Charles, can you imagine it? You think I spend too much, and this chit—and I do mean chit, for I believe she is but an ignorant little country girl of only eighteen or nineteen—has ordered one hundred gowns for the Season!"

Elizabeth stared at her in shock and dismay, clutching her book tightly to hide the trembling of her hands. *Is it starting already? Gossip is being printed about me before I am even in town. I did not order one hundred gowns!*

She was having a great number of gowns made, but Lady Matlock had insisted that she would need each of them for the demands of the Season. Some were not even new but re-workings of older gowns to make them more current with the fashions.

Mr Bingley showed no interest in Miss Bingley's report. "If Lady Courtenay requires a hundred gowns, and has funds for a hundred gowns, I am sure it is nothing to me."

"Yet, how you do go on when you think I have ordered an excess of finery!"

Mr Bingley shrugged, his attention still on his newspaper. "If you had funds for a hundred gowns, you would likely order a hundred and fifty. No matter what you have, Caroline, you will always spend more."

His rebuke went unnoticed, for Miss Bingley's mind had already landed on another thought. "I simply cannot wait to make her acquaintance. Imagine the arts and allurements one must know to entrap such an eligible man! I daresay, we all have much to learn from her!"

Mrs Hurst opined, "The telling of her arts would not be fit for a true lady's ears."

"True," Miss Bingley snickered. "Very wanton, I am sure—or rather, I believe. Only a harlot could know for sure."

Mr Bingley scolded her, but she continued. "No one of consequence will receive her. She is entirely uneducated, from what I have heard, and silent as a nun!"

"I heard she is a bluestocking who speaks too much and is unattractively opinionated," Mrs Hurst said in complete contradiction of her sister, who forgot the prior two seconds and nodded vigorously in agreement.

"Neither is she attractive. I heard she is almost painfully thin, her figure much like that of a boy, with no bosom at all to speak of! Did you hear it said so?"

"Oh yes! And that her hips were broad and fleshy like a common fishwife."

Elizabeth felt tears spring into her eyes. She looked down at the book on her lap, hoping no one would take notice of her consternation.

Why do I care what these ridiculous women think? They are silly and vain and do not know me at all. Henry knew I loved him as I know he loved me. His fortune and his title meant nothing to me. Indeed, I wish he had not any such consequence, for had he not, he would likely still be with me. I would much prefer that to ordering an absurd number of gowns for social events I do not wish to attend to find a husband I do not want.

"He did not love her, you know," Mrs Hurst told her sister in a grave and knowing tone. "I believe she arranged a compromise."

Caroline gasped. "No! She did not!"

"Oh yes! Who knows whether it was true? I think some sort of obscene allurements were used to—"

"I beg your pardon." Elizabeth found herself rising on shaking legs, hoping her face was not blushed scarlet. "I believe I must check on Jane."

She scarcely dared curtsey. As overset as she was, she felt sure that, if she bent her knees even slightly, they would give way completely and cause her to topple over. She left the room, trembling with anger, mortification, and an intense wish to deliver a vicious set down to those two. Only the certain knowledge that she could not do so without bursting into tears stayed her tongue.

Large, hot tears began coursing down her cheeks almost as soon as the door closed behind her. She paused, pulling her handkerchief to her face and pressing it into her eyes.

She was angry with herself for being bothered by the sisters and their gossip. She had to accustom herself to the notion that people would speak of her. Regardless of what she wished, she was an interesting story: an unknown young girl from the country who had found herself spectacularly wealthy and titled and at the centre of some political intrigue, complete with traitors and murderers. It was too delicious not to be talked of, and she must accept that and not let it distress her so.

She scolded herself in the hall. "Stop being so ridiculous. It does not matter what those two think; they are feeble-minded."

"I must say, I agree," a deep voice informed her, "about the latter part, of course, not the part about your being ridiculous."

Her tears ceased immediately as Elizabeth emitted a slight shriek. "Oh!" She turned towards the voice. "Mr Darcy, I did not realise you were there."

Mr Darcy had silently exited the drawing room and followed her into the hall. *Oh, this man! Why is he always lurking about?*

"Are you well?"

She summoned as much dignity as a weeping woman could when caught talking to herself. "Perfectly so, Mr Darcy."

Her handkerchief had grown soggy, and he pulled his from his pocket. She took it reluctantly, swallowing hard in an attempt to control herself. It was not so easy with Mr Darcy's intent stare on her, and she wished desperately that he would simply walk away.

"Forgive me for following when you clearly sought privacy. I did not mean to intrude."

"It can hardly be termed privacy when I am crying in the hall."

"I hope Mrs Hurst and Miss Bingley did not insult you in some way."

She shook her head, not looking at him.

There was a slight pause before he spoke again, softly. "Permit me to apologise to you for my grievous insult this morning."

"Of course."

"I should not have thought such a thing of you when your character and your manners have been nothing less than exemplary. I cannot imagine what madness compelled me to speak as I did, and I am deeply sorry."

"Consider it forgiven."

"Thank you."

How she wished he would turn his stare away, or walk away, or in some manner break this interminable moment between them. "I believe I must go check on my sister now. Please excuse me." Giving him no opportunity to refuse, she turned and fled.

SEVEN

In London, George Wickham was contemplating his opportunities for the next months and found none that met with any degree of satisfaction. *No matter how close I come, fortune always eludes me.*

For surely, he had been born to be a gentleman—a wealthy gentleman—he just knew it. He had the sense, the education, and the manners; indeed, he was a gentleman in every aspect save for one: the fortune. Thus was he continually forced, in a habit most undignified and unbecoming for a man of his character, to stoop to working for a wage.

When old Mr Darcy, his benefactor and the master of the estate on which he had been raised, had died, he had expected a substantial legacy. Twenty or thirty thousand pounds would have done nicely. With fifty, he could have purchased an estate of his own and finally assumed the place meant for him among the landed gentry.

Instead, he was left one thousand pounds and the promise of a future living at Kympton.

At least, he had managed to obtain three thousand pounds in place of the living. He had intended to increase these funds at the gaming tables, but fortune shunned him, and soon his legacy was a distant memory. His ready funds continued to dwindle until it was all he could do to scrape by.

Then one fine day, in a public house in London, he learned of a very promising opportunity. For a mere day's work, he would be given a sum of five and twenty pounds—paltry, but he saw immediately how he might increase it.

The payer of the wage was the twin brother of a wealthy earl. Wickham's work would ensure the man received his due. Surely, once the work had been completed to the gentleman's satisfaction, he would realise the invaluable service Wickham had provided and that his compensation was woefully inadequate. However, if he did not understand it, Wickham would certainly help him to, perhaps with a few selected hints that their sovereign might not look upon the situation with sanguinity.

Alas, once again, fortune spat on George Wickham's head. He made of it what he could, but nothing had gone as planned, and in the end, he had not even received his promised wage. To make matters worse, Wickham found himself tossed in with a group of nothings who were embroiled in an accusation of treason. He was forced to go into hiding, spending the next years going from one miserable situation to the next, avoiding notice and barely subsisting on what few shillings he was able to obtain from occasional games or wagers.

Now, he found himself in desperate circumstances. Funds were non-existent and prospects even worse. Winter was about to set in, and he was nigh on being evicted from what had to be the meanest lodgings in London. Here he sat in a tavern with nothing but the shillings in his pocket, debating whether to eat or gamble.

He strolled back towards the game tables when a man he had once known stopped him.

"Willingham! How marvellous to see you!" Lieutenant Denny was effusive in his greeting. "Allow me to buy you a pint, old friend; I have not forgotten your assistance to me with that, ah, situation in Birmingham, my good sir."

The two men easily settled into the banter of a long-time alliance that, before too long, centred on Wickham and his current plans, or lack thereof. Lieutenant Denny had a solution: entreating Wickham to join his regiment.

"Room and board is assured, Willingham, and the work is easy enough. The pay is not much, but it will get you by, and the ladies do favour the uniform."

Wickham considered it. As a long-term solution, a military life did not tempt him as it tended to be characterised by hard work and dedication to service, two things he found uninteresting. However, for the present, with winter rapidly approaching and little else to occupy him, a stint in the militia might just be the thing. Of course, he lacked the funds to purchase a commission, but perhaps Denny might spot him a bit, just until things turned around at the gaming tables.

He offered Lieutenant Denny a lazy grin. "Let us speak with your colonel, then."

THE NEXT DAY, WICKHAM FOUND HIMSELF ONCE AGAIN IN THE PUBLIC house with even fewer shillings in his pocket and prospects so dim that even a commission in the militia was beyond his touch.

Denny had laughed at the idea that he might provide the funds for George to purchase his commission. "Willingham, you and I both know that would be money never again seen, and though I enjoy your company, I do not wish to purchase it. If I want to waste money, I shall go to the tables and have at least a chance of a return."

The more Wickham considered it, the finer an idea the militia seemed. There was little danger, and further, he had to believe that military service to the king must surely erase whatever suspicion he might be under for the little matter in Coppenhall. Lieutenant Willingham of the __shire militia could have nothing to do with the man who had murdered a peer of the realm.

Once again, fortune—or lack thereof—stood in his way. With a sigh, he rose, preparing to walk to Mayfair and the one person he knew would forever answer to the call of family and obligation and provide a bit of comfort for the son of his father's esteemed steward.

It was a short distance to Darcy's house, though a world away. The filthy streets teeming with grimy, downtrodden people and miserable cattle gave way to large, stately homes and the graceful movement of fine horses pulling luxurious carriages.

Wickham smiled broadly and smoothly, tipping his hat at the disapproving manservant who opened the door. "Is Darcy in?"

Hobbs was already closing the door. "He is not receiving today, sir."

"It is a matter of some urgency." Wickham tried to slink into the house, but Hobbs blocked his movement.

"You will have to return another day, sir." The door pressed against Wickham's shoulder.

"I must see him straightaway."

"Absolutely not, sir."

"Mr Hobbs, I shall receive Mr Wickham." A female voice interrupted their struggle.

Wickham looked up to see his alternate plan descending the stairs. "Miss Darcy, is it really you? Why I should not have known you! What a beauty you have become. I am certain you hear it from your suitors nearly every day."

Georgiana blushed and giggled. "Perhaps I do, but it does not mean the repeating of it is unwelcome. See me to the drawing room, and we shall have a good discussion of all that has passed since last we met."

With Mr Hobbs frowning in disapproval, Wickham led Georgiana to the drawing room where they sat and chatted amiably about all Georgiana had done since leaving school, which seemed to amount to little more than to shop, rebel against her brother, and act petulant. Needless to say, he did not express this opinion; rather, he pretended to be occasionally lost in admiration of her, alternately playful and bashful.

When she asked of his doings, he affected an air of humble embarrassment. "Oh, please do not make me say it. I feel quite the lazybones, I assure you, but after my bout with pneumonia…no, I would not have you be sorry for me."

"Pneumonia! How dreadful!"

"The fever was almost gone in just a few weeks; however, the coughing lingered for some time. Many believed I might have consumption, but I proved them wrong at the last."

She gasped appropriately.

"I am grateful for the gift of my good health, I assure you. Then again, one cannot exactly call it a gift when the apothecary's bills come due!" He laughed riotously.

"Oh, were the bills very bad?" Georgiana asked, her blue eyes round with concern.

"He was a very reasonable fellow, first to last, and has given me due time to produce the funds. Alas, I could hardly work when I was so exceedingly ill, could I? Never mind that; I am sure I shall find a way."

"But what will you do?"

"I am hoping I might join in with the army. Perhaps I shall soon be an esteemed colonel like your dear cousin Fitzwilliam!"

"How unfortunate that he is not here this afternoon. He stays here with me this week as my brother is in the country with Mr Bingley and his sisters."

"Darcy is in the country? How unfortunate; I so wished to see him," Wickham lied smoothly, thankful he had at least sufficient luck to avoid seeing the colonel. "I am sure you are enjoying time with your cousin."

That led to a discussion of Fitzwilliam and his doings, reported by Georgiana to be regimental training exercises—which caused a great deal of relief on Wickham's part as he had frequent dreams of the colonel coming for him. After this conversation had run its course, Wickham rose, pretending to excuse himself. It was a calculated effort to make Georgiana wish to keep him there and do what she could to retain his interest.

"I must be off. I must somehow find a wage sufficient to purchase my commission." Wickham put a wistful look upon his countenance. "It is the life your father always wished for me. I do hope to honour him in some way."

"Did he not intend you for the church?"

"Oh, he made provision should I select that for myself, but he told me often that service to God and service to king were one and the same —both a noble calling. In such a time as we live in, though, an able-bodied young man such as myself must do his duty to England. Let us have the elders among us lead by example and sermons while the young fight the good fights."

"How much is a commission? It cannot be so dear, can it?"

Wickham shrugged and named a sum which was approximately twice that needed.

Georgiana, delightful girl that she was, leapt at the bait. "Allow me to be your sponsor! I could do no less for my dear father's protégé!"

George immediately demurred, skilfully arguing against himself until Georgiana was so deeply convicted that she not only gave him the sum named but a good bit more besides.

"I shall only take this as a loan. You will be repaid."

Georgiana smiled and shook her head then escorted him to the door, half in love with him already and profoundly grateful that her stupid new companion had not interrupted them while they chatted.

THE DAY WAS PARTICULARLY FINE FOR THE MIDDLE OF NOVEMBER, AND the streets of Meryton were crowded. The ladies of Longbourn had been wandering for some time and inspecting the shop windows when Kitty collided with a handsome, tall gentleman who was standing with Lieutenant Denny of the militia quartered in Meryton. Although their contact was slight and Kitty was in no danger of losing her balance, the man grasped her elbow as if she were about to tumble from the edge of a cliff.

Elizabeth glanced behind her to where Jervis lingered in the alleyway, ready to act if needed. She spoke quickly, hoping to avoid a scene. "My sister is unharmed, sir. Please remove your hands from her."

The man laughed amiably. "Pardon me, ladies. I am Mr Geoffrey Willingham, and I am very pleased to make your acquaintance. And you ladies are…?"

"Leaving." Elizabeth brusquely took Kitty's arm.

Lieutenant Denny stepped forward. "I beg your pardon, Miss Elizabeth. Willingham intends no disrespect." He looked at his friend with meaning. "Do you?"

Willingham smiled charmingly. "Certainly not. Forgive me. I lose all sense of decorum with such beauty before me."

This made Lydia giggle, but a quick squeeze to her arm from Jane stopped it immediately.

Elizabeth pursed her lips sternly and said, "Excuse us, please," and turned to leave. She was shocked to find herself facing Mr Darcy and Mr Bingley on horseback.

Jane and Mr Bingley were at once in conversation, halting the Bennet sisters' escape. Mr Darcy greeted everyone succinctly, including Lieutenant Denny. Mr Denny began to introduce Mr Willingham, but Mr Darcy stopped him. "We are acquainted. What do you do in Hertfordshire, Wickham?"

Mr Willingham had his back to the street when Darcy rode up but turned when he noticed Elizabeth's surprise. When he saw Darcy, his face turned ashen, and he eased away from the group. "Forgive me. I have forgotten an urgent appointment." He then made off at a quick pace.

Denny stared after his rapidly departing friend. "Strange…I wonder what ailed Willingham."

"Willingham?" Mr. Darcy rolled his eyes. "Do you mean Wickham?"

"Mr Geoffrey Willingham. He just purchased his commission. I saw his papers myself."

Mr. Darcy exhaled forcefully. "No, his name is George Wickham. I have known him nearly all my life. He is clearly up to nothing good then, using an assumed name."

Jervis could scarcely wait to get back to Longbourn and send an express to his superiors.

TWO DAYS AFTER THE ENCOUNTER IN MERYTON, DARCY WAS surprised to hear Bingley's butler announce none other than his cousin and closest friend, Colonel Richard Fitzwilliam. "Fitzwilliam! What do you do here?"

Having served his country well in the past years on the Continent, Colonel Fitzwilliam had been returned to England and given his choice of orders in London. His father had urged him to join in on the matter of Lord Courtenay's murder, believing it would be a short assignment and not dangerous. The investigative group was pleased to have him because of his prior connexion to the gunman, George Wickham, and sent him to Hertfordshire when they learned Mr Wickham had been seen there.

Colonel Fitzwilliam gave Darcy a quick clap on the arm. "Some regimental business, Cousin."

"Georgiana is well? Has she behaved?"

"She is with my parents. I am not sure of the use of that companion of hers. Less a companion than a co-conspirator, I think, but nothing for you to be concerned about at present."

He paused, looking around him. "So, this is Bingley's place, then? Quite nice, I must say. Any local lovelies to hold his interest?"

Darcy groaned. "You know Bingley—always a local lovely to interest him, though whether they can hold that interest is more doubt-ful." The two men laughed and settled into conversation for the remainder of the afternoon.

As evening approached, they became restless and decided to take a quick ride about the countryside. As they approached Oakham Mount, Darcy could make out the figure of a young woman walking alone with only a hound as her companion. As she turned to descend the rise, he confirmed it was Miss Elizabeth Bennet.

Darcy's first instinct was to turn away and hope she had not seen them. Although he wished to greet her, he disliked the notion that she would meet his cousin.

Fitzwilliam was not considered conventionally handsome; however, he cut a fine figure in his regimentals and had a bearing that suggested manliness and danger. Furthermore, he was easy, gregarious, and could flirt with impunity, knowing his position as a second son kept him safe from most matrimonial designs. Darcy had no doubt that, within ten minutes, Miss Elizabeth would be utterly charmed by Fitzwilliam, and the very thought of it made his stomach turn.

Just then, she looked up and witnessed his indecision. Resolving himself to the meeting, he gestured to his cousin, and soon they had dismounted and stood with her.

"Miss Elizabeth, may I present to you my cousin Colonel Fitzwilliam? Fitzwilliam, this is Miss Elizabeth Bennet."

The youngest son of Lord Matlock! Elizabeth was alarmed. She had never met Colonel Fitzwilliam, who had been off serving his country throughout most of her ordeal, but she had heard of him, of course, and assumed he had heard of her as well. *Does he know me?*

She curtsied quickly and raised her eyes in time to see a brief flash of question in the colonel's and prayed he would say nothing to give her away. She was agitated, unaccountably distressed by the notion of Mr Darcy knowing her identity.

"Miss Elizabeth Bennet!" Colonel Fitzwilliam did not conceal his delight. "I am delighted to make your acquaintance at last."

"At last, sir?" Elizabeth decided that the best course of action would be to dispel any suspicions in the good colonel's mind that she was the countess about whom he might have heard.

The colonel spoke warmly. "I have heard much of you, and none of the praise has been exaggerated, I see! I believe you are acquainted with my parents, are you not?"

As Darcy looked on with confusion clear on his face, Elizabeth enquired, "Your parents, sir?"

She felt quite the actress as she maintained a coolly polite yet questioning look upon her countenance. Inside, however, she was shaking and could not wait to get away from the two men. She felt unreasonably but adamantly opposed to the notion that Darcy, and thus the Bingleys, would know about her title and her wealth. She was not exactly certain why she felt so strongly about it; everyone in London would know in a short time. *In a short time, perhaps, but not now.*

The colonel leaned back, looking puzzled. "Yes—Lord and Lady Matlock are my parents."

Elizabeth saw the moment that the colonel understood she did not intend to give away her identity. With a smile, he said, "Perhaps I am wrong. I believed they knew the Bennets of Hertfordshire, but I must be mistaken."

She smiled back. "Regardless, I am pleased to make your acquaintance, sir."

I like him. Elizabeth fell into easy banter with the colonel, her esteem for him increasing with each passing moment. She could not miss the blistering glares Mr. Darcy sent in his cousin's direction; no doubt, he despised every moment he was forced to bear her society.

She soon excused herself, telling the gentlemen she was needed at home. Both indicated they wished to escort her, but she was successful in evading their assistance, not wishing either man to realise she had a footman hiding in the shrubbery.

EIGHT

"You look beautiful," Jane whispered to her sister. "Is that the necklace Henry gave you?"

"Yes," Elizabeth choked out. "Yes, he…oh, Jane! This is a terrible mistake."

The days leading up to the Netherfield Ball were filled with anxiety for Elizabeth. She vowed nearly ten times a day that she would not attend, and she spent the rest of the day convincing herself that it would be best to go. She would then recall the few times she had the pleasure of dancing with her husband. This would inevitably lead to some weeping, during which she would vow not to go to the ball, and then the cycle would begin anew.

At last, she hit on the idea that, if she confronted her memories, they would be exorcised. She sent to her home in London for a gown she had worn to a ball with Henry, as well as the jewels she wore with it, including a necklace he had given her when they were first betrothed.

Now she stood on the threshold of Netherfield's ballroom, resplendent in all the trappings of Lady Courtenay save for one thing: Lord Courtenay. She almost expected to see him, laughing about this or that. He had always been in such a fine, jovial mood, her Henry, loving a laugh and ever of a mind for a good party. Like her, he delighted in the follies and whims of others, and she imagined his voice in her ear, playfully remarking on the profusion of feathers adorning the ladies in the room or observing that her cousin Mr Collins appeared to be stomping grapes for wine rather than dancing.

The memories accosted her at every turn. She searched the dancers, wondering whether she might find a younger version of herself, gaily dancing with her love.

This will not do. She inhaled deeply, pushing away the tears that stung her eyes and vowing to put any thought of her past behind her so she might endure, if not enjoy, the evening.

Darcy tossed and turned on the nights preceding the ball, alternately permitting and denying himself the pleasure of dancing with Miss Elizabeth Bennet. Finally, he came to the decision to allow himself one set—thirty minutes in which he might claim her as his own and indulge himself in the painfully sweet pleasure of seeing her eyes on him, feeling her hand in his, and hearing her conversation in his ear. Then he would depart Hertfordshire and see her no more; in that, he was resolved.

He roamed the ballroom, awaiting her arrival for what seemed to be hours. Colonel Fitzwilliam, who had obtained permission from his regiment to remain for the ball, teased him mercilessly about his unrest and mocked his pacing, but Darcy was not mindful of him.

Suddenly, he saw her, and for a moment, he could not breathe. She was stunning, extraordinary, the very essence of feminine beauty and grace. He was surprised at the immediate, intense yearning he felt for her.

Some part of him observed the fineness of her dress and her jewels, but these thoughts were forgotten almost as soon as he considered them. S*he has that look about her, a fragile sort of sorrow. How odd. Why would a young, beautiful lady be sad at a ball?*

As he watched, he saw her remove the diffident air from herself. She inhaled deeply, arranging her features into a picture of confidence. She raised her chin and assumed a faint smile that had all the appearance of pleasure. He was puzzled by it but could make nothing of it, and he soon forgot it in favour of studying the pleasing way her hair bounced softly against her neck and her gown fluttered gently around her ankles as she walked.

The music began, signalling the next dance, and couples began taking their places. Some arrangement for her first dance must have been planned previously, for Darcy saw Miss Elizabeth immediately being claimed by young Mr Philips, her cousin. He settled himself to the pleasure of watching her dance, all the while considering his plan to request a set.

ELIZABETH FELT SHE HAD GATHERED HER EQUANIMITY TO THE GREATEST extent possible, and still, as she greeted her hostess and made her way towards the dancers, she was filled with fear and the desire to burst into tears. She had left nothing to chance for this evening. Her first dance had been prearranged with her cousin, Mrs Philips's youngest son, who had been her preferred childhood companion and remained a dear friend.

Philips squeezed her hands in reassurance as they began the dance, weaving through the pattern and chatting lightly of inconsequential things. Slowly, the anxiety began to ebb from Elizabeth's body.

Then it happened. While moving through the pattern, she chanced to look over at the refreshment table, and a vivid memory fell upon her with ferocity.

The first event we attended in Italy was a ball given in a lovely, old estate just outside the town in which we stayed. Henry and I opened the ball, but my hand was requested for the next set by another gentleman of our party: Mr Arthur Moore, a wealthy landowner from Yorkshire, also on his wedding trip. He was an amiable gentleman and a fine dancer, and I was enjoying myself quite well when I happened to glance towards my husband.

Henry stood with his good friend Lord Belmore, a portly, amiable gentleman with a decided bent towards irreverent humour. Catching my eye, Henry daringly blew me a kiss. I blushed and looked down as I moved into the pattern, thus my back was turned to the two men. When I came around again, Lord Belmore nudged Henry's ribs as he caught my eye and mimicked Henry's kiss. I gave Lord Belmore a mock scolding look and then the pattern turned again and my back was to them.

When I faced them once more, the two were acting like school-boys, conducting a duel in my honour with spoons from the refreshment table. I could not contain my laughter at the sight, and I knew an exquisite felicity that I felt would never leave me.

Lost in her memory, Elizabeth looked towards the refreshment table, almost expecting to see Henry, his daring kiss, and the mock duel. When truth intruded upon memory, the force of loss hit her all over again. She stumbled, and Philips caught her, noting her pallor. "Lizzy, are you well?" Mutely, she shook her head.

"Shall we leave the floor?" Again, she shook her head, summoning her courage and refusing to bow to the intimidation of her own sorrow. She could not fail at this, a simple ball in her home county. If she did, how could she ever face London?

Do not cry, Lizzy, just dance. Look at the flowers. Look at Jane dancing with Mr Bingley. Look at the musicians. Think about anything but Henry.

When the interminable dance ended, Philips escorted her from the floor. "If anyone asks for me, I am taking air on the terrace," she whispered then turned and walked briskly away, determined to make it outside before her tears began to flow.

Mr Darcy came upon her as she fled. "Miss Elizabeth, if you are not otherwise engaged, would you do me the honour of dancing the next with me?"

Elizabeth did not comprehend what he said—her mind was filled with nothing but the need to restrain her tears. It was as if he spoke through a fog, but whatever he had said, he seemed to expect a reply, so she offered a tremulous smile and said, "Yes, it is."

She hoped her response matched his question, which she assumed to be something about the ball or the weather or some such nonsense. It hardly signified; she just needed to get away from him before she made a fool of herself by bursting into sobs.

He left her just as tears flooded her eyes, obscuring her vision as she rushed from the room, blindly stumbling through the hall and onto a balcony where the cold night air welcomed her into solitude. Elizabeth was dimly thankful for the chill of the night keeping potential companions inside.

"Henry." She said his name in a sob, unleashing all of the anxiety, pain, and loneliness of the past two years. She suppressed nothing, permitting her sorrow to overwhelm her as she soaked her handkerchief, which was soon too wet to be of use.

She startled when she felt a dry handkerchief pressed into her hand, but she did not look at its owner in the vain hope that whoever it was would go away and leave her to her agonies. He did not, and at length, she forced herself to regain her composure.

Colonel Fitzwilliam was looking at her with compassion. When it was apparent he would not go away without some explanation, she admitted in a voice that was hoarse and sounded damp, "Your parents have been so good to me these two years, helping me arrange and manage my affairs."

"They think very highly of you." He hesitated and then asked, "How is our young earl?"

Elizabeth shot him a quick look. Disregarding his question, she asked her own. "So you know...?"

"Everything...though I must admit, it escaped me that I might make your acquaintance here in Hertfordshire. I have recently assisted the group from the Home Office that seeks the last man involved in the plot."

"My husband's killer."

Colonel Fitzwilliam nodded silently, and the two fell silent.

Finally, Elizabeth spoke again. "I must go to London in January and remain for the Season. It is not my wish to do so. Except for desperately missing my son, hiding in Hertfordshire has been perfect."

"I certainly appreciate the desire to avoid the marriage mart. I have been doing so for nearly a decade now." The colonel laughed at his own joke, bringing a wan smile to Elizabeth's face.

She looked down at Colonel Fitzwilliam's now soggy handkerchief, which she was twisting in her hands. "I used to find balls and parties quite enjoyable."

"But not tonight?"

Elizabeth sighed. "I have been beset by too many memories of late, and the dance I shared with my cousin was one Henry particularly enjoyed. With my already melancholic state over returning to London, it was enough to cause the storm of despair you just witnessed."

"I admire your courage. You have endured much, Lady Courtenay."

Elizabeth heaved a great sigh at the appellation. "I am not feeling very courageous at the present time. I want to go home and hide."

"Perhaps you should do just that. I shall tell Mr and Miss Bingley you took ill if you would like."

It was an appealing idea, but Elizabeth was disappointed in herself for failing to achieve the two sets she had sworn to endure. Temptation won out, and she smiled at the colonel. "I believe I shall. My appearance is surely beyond repair."

Colonel Fitzwilliam gave her a kindly smile. "It would take more than a bit of weeping to mar your beauty. Well! I must be of use here. May I call your carriage?" At Elizabeth's grateful nod, he was off, and she, after a quick look around to be sure none had observed them, hastened towards home.

In the ballroom, Darcy was eagerly anticipating his dance with Miss Elizabeth. *Where is she? The dance should begin soon.*

Ten minutes later, Darcy still did not see her. He circled the ballroom, growing increasingly anxious. He had seen most of her friends, but she was with none of them, nor her sisters or parents. *Does she avoid me?*

After several minutes, he concluded she *was* avoiding him. She did not want to dance with him, but instead of refusing and being forced to sit out the rest of the evening, she had accepted him and then absented herself. *Such cunning!* It enraged him.

Ridiculous, vulgar girl. It is insupportable to treat a man of my consequence in such an infamous way.

Sudden realisation caught him short. Where is Fitzwilliam? He is never one to miss a dance.

Darcy recalled the easy conversation between his cousin and Miss Elizabeth at Oakham Mount, and he wondered whether the two of them might be off somewhere sharing a private moment. The very thought of it raised his anger to near apoplectic levels.

Miss Bennet stood with the Bingleys in the corner by the refreshment table, smiling demurely as Bingley fawned over her. Darcy frowned as he strode towards them, realising he needed to take more notice of his friend's situation before Bingley found himself bound to a woman who barely tolerated him and whose family scorned him.

Colonel Fitzwilliam entered the room just as Darcy was approaching Bingley, and he also walked in that direction. He and Darcy converged upon the group nearly simultaneously.

"Bingley, I have been asked to pass along the regrets of Miss Elizabeth Bennet. She was taken ill and has returned to her home."

Darcy stared at his cousin in fury as Bingley made the appropriate noises of dismay about Miss Elizabeth's purported illness. He did not miss the look of concern on Miss Bennet's countenance or the manner in which she excused herself to hurry over to her parents, but he was too filled with anger to comprehend it.

Fitzwilliam's nose and cheeks appeared a bit red, as though he had been out of doors for some time. As an entire set had passed since Darcy first began to look for Miss Elizabeth, it was likely they had been on the balcony the whole time, which would indeed make one cold, standing in the chill of late November for nearly half an hour.

Darcy inhaled deeply, steadying himself and balling his shaking hands into fists at his side. Was it a planned assignation? Or did Fitzwilliam just go outside and brazenly approach her? Had he forced himself on her in some way? Stolen kisses perhaps?

Fitzwilliam caught Darcy's black look, and his eyes widened. "Miss Bingley, if you would excuse me, I believe I must find—"

"Fitzwilliam, a word please. The library?" Darcy spoke to his cousin through clenched teeth.

"Certainly." The two men excused themselves and strode towards the library, Colonel Fitzwilliam quickening his step to keep apace of his taller cousin's infuriated stride.

Darcy closed the library door behind them, and reached for Bingley's decanter. He poured two brandies and, handing one to Fitzwilliam, muttered, "Something to warm you, Cousin, or shall I say, something *else* to warm you?"

Colonel Fitzwilliam took the glass and found a comfortable chair. "I have not the pleasure of understanding you."

Darcy crossed the room with quick paces. Looming over his cousin, he demanded, "What did you do?"

"What do you mean?" Fitzwilliam calmly sipped his drink.

"Do not play me for a fool!" Darcy thundered, blood pounding in his veins. "You made her leave. Did you attempt to seduce her? Impose your-self on her? Or perhaps the whole thing is an assignation? Maybe you are planning to be off to call on her while the rest of her family remains here?"

Colonel Fitzwilliam stared agape at Darcy and with no little anger in his eyes. "I would hope you know me better than to accuse me of such vile doings, but I certainly shall not stand here awaiting more." He placed his glass down firmly on a nearby table and stood to quit the room.

"Can you deny you were outside on the terrace with Miss Elizabeth?"

"And if I was?"

"What were you doing out there?"

"What is it to you?" Fitzwilliam glared at him fiercely. "How dare you say such things to me. While I would never deny that I enjoy the company of a beautiful woman, never have I been dishonourable, and I would expect you to know that better than anyone."

It was a silent standoff until, at length, reason intruded, slowly dimming Darcy's ire. He took a step back and a deep breath. He sank into a chair and raked his hand through his hair with a heaving sigh. "My apologies," he muttered.

"What is this about?"

"I hardly know."

Fitzwilliam sat in the chair next to his cousin. "I went outside to get some air and saw her weeping. I spoke with her briefly and, in light of her distress, assisted her in calling for her carriage to take her home."

"Why was she upset?"

Fitzwilliam hesitated. "What she told me was in confidence though she did not necessarily intend to confide in me. I happened to be there in a vulnerable moment." He paused a minute and then added, "She is a magnificent creature, is she not?"

Darcy sighed, disgusted with himself for his unreserved and undig-nified behaviour but grateful that it had only been his cousin who had witnessed it. *Any other man would have called me out by now.*

"Magnificent or not, Fitzwilliam, she is completely unsuitable. I cannot have designs on a penniless country miss. It is for the best that we did not dance; it would make it that much more difficult to put her behind me."

Colonel Fitzwilliam leaned back, crossing an ankle over his leg.

"So, were she not a penniless country miss, you would do what? Marry her?"

Darcy rolled his eyes. "Were the situation different, I would offer for her immediately. It cannot be though. I must be reconciled to that fact. and I must forget her. I must forget that she is the only woman I have ever met who makes me feel truly alive."

To his surprise, Fitzwilliam chuckled. "Do not be so gloomy. These things have a way of working out, you know."

NINE

LONDON, WINTER 1812

Expecting the return of Mr Bingley to Netherfield in December, Jane was disappointed. She learned through the servants that Netherfield was closed and its master was not expected imminently. This was confirmed by two letters from Miss Caroline Bingley informing her they would not return from London and hinting at an attachment between Mr Bingley and the young sister of Mr Darcy.

To Mrs Bennet, such news could only be a blessing. She told her sister of her great relief in having been spared the pain of seeing her most beautiful daughter in such an unequal match. Mrs Philips privately thought that Jane would fare very well with such a handsome and kind gentleman who was much like Jane in terms of temper, but she did not share this thought with her sister.

Elizabeth was able to raise Jane's spirits about the matter of Miss Bingley's letters. "Those are Miss Bingley's words, not his, and I daresay she will sing a different tune once she has learned of your connexion to the house of Courtenay." Elizabeth giggled, feeling a bit uncharitable but unable to resist. "Then we shall tease her and refuse her entry into our society, saying that, since her brother is nearly wed, we have no use for him in our assemblies."

"Oh, Lizzy." Jane smiled through her downcast countenance. "You would never do any such thing."

"No, I would not," she agreed. "If I began by excluding those who only liked me for my standing in society, I should soon have no one left to call upon."

Despite her anxiety over going to London, she found it far easier in December to be teasing and happy than she had in some time. Her beloved son had come to Hertfordshire and nothing could have brought her more joy.

Henry was always a welcome addition to the family circle. Although Mrs Bennet found the noise of a young child rather trying for her nerves, Mr Bennet was fond of his young grandson, and his four aunts eagerly embraced the chance to spoil him and indulge his every whim. There was nary a moment when someone was not putting themselves forward to play with him or read to him or feed him some little treat. Young Henry loved the country, remaining out of doors until his cheeks were painted a scarlet red and his nose ran unceasingly.

The decree on Elizabeth's identity would lift on 31 December and the New Year would bring with it a new life for Elizabeth and her son. She found herself in the grip of a feeling that was largely anxiety but also eagerness to be a proper mother for her son.

Watching him caper about in the chaos of Longbourn, she hoped it would not be too great a change for him to go from the Gardiner household, where he was one of several children, to hers, where he would be the one and only. *Yet another reason to get this marriage business settled: Henry needs a brother or sister with whom to run about.*

On December 30, a caravan of carriages set out for London: one contained Elizabeth, Jane, young Henry, and his nurse; another had the Gardiner family; and a third carried all their servants. The journey was easy, and by the middle of the afternoon, Elizabeth found herself at Towton Hall.

Towton Hall was completely unchanged from the beautiful, elegant home it had been when she had lived there last. It was an exceedingly grand place, reflective of the large fortune of the Courtenays, and was decorated accordingly. Some of the rooms were a bit uselessly fine for Elizabeth's taste, but she was not inclined to change it as, when she married again, she would spend little time there.

Henry had thought that many of the furnishings of his parents' home were rather gaudy, and in some manner, it soothed her to remember his comments. *"Francis told me they had the very same wall covering in a brothel he favoured,"* and *"Try that chair there; I shall not swear it is the most uncomfortable in all of London, but I daresay it comes close."* If those items were replaced, then his comments and their laughter would be forgot, and so she would leave them.

DARCY REMAINED IN TOWN FOR THE FESTIVE SEASON. HE HAD BELIEVED he might prefer some time to himself before the Season commenced, but the time drew long. He thought of Miss Elizabeth Bennet far too often and in a manner far too familiar. He found his mind often occupied with dreams of not just seeing her in town but actually being with her.

Darcy informed Lady Matlock that he desired her assistance in securing a wife. She had said little about it, but he had no doubt that a full scheme was already in motion. Some days, he wondered whether he would live to regret it.

His cousin Viscount Saye was the first to arrive back in London after spending Christmas at Matlock. Although five years older than Darcy, he was yet unwed, much to the consternation of his parents. Darcy suspected an alliance was in the making and decided to speak of it to him. His cousin would understand his dilemma even if Saye was a bit of a rattle—and certainly a rake—and might disparage him for fancying himself in love with some girl he met in the country.

"So you are returned early," Darcy remarked nonchalantly when Saye called. "I wonder why."

Saye shrugged, his eyes on the fire in Darcy's study. "Heard of a bit of a thing here in town and wanted to see to it. I cannot abide missing a good party."

"No ladies to call upon?"

Saye's eyes went to Darcy, his gaze wary. "What have you heard?"

Darcy was inscrutable, doing nothing but staring at his cousin, who finally gave way.

"My mother wished me to call on Miss Redgrave."

"She is a handsome girl."

"Very pretty," Saye agreed. "With a figure a man could admire for hours."

"Niece of Lord Arundel if I am not mistaken."

"Her father is Sir David Redgrave of Rokeby Park in York, and her mother's brother is the earl. My father is keen for the alliance. Arundel has much influence in Parliament. The two of them together could likely accomplish anything they wished."

Darcy studied him as he spoke. "So will you...?"

"I suppose I must. She is an amiable girl. A bit dull, but perhaps she will be less so once we are married and she does not feel such anxiety to say what she thinks I wish to hear."

Without meaning to, Darcy winced. Seeing Saye make a choice that he himself would soon make was disheartening and more than a little frightening.

Saye observed his wince and spoke with more than a touch of defensiveness. "It is the responsibility we bear as first sons. We get all the fun of fortune and position as well as the smothering obligations that come with it."

Darcy did not reply; he rose and went to stoke the fire then returned to his seat. He crossed his legs and stared off to the side for a moment. He then picked up his brandy, took a drink, and set it down. Saye's eyes were on him throughout.

Darcy finally spoke. "You are reconciled to it then?"

With some surprise, Saye replied, "I have known my life long that this is how it is. Perhaps it is easier to stomach for I am nearly five years your senior. I felt the hangman place his noose about my neck some time ago, and I have grown accustomed to the feeling."

"Have you ever been in love?"

"In love?" Saye considered for a moment. "No, I do not believe so. You?"

Darcy did not answer for a moment, which caused Saye to chuckle gleefully. "Darcy! You, in love? I can scarce believe it. Who is she? Will you offer for her?"

"I cannot."

"No? Why ever not?"

"She is a lady," he began, wondering whether he was mad to confess to Saye, who commonly lacked both sympathy and discretion. However, it would bring relief to give voice to it, and he had hope that, in so doing, the curse would lift. "The second daughter of a country gentleman of little consequence. The father has two thousand a year; the mother's people are in trade. They are connected to no one of consequence, and I loved her the first moment I saw her."

Saye regarded him sceptically. "First moment you saw her? That seems unlikely."

"I have always thought the notion of love at first sight an absurdity, but there it was, and I could not deny it. It was as if I had searched for her my entire life, and at last, I found her. Each time we met, I expected my feelings would be disproved, but it was not so—quite the opposite in fact."

"Are your affections returned in equal measure?"

Darcy laughed. "No. Mostly she seemed rather indifferent to me."

"There you have it," Saye pronounced smugly. "You do not love her; you only want what you cannot have. No doubt, had she forwarded herself to you as ladies of the *ton* have done, you would be disinterested. It was an art like any other, only one less commonly employed."

Darcy drummed his fingers slowly on the arm of the seat while he considered it. "She does not seem the kind to act in that manner."

"All ladies are that kind," Saye pronounced with authority. He drained the last of his drink. "In any case, whether or not she sought to secure you is immaterial. She cannot have you, and you cannot have her. Unless you think she might be your mistress?"

Darcy gave him a disgusted look.

Saye held up his hands in a gesture of surrender. "I am only asking. I do not even know the lady."

"That is why I am finally allowing your mother to find me a wife. I must put aside fanciful notions of loving a woman so beneath me and do as my duty compels."

"That you must," Saye agreed. "Both of us at last succumbing to my mother's machinations—how pleased she must be. Pray, do not mention your farm girl from Hertfordshire to my mother. You will see no sympathy in that quarter. She is determined to make a brilliant match for you."

"I have no desire to incite the wrath of your mother or sit under the sound of your father expounding on duty and obligation."

Saye clapped Darcy on the shoulder. "You and me, Cousin: the next generation of lambs led to the slaughter of dutiful matrimony. Let us hope 'tis better than it seems."

WITH A DEEP SIGH, DARCY LOOKED UP AT THE FACADE OF THE HOUSE where Mr and Mrs Hurst resided. Having already declined two invitations to dine in the six weeks since they had all returned from Netherfield, he had not felt he could beg off another. This night he expected to be particularly trying as the invitation from Mrs Hurst had included an entreaty from Miss Bingley to join them and "speak to Charles, as only you can, sir, of his unseemly attachment."

Darcy knew not what Bingley's sisters might have already said, but he would offer that which he had opined before: the match was less than Bingley might reasonably hope to attain. Beyond that, he had no conjecture or suggestion, save that Bingley allow a bit of time to pass and then revisit his feelings. Darcy suspected this dinner was being convened because Bingley felt enough time had elapsed to make him certain of his attachment.

The hour before dinner passed with a measure of relative delight. Although it was rarely seen, Hurst was, when not in his cups, a good host and often had amusing anecdotes to share. He had the group laughing within minutes of Darcy's arrival, and their enjoyment carried them into the meal itself.

The topic of true interest was raised in the drawing room after dinner. Caroline swooped towards Darcy the moment he entered, hissing, "Come turn pages for me." He had no excuse to decline and joined her by the instrument.

She began to play, speaking in an agitated whisper. "He says he will return to Netherfield in February and wishes me to go with him to serve as his hostess. I shall not be a party to my own destruction!"

Darcy turned the page, taking a moment to restrain his amusement at her dramatics. "I should hardly call it your 'destruction.' Miss Bennet is gently bred, after all."

"Gently bred? Pah!" Caroline shook her head derisively, her fingers punishing the keys of the instrument. "She is not suitable. You must speak with him, sir, I beg you! You are my last hope."

"I will speak to him, but I shall not exert undue influence."

"You own my gratitude," she told him. They were quiet while she completed her frantic concerto.

As they rose from the pianoforte, she added, "And now, you must permit me to do you a good turn as well. I know of a lady in need of a situation. She has excellent references, and though her wage is a bit higher than most, I have heard she is well worth it."

"For Georgiana?" He was surprised. It was indeed a good turn if Miss Bingley helped him find a companion for his sister.

"Mrs Younge is an expert at helping more lively girls settle into demure womanhood. I am certain she would do very well with dear Miss Darcy."

"I shall be glad to take her information and arrange to meet her," Darcy answered as they reached Bingley, who was sitting with his eldest sister. Hurst had long since fallen into a stupor on a chaise near the fire, and Miss Bingley immediately importuned Louisa to walk around the room with her.

For a moment, Darcy sat with his friend in silence. Bingley proved first to speak. "Darcy, I see by your expression that you are preparing to have a serious talk. Pray, save yourself the trouble. My mind is made up; I cannot be happy unless I am with Miss Bennet."

"You are reconciled to any consequence of offering for her then?"

"Society's nonsense? I cannot be bothered with it. I love her, and I cannot live without her. If that life is outside of the *ton*, so be it."

Darcy spoke carefully. "My greatest concern is that I had not detected any symptom of peculiar regard in her. I should not wish you to sacrifice your standing if the lady is not sincerely attached."

"Do you know her so well that you could discern the truth of her feelings?" Bingley looked at him with raised brows.

"I suppose not."

"Miss Bennet is a demure, proper lady. I would not expect to see more overt regard from her than I have. I am satisfied in my understanding of her esteem."

"Very well, then. Your mind is decided, and I applaud your resolve. What, though, of your sister? She is unhappy and could grow bitter if she feels her prospects have been altered."

Bingley smiled, seeming a bit triumphant. "I have had success with some of the investments you recommended. With the gain, I shall augment her fortune, either to induce a suitor into matrimony or to provide her a better living. I cannot sacrifice my happiness for hers."

Darcy looked at his friend and felt a deep pang of sour jealousy that he swallowed like a hard, bitter pill. He forced a smile to his face. "Then I hope to soon wish you joy."

"Thank you. Will you accompany me to Hertfordshire?"

After considering for a brief moment, Darcy said slowly, "You would perhaps wish to delay."

"Delay? Whatever for?"

Darcy regarded his friend a moment. *First sworn to dissuade him and now moved to assist him?* "I overheard a conversation while at Netherfield between the two eldest Miss Bennets, and Mrs Bennet spoke of it at your ball. To wit, Miss Bennet and Miss Elizabeth intend to be in town for the Season."

"In town? Splendid! But are you certain?"

"They were to arrive for the New Year. I should not imagine they will be invited to any parties of the *ton*. Will you go to their uncle's home to meet them?"

"Gladly." Bingley grinned broadly. "In Cheapside, or wherever he is; it will not keep me away."

"Say, Cousin, will you attend the opera tonight?" Saye helped himself to a generous serving of Darcy's port and sprawled comfortably in the chair across from the desk where Darcy was tending to his correspondence.

Alas, it was a poor attempt, for little could be accomplished when his mind refused to think of anything except Elizabeth Bennet. Bingley's decision plagued Darcy, stirring within him all manner of envy for his friend's situation, coupled with wistful longing for a marriage so unlike the one to which he would be subjected.

With Saye's question, his wandering mind instantly imagined taking Elizabeth to the opera. With just the two of them in his box, he would pull her close and immerse himself in the scent of her, the feel of her as the beautiful music washed over both of them…

"Darcy!"

He jumped at his cousin's raised voice. "I beg your pardon. What did you say?"

Saye regarded him with a look that was both amused and concerned. "I said, will you be going to the opera tonight? It promises to be a crush."

Darcy frowned. "A crush in early February? Why? Town is yet rather sparse."

"The rumours that have been circulating—and I happen to know they are true—indicate that Lady Courtenay will make her first appearance tonight. Naturally, everybody wishes to get the first glimpse of her so they can gossip about her with their friends."

Darcy thought that little could interest him less than the *ton* and the comings and goings of ladies of the peerage. "I cannot imagine why that is of such significance."

"You, sir, are a dull boy. Lady Courtenay is a highly desirable, highly eligible prospect for any gentleman, and I have it on good authority that..." He paused to vex his cousin who, true to form, shot him an annoyed scowl.

"That what?"

"She seeks a husband, and soon."

Darcy scoffed. "I am sure she does. Did the jointure disappoint?"

"Certainly not. By all reports, the terms of the jointure were scandalously generous."

"Then why the haste?" Darcy could not even think why he was asking as he felt a decided lack of interest in the lady.

Saye stood and went to the fire, stirring it with the poker. "Have you heard none of the reports of her?"

Lord and Lady Matlock had spoken a great deal about Lady Courtenay. Darcy scarcely listened to a word of it, choosing to retreat into his thoughts and daydreams about Elizabeth Bennet whenever they prattled on about her ladyship. "I must have forgotten."

Saye rolled his eyes. "Husband killed in cold blood by his own brother and a band of treasonous radicals, forced to hide out for two years in the country until his assassins were apprehended, separated from her child and her husband's heir during all that time—is none of this familiar to you?"

Darcy thought for a moment. "I remember it now. Forgive me, but my mind generally has more pertinent matters on which to rest than gossip about those wholly unrelated to me."

"Wholly unrelated to you? Not if my mother has anything to say of it."

Darcy sat up straight. "What? Why?"

Saye sat down again, his face wreathed in a broad grin. "Her ladyship is the catch of the Season, and as you have been nearly the most eligible bachelor for some time now—second to yours truly, of course —it only makes sense to pair you up. As you so generously gave leave for my mother and father to arrange matters for you—"

"No!" Fierce nausea immediately roiled in Darcy's gut. "Blast! I have had second thoughts already about involving your mother, and now...a moment of weakness and I find myself honour bound!"

Saye snorted with laughter. "Let us not give way to our sensibilities just yet, Darcy. You will meet her, no more."

Darcy rose from his desk and began pacing. "What do you know about her? Have you been introduced?"

"I shall meet her tonight. Richard is her escort."

"And? What did he say of her?"

"I believe he finds her quite delightful."

"Yet, they do not try to pair her with him—or you, for that matter! I wonder why."

"Fair-haired men recall her husband to her mind." Saye tried to smile in a placating manner. "Regardless, my duty was to visit you today and determine whether you would be at the opera so that my mother can introduce you. That is all—a meeting. My mother will not bring the vicar; you have my word."

Darcy huffed with disgust, far from appeased. Saye watched him for a moment before rising and shrugging his shoulders.

"Merely an introduction, no more. If you have no desire to further the acquaintance, that is up to you. However, if you are serious about taking a wife, do not delay. The lady is highly desirable! No doubt she will have a number of offers even before the Season begins. It is fortunate that Richard is trained in combat else some might be tempted to elbow him right out of the way tonight."

"How splendid for him," Darcy muttered. "Perhaps she will fall in love with him, and I shall avoid the shackles yet again."

"Careful what you wish for, Cousin," Saye said as he departed.

When Saye had gone, Darcy gave way to his anxiety and regret, alternating between pacing, shaking his head at his own foolishness, and wondering how vexed his aunt would be if he cried off of the entire evening. Reason intruded on occasion, insisting that he needed to marry and this was merely an introduction. His natural tendency to worry soon overcame reason, allowing him to pace and fret some more.

As Elizabeth's carriage travelled towards the opera house, she felt nearly faint from her anxiety, which seemed to increase with each beat of the horses' hooves. *I cannot do this. What if no one speaks to me? What if they make hurtful remarks and mean judgments of me? Oh, how I long to be home!*

At least, she had a pleasant escort. Although her prior acquaintance with Colonel Fitzwilliam was brief, she had liked him a great deal at Netherfield and found it easy to be in his company. Even now, he was regaling them with amusing stories of his travels, which Elizabeth suspected he did with a purpose: to distract her from her anxieties.

Lady Matlock said her attendance was the talk of London. No doubt most of the *ton* would be at the opera. Elizabeth vowed she would stay next to Colonel Fitzwilliam, speak as little as possible, and just concentrate on making her way to her box. Lord and Lady Matlock were with her along with Jane and Aunt and Uncle Gardiner. Surely, it would be well, and perhaps, after tonight, the *ton* would lose interest in her.

With a sly look, Lady Matlock leaned towards Elizabeth. "My dear, is it possible you met my nephew last autumn? He told me he spent a great deal of time in Hertfordshire, and I wondered whether he had met you—or rather, met Miss Elizabeth Bennet."

Although she suspected she already knew, having put it together when she met the Colonel, Elizabeth asked, "Who is he?"

"Mr Fitzwilliam Darcy." Lady Matlock beamed with delight. Elizabeth congratulated herself on not emitting some sort of rude word or gesture. "Yes, I did."

Her ladyship giggled like a girl. "I teased him a little to see whether he would admit to the acquaintance, but he did not drop a word of it. I knew he must have been introduced, for Richard told me he had met you, and I presumed he was in company with Darcy."

Elizabeth gave her a tight smile. "I believe he found Miss Elizabeth Bennet far beneath his notice and certainly not worth discussing with his exalted aunt and uncle."

"He will attend tonight with his sister. Shall I ask them to join our party?"

Elizabeth could not imagine anything she would like less but reasoned that she might as well greet him now and get the pleasantries over with. "As you wish."

The carriage came to a halt, and Lord Matlock and Colonel Fitzwilliam exited, preparing to hand out the ladies. Elizabeth was the last to depart, and she looked at the carriage behind to ensure Jane and the Gardiners were with them. Then it was time to face society.

THE OPERA HOUSE WAS FULL TO OVERFLOWING, ALL OF BETTER SOCIETY agog with their desire to see the countess. Her story was repeated in excited whispers among the knots of elegant ladies and gentlemen. Speculation abounded as to the identity of her fortunate escort, the style of gown and the jewels she would wear, and how soon she might marry again. Tales of her beauty, grace, and wit ran rampant. In general, the *ton* was much disposed to approve of the young countess, courtesy of her large fortune and heartbreakingly dramatic story.

Darcy heard the bits and pieces of varying—and sometimes contradictory—rumours swirling about him as he made his way through the crowd, his sister on his arm. Having decided he would oblige his aunt with an introduction, he was resolved to meet Lady Courtenay with a mind unfettered by prejudice. It was exceedingly unlikely that he would marry this lady, no matter what his aunt believed, but it would do him no harm to meet her.

You cannot marry some insignificant country girl. Think of your family name. It might as well be Lady Courtenay as any other lady, for it can never be the one who owns your heart.

Darcy and Georgiana had advanced halfway up the stairs leading to the boxes when Georgiana looked back and espied Lord and Lady Matlock slowly entering the grand hall. She tugged her brother's arm to inform him of their presence.

Darcy was thankful for his height in these situations as he easily spotted his aunt and uncle amidst the crowd that had set upon them nearly immediately. Finally, Darcy saw his cousin enter, but the lady on his arm was evidently petite, for she could not be seen through the crowd around her.

Later, Darcy wondered whether his recollection had taken on a false hue, tainted by the knowledge of what came later, or whether it was truth and understanding that caused him to remember his view of her approach being painstakingly slow. It seemed as if she moved towards him in a dream with the sea of people moving and undulating about her. The hum of the crowd grew to a roar, but he discerned nothing of the words spoken, just an indistinct cacophony in his ears.

It was obvious that the lady would have no difficulty making her return into society, for society thronged about her, desperate to catch a look or a word. Those afforded a conversation were among the most fashionable: young Lady Jersey, Lady Cowper, and Mrs Drummond Burrell, along with their husbands. *Splendid, she is one of those ladies whose greatest concern is gaining admittance to Almack's.* He rolled his eyes even as he thought it though he could not discount the excellence in such connexions.

He tried to see her even as he attempted to appear disinterested—no mean feat. He was soon punished for his inattention as, before he knew what she was about, Caroline Bingley had appeared and attached herself to his arm.

"All these people to see some little country nobody," she hissed. "You shall not see me paying her court, I assure you."

I doubt you could get near her. Darcy was about to invite Miss Bingley and her brother to join him in his box when Bingley suddenly gasped.

"Bingley? What is it?" Darcy asked. "Are you ill?"

"I believe I just saw Miss Bennet," Bingley reported breathlessly, his eyes wide.

"Oh, Charles." Miss Bingley rolled her eyes, explaining to Darcy, "We have had a number of reports of Miss Bennet's whereabouts this week. Let us see, she was on Bond Street—at the most fashionable dress maker, of course—and she was seen leaving Towton Hall in Mayfair as well!" She lowered her voice. "Pray speak to him; his obsession is truly unseemly."

Darcy did not hear her, having turned to look in the direction Bingley indicated. As it turned out, Bingley was correct: the lady he saw was unmistakably Miss Bennet making her way towards the boxes along with an older couple. However, it was not the sight of Miss Bennet that most astonished Darcy.

The sound of his own pulse filled his ears as his mind struggled to make sense of the sight before him, and time slowed to a merciless crawl. His eyes seemed to have developed extraordinary capacity as they noted the bit of a dark curl on the delectable, snow-white skin of a graceful neck, the flash of an impish smile, and the flutter of her gown.

There was a murmuring of Georgiana attempting to speak to him, but he was deaf to her words, hearing nothing but the pounding of his own heart. Bewildered, he shook Caroline Bingley loose and took two steps forwards. His lips parted and his mouth opened, but no sound would emerge.

The four had converged upon their little group. Lord and Lady Matlock stared at him, and Fitzwilliam smirked; he did not care. His eyes were fixed onto the eyes that enchanted him, the figure that

enthralled him, and the face that reached into his dreams and captivated his heart.

"Miss Elizabeth Bennet," he whispered.

She offered him a curtsey, her eyes remaining locked in his gaze. "I
beg your pardon, sir. Please call me Lady Courtenay."

TEN

The opera house continued to buzz around them. Darcy felt undeniably stupid, unable to pull himself from his astonished trance. It was Elizabeth who broke the spell, saying kindly, "Will you introduce me to your friend?"

Georgiana was greatly pleased by her notice and flushed becomingly as the introductions were made.

"Darcy, will you join us in our box?" Lady Matlock asked.

"We would be delighted." He possessed himself of Elizabeth's hand, placing it within his arm and moved her through the crowd. He was aware of Fitzwilliam's scowl behind him, but Lady Matlock nudged the colonel towards Georgiana, and that was that.

Progress was slow as they made their way to the boxes with Elizabeth subjected to introduction after introduction, including to Saye who met them just outside the box. Their comfort did not improve when they finally gained their seats as doing so enabled the rest of the crowd to stare at and discuss them. Speculation on the exact nature of the relationship between Elizabeth, the Fitzwilliams, and the Darcys was rampant, but for once Darcy cared nothing for the indignity of being an object of scrutiny and speculation.

At once, so much made sense: Mrs Bennet's airs, the inexplicably fine horse, the expensive jewels, and the trip to Italy of which he had heard Elizabeth speak. The sadness he had thought he saw in her at times—it was only to be expected for one who had lost a husband at such an early age.

Thinking of her deceased husband brought a brief pang to him. He could not like the thought of Elizabeth pining for another man, but it was several years gone by. Surely, if she sought a husband, she was inclined to put her past behind her.

I can marry her now.

Although it was an obvious notion, its realisation made him almost giddy, and he fought against breaking into laughter. He pinched his arm rather roughly, wishing to be certain this was not some sort of dream from which he would wake and then plunge into disappointment. The pain of his fingers bruising his arm made him wince.

He glanced over to see Elizabeth watching him. She arched one eyebrow, and he grinned sheepishly in return.

"Are you well?" she asked.

"Very well," he told her expressively. "Better than I have been in some time."

As the first act began Darcy continually stole glances at Elizabeth, admiring her calm acceptance of all the attention she drew. He might have been inclined to act peevish or a bit aloof, but Elizabeth smiled kindly and spoke with ease to their entire party, which included her aunt and uncle, Sir Edward and Lady Gardiner. Darcy was surprised to learn that Sir Edward was in trade. He had recently been knighted for a service that was unspecified, but Darcy thought it likely had something to do with Elizabeth's situation.

There was much speculation about Miss Jane Bennet. Although she had only a small fortune, she was desirable by virtue of being the sister of Lady Courtenay and possessing extraordinary beauty. Her warm greeting of Mr Bingley led many to wonder about the nature of their attachment. Darcy was pleased on behalf of his friend to see her demure glances in the direction where Bingley sat with his sisters and her pretty blushes on the occasions when Bingley caught her with his gaze.

Elizabeth showed great condescension to Georgiana as well, speaking to her far more than was required, given that his sister was not yet out. Darcy was relieved to see that Georgiana was well behaved for once and even a bit timid in Elizabeth's presence.

It was not surprising to see the Bingleys set upon them at the intermission. Darcy found it enjoyably odd that for once, he was *not* Miss

Bingley's first object of admiration. On this night, that honour would go to Elizabeth.

"I cannot say I am entirely shocked by this revelation, Lady Courtenay," Miss Bingley preened, seeing the eyes of the *ton* upon her as she was admitted to their box. She immediately took the liberty of drawing Elizabeth to her in a tight, far-too-familiar clasp. Darcy saw that Elizabeth was startled, but she did not embarrass Miss Bingley with overt hesitation.

"No? That is a surprise."

"When we were introduced, I immediately noted something in your air, a refinement that can only come from exposure to higher society and a better class of people than is seen in the country."

Elizabeth looked amused. "As I only spent a few months in the company of better society, and most of that on the Continent, I must credit the environs of Hertfordshire for my 'air.'"

"Hertfordshire is a delightful place, simply delightful! I told Charles just the other day that I longed to return to Netherfield." Miss Bingley was effusive in her falsehoods.

"We see it the same way, Miss Bingley."

Seeing Elizabeth was weary of Miss Bingley's conversation, Darcy thought it a fine time to interrupt the discussion. "Lady Courtenay, some wine perhaps?"

"Too late, Cousin, I have beat you to it." Saye had risen, unseen, and gone off to stretch his legs, returning with the drink for Elizabeth. She accepted it graciously, giving him a smile.

"After such an arduous trip through the entrance hall, I am thirsty!"

"I am certain you are!" Saye leaned abominably close to her, smiling engagingly as though it was his right. "After all, though it is an opera, one cannot deny that you are the belle of the ball."

Elizabeth regarded him sceptically as he spoke and finished his compliment with a deep bow over her gloved hand. When he had risen, she smiled sweetly. "You are gifted in the art of flattery, my lord."

"With such beauty before me, I am overflowing with admiration and give voice to only a small bit of it." He again smiled, looking a bit wolfish in Darcy's estimation.

The intermission was coming to its end, and Elizabeth, with no apparent pleasure, made a generous gesture to Miss Bingley that Darcy knew must be a compliment to his friend.

"Miss Bingley?"

"Yes, my dear Lady Courtenay?"

"I shall not receive everyone who calls this week, as I am exceedingly busy, but should you wish to call, my sister and I would be pleased to receive you."

If possible, Miss Bingley preened even more, announcing loudly, as she prepared to depart the box, "How pleased I am that we shall further our intimacy here in town. What a splendid time we shall all have together!"

The last sight Darcy had of Miss Bingley was her head turning, with feathers bobbing madly, as she eagerly looked around to see who had noticed her friendship with Lady Courtenay.

The remainder of the evening's entertainment passed much as the first part had: Elizabeth watching the opera while the rest of the house watched her. There was a second intermission, during which they were besieged by more callers. Elizabeth looked nearly faint with exhaustion by the time the opera finally drew to an end.

It was painful to part from her at the end of the evening, but Darcy knew he would call on her the next day. Tomorrow, my beloved. He hoped rather than believed that his anticipation would afford him sleep that night, if only so that he might dream of her.

In the morning, Elizabeth was surprised to find that she was not alone in her bed. As she opened her eyes, she felt wet kisses being pressed to her cheeks while a tiny hand wound its way into her hair. She opened her eyes to see her son's small face inches from hers. "Mama!" he cried out happily on seeing she was awake. She smiled, feeling a surge of pleasure and relief in beholding him.

It had been a particular sort of torture to be separated from young Henry for such a long time. It was a mother's instinct to protect her child from danger, and to be forced apart, knowing he was in danger and she could do nothing for him, had been horrific. Nearly every night of their separation, she had dreamt he had been hurt and killed while she watched helplessly. Almost as awful was the understanding of how much she had missed not seeing him as he grew, but she persuaded herself time and again that it was for his safety, and she could not possibly protect him as well as trained soldiers could.

Each day that she awoke and knew she had only to go down the hall to his nursery to see him hale and whole was relief anew. She had not yet grown accustomed to the luxury of seeing him whenever she wished. She counted it a blessing now, even though she had slept only a few hours and felt as though her body was too heavy to move and her eyes were filled with sand.

"Good morning, my darling angel." She sleepily put her arm around him and pulled him tight. He snuggled in close, playing with a bit of her hair that he had wound about his hand. For a few minutes, she relished holding him, revelling in the feel of his round little body pressed against her, his warm breath on her neck.

Soon, however, he began to squirm, and she knew that she would be called upon to play blocks or soldiers or whatever small game captivated him that day. With a shake of her head, she roused herself. Although her knocker was not yet up, callers would besiege her, beginning with Lady Matlock. If she wished for any time to play with her son, this was it.

TWO HOURS LATER, HER TIME WITH HENRY IN THE NURSERY HAVING passed in a wink, she was indeed in her drawing room with Lady Matlock discussing the prior evening. The countess assured Elizabeth of her certain social success and distinction, and Elizabeth thanked her for an enjoyable evening.

Very delicately, the subject dearer to Lady Matlock's heart was raised.

"Concerning the matter of your marriage, my dear…" She smiled hopefully. "My nephew Darcy is a very handsome man."

"Very handsome, indeed," Elizabeth agreed without enthusiasm.

"You heard, I suppose, of his estate in Derbyshire? It is quite grand."

"Ten thousand a year. Yes, I know. It was often mentioned in Hertfordshire, as you might imagine." The two ladies shared an awkward chuckle.

"He practically raised his sister."

"She was very sweet."

Lady Matlock paused, studying Elizabeth for a moment. "I think the two of you—"

"Absolutely not," Elizabeth said firmly. "Do not waste another thought on it."

Lady Matlock regarded her with dismay. "But why?"

"Forgive me, but your nephew is—" Elizabeth stopped herself. "Mr Darcy and I are not friends. Let us leave it at that."

"Did something happen last night?"

"No, Mr Darcy was gentlemanly enough last night."

"Did something occur in Hertfordshire that has coloured your opinion of him?"

Elizabeth shook her head. "It hardly signifies. He made his opinion of me and my character known in the autumn, so any overture he makes towards friendship now can only be seen for what it is—false, and based solely on my name and station. It is one thing to enter into an arranged match with a man who I can at least hope has some affection for me, but it is quite another to marry one who I know disdains me and settles with me only for fortune."

Lady Matlock frowned, her disappointment plain. "I do not understand."

"You said yourself that he had not mentioned meeting me in Hertfordshire. Would it surprise you to know that, not only did I meet him, but I also resided at Netherfield with their party for nearly a week? It was the most uncomfortable, awkward week of my entire life, made bearable only by the fact that I knew my dear sister, who had fallen ill, needed my assistance—assistance she would not have received from either of those sisters of Mr Bingley."

Lady Matlock nodded. "Those two would not spare a glass of water to one dying of thirst on their doorstep. But what did Darcy do?"

Elizabeth sighed. "He insulted me at an assembly, he accused me of having a liaison with a footman—Jervis, by the by—and we argued constantly. He lurked about, following me into halls and eavesdropping on my conversations as though he expected to catch me in some mischief. It was clear he thought little of my character; and that, I cannot abide. Regardless of what title or fortune you might put upon me or take away from me, I am a lady."

"He is not always easy in a society unknown to him, perhaps—"

"It is one thing to be uneasy," Elizabeth retorted, "and another to be rude, disagreeable, and haughty. He recommended himself to no one, least of all me. Forgive me, madam. You have been nothing but good and kind to me, far more than was ever required, and I feel your solicitude keenly. However, this match cannot be made. I am resolved to have no part with that odious man."

Lady Matlock released her breath in a huff of disappointment. "If that is how you feel, I would not try to persuade you otherwise."

"Thank you." Elizabeth gave her a slight smile. "Let us speak on other things then, shall we?"

WHILE LADY MATLOCK CALLED ON LADY COURTENAY, COLONEL Fitzwilliam and Lord Saye presented themselves at the Darcy town home, eager to discuss the night prior. Darcy received them as he broke his fast, overcome by an unusual feeling: utter happiness and eager anticipation. He could scarcely eat, as chewing required him to stop grinning, a near-impossible task.

Fitzwilliam sat down beside him as Saye poured himself a cup of coffee. Darcy said nothing at first, valiantly attempting to make his way through a muffin.

"Well?"

Darcy took a bite, chewed, and swallowed, and then allowed his grin to overtake him again. "Well, what?"

"Come now! You know what. I could see in Hertfordshire you were taken with the lady, and it has required all I had to remain silent!"

"I must ask what it was that made you be silent after all. Not that the surprise was unpleasant, but I have fancied myself heartbroken all these months."

"Heartbroken!" Fitzwilliam rolled his eyes. "It was a decree, in case you had missed that. All of Hertfordshire was silent, not only me."

"Fortunately for you"—Darcy managed to swallow another bit of his breakfast—"I am too happy to care."

"'Tis like a novel," Saye commented. "A fairy tale where you fall in love with one you cannot marry, only to find by miraculous and unlikely circumstance that you can. I am astonished you did not offer for her on the spot."

"I shall not waste another minute," Darcy informed him. "We shall be betrothed yet today if she will have me."

"My mother has gone to call on her this morning. Evidently, it is all nearly settled. Lady Courtenay, like yourself, has requested my mother's help in arranging her marriage."

Darcy felt a warm flush of pleasure come over him, excitement mingled with anticipatory delight. "Did she know that last night?"

"No," Fitzwilliam interjected quickly. "My mother asked her as we travelled to the opera house whether the pair of you had met in Hertfordshire, and she said you had. My mother was amazed you had not mentioned it."

"With your parents urging me to marry, I could hardly tell them that I had fallen in love with an unsuitable miss from the country."

"How fortunate that the unsuitable has become suitable," Saye remarked.

The gentlemen laughed and talked as Darcy finished his meal. The men had just risen with the intention to walk to Lady Courtenay's home when Lady Matlock was announced.

Her sons greeted her with surprise, having planned to collect her at Towton Hall, but she waved off their exclamations impatiently. "Darcy," she scolded, "what have you done, foolish boy?"

As soon as Lady Matlock had departed Towton Hall, Mr and Miss Bingley were announced. Elizabeth was mildly amused by the hour; at Netherfield, it had seemed that none of them rose before noon. Yet, here they were at nearly the earliest possible hour for calls. Miss Bingley was resplendent in feathers, jewels, and a very fine gown; the lady obviously wished to impress.

Jane joined her sister in the drawing room and immediately fell into a deep blush, casting her eyes downwards. She and Mr Bingley were drawn together in a quiet little conversation almost instantly, leaving Elizabeth with Miss Bingley.

She looked at Miss Bingley's face, which, unlike in Hertfordshire, had the expression of greatest pleasure upon it when looking on her brother and Jane. *This is how it is. Miss Bingley and Mr Darcy are no worse than anyone else. Would Lady Matlock receive Miss Elizabeth Bennet? Would the opera house fill to see a Miss Bennet appear?*

Elizabeth forced a gracious smile onto her face, reasoning that she did not have to like Miss Bingley even though she had to be cordial to her. Jane was falling in love with Mr Bingley, and thus Miss Bingley would become family of sorts.

"Lady Courtenay, your home is exquisite. How lovely it must be to have such a fine situation! It must have grieved you considerably to leave it all behind while you were in Hertfordshire."

Elizabeth stopped herself from rolling her eyes. "I am more grieved to be apart from my family and friends in Hertfordshire. My husband's home is lovely, but I spent little time here."

Miss Bingley looked like she could not possibly apprehend what Elizabeth might have missed about the country, but she continued on. "Hertfordshire is lovely. I do hope my brother will settle there, which I think he must, particularly if a certain…desirable event, shall we say… should occur." She glanced eloquently at the two lovers, still in close conversation.

With another forced smile, Elizabeth asked, "Would you like to see the rest of the house? I can summon a maid to perform our office here."

Miss Bingley eagerly agreed, and Elizabeth took her on a tour, showing her the many fine furnishings and priceless heirlooms of the Courtenay family. As the two ladies walked, Elizabeth realised a greater retribution could not have been found for the slights Miss Bingley had put upon her in Hertfordshire than was had in their present activity. She almost pitied the woman, seeing her nearly swoon at the tapestries and wall coverings and fondle some of the sculptures in the gallery as if they were her lovers.

As they walked on, Elizabeth had to admit to a grudging sort of admiration for Miss Bingley in terms of house decoration. Although she might have imagined her tastes to be rather garish, in actuality, Miss Bingley had some fine ideas for some changes that might be made here and there to integrate new with old and enable Elizabeth to modernise without eradicating too much.

"Lady Courtenay, if I might be so bold…" Miss Bingley stood in a diffident posture, a deep blush spread over her face and neck. She gave an embarrassed little laugh. "Fashion is something of my passion, and I read about all of your gowns. I would be so honoured to have just a small peep at your dressing room…Oh! I am aghast at my impertinence!"

Elizabeth regarded her with cool amusement. "I do recall you and Mrs Hurst reading of my gowns one day while I was at Netherfield."

"Oh, yes." Miss Bingley had the grace to look discomfited by the recollection and so Elizabeth took pity on her.

"Come, let us go to my dressing room."

Elizabeth smothered her smile upon seeing Miss Bingley emit gasp after gasp as her gowns were shown. Miss Bingley looked almost green with envy as Elizabeth showed her the Courtenay jewels Henry had given her, as well as numerous shoes, bonnets and hats, scarves, shawls, and other ladies' accoutrements. Miss Bingley was reverential as she gazed upon all the finery, peppering Elizabeth with various questions about her preferences and choices.

"Oh! Now this is a colour I might not have considered for you, but I daresay it is very nice against your skin. What are your favourite colours? … What think you of shorter hair? I have considered it, but I do not know whether I would like it. … Have you ordered any ankle length gowns? … Your late husband must have been quite fashionable."

The last made Elizabeth chuckle. "Heavens, no. If ever a gentleman required the assistance of a good valet and a wife, it was my Henry. When I first met him, he was dressed so poorly, I had no notion that he was of fashionable society.

"His clothes were well made, but Henry had little interest in his attire. As long as it was not damaged or stained beyond repair, and still kept him warm and dry, it remained in his service. The notion of whether something was the latest fashion would never have entered his mind, and even his newer purchases were of a staid, unremarkable variety. When I met him, I thought him to be a gentleman, or possibly in trade, but certainly not as wealthy or as high as he was."

Miss Bingley laughed. "I might say the same of my brother."

"Mr Bingley always seems well-dressed to me."

"Charles looks as he does because he has an excellent, fashion-conscious valet, and he has me in his ear, urging him towards certain selections. Left to his own devices, he would likely wait for his clothing to dissolve into its individual threads before he purchased new."

"You and his valet have done a fine job, then. He is always well-dressed." She glanced at the mantel clock. "Speaking of your brother, I believe we have left him alone with my sister long enough."

Miss Bingley rose from her seat. "I am sure he had no idea of being so indulged when we came here today."

As they descended the stairs, Miss Bingley spoke. "May I speak frankly?"

"Of course."

Miss Bingley hesitated, as though searching for the correct words. "My brother was quite taken with your sister when we were in Hertfordshire. Charles is known for his tendency to fall in and out of love rather quickly, but his regard for her did seem different. He had every intention of returning to Hertfordshire and offering for her.

"I must admit—the things I wrote in my letter to Miss Bennet were of my own design, and I hope it will not affect your good opinion or your sister's regard for my brother. He heard the opinions expressed by me and by his friend, but he intended to return to Hertfordshire nevertheless."

So Mr Darcy had a hand in this as well—that does not surprise me. "I am not in the habit of influencing my sister's decisions, and I would not begin now. Despite my elevation and its effect on the future prospects of my sisters, Jane has not changed. My mother might feel otherwise, but Jane is of age and has my father's support. She will hear the longings of her heart when she chooses to marry, and nothing else."

With a faint smile, Miss Bingley acknowledged her, and then the two proceeded back to the drawing room.

ELEVEN

Darcy's aunt wasted no time in upbraiding him for his behaviour in Hertfordshire, and Darcy sat quietly and accepted her censure as his due. His mind was far beyond thinking of the indignity of his aunt scolding him like a schoolboy; rather, it was set on the fact that he had destroyed his chance at happiness.

Given the summary his aunt presented, he could not wonder that Elizabeth despised him. Yet, how she misunderstood him! If she only knew that his absurd accusation of impropriety with her footman had its root in insane, irrational jealousy. The stares she thought were meant to censure her were his eyes yielding to the wish that the rest of him held, which was to know her, everything of her. As for the rest of it—the haughtiness, the disdainful appearance—it was neither arrogance nor pride but discomfort in a strange surrounding. Surely, she could forgive him that if she knew the rest to be untrue.

When his aunt had finished, he excused himself, intending to go to Elizabeth and throw himself at her feet. Once she knew how he loved her, they would overcome the rest.

ELIZABETH WONDERED WHETHER MR DARCY KNEW OF HIS AUNT'S design for the two of them, and if so, how he felt about it. She did not have to wonder long as, before the day was ended, he called on her.

She sat quietly, waiting for him to be shown in. She stood when he entered, curtseying as she greeted him.

"Lady Courtenay, I wonder whether you would be so kind as to grant me a private audience."

Oh no. Elizabeth dismissed her housekeeper with a sinking feeling in her heart and indicated he should sit, but he did not. Instead, he paced slowly as he appeared to gather his thoughts.

At last, he cleared his throat and abruptly sat down on the seat across from her. "I was dismayed to learn of your opinion of our acquaintance in Hertfordshire. I wish to apologise for any offence I have caused you. It was not intended."

"I thank you for your apology, sir, but as you have already offered me your regrets for the incidents at the assembly and at Netherfield, I assure you, further expression is unnecessary."

"Thank you." He took a deep breath and paused for several moments. "In addition, you must allow me to tell you that I ardently admire and love you. I have struggled with these feelings but it will not do. I beg that you would relieve my suffering and marry me."

For a brief, mad moment, she wondered whether she had heard him aright. She resolved to be courteous as she declined him. "Thank you, sir, but I am afraid I cannot accept you."

He appeared to receive the information with equanimity, and he stood. She assumed he intended to take his leave and so rose with him. It was then that she saw it: the slight spasm of a muscle near his jaw that betrayed he was barely clinging to his self-control. "Might I ask why?"

"What?"

"I am rejected, and I ask only that you kindly explain why. I apologised for the hurt I caused you and told you that I love you. You, in turn, coldly dismissed me with nothing more than a few polite words. I believe I deserve more than that."

Elizabeth's jaw dropped. "What more do you want?"

"An explanation!" he exclaimed, a flush coming across his cheeks. "Surely you see, as my aunt did, how alike we are in wit and temper, and with the obstacles before us having been removed, I would wish to understand what it is you seek!"

Elizabeth's temper was rising, and she struggled to retain control of her emotion. "Mr Darcy, I do not expect to find the sort of love that I had with my husband. However, what I shall not do is unite myself with someone who disdained me so thoroughly as Miss Elizabeth Bennet yet has decided that I am acceptable due only to my fortune and consequence. Such unabashedly mercenary motives cannot be rewarded."

"Mercenary?" Mr Darcy looked incredulous. "Do you accuse me of being mercenary?"

"Mercenary, prudent, practical—call it what you will. Your disgust of me in Hertfordshire was plain, and now you dare to profess affection for me? Furthermore, do not think me ignorant of your actions against Jane. Your opinions are well known to me, sir, and I abhor them."

"What opinions are those?"

"Nothing about me has changed, sir, only my circumstances. Therefore, I must conclude it is my circumstances you love and not me."

"You could not be more wrong."

"How can you say so?" she cried out. "Surely, you would not think me so foolish as to imagine that your professions of affection are true."

"Disguise of every sort is my abhorrence. I fell in love with Miss Elizabeth Bennet of Longbourn in Hertfordshire. The fact that you are now known to me as Lady Courtenay has neither increased nor decreased my ardour or my desire to have you as my wife. Should my word be insufficient on this matter, I would urge you to apply to my cousin Saye, who heard all the particulars long before you came to town."

"Ah! So you loved me and wished to have me as your wife in Hertfordshire? Tell me, Mr Darcy, when did you plan to return to Longbourn and speak to my father? Does Lord Saye know that too?"

Mr Darcy was silent.

"I did not think so," she said triumphantly.

"You are now part of a higher circle of society, and you see how these matters occur. My feelings for you were not all that I had to consider in my selection of a wife. I have my family name and reputation, my fortune, and my sister to consider, and I take those responsibilities seriously. I could not be run away with sensibility; reason had to be my counsellor."

"Was it your reason that caused you to act so rudely to nearly all whom you met in Hertfordshire? My opinion of you was decided the first night we met at the assembly where you not only insulted me so grievously but also held yourself above the entire populace of Meryton.

You did not enter into conversation, nor did you so much as consent to introduction. You spurned the kindness extended to you by Sir William, Mrs Long, and many others and raised an almost uniform disgust in your manners."

Not unexpectedly, he attempted to justify his actions. "I am not at ease in a society so wholly unknown to me."

"You did not try to know anyone in Hertfordshire because they were not of your circle. You did not trouble yourself to form an acquaintance with people so beneath you."

Darcy clenched his jaw and looked to the side. "It was unlikely that I would ever spend much time in their company."

"Nevertheless, they deserved your respect." Elizabeth inhaled deeply. "You claim to love me, but that is mere trumpery. Regardless of my position, the truth is, I am Elizabeth Bennet, a simple girl raised in a modest way in an insignificant place no one cares about, save those who live there.

"Those people you scorned are the people who raised me, who loved me, and who protected me these two years when my life was endangered. You cannot claim to love me when you have so determinedly despised what is an essential part of me."

He said nothing, but his eyes were intent upon her.

"While I appreciate your apologies for your actions, what you could never deny is the opinions that supported them. If I were still Miss Elizabeth Bennet, you would not have condescended to know me, nor would you have encouraged your friend to re-acquaint himself with my sister.

"You are unfortunate to follow after one whose love easily and rapidly overcame all the same objections that you have just put forth. A man whose fortune equalled yours and who thought nothing of taking an inconsequential country girl of only eighteen and making her his countess. A man who treated my family as kindly as though they were his own, who had no shame in my background or my upbringing, and all because he loved me. So forgive me if your notion of love and admiration pales in comparison."

She walked away from him, returning to the settee, picked up her tea, and took a long drink.

Mr Darcy imitated her actions. He had remained silent throughout her speech and now seemed pained as his eyes changed from angry to melancholy.

Elizabeth inhaled deeply, regaining her composure along with her civility. "Mr Darcy, you have honoured me with your offer, and I do recognise the compliment of your affections. And yes, I do apprehend the reality of marriage in the world in which we live, and I do not fool myself into thinking I may marry where I like. There are obligations to be fulfilled for us both.

"However, if nothing else, I hope to enter into a marriage with someone who might have liked Miss Elizabeth Bennet as much as he likes Lady Courtenay. I cannot have that belief where you are concerned because I know, without a doubt, that you rejected me as Miss Elizabeth Bennet. You doubted my character, and you insulted my person, and those things cannot be changed by the lustre of fortune."

Darcy did not speak for several long moments. Finally, he said, "I shall not take any more of your time. Pray forgive me for expressing these thoughts that have so disgusted you. You may be assured that you will not hear of this subject from me again."

He then departed.

DARCY SCARCELY MADE IT TO THE BOTTOM OF THE FRONT STEPS OF Towton Hall before he wished to turn back, to go to her, and to tell her how very wrong she was about him. He longed to defend himself against her accusations and to force her to accept the fact that he loved her.

Over the subsequent days, in reflection, he was glad he had not yielded to this impulse, for to do so would have been sheer folly. Once his anger subsided, he came to realise that she was entirely correct in her refusal. He had looked meanly on those who loved her, and he had judged her wanting. He had shown very little respect to the people of Hertfordshire, including her, and thus was his profession of love made ridiculous. He realised now that, although he loved her in word, he had not loved her in deed. His actions contradicted his feelings: his ardour was unsupported by respect, honour, and esteem. He had yielded to the strictures of society rather than his heart, and now he paid the price in the form of a lost love.

He wallowed in these musings for a fortnight, certain he had missed his only chance to love and be loved until Lord Matlock sought him out.

"Darcy, you must not waste the Season in this study of yours. If Lady Courtenay has a poor opinion of you, try to redeem yourself."

"Impossible. She thinks me the lowest of the low, and I must say, I begin to see her way of it."

Impatiently, his lordship demanded, "Do you or do you not love her? You said you did, and your aunt and I are making every effort to forward the match, but you go about thwarting us at every turn."

"Had I any notion that Lady Courtenay—"

"You should not have insulted her and acted curmudgeonly, regardless of who she was."

Darcy threw up his hands in disbelief. "You would have been the first to censure me had I even suggested that I might form a union with an unknown girl from the country."

"I never told you to look meanly upon anyone!"

"You would have told me not to look at them at all!"

So it went, round and round, until Lord Matlock left in a huff. Darcy sent a note within the hour, apologising for arguing with him, but he could not concede the point. Miss Elizabeth Bennet never could have been regarded as a good, or even an adequate, match. His error arose from the fact that he had cared for such notions above his affection for her.

Lord Matlock returned a note to him within an hour of receiving his.

I shall forgive your temper, but I shall also insist upon reparation in the form of your promise to attend the dinner at Lord Fane's two nights hence. Lady Courtenay will be there; do your best to make amends. Your aunt remains steadfast in her belief that the two of you should marry.
— M

THERE WERE NEARLY SEVENTY PEOPLE IN ATTENDANCE AT THE FANE home; Darcy saw Elizabeth almost immediately upon entering the house. He greeted her awkwardly and then beat a hasty retreat to the mantel, where he stood drinking his wine and attempting to gather his equanimity while surreptitiously admiring her. It was an impossible task; she was exceptionally lovely in a claret-coloured gown that clung to her and gave her eyes a special glow.

He could not expect her to regret her refusal—not after he had behaved so miserably—but he did hope they might be agreeable in company together, particularly as it seemed Bingley was nigh on proposing to her sister. He saw his friend now, standing in the midst of three gentlemen paying court to Miss Jane Bennet and utilising a version of Darcy's scowl in an attempt to push the others off.

When he chanced another look at Elizabeth, he saw she was in a close conference with Mr Abell, a handsome gentleman from Berkshire. Abell was charming her; Darcy could see it in the way her eyes sparkled when she spoke. He swallowed, hard, feeling a large lump of regret lodge itself in his throat. Elizabeth caught his look for a moment but quickly looked away, as did he.

He was attempting to recover his composure when Miss Greenbough and her sister, Miss Rose, approached him. The two ladies were pretty girls with good fortunes. They were accomplished in all the usual ways, and they both flirted with him. He tolerated it fairly well but was relieved when dinner was called.

Lady Fane, their hostess, came to him just as the dinner bell was rung. "Mr Darcy, escort Lady Courtenay, please."

Although he believed she might despise it, he could not deny his hostess and so did as requested. His pulse raced as he approached her, both for fear of her response and with desire to be near her. She smiled stiffly and quietly took his arm.

Despite the discomfort between them, Darcy enjoyed having her on his arm. He glanced down at her hand, admiring the pale elegance of it. She glanced up and caught him staring at her hand like a fool. He quickly moved his glance to his other side, cursing himself for being so stupid.

They settled into their seats without speaking. He had Lord Fane's ancient, and mostly deaf, mother to one side of him and Elizabeth, who he was certain did not wish to speak to him, on the other. Darcy resigned himself to a long and silent dinner.

When some time had passed, he decided to brave speaking to her. "Lady Courtenay, I believe we must have some conversation. It would look odd for us not to speak at all for several hours altogether."

"Very well. Yours shall be the subject."

Careful Darcy. Say nothing to offend but everything to appease. He took a drink of wine and then set his glass down. "Let us speak on first impressions."

"First impressions?"

"They are dangerous things. Unless a person exercises great caution in the avoidance of prejudice and hasty opinion, a faulty judgment is nearly unavoidable." He gave her an uncertain smile.

She raised one eyebrow at him. "I do suppose you would think so."

Blast! He intended to obliquely apologise to her, to tell her he knew he made a poor first impression; however, as was common for them, it seemed he had angered her instead. "You do?"

"You mentioned to me several times the other afternoon that I was in error in my understanding of your character in Hertfordshire. Are you blaming my misunderstanding on hasty opinions and prejudice?"

As he struggled for something to extract him from the mire of his thoughts, Elizabeth spoke again, her tone milder. "You are likely correct, though I must mention that our present discord is also due, at least in part, to your hasty opinions and judgement."

"I do not disagree with you, and I am not blaming you. I was referring to myself. I went to Hertfordshire expecting to find a savage society and formed my opinions of the populace based on that prejudice. I wish I had not looked so meanly upon people who, by and large, were exceedingly welcoming and kind to my friend and to me."

When he mentioned Bingley, he saw her glance towards Miss Bennet, who sat across from Bingley. They were both speaking to other people, as politeness would dictate, but their conversations were interspersed with frequent glances and small smiles at each other.

"I do not desire ill will between us, Mr Darcy. I believe we shall often be together in company. I am receptive to whatever second impression you choose to bestow."

"Thank you," he replied then lapsed into silence, his eyes mostly trained on his plate. He knew he needed to speak more to her, to take advantage of the second chance she offered, but he could not think how best to go about it. He offended at every turn, no matter his intent.

There was a pause, much too long to be anything but awkward, until he hit upon a subject. "What think you of books? Do you find pleasure in reading?"

Her eyes had a distant look, and she startled when he spoke. Her answer to him was unguarded. "I have found pleasure in little else but books these last two years. I daresay, I could keep you all night long discussing everything I've read."

"Just these two years?"

Roses bloomed on her cheeks as she laughed lightly. "I have always enjoyed reading, but in the recent past, I have been nearly voracious. When one is in exile, books are a great companion. They do not require you to feign a happy spirit nor to amuse or comfort them, yet they do all these things for you without fatigue. But I shall ask your forgiveness, Mr Darcy, for speaking in such a frank way."

"Meryton seemed a lively enough place. I would have supposed there to be much more to occupy you than books alone."

"I was not of a mind to be in society very much after my widowhood," Elizabeth explained with a small shrug. "When I met you and the rest of Mr Bingley's party in October, I had not been to an assembly for over two years."

"Why not?"

"I was anxious and unhappy at parties. I could not be easy, feeling endangered and feeling as if I betrayed my husband. It felt vulgar to me to go out and laugh and chat when he had suffered as he had."

She gave him a rueful smile. "I became so wretched with nerves, I could scarcely speak. My heart would pound as though I was having some sort of an attack. It was terrible."

"And that was your experience at the assembly in Meryton?"

"Yes, and at Mr Bingley's ball too. I expect it will improve with time. At the very least, I have grown somewhat accustomed to it."

Could you have been a more dreadful brute, Darcy? He was pained by the understanding of her injury as the result of his insults, and he was heartily ashamed of himself.

How could I have been so idiotic? Am I truly such a brute? Countess or country maiden, she did not deserve to have a rude stranger behave so cruelly to her.

Elizabeth was a singularly worthy lady. An entire town had rallied around her, shielding her due to their esteem. She tolerated his insults and slights when she should have publicly humiliated him. If not for his aunt's design to unite them, he might never have known of her dislike. She was unfailingly kind to him despite his decided unkindness to her. She was even kind to Miss Bingley, who had barely been polite to her in Hertfordshire.

"Mr Darcy, you are lapsed into quite the brown study." Elizabeth had been released from a conversation on her other side and had turned her attention back to him.

He looked at her and felt the fullness of his remorse. She was extraordinary, and even had she nothing—no title, no fortune, or anything of the sort—he would have been honoured to bind his life to hers. Theirs would have been a happy union, filled with love and laughter, and he would have had a life unlike any he had ever known.

"I am heartily sorry for my treatment of you," he told her in a voice hoarse with regret. "I should have known it sooner, but I did not, until now, apprehend the fullness of my stupidity or my cruelty."

She smiled at him rather benevolently, seeming inclined to grant him some measure of clemency. "I know. Pray, let us speak of it no more."

"You are too generous."

She waved her hand in the air, seeming as though she wanted to brush away the conversation. "I believe we were speaking of books. Tell me, what do you think of *The Lady of the Lake?*"

She was successful in redirecting his interest. He soon found himself agreeably engaged in discussing the various themes and notable questions within that work, and many others as well. He found her well read and conversant on a wide variety of works, both fictional and not.

"My father's library is extensive, and we have added to it. He enjoys a spirited debate."

"I believe his daughter does as well. There were several times during our conversation when I suspected you were expressing an opinion not your own to provoke the discussion."

"You found me out." She laughed, her eyes twinkling and enchanting him. "Why do so many ladies believe they must mould their opinions to those of their partners? It suffocates any possibility for discussion. Do they not eventually run out of things to say if no one ever has a differing thought?"

Darcy nodded, too deep in his admiration to say more. *Oh, that this conversation and the conviviality we are sharing would never end!* Her sparkling repartee and evident enjoyment of the moment was too enthralling. He felt himself tempted to do something unwanted and ridiculous, like kissing her or professing his love again, but he did not wish to mar this tentative peace.

The ladies soon rose to withdraw, and he simultaneously exhaled in relief and mentally groaned in disappointment. She offered him a brief smile as she left; he supposed it would have to sustain him.

THAT WAS FAR BETTER THAN EXPECTED. MR DARCY WAS RATHER agreeable.

Elizabeth was happy for Jane's sake that she and Mr Darcy could tolerate one another in company. She believed his friend would soon offer for Jane, and Jane would accept. Then they surely would all be often together.

Mama will not be pleased.

Thinking of her mother's response led to further reflection on her own marital expectations. She could not marry a man like Mr Bingley, and not because of her mother's disapproval. Her son required a suitable father, and a man without a family estate would not do, no matter how large his fortune or how amiable his temper.

So she must understand why Mr Darcy left Hertfordshire without expressing his feelings. He had been encouraged to make a brilliant match his whole life, and as she had her son, he had his sister to consider. Although she despised it, nevertheless, it was the way of the world.

What might society say were she to announce a desire to marry someone like Mr Goulding's son Jasper? Jasper was handsome, kind, and heir to Haye Park, which had an income of nearly three thousand a year. She had known him since she was a child, and prior to her elevation, he would have been a good prospect. Now, however, he could not be a consideration.

Mr Darcy entered the room with the other gentlemen and stood in an out-of-the-way spot near the pianoforte. He did not look her way, so she indulged herself in consideration of his character and person.

To compare him to her departed husband would be unfair. At their essence, they were different men. Henry was amiable and gregarious, at ease in nearly any society, whereas Mr Darcy was easy nowhere. Even now, among a company of his equals, he appeared aloof.

She shook her head a bit, still unable to imagine what absurd impulse had led to his declarations. He did not seem the sort to deceive or to be carried away into flights of fancy. It made no sense unless he truly—No! She stopped that thought at once!

Perhaps he did feel a sort of affection or attraction, and perhaps he was so unaccustomed to such feelings that he believed it was love. That must surely be the case, and if so, he was to be pitied. To fancy himself in love would subsequently cause him to fancy himself heart-broken, and she would not wish to hurt him, no matter how he had treated her.

I must be kind to him.

Her thoughts were interrupted as she was joined by two gentlemen she had met earlier that evening, Viscount Milbank and his friend, Mr Donning.

"Lady Courtenay will you join us in a game of cards?" She agreed and accompanied them to the tables.

Elizabeth thought she had rarely laughed as she did at the card table that evening. Both Milbank and Donning were older than she, in their thirties, and had a store of amusing tales dating back to their time together at Eton, which they had attended with Henry and his brother. Their stories were full of the boyish pranks in which the foursome had engaged although Elizabeth noted that much of Francis's "fun" was somewhat mean spirited.

Donning flirted with her in a circumspect manner. It was almost amusing to see him defer to her opinions and pander to her as they played. She enjoyed his sense of humour, however, and he seemed to be a learned and witty man. On the whole, she found him rather engaging.

When Viscount and Lady Milbank rose from the table, Donning lingered with Elizabeth. "I do hope the conversation about your late husband was not distressing."

"Not at all; I enjoyed it. These are stories I otherwise might never have heard."

"They are likely all in his journals." Donning laughed. "I never knew someone as eager to chronicle his life as Henry was. His father encouraged it; he felt it a good practice for young gentlemen."

"I have not seen his journals," Elizabeth said thoughtfully. "Perhaps they are at Warrington."

"Perhaps," Donning agreed. "He would not have discarded them. They were prized, almost above all else."

"I must find them." Elizabeth smiled up at the man. "Thank you; you might have found a bit of my husband for me that I had not known existed."

He bowed lightly. "Pleased to be of any service, madam."

The two spoke of inconsequential matters for a short while after that and soon prepared to depart as the party was coming to its end. As Elizabeth turned to look for Jane, she found Mr Darcy close by. He was staring out a window with a displeased frown. When he saw her, he came to her immediately.

With no preamble, he spoke. "The estate of the Donning family is in significant arrears. Donning's father is too fond of ladies and gambling; he has lost his wife's fortune and his son's inheritance. He spends his days in idleness and dissipation, seeking a scheme to make a quick fortune sufficient to save their land."

Elizabeth replied teasingly, "If his father offers for me, I shall certainly remember that."

Mr Darcy frowned. "I only tell you this that you might be aware of his situation. Donning will inherit his father's estate, as well as the problems and debts that come along with it."

"That is important information, but I only played cards with the gentleman. We made no arrangements beyond that, nor had I planned to do so."

Mr Darcy's colour was high and his speech was stiff. "I beg your pardon; you are not in need of my protection, but I would not wish you to be taken in by someone whose motives were self-serving."

They found themselves the last remaining in the room and slowly strolled towards the door. Elizabeth noticed he wore the same expression as when he had accused her of the assignation with Jervis. *He is concerned about me though it is seasoned with a healthy dose of jealousy.*

She laid her hand on his arm, squeezing lightly. "Thank you. I do appreciate your assistance, particularly as I know so few people."

The look on his face softened. "It is not my place, I know."

She smiled at him gently and then withdrew her hand. Bingley was handing Jane into the carriage as they approached, and Mr Darcy reached out to do the same for her. She thanked him as she climbed in, and then they departed.

TWELVE

An unusually warm spell in February brought with it a desire to stir abroad, and Georgiana Darcy took advantage of one fine day to shop on Bond Street with her new companion, Mrs Younge. The lady had been in their employ only a few weeks yet already seemed to have a bit more wit than those who came before her. Mrs Younge was strict and quick to step in when she saw Georgiana flirting with a gentleman, even if only by glances and shy smiles.

"We shall get along to the extent you allow it, Miss Darcy," Mrs Younge informed her. "I can be your disciplinarian, or I can be your friend. Your actions and behaviour will decide it."

Thus, did Georgiana soon come to find that her life was made more pleasant if she behaved herself. She began to see that there might be at least some enjoyment in doing that which was expected of her.

Given Mrs Younge's strictness as a companion, her approval of Georgiana's friendship with Mr Wickham carried much weight. Georgiana knew Mrs Younge never would allow it if it was the least bit improper.

"Should we tell my brother he calls on me?"

Mrs Younge's attention was on her needlework. "Your brother hired me to have charge over such concerns. Let us not trouble him; after all, you did not mention that Miss Latymer called today, did you?"

"No..."

"Your brother has far weightier concerns than the fact that an old friend of the family called. Was not Mr Wickham raised at Pemberley?"

"He was."

"Indeed he was!" cried Mrs Younge with cheerful assuredness. "A friend of the family, almost a brother! Who could refuse him? I should as soon deny Colonel Fitzwilliam entry."

Georgiana laughed. "Quite true. As intimate as Mr Wickham and my brother are, it is likely Fitzwilliam is already aware he has called."

Unknown to the Darcys, Mrs Younge was a long-standing associate of Mr Wickham, dating from her first position as a companion. Their relationship had begun when she was in the employ of Miss Edith Williams. Miss Williams's previous companion had been dismissed because her charge had been caught in a liaison with the young Mr Wickham, then only a boy of eighteen. The Williams family had paid him a pretty sum to silently depart from Miss Williams's life with additional payment promised on her marriage. In that situation, Mrs Younge saw her opportunity.

They did not enact their scheme often. Judiciousness was required to avoid suspicion falling on Mrs Younge, but as she rapidly gained a reputation for success with "spirited" young ladies, the rest came easily. Every so often, she would introduce her charge to Mr Wickham. He would do what he did best, Mrs Younge would "catch" them, and the payment would be shared.

The families never suspected a thing. Mrs Younge was known for her ability to take a headstrong miss and bring her to heel, and Mr Wickham wisely prevented their association from becoming known.

Miss Darcy was almost too good to be true. The Darcys were an old family with a good name and connexions to the peerage. Few families were more concerned with honour and reputation or so willing to do whatever was needful to protect its dignity.

Mr Wickham was eager for this one; he was desperate for money and equally desperate to settle his grudge against Darcy. Mrs Younge was uncertain of the details, but she knew he needed funds to escape the country. He spoke longingly of the Indies or America but desired enough money to situate himself well once he arrived. Payment for silence would not suffice. It would need to be an elopement and Miss Darcy's fortune, split two ways.

"Seduce her," Mrs Younge told him at their last meeting. "She reads these romance novels like a horse drinks water. She's ripe for the plucking."

"Persuade Darcy to let her go to Bath. I cannot seduce her in the house. Darcy's servants know me."

"I shall see what I can do. Perhaps when he is out some night?"

"That will give me very little time."

"How long do you need?" Mrs Younge laughed, a bit coldly. "I am not asking you to prove yourself the world's greatest lover. Take what you need; she will understand afterwards that marriage is necessary."

"I shall try to make her fall in love with me first. This cannot be distressing for her—I must honour old Mr Darcy at least that much."

Mrs Younge rolled her eyes. "Oh yes, you are the paragon of honour."

ELIZABETH SAW LITTLE OF DARCY IN THE REMAINING DAYS OF February: only once at the theatre and another time at a card party. As in Hertfordshire, when they were in company together, she often found his gaze upon her. Given his most recent declaration of affection, it hardly seemed that he was looking at her in an effort to find fault, but she would not entertain other ideas.

Elizabeth's obligations to society exhausted her. She was inundated by callers and the necessity to return calls, she had a relentless need for new clothing and fittings, and there were endless rounds of amusements in the evenings.

On February 28, Elizabeth marked the third anniversary of her wedding to Henry. The occasion, and the weeks leading up to it, deepened her usual bouts of melancholy, and she found herself unable to sleep or eat. Jane, who had been invited to spend the day with the Bingleys, was loath to leave her, but Elizabeth urged her to go. Once her sister was gone, however, she wished she had company.

Therefore, later that day, she was gratified to receive a call from a friend of her late husband, Mr James Hanley, and his sister Mrs Newland. "This is an unlooked-for pleasure, Mr Hanley. It has been far too long since we have met."

Mr Hanley and his sister both smiled at her kindly. "Do not think me ignorant of your trials, Lady Courtenay. Henry would be proud of you for having managed with such grace and composure and for protecting his heir as you have done. I wonder whether I might meet the boy."

Elizabeth agreed with much surprise, and young Henry was brought into the room by his nurse. After the requisite period of cooing over him, Mr Hanley pronounced him a fine young gentleman, certain to have been the pride of his father.

The rest of the visit was pleasant enough although Elizabeth privately thought Mr Hanley and Mrs Newland were kind but dull. Mrs Newland did little more than gaze placidly about the room with a demure countenance.

She was relieved when Lady Matlock was shown into the drawing room, prompting both Mr Hanley and his sister to rise and end their visit. As they departed, Mr Hanley said in a low voice, "Lady Courtenay, Henry was one of my oldest and dearest friends. If there is anything you need that I have the power to give, please ask. It would honour me to be of use." His speech brought a tear to her eyes as the door closed behind him.

Lady Matlock immediately noted her low spirits. "You seem rather melancholy today, my dear."

"Do I?" Elizabeth forced a small smile to her lips. "I am only a little tired."

"I hope you will not be too fatigued to dine with us this evening. It is a family dinner, and my nephew will join us." The housekeeper entered with fresh tea for the ladies, and the two were silent for a moment, awaiting her departure.

Elizabeth smiled again faintly as she poured the tea. "You are not yet ready to allow that I shall never be Mrs Darcy, I think."

"Perhaps not," Lady Matlock replied with a slight smile of her own.

Carefully, Elizabeth said, "Mr Darcy and I are becoming friends after a fashion, but please relinquish any idea you have of a match. It simply will not do."

"Even if he is in love with you?"

"He is not in love with me."

"What makes you so certain of that?"

"What makes you so certain that he is?" Elizabeth retorted.

"He told both my sons before he knew you as Lady Courtenay and his uncle afterwards. Darcy is not a man to speak lightly of such things. If he said it, I assure you, he meant it."

Elizabeth stood and went to a nearby arrangement of flowers, plucking absently at dead leaves and imperfect petals. "Perhaps he merely *thinks* he is in love with me."

Lady Matlock rose and followed Elizabeth, laying her hand gently on her arm. "Do not be immovable in your decision not to love him. He has made many mistakes, it is true, but I am certain he will learn from them."

There was silence as Elizabeth continued her pruning and plucking.

"He has had a great weight on his shoulders since the death of his father," Lady Matlock continued. "So many depend on him, and he has risen to it with nary a complaint. He is good to his servants and his tenants, and he has done his best by Georgiana. There are many ladies who could decorate his arm, care for his homes, and give him an heir—but only you can fill the needs of his heart."

Elizabeth still did not speak.

"The advantage would be yours as well. Darcy is unequalled in his care of those he loves. He would be an excellent husband; I would never forward him to you if I thought otherwise. As highly as I regard him, so too do I wish for your happiness."

Elizabeth stopped her attack on the flowers and stepped back, dusting her hands together briskly. "I shall never marry him, but I shall try to like him. Will that do?"

Lady Matlock smiled. "For now."

DARCY FROWNED UPON HEARING THE HEAVY STEP OF HIS COUSIN'S boots coming down the hall towards his library, where he sat with his book and a cold cup of coffee. He wondered whether he should feign sleep to avoid the conversation, but it was too late. Fitzwilliam came bursting through the door with Saye close behind.

"There you are. Mother believed you died, but I told her we surely would have seen that in the papers." Saye sat down in a chair, poured himself a bit of coffee, and added a healthy dose of something from the flask in his pocket. "You have gone to ground, Cousin. What ails you?"

"Nothing," Darcy replied though it was not precisely true. In the weeks past, he had been forced to suffer watching Elizabeth being paid court by nearly every unmarried man in London. He stood by at several balls, not daring to risk rejection by asking her to dance but watching her do so with other men, knowing that, at any moment, an announcement of her betrothal could come. He looked for it anxiously each time he saw her, seeking any indication of a peculiar regard for one to whom she spoke or with whom she danced. He knew not how he would bear it when he saw it.

Darcy's cousins continued to stare at him, causing him to protest, "I have been out with a few people."

"I am not among that number," Saye informed his brother gravely. "I have tried several times to have him join me at Jackson's or Angelo's, even his own club, but nothing has tempted him from this chair."

"Not tonight," Fitzwilliam informed Darcy cheerfully. "My mother is having a dinner party, and your attendance is required even if my brother and I must pick you up and carry you there ourselves. Pray, do not oblige us to do so."

Darcy gave no response to this edict. He rose and went to stir the fire.

"Lady Courtenay will be there," Saye said.

"What is that to me?"

Saye blithely poured himself another of his special coffees. "So, you love her. You will hardly win her from your nest in the dark library."

"Someone who has offended her as I have could never reasonably hope to win her no matter my position."

"Your gloom bores me," Saye informed him. "Stop moping about like a simpleton."

Darcy frowned in annoyance. "You are not aware—"

Saye waved his hand, increasing Darcy's annoyance. "I do not need to be aware of anything. See here; if you saw a jump you wished to clear on your horse, you would practise until you could do it. When you meet one who can best you with his blade, you practise until you can beat him. If this were a game of chess and you found yourself in a corner, you would manoeuvre your way out of it. To win a lady is not different from any of that. Persuade her she needs you, and the rest will come."

As if that would be easily done.

"Your problem," Saye continued, "is that first, you attempted not to court her, and then, you tried rather unexpectedly to court her. You changed direction too quickly."

Strangely enough, Saye was beginning to make sense.

"What you must do is put aside romance and befriend her. She has suitors lined up throughout London; distinguish yourself by not being a suitor but a friend."

Fitzwilliam took his brother's flask and added to his coffee. "You astonish me, Saye. Every so often, you say something rather wise."

Saye gave a little nod, admitting modestly, "Even a blind squirrel occasionally finds a nut."

Reluctantly, Darcy said, "Very well, then. When is dinner?"

"Her ladyship says if you are not there by half-six, one of Lady Courtenay's beast-like footmen will be dispatched to retrieve you."

Darcy rolled his eyes. "I shall be there."

DARCY DRESSED WITH ALMOST RIDICULOUS CARE THAT EVENING, turning away four of his valet's suggestions before finally settling on a waistcoat. As he was shaved, his mind lingered on the words his cousins had said to him.

It was unlike him to surrender when presented with a challenge, and in truth, that was all this was. He had made a horrid first impression because he had behaved proudly in Hertfordshire, but he changed that. He would no longer be haughty, and he would no longer designate people as beneath him. Such thinking could only be counter to his purpose. He would regard everyone as a person worth knowing, irrespective of standing.

He entered the drawing room wherein waited his aunt, uncle, and two cousins. Minutes later, Lady Courtenay and Miss Bennet were announced. Elizabeth was pleasant to him, Darcy noted, seeming to look on him kindly, and from it, he drew some hope. *Be her friend. Put aside notions of marriage for now, and just be her friend.*

It was a familiar group, and soon, friendly conversation and laughter filled the room. Lord Matlock was in high spirits, regaling Elizabeth with some amusing tales that she appeared to tolerate with good humour.

After a time, his lordship abruptly ordered, "Darcy show Lady Courtenay that little sculpture in my study."

Darcy had been speaking to his aunt, and he looked at his uncle at once, a bit chagrined by his rather obvious machinations. It seemed Elizabeth was surprised as well though she quickly covered it.

Lord Matlock tried belatedly to make his design less obvious. "I was speaking to Lady Courtenay of sculptures or, rather, the gardens at Matlock, and it came to my mind. I am sure she will enjoy it."

With a smirk on his lips, Saye said, "Ladies do love military statuary more than anything, do they not?"

Elizabeth laughed at him but rose, saying, "Oh, yes. It is my passion."

Darcy stood and offered Elizabeth his arm. Saye, after a look from Lady Matlock, followed behind as though he would accompany them for the sake of propriety, but he disappeared almost as soon as they had cleared the room, wandering down a different hall with vague words of looking for something somewhere.

"Lady Courtenay, I apologise for my family's rather obvious designs."

"You need not apologise."

"I would not embarrass you."

"I am not embarrassed." She smiled as they entered the book room wherein resided a little bronze sculpture of Wellington on his horse that Lord Matlock had commissioned.

Elizabeth picked it up, studying it closely. "So lifelike, other than the size, of course." They both laughed a little, and then she turned to him, setting the sculpture back in its place.

"I have seen very little of you of late."

"I tend to be disinclined towards more invitations than not, and"— he took up the sculpture and examined it—"I have been spending my time engaged on a course of introspection and improvement in my character."

"A worthy endeavour for us all," she said gently. "But I do hope our past disagreements have not prompted it."

He put the sculpture back into its place and turned to her. "Your reproofs were well-laid. I cannot deny, as I think back over my behaviour—not only in Hertfordshire but for many years—that I am ashamed of how I have acted. I was given good principles by my excellent parents but left to follow them in pride and conceit. I have grown accustomed to looking at those outside my immediate circle with meanness and disdain. I can only thank you for bringing it to my attention and permitting me to see, with candour, the error of my ways."

Her eyes were fixed on the sculpture. "I spoke too freely. I must be more temperate in my expression."

"I cannot despise your honesty. I have seen much to improve in myself, and I am grateful for that." He hesitated a moment and then went on. "Though I must say, while you were correct in many things about me, in one thing you were mistaken."

"Yes?"

"You think my regard for you is untrue, but I do love you, more so each time I see you. My expression of it is wanting; I have not known what it is to love or how to love another. Yet, already you have taught me that love must not be selfish. It must be courageous, placing itself above all other considerations."

She blushed, still not able to raise her eyes to his. "You should not alter your character to please me. Whatever regard you might hold for me, I am unable to offer you more than my friendship."

"My greatest honour would be to call myself your friend," he responded gently.

She raised her eyes and offered him a smile. "Then we are friends, Mr Darcy. It is settled."

THIRTEEN

LONDON, SPRING 1813

March began in an unseasonably warm manner, affording Elizabeth the chance to walk among the burgeoning trees and flowers in Hyde Park. It did much to relieve her spirits.

Bingley had proposed to Jane towards the end of February, and he was accepted with tearful joy. Elizabeth was happy for her dear sister though Mrs Bennet was excessively unhappy, uncomprehending of the notion that Jane could love a man who lacked a title and had ties to trade. Mrs Bennet had been so distraught that she had hastened to London to talk sense into Jane, leading to several days' worth of disagreement and sobbing.

At last, Elizabeth had intervened, telling her mother that she must accept Jane's decision else risk estrangement from both daughters. She then offered for her mother to hold the breakfast at Towton Hall at any expense. Mrs Bennet's ire had not been completely lost, but it was subsumed by the need to plan an elegant wedding. This was its own sort of vexation as her mother was alternately demanding, petulant, and unreasonable with only occasional bursts of good sense.

Jane bore the largest share of it, occupied as she was in shopping and planning for the breakfast with her mother, but Elizabeth heard enough to make her want to run off. Miss Bingley, too, wished to be a part of the preparations, and soon enough, Elizabeth saw the three forming an alliance.

Jane and Mr Bingley were to marry at St. George's in Hanover Square. Mr Darcy would stand up with his friend and Elizabeth with her sister. All was set for March 19, and Jane's wedding clothes made her obligations to the dressmaker nearly as great as Elizabeth's. Seeing her sister so happy and so in love with her betrothed made Elizabeth equally felicitous, but it also made her lonely, particularly when she considered her sister living apart from her, perhaps even returning to Hertfordshire.

You will have your son, and the Gardiners are nearby. What else could you want? A look at Jane and Mr Bingley whispered the answer —she should marry, not just for her son, and not just to fulfil some obligation, but for herself. For companionship, for friendship, and to have someone by her side…it might be quite nice.

ELIZABETH BEGAN TO LOOK A BIT DIFFERENTLY AT THE GENTLEMEN AT the various soirees, balls, and events she attended. One gentleman she favoured was Mr Copley. She had danced with him at one of the first small balls she had attended in town and frequently saw him elsewhere in the later weeks. He was the eldest son of Viscount Beauchamp and a well-favoured man, intelligent and well read. He had no sense of humour however; her attempts to tease him were met with a blank look or a misunderstanding. Perhaps that would come later. Despite her more sombre demeanour of late, she still loved to laugh and could not imagine being with one who could not be diverted by follies and whims.

Then there was Mr Hanley.

Mr Hanley, her husband's dear friend, called frequently—never more than was proper but enough to make her wonder about his interest in her. She danced with him once and saw him at the theatre several times. He was a fine man but very dull, speaking little and seeming disinterested in most of what was occurring around him.

Colonel Fitzwilliam had also crossed her mind more than once as a prospective marital partner. Perhaps not handsome in the classical sense, the colonel had a rugged manliness she found appealing. He needed to marry a woman of fortune, and she, courtesy of her late husband, was now in possession of a fortune as well as a home in which they would live. They got along famously when they were together, and she was already nearly a part of his family. It was, in many respects, favourable for a union.

In the weeks since Elizabeth had appeared on Colonel Fitzwilliam's arm at that first, and often discussed, night at the opera, he had enjoyed a great enhancement in his popularity. The situation had been furthered by a report, the origin of which Elizabeth could not apprehend, of a rather salacious comment made in his favour, ostensibly by her.

As the story was told, an unnamed someone asked Elizabeth why she was always going about with "that soldier...a second son, is he not?" Where and when this had occurred varied: sometimes at a ball, sometimes the opera; that part of the rumour did not signify.

Supposedly, Elizabeth raised one eyebrow and said, "Second sons, if you can afford one, are much to be preferred in my opinion." When the person asked her why, Elizabeth smiled and replied, "Because they...*work*...harder."

Elizabeth had never said this; nevertheless, the story was told with increasing delight in many a drawing room. It was all part and parcel of the belief that widows, especially young ones, were a licentious, unfettered bunch. Even though she was appalled to be so considered, she could not be too distressed over it; apparently, a widow's reputation was as sturdy as a maiden's was fragile. Such a witticism could only add to her appeal in many quarters. And those she called her friends knew she would never say such a thing.

Colonel Fitzwilliam found himself very nearly hunted courtesy of his particular friendship with Lady Courtenay. In his presence, fans and handkerchiefs were dropped with alacrity, bodices were strained against dangerously, and hair was toyed with madly. For his part, the colonel quite enjoyed these displays, almost insufferably so.

Elizabeth watched him one night at a concert. She had been speaking to him, but his attention was drawn by a gaggle of young ladies eyeing him from across the room. He was so enamoured of their interest, he did not notice that Elizabeth had stopped speaking in the middle of her story. It recalled to mind another occasion when they had danced while he exchanged glances at a lady nearby, neglecting Elizabeth.

She could not despise him for it, but it did make her understand the sort of husband he might make. She would not wish to vie for attention; devotion was important to her. With Colonel Fitzwilliam, amiable as he was, she could not truly feel she had him. He did not seem to be a man content in domesticity or satisfied within his family circle.

THE WEDDING DAY OF BINGLEY AND JANE WAS SOON UPON THEM. Elizabeth thought her heart would burst with happiness for her dear sister.

Mr Darcy had done a great deal for his friend, assisting him with the legal matters associated with marriage and giving him advice on a permanent home. Elizabeth could have no quarrel with him in terms of the friendship he offered to Mr Bingley and, by extension, her sister. They spoke amiably at the breakfast when he complimented her on the arrangements.

"It is no credit to me," she assured him. "My mother and my household had the run of things."

"I think Mr and Mrs Bingley will be very happy together."

She tilted her head, allowing a mischievous smile to play upon her lips. "I am surprised you would say so."

"Why?"

"I understood you were not inclined to look favourably upon the match. I have it on the highest authority." She glanced towards Miss Bingley, ensuring that her words remained light and teasing.

Mr Darcy paused a moment then returned her teasing. "I did it for you."

"For me?"

"Wholly for you."

"How so? If my sister had not known she would see your friend in town, she might have been rather miserable, and I must have hated you for ruining the hopes of a most beloved sister."

"How fortunate *that* did not occur. Instead, you will have the most sublime pleasure of all. We shall be old and grey and see the happy Bingley family with their many children and prosperous estate around them. On that day, you may tell me that you were right and I was wrong, and I shall be forced to cede to your much greater authority. Could anything be better?"

She laughed, her spirit delighted with his unexpected remarks. "No, I do not believe there can. I must always maintain our acquaintance so that I do not lose the privilege."

"Once I have won your hand, maintaining our acquaintance will be easy."

"That again! You must take Lady Matlock's view that a demurral is not a finality."

"There is a certain stubbornness in our family, coupled with an innate and fervent desire towards having things to our liking. Have you not seen it before?"

"I have now." Elizabeth shook her head at him. "Yet, despite this fervent desire to marry me, you do not even ask me to dance. We have been at three or four of the same parties these past weeks, and you have not asked me once."

She kept her words light-hearted although it was a subject that had unaccountably plagued her. He had offered friendship, along with a wish to let their past be laid to rest, and she had agreed. So why did he never ask her to dance? And why did it bother her so?

She had seen him at a large ball the previous week, dancing with a beautiful lady who she learnt was a distant relation of Lady Matlock. Elizabeth was equal parts jealous, curious, and vexed with herself for thinking of him at all. *Mr Darcy and I are only friends. He may dance with whomever he chooses.*

He was quiet. Had she gone too far with her banter? "Forgive me. You may dance with anyone you wish. I did not intend to beg for a partner."

He laughed, much to her relief. "Nor do you need to. I assure you, I would like to dance with you. I have not asked because…" He stumbled over his words, seeming embarrassed. "Well, it does not signify. May I ask you now to reserve me a set at the next ball we attend together?"

"Yes, you may. However, I fear it might be some time as I am for Kent soon."

"Lady Catherine told me of your visit. I, too, plan to be in Kent at that time. I go every year to provide any assistance she should require with her spring plantings and her tenants."

"You are a dutiful nephew."

"Is there a particular reason for your journey?"

"To see Mrs Collins. I have had several letters assuring me of her felicity with my cousin, but I need to see my dear Charlotte's face to know the truth."

Darcy seemed puzzled by her answer. "Do you have cause to suspect otherwise?"

"No particular reason. It was a prudent match. I only wish to satisfy myself that she is content with it."

"Do you intend to stay at Rosings? My aunt must surely have extended an invitation."

"I thought I would reside at the parsonage."

She saw his surprise and then watched as he restrained himself to say neutrally, "Of course; you must wish to spend as much time as you can with your friend."

A smile crept over her face. "Well done, Mr Darcy! You covered your alarm very well, but I am teasing you again. Lady Matlock has arranged an invitation for me to stay at Rosings. With the servants I must bring with me, to reside at Mr Collins's house would be difficult and disruptive to them."

He appeared relieved. "Would you do me the honour of travelling with me, then? I always find such journeys made more agreeable with a companion."

She was surprised by his request but could not think how to politely refuse. Surely, she did not dislike him so much that she would insist on her own arrangements, not when they both went to the same place at the same time—in fact, she did not dislike him at all. She enjoyed spending time with him. Thus, what could be more sensible than to travel together?

"I have promised Charlotte I would bring her sister to her."

"Oh yes. I was surprised to see Miss Lucas in town for the wedding and wondered why she had travelled that way, but having her along will do very well. We require a chaperon in any event."

"Quite right," Elizabeth replied with an arch smile. "I would not wish you to think I wanted to compromise you."

He laughed a bit awkwardly but then offered plans much to her liking. They would go to Rosings together on Monday next.

THE JOURNEY TO KENT WAS AN EASY ONE UNDER THE CARE OF MR Darcy. Lady Matlock joined them at the last, having decided to pay her sister a visit.

Rosings Park was quite grand, as was the lady who inhabited it. When they had settled into their rooms and changed from their travelling clothing, the group assembled in the drawing room for tea and refreshments. Elizabeth was quick to congratulate their hostess on her daughter's nuptials.

"I understand your daughter is recently wed. You must count it a joy to see her so well settled and at so easy a distance."

Lady Catherine disagreed. "If you should call such a distance easy —it is nearly twenty miles. My daughter is of a delicate constitution and cannot be subjected to frequent travel."

"You will go to her, then. I understand the roads are good. It will be but half a day."

Lady Catherine made some sort of indignant noise.

"And how is Mr Maddox?" Lady Matlock asked. "Is he accustomed to his new position as yet?"

Another noise of disgust. "My new son is an artful sort and is all for what he can get. I have no doubt he will continue as much the same." Lady Catherine screwed up her mouth in a disapproving frown and would say no more on the matter.

With Lady Catherine in such an evident ill humour, it was difficult to know how to continue the conversation. It seemed their hostess was determined to meet any topic with vexation. They stumbled about a bit, making an attempt at various topics, until Darcy abruptly stood.

"Aunt, if your custom has not changed, I believe we have well over an hour until we dine. Is that so?"

"Why would my custom alter? It has long been the practice of fashionable society to dine—"

"Excellent," Darcy interrupted and held out his arm. "Lady Courtenay, would you join me in a call on the parsonage?"

Elizabeth looked up at him in astonishment as Lady Catherine expressed her clear disinclination for the plan. "A call on my parson! Darcy, whatever can you be about? I assure you, such condescension is neither required nor expected."

"I made the acquaintance of Mr Collins and his wife in Hertfordshire," Darcy informed her. "As you know, Mr Collins is heir to the estate of Lady Courtenay's father and Mrs Collins is her dear friend from girlhood. I would not overlook them. Come, my lady." The last was directed at Elizabeth as he took her arm and tugged her from her seat. She recovered her surprise sufficiently to send for her bonnet, and they quickly departed, Lady Catherine's displeasure ringing in their ears.

As soon as the door to Rosings closed behind them, Elizabeth looked up at Darcy. "This is unexpected."

"Knowing my aunt as I do, I would not be surprised if she had discouraged Mrs Collins from any familiarity or intimacy with you during this visit. I do not know Mrs Collins sufficiently to predict how she might react to such a directive, so I thought it best if we began early to encourage comfort and ease."

"You are kind," Elizabeth said, looking at him thoughtfully. "I would be sorely grieved to be here without seeing my friend often."

Darcy gave her a half smile. "I do, on occasion, like to break from my usual routine of selfish disdain for the feelings of others."

She laughed. "You will surely pay a price for it; while Charlotte and I share all the gossip of Meryton, you will be the captive audience of Mr Collins."

"We have already been through all the bowing and scraping; he will surely be able to meet me as an established acquaintance and speak of sensible, if not witty, things."

Not likely. "Let us hope your kindness is not punished too severely."

Darcy proved utterly wrong in his belief as Mr Collins, overcome by the presence of elevated personages in his home, was merciless in his attentions and effusions. Darcy bore it with continued good grace. The time passed away too quickly, and soon, Elizabeth knew she must leave, not wishing to be a poor guest within her first hours of being in Kent.

As she and Darcy strolled back to the house, she sneaked occasional glances at him as he remained deep in thought. Finally, she said, "Mr and Mrs Collins were pleased with our visit. I must again thank you for thinking of their concerns in this."

"It is what any feeling person would do."

"It required quite a bit of consideration and forethought, much more than many would give. Even I, who had spending time with Charlotte as my object, did not consider how she might have been discouraged from approaching me. So, I must persist in my gratitude, sir."

"I believe that I must thank you as well."

"Me? Why?"

"You demand of me a better man," he told her quietly. "I find I rather like the version of myself that meets with your approval."

Elizabeth seized upon the warmer weather of Kent gratefully, departing on an early walk the first morning she was in residence at Rosings. She strode towards the parsonage, uncertain of Charlotte's daily routine but hoping to catch her at it. Charlotte was feeding her poultry and instructing her housekeeper and could not come away. Elizabeth promised to call later that morning.

Free to walk, Elizabeth chose a lane at random, delighting in the burgeoning verdure before her. She inhaled deeply, drawing the fresh spring air into her lungs and feeling the bounce return to her step. She soon came upon Mr Darcy.

"May I join you?" he requested. "It is a lovely morning, is it not?"

"It is splendid, and yes, you may join me." They began to walk, and Elizabeth asked, "Do you always rise early, or did the sounds of the country awaken you?"

"I am an early riser. Are you?"

"I am," she admitted. "Not the mode, I know! I much prefer a walk at dawn to a promenade during the fashionable hour."

"As do I."

They walked on, sometimes silent and other times voluble. Elizabeth had many questions about the grounds, the house, and the parish that Darcy was happy to answer.

From that morning on, their rambles together became a regularity. At first, Elizabeth counselled herself to be kindly to him, honouring her promise to Lady Matlock, but she was soon surprised to realise she anticipated his company. When at ease, Darcy was a good conversationalist with a wry sense of humour.

The length of their walks increased daily as they found more and more to speak of, from his home at Pemberley to her closeness with the Gardiners. He had formed, independent of her praise, a good opinion of her aunt and uncle, and it pleased her. She told him they had always been good to her and had taken pains to see to her education and the development of her manners in a way her own parents had not.

"I saw early on that my parents were not like others I knew."

"How so?"

She shrugged. "My mother is vulgar and silly, and my father is unconcerned and sarcastic. It is, for both of them, a means of surviving a situation they both abhor, but it puts them in an exceedingly poor light as spouses and as parents."

Darcy spoke of his family as well, confiding his struggles with Georgiana.

"There is nothing a girl of that age wishes for more than to be seen as an adult, yet there is a girlish sensibility present that cannot be denied," she advised.

"Her behaviour is so brazen at times; it perplexes me."

Elizabeth considered for a moment and then continued with delicacy. "If I might say—and this is purely conjecture on my part—that I saw in my father an awkwardness that arose when my sisters began moving from girlhood to womanhood. They had all the appearance of women, and it was disconcerting for him. He showed them less interest, and they, in turn, behaved in silly ways to get his attention."

"Do you suggest that Georgiana sees I am at ends in trying to manage her?"

Elizabeth smiled sympathetically. "Your relationship must change. I would imagine it is difficult enough, being that you are not her parent but her brother. You have been more the father, but now, you might attempt to form a friendship of sorts as adults. There is bound to be some difficulty and some discomfort. She might behave as she does to draw your attention or because she does not know how to act."

He appeared dubious. "Drawing my attention can hardly be her object as I am most often admonishing her."

"Perhaps," Elizabeth replied. "But if I might be so bold as to offer a suggestion? Put aside your feelings of awkwardness and seek to understand her and spend time with her. It will serve your purpose far more than admonishment could."

"You may be right. In any case, nothing I have done has worked; a new tactic can hardly do worse."

As they continued on their stroll towards the house, Elizabeth considered him. Their conversations these past days had revealed a side to him she would not have suspected: a well-intentioned man with an honourable character and true heart and with similar frailties and problems to anyone else. It was endearing. When she had sketched his character in Hertfordshire, she had seen only a small portion of his true self.

"May I enquire as to your thoughts, my lady?"

"Forgive me." She blushed lightly. "You have caught me in recollection."

"Of what?"

"I was thinking of my initial impression of you. My opinion has improved markedly now that I know you better."

He looked down, the brim of his hat putting his face into shadow. "How far improved is that opinion?"

She glanced at him quickly, her heart skipping a beat.

He stopped them, turning to her and looking into her eyes. Her hand, which had been in his arm, dropped and somehow found a place within his grasp. "You must know my feelings and wishes are unchanged. You may have me; nay, you already have me. On your word, we shall be husband and wife."

Dismayed, Elizabeth spoke quietly and as gently as she could. "Forgive me if I have led you to think my feelings have changed. I treasure the time we spend together, but I cannot marry you."

There was a bench nearby and he led her to it. "You do not doubt the sincerity of my love for you?"

"No, not that." She looked down at her lap.

"Then what? Do you not think we would be as happy in marriage as we are in friendship?"

"No, I confess, I do not. We would argue and fight; you would grow resentful over what I could offer you, and I would grow weary of trying to love you well enough to satisfy you. I already know the pain of losing love, and I could not dare begin with a love that burns hot and see it grow cold. I could not bear it."

She looked up; pain smote her chest in seeing the sadness in his eyes. She caressed his arm. "I am sorry. I have pained you."

"I am only pained with my understanding of your sorrow. I should not be surprised. To have lost all you did and endure all you have, that you should be care-worn is expected. You do such an excellent job of appearing content and in good spirits, it deceives me into believing you truly are well."

He removed her glove and brought her hand to his lips for a gentle kiss. "I am happy to wait for the day when you again have the courage to be loved as I intend to love you."

FOURTEEN

The days in Kent went by with relentless haste. Elizabeth thought that most of her joy was due to the ease inherent in being in the country. Her routine of taking walks, visiting Charlotte and Maria, and reading was similar to that which she had maintained in Hertfordshire, and it pleased her. Lady Catherine had habitually invited Mr and Mrs Collins to dine twice a week prior to her guests' arrival, and in light of Mrs Collins's relationship with Lady Courtenay, she did not break custom during their stay.

Elizabeth continued to enjoy long rambles through the extensive lands around Rosings, usually accompanied by Mr Darcy, sometimes by design and sometimes by chance.

They had been in Kent a week when, on one of their morning walks, Mr Darcy unexpectedly remarked, "It surprises me how little you speak of your marriage or your deceased husband."

"For so long, I was unable even to speak his name. I grew accustomed to being silent on the subject."

"Of course, for the sake of your disguise. Surely you spoke of him within your family circle?"

"Not often. For the first months of my bereavement, I was increasing. I spent the time on a remote estate in Northumbria near Morpeth. I was in a state of shock when I arrived, hardly believing Henry was dead, and I had this great conspiracy surrounding me. It seemed absurd, particularly for a girl of eighteen to whom nothing of note had ever happened before." She tried to laugh, but it emerged devoid of humour.

"When I returned to Hertfordshire, my father reminded me of the need to maintain the appearance of a carefree, unencumbered young lady. I think they supposed my months in Northumbria should have been sufficient to mourn Henry.

"My father did not wish to hear about it, and my mother could not comprehend that having his fortune was not the same as having him. Jane did the best she could, but she had no idea what it was to lose a husband you love. So all I could do was to put on the most cheerful mask possible, both at home and on the rare occasions I was in company."

Darcy was silent a moment and then ventured, "When my mother died, we were encouraged not to speak of her. I recall Mrs Reynolds saying it pained my father to hear her mentioned. However, when my father died, only Georgiana and I remained. Georgiana wished to hear about him frequently, and it was rather soothing to speak of him."

After another pause, Elizabeth confessed, "I did sometimes long to speak of Henry. All I had left were my memories of him, and those seemed to slip away more each day."

They were diverted by a field of wildflowers, causing Elizabeth to exclaim over them although they were not yet in full bloom. She closed her eyes, inhaling deeply to catch any whiff of their developing fragrance and enjoying the feel of the spring sun on her face.

As soon as they resumed walking, Darcy asked, "How did you meet him?"

She glanced at him. It baffled her that Darcy, who by his own account was a jealous man, would wish to hear of her romance with her departed husband.

He added softly, "I would be honoured if you would tell me."

After a brief hesitation, she agreed.

"I had gone to Bath with my Aunt and Uncle Gardiner. My aunt, you see, had then two daughters and dearly wished to give my uncle a son, but several pregnancies had been lost, and she despaired of ever having another child. They took a house for the whole of the winter and spring, and I accompanied them. One day, I stood looking in the window of a shop while my aunt stepped inside to consult with the proprietor, and I was approached by two gentlemen."

The man who approached was kindly looking, not very tall, and slightly built. His fair hair was mostly straight and looked as though it needed cutting. He was, perhaps, not conventionally handsome, but he had the sort of face that inspired trust, with warmth and the suggestion of home in his smile. I knew I would like him before I even heard his voice.

"Pray, forgive me, Miss."
"For what?" I asked.
"For what I am about to do. You see, I find you the loveliest

creature I have ever beheld, but alas, there is no third party here to introduce us. So I face a difficult choice."

I struggled to contain the broad smile that threatened my countenance. "Which is?"

"Either I can yield to propriety and leave this place still unacquainted with you, or at the risk of offending you, I shall introduce myself and ardently hope that I am afforded your mercy. You seem a good, merciful sort of girl— what say you to overlooking my indiscretion?"

"Miss Elizabeth Bennet of Hertfordshire, sir."
"Mr Henry Warren of Lancashire."
We both stood, smiling at each other, until the other man

with Mr Warren made himself known by clearing his throat. Mr Warren did not remove his eyes from me, saying, "May I present my friend to you? Miss Elizabeth Bennet, this is Mr James Hanley."

The three of us talked as if we had known one another for years though Aunt Gardiner was displeased to find me speaking to two strange gentlemen when she came out of the shop.

"Elizabeth, dear, come along."
Henry gazed at me as I departed, and I just knew that what had happened on that street was the most significant moment of my life thus far.

Our next meeting was just hours later when I went with my aunt to a nearby garden for a stroll. "Quite a coincidence that we should find ourselves here at the same place and time," I said as Aunt Gardiner looked on suspiciously.

Henry whispered, "Not really...I have lain in wait for you for hours. Once I discovered your place of residence, I assumed you would be along sometime. If not today, then I planned to return tomorrow."

I should have scolded his impertinence, but I could not. Instead, I laughed delightedly at his words, took his offered arm, and strolled with him under the watchful and uncertain eye of my aunt.

The next week passed in a happy haze of assemblies, balls, and card parties. With Aunt Gardiner's maid trailing us determinedly, we went for long walks, speaking of anything and everything. Henry told me he was an orphan with his sole claim to kinship being his twin brother, Francis. I regaled him with tales of my mother, my father, and my four sisters. We learnt that we both loved to read, dance, and be out of doors. We discovered we liked the same foods and had similar taste in music.

Had I cared to look, I might have noticed that Henry was a man of some means and standing; he was given a certain deference in society, which should have betrayed his consequence. But I was young and falling in love, and I did not care to think of much beyond that.

On the eighth day of our acquaintance, we visited in the drawing room of the house that Aunt and Uncle Gardiner had let. I played for him on a pianoforte that had seen better days, hoping my voice compensated for the poorness of the instrument.

When I finished, Henry clapped enthusiastically then turned strangely timid. "May I speak to you in private?"

My heart raced as I dismissed the maid and joined Henry standing by the window. He took my hand and brought it to his lips for a gentle kiss. "I know not the words to persuade you nor the way in which to act the ardent lover, so I will speak in a way that might seem dull and stupid. Please know, it is only my deep affection for you that renders me thus; I am helpless to your charms, to your wit, and to your beauty.

"Even though it is but a week that I have known you, I believe—nay, I know—that I love you. I love you deeply, passionately, and abidingly, and I beg you to be mine from this day forward."

I could barely speak, but I had to be certain I understood him. "To be yours?"

"My wife, dear Elizabeth. Please marry me. Please be my wife." His eyes met mine with an earnest longing that took my breath *away. I gasped out my reply, "Oh yes, sir, yes, I will marry you. I will marry you."*

In a trice, he pulled me to him. I thought he might kiss me, but he restrained himself admirably. We spent the rest of the day dreaming happy dreams and planning for our life together. Uncle Gardiner was due in Bath the following day. We decided to tell him our news first and then my parents.

Even then, having accepted his offer, I had no idea he was an earl. It seems rather extraordinary to me now, but some allowance must be made for youth. I was only seventeen and had been in society very little. He had introduced himself as Mr Henry Warren—I did not imagine for even a moment that he was of the peerage. It was my aunt who first questioned what I knew of his prospects.

"Affection is important, and you should not marry without it," she cautioned me. "However, you will still require a home and something to feed you. Your parents will not give their daughter to a man with nothing to recommend him."

Uncle Gardiner had no scruple in asking Henry pointed questions about his situation, knowing that Papa would wish to know all. What he learned astonished all of us—me, most of all. We took a walk along the shore shortly after Henry's conversation with my uncle, and I must admit, my first inclination was to cry off.

"I do not think I can—"

"Elizabeth, I love you with all my heart, and you can do this; you can be my wife and my countess…"

Tears immediately sprang to my eyes. "I have not been raised as you have, Henry. My father is a gentleman, but our estate is entailed on my cousin and brings in only two thousand a year. My sisters and I have each a portion of only one thousand pounds. We are not known in London Society and—"

"Do you think I did not realise that?" Henry laughed. "My darling, I have fallen in love with you, not your fortune or your family estate.

"I have seen too much misery in unions of great families and great fortunes. My own parents were the perfect example of two exalted lineages coming together, producing their sons, and then going on to debauchery and infidelity. I do not want that for myself. Money and standing are nothing to love and affection, and I choose the latter." He took my hands, pressing them earnestly to his lips. "Please?"

I could not refuse him. I tossed my fears aside and promised myself to him forever.

Elizabeth sighed, forcibly removing herself from her reverie as she recalled that she was not in Bath but in Kent, and not with Henry but with Mr Darcy, who was strolling beside her, his eyes trained upon the ground beneath his feet.

"As I am sure you might imagine, my mother was nearly uncontrollable in her effusions over the fact that a wealthy earl had offered for me. It was much to her regret that she had not sent Jane to Bath, for she was certain Jane would have come home with a marquis or a duke." Elizabeth laughed though she was only partly in jest.

Darcy replied, "If it will console her, I will be more than happy to tell her that nearly all of the dukes with whom I am acquainted are old and already married."

"That should be a comfort," Elizabeth agreed.

"Was your father in support of your marriage?"

"He never had any idea of my marrying at such a young age, but he knew it was important for one of us to marry well. This was an excellent opportunity to raise the prospects of not only myself, but my sisters too.

"The wedding was held within a few weeks," Elizabeth continued. "Henry had taken a villa in Italy for a holiday, and he suggested it should become our wedding trip. The entire thing, start to finish, was truly a fairy tale."

They had returned to the house by this time. As they prepared to enter, Elizabeth was struck by the kinship she felt with Mr Darcy. She observed him as he climbed the stairs beside her. *It must be difficult for him to hear these things, the tales of my romance with Henry. How kind of him to ask.*

Despite the bittersweet pang associated with her recitation, when she was done, she felt only the joy of her memories. *Too often, I recall the end when to relive the beginning is far more profitable.*

"Mr Darcy?" When he looked at her, she said, "Thank you. It has been good to speak of this. I should think of these memories more often so they do not leave me."

"You should, perhaps, write them down in a journal. When your son is grown, you will have a record of his father to share with him."

"An excellent idea," she exclaimed, wondering that she had never before considered it. They parted, Elizabeth's mind filled with memories and the plans to record them.

She began that very night, taking paper from her writing case and starting with what she had told Mr Darcy. She wrote until her eyes grew too heavy to continue, but when she retired, she could not sleep.

For a time, she lay there, studying the canopy above her. The idea of marrying again had plagued her, for she believed that Henry would need to be forgotten for the benefit of her new husband. Just as she would take off the name Courtenay for whatever came next, so must she replace Henry in her heart—or so she had thought.

Now she understood that it need not be so. Marrying Henry had not erased her life as Miss Elizabeth Bennet, nor would her second marriage erase her life as Lady Courtenay. It would always be a part of her. Whoever she married would need to know that to love her would mean accepting the part of her that would always love Henry.

Having come to this understanding, she knew a peace she had not felt since Henry's death. She would not be required to forget, a notion that had built her anxiety these many months. She could go on, and she could pledge the rest of her life to another man without forsaking the part that had been dedicated to Henry.

THE DAY BEFORE THEIR PLANNED RETURN TO LONDON DAWNED FAIR and bright. Elizabeth awoke with a smile on her lips, eager for her walk with Mr Darcy and anticipating the return to her son on the morrow. She was dressed quickly, her hair put in a simple style, and she descended the stairs, intent on having a cup of tea before leaving.

Entering the breakfast room, she saw Lady Catherine sitting alone, her hand on a broadsheet beside her. She looked at Elizabeth with a compassion that was alarming and gently moved the broadsheet towards her.

"The record of the death of your husband's brother."

Shock, cold as ice, washed over Elizabeth. She sat without thinking and took the page set before her.

The trial of her brother-in-law was recounted in solemn detail: the breakfast he had been served, and the fact that he had been given a glass of wine. His defence to the court and his denial of all wrongdoing were detailed. Then came the testimony, the cold recitation of the facts from the Lord Chief Justice Ellenborough, showing clearly that Francis

Warren was responsible for the death of his brother and for conspiring against the Crown and the government in scheming and in financial support of the misdeeds. The letter was produced in which he had lured his brother to their ancestral home, during which journey, Lord Courtenay was ambushed and killed.

The jury had deliberated only a short time before returning to say Mr Warren was indeed guilty of high treason and would thus be sentenced to death. The final paragraph read:

"The prisoner, who was found Guilty, received a Sentence of Death this day (Monday), to be drawn on a hurdle to the place of Execution, and then be hanged by the neck till he is dead, his head to be struck off and his body to be divided in four, and to be disposed of as the Regent shall see fit."

She could not bear to read his dying speech. It was enough to read the report stating Mr Warren had ranted as a madman to the crowd's delight. Then she read the prayers for mercy on his soul as well as pleas for forgiveness by all who knew him. The account of the actual hanging was mercifully brief but nevertheless chilling.

When she had finished, she rose on shaking legs. "Excuse me," she mumbled to Lady Catherine before turning and leaving the room, stumbling over nothing in her haste to escape.

DARCY MET LADY MATLOCK ON THE STAIRS AS BOTH DESCENDED towards the breakfast room.

Lady Matlock smiled at him in a knowing way. "I noticed that you have been taking a great deal of air these past days. This must be helping you sleep well."

"I cannot complain," Darcy replied. "My rest has been very good, and I would say that this time we have spent in Rosings is above anything I have ever experienced here."

Lady Matlock could not conceal her triumphant grin, causing Darcy to add, firmly, "We are friends, Aunt."

"Friends do not always remain friends. Friendship can be a place to change horses, if you will, on the journey from indifference to love."

"I suppose I had always believed Aesop, in that familiarity breeds contempt."

Lady Matlock pursed her lips and then warmed to her analogy. "I suppose it depends on which side of the road you travel. My thought is that it might be time to change horses on this journey."

He gave her a puzzled look as they entered the breakfast room where Lady Catherine sat with her tea. Darcy went to the sideboard, seeking something quick to eat. Without looking at his aunts, he enquired about Elizabeth's whereabouts.

Lady Catherine replied, "She read the paper and left."

Darcy turned towards the table. "How odd; we had planned to see the folly this morning." He seated himself and took up the papers that Lady Catherine had indicated. Understanding immediately their significance, he turned to his aunt, incredulous. "She read this? Where did she go?"

Lady Catherine shrugged, taking another sip of her tea. "She did not say."

Lady Matlock asked, "What is it, Darcy?"

"An account of Mr Francis Warren's trial and execution." Darcy rose hastily. "Excuse me, I must find her."

Two hours later, he finally found her sitting on a rise overlooking the wildflowers she had so admired days earlier. She was motionless, staring at the flowers. In her hands, she held a handkerchief, but there was no evidence of tears.

He sat next to her on the ground, unknowing what he should say or do.

She looked at him once and then without speaking, she moved to him and buried her face in his shoulder. He embraced her instinctively. For some indeterminate time, she was soundless and wordless until he felt her draw a deep, shuddering breath. The handkerchief went between them, and then she pulled back, her eyes swollen and red.

"Did you see it?" Her voice was low and a bit rough.

He nodded.

"I…I feel so…so odd…I have no idea. I am sad and horrified and ill. What should I think? How should I feel? I hardly know. Should I not be happy? My husband's killer has been brought to a just end. Is that not cause for elation? Yet I am not joyful, but I do not know precisely what I am."

He decided to chance pulling her back into his arms, pleased when she leaned into him willingly. "You have a kind and compassionate soul. I cannot think it easy for you to read of the death of anyone, never mind someone connected to you."

"It is ended. It is a grisly, mean finish, but a finish nevertheless."

They remained there for nearly two hours more, talking over the details of it at times and other times silent, sitting and regarding the flowers as they took in the sun and blew with the breeze. At length, Darcy asked whether she was ready to return to the house.

"Must we?" she asked with a weak laugh. "It is our small slice of Eden here. I could almost forget the very existence of London and all its conspiracies, trials, murders, and hangings so long as I have the view of these lovely creations before me."

"You must come to Pemberley," Darcy blurted with no forethought. "That is exactly how I feel when I am home. It has much natural beauty to recommend it. When I am there, I can scarcely bear to leave it."

She smiled at him. "I would like to come to Pemberley, then. You might have made your invitation in jest, but still, I hope you will not withdraw it."

Darcy was pleased and more than a little excited by the notion of having her there, but he still spoke calmly. "When your obligations of the Season are done, we will go."

ELIZABETH HAD GONE TO HER BEDCHAMBER WHEN SHE AND DARCY returned from their visit to the wildflowers, and she seemed better prepared to meet the rest of their party by the end of the day. Darcy watched her carefully throughout the evening. It could not be denied that she was affected by the news of the morning, but he could tell that she was doing her best to behave as usual.

They returned to London the following day after having learned from Lady Catherine the surprising news that she would go to her house in town within the fortnight to enjoy the Season with the rest of the beau monde. She intended to host a large dinner party soon after her arrival to reacquaint herself with many of her old friends. Elizabeth agreed to attend.

The carriage was quiet on the way to town. Maria Lucas had remained with the Collinses, and Lady Matlock read a book. Elizabeth also looked at a book, though several times when Darcy observed her, she was doing little more than staring out the window.

His heart ached for her; he had seen how much distress lay within her. He longed to be her confidante, her rescuer, and anything else she might wish him to be.

You have gone from despising me to enjoying my friendship, and now... something else? What have we become, Elizabeth? Do you feel it as I do?

FIFTEEN

The late April day was fine with sunny skies and a refreshing springtime breeze. Elizabeth resolved to take a bit of air as soon as her son was in the nursery for his afternoon nap. With her footmen attending her, she strolled through the park, inhaling deeply and enjoying the loveliness and lightness of the spring air.

"Lady Courtenay!" Colonel Fitzwilliam called out to her with a hearty wave. "How fortunate to find you here. I intended to call on you later, but this is much better. May I join you?"

She agreed, and he fell in step beside her.

"I believe my aunt has bid you to attend this evening's entertainment?"

"She has. I understand it has been some time since she has been in town."

"Yes, it has. When my cousin Anne was seventeen, Lady Catherine brought her to town to begin the arrangements for her coming out the following year. While they were here, Anne became ill with pneumonia, which lasted for months and nearly took her life. My aunt decided that the filth of London was too much for any decent person to bear, and she took herself back to Kent as soon as Anne was able to go, vowing never to return."

"Yet, she is come back. I wonder why?" Elizabeth gave Fitzwilliam an impish grin, having become well accustomed to Lady Catherine's opinions in Kent.

"Monotony, and the understanding that none of us intend to leave the amusements of town to go to Rosings and entertain her. I do think she had dreams of being a bit of a society hostess before Anne was born. Perhaps she intends to begin living those dreams." They shared a brief laugh at the notion.

The two strolled for a bit, chatting amiably about inconsequential matters until the subject of her brother-in-law's execution arose.

"It was a shock," Elizabeth said. "Such detail!"

"You should see the crowds that come to watch these wretched souls lose their lives. Bloodthirsty savages—the ladies included!"

Elizabeth shook her head in astonishment. "At least it puts some sort of finality to this matter. It has come to its end."

"I would agree if I could but find the gunman. I despair of finding him, bit part that he was. Would that I might have been one day earlier to Hertfordshire!"

"The gunman was in Hertfordshire?"

"On business unrelated to this," he assured her quickly. "It was in the autumn. Jervis apprised the Home Office that a man bearing George Wickham's description had tried to take a commission in Colonel Forster's regiment. Alas, Wickham saw Darcy in Meryton and left before we could apprehend him."

"George Wickham." Elizabeth puzzled over the name. "Did I make his acquaintance?"

"Darcy told me you met him briefly on the street one day. I do not think it was an acquaintance that pleased you. He might have been introduced as Geoffrey Willingham, friend of Lieutenant Denny."

"Oh!" Elizabeth recalled the day on the streets of Meryton. "Yes, I do remember him. A bold and impudent man. Why did he go? I do not believe he ever joined the regiment, did he?"

"He had just joined the very day he saw Darcy. The trick of it was, he had joined under an assumed name only to then meet a man who had known him since childhood! Singularly unlucky, but I suppose the luck he has had in eluding capture more than compensates for it."

It made Elizabeth oddly cold inside to imagine that she had looked upon the countenance of her husband's killer. Had he known her? "I wonder whether anything will bring Mr Wickham back into the light of day."

"Whoever would have believed that dissolute reprobate would exhibit such cunning in avoiding capture for so long? Not I, I assure you. I should not have believed he would remain free for two weeks, much less two years."

"I can only suppose that the payment he earned has been sufficient to aid him in the endeavour."

Colonel Fitzwilliam snorted derisively. "Twenty-five pounds is a trifle to George Wickham. No, I assure you, it was spent before ever his hand touched it."

Elizabeth went cold, a sharp pain lancing her heart. "Twenty-five pounds?"

Colonel Fitzwilliam continued on, failing to notice the expression on Elizabeth's face. "Yes, the investigators imagine that he was probably promised another payment on completion of...but everything happened so quickly he probably never—"

Elizabeth heard nothing of what he said after the impossible sum of twenty-five pounds was mentioned. A loud buzzing seemed to fill her ears as she fought to remain calm. *Twenty-five pounds!*

She never wanted to think of the profit the man—now known to her by the name of George Wickham—had gained by murdering her husband. Somewhere in her mind, she believed it had been a sizeable fortune, something a person could use to survive for a long time. Not something so little, so meaningless, as twenty-five pounds.

Twenty-five pounds to end a man's life. Twenty-five pounds to make her a widow. Twenty-five pounds, and her son would never know his father. The pain of it was agonising. Oh, who, who was so cruel as to place a mark on Henry's dear, wonderful head for such a paltry sum?

She dimly realised that Colonel Fitzwilliam was speaking to her. "Lady Courtenay, are you well? You seem pale my lady. Are you ill?"

She answered distractedly, "No, I...I seem to have a headache. I believe I have walked too far today."

Colonel Fitzwilliam was solicitous and offered his arm immediately. "Let us turn back then."

TRY AS SHE WOULD, ELIZABETH COULD NOT LEAVE THE TORMENT OF the twenty-five pounds behind her that afternoon, and she wandered through her home, lost and bereft, thinking of little else. Some small corner of her mind protested, attempting to draw her back into the realm of reason: was any sum sufficient for the loss of dear Henry?

Still, the rest of her mind, the largest portion, railed and cried against the injustice, the sheer thievery of her beloved husband for a mere twenty-five pounds.

Alternately, she was angered and saddened, felt kicked and cried, until suddenly, she was overcome by a longing for something—some small bit of Henry—to console her. She went to his study, a room never entered but for the occasional cleaning, to search his papers, longing to see his handwriting, desperate to find a note or a letter that contained his thoughts.

Elizabeth entered the room and rifled through his desk drawers, yearning for anything of him. She was pleased to find a flask engraved with Henry's initials, and she opened it instantly. It had been there for two years and contained a drink not usually enjoyed by ladies of gentle breeding. However, it was also probable that the last things to touch the flask were Henry's lips, and that was reason enough for her to imbibe freely.

The first drink burned her throat painfully, and she gasped, wondering who on earth could enjoy such torture. The second drink was far less painful, and the third was almost pleasant. Elizabeth sat on the floor behind Henry's desk, looking through his correspondence, which was, by and large, a mess. Henry did not excel in the art of organisation and filed things every which way: investment dealings and information on various charitable ventures were mixed with personal letters to his brother and other correspondents. *His writing is truly awful. Just like Mr Bingley's—blots and blotches in abundance.* The thought made her giggle. Elizabeth sipped from the flask, reviewing the letters, occasionally weeping and sometimes kissing his signature and in general, enjoying a bit of a nervous fit.

It was well past the time when she should have been dressing for dinner at Lady Catherine's that her maid entered. Burney pursed her lips into a little frown upon seeing her mistress on the floor, surrounded by her late husband's papers.

"I beg your pardon, madam, but it appears your...headache has worsened. Shall I notify Lady Catherine that you will not be in attendance at her dinner this evening?"

The task of repairing her appearance and attending a dinner, making witty conversation and fending off advances, seemed both impossible and insupportable. "Yes, I fear my headache will keep me home this evening."

DARCY DRESSED FOR DINNER AT HIS AUNT'S HOME, A FRISSON OF excitement going through him at the thought of seeing Elizabeth. He had noticed a marked change in her regard since their time in Kent. She looked at him at times, and he hoped he did not deceive himself in seeing a tender regard. He could not be so bold as to suggest it was love, but there was an admiration present that was sufficient for him.

He would offer for her again, perhaps even tonight, believing that, by now, she was merely afraid—afraid to give herself to another and take the chance, once again, of permitting herself to care. He hoped to push her a bit, to help her move past these obstacles to happiness, obstacles she had set herself. All he needed was the assurance that a push would not send her running, assurance that he hoped to obtain this night.

Elizabeth was not at his aunt's home when Darcy arrived, and he became increasingly anxious each time the butler announced a new arrival who was not her. At length, the butler arrived bearing a note to his aunt. She read it and offered some instruction, which the man noted before departing.

Some minutes later, Darcy made his way to his aunt's side. "Lady Catherine, I notice that Lady Courtenay is not yet arrived."

Lady Catherine waved her hand indifferently. "She has taken ill this evening and cannot join us."

"Ill?" Darcy exclaimed. "What ails her?"

"Lady Courtenay did not specify," she replied then turned to draw Sir Gerald Crane into conversation.

At once, the night seemed unbearably long and tedious, as well as utterly pointless. He longed to see her, to speak to her, to understand what she was feeling. He could think of nothing to excuse himself from the evening, however, and knew his aunt would not allow him to depart without extensive questioning and undue notice.

The excuse came so readily, and with so little intervention on his part, that it seemed an act of fate. A day servant, hired in for the evening, leaned towards Darcy to offer a glass of wine. The hapless fellow overbalanced himself and his tray, and in one fell swoop, tipped several glasses of wine onto Darcy's trousers.

The servant was appalled and repentant, stammering and shaking as he and another footman attempted to clean Darcy's attire. Lady Catherine was furious, motioning to the butler to remove the man immediately.

The devastated man left the parlour, no doubt thinking of his lost wages and damaged prospects for future employment. Darcy watched him go as he apologised to Lady Catherine, explaining he must be immediately away to the care of his valet or risk ruining his apparel.

As he left, he took Lady Catherine's butler to the side, giving him several coins and asking that the servant be fully recompensed for his evening. The man protested, knowing the amount offered by Darcy was well in excess of the earned wage, but Darcy was firm.

I HAVE HAD TOO MUCH TO DRINK, AND IT WOULD BE SENSIBLE OF ME TO retire directly.

Instead, Elizabeth replaced the papers in her late husband's desk, causing them to be in a state of even greater disorder than they were previously. One letter refused to remain in the drawer, and she eventually gave up on it, holding it in her hand and promptly forgetting it. She then left the study and walked towards the drawing room, intent on collecting the book she had been reading several days prior.

Although she was still enjoying her slight state of inebriation too much to feel ashamed of indulging, part of her did recognise that to drink spirits in such a way was neither proper nor ladylike. *Surely because gentlemen do not want us to know how nice it is to have a bit of strong drink now and then! At least I am not drunk—that would be truly unseemly. No, I am most certainly not drunk so much as I am... happy. I feel quite happy, happier than I have in months.*

She arrived in the drawing room, stumbling a bit over the threshold. *Why did I come here?* She had no notion and stood a moment, trying to recall. As she did, she was surprised to hear Mr Darcy announced.

What is he doing here? Is it not the middle of the night? She looked blearily at the mantel clock but could not make out precisely where the hands rested.

As Darcy entered, she noted how handsome he was in his evening clothes. *He can be rather arrogant at times, but a man who looks so fine in evening wear certainly has just cause.* She believed she had only thought the words, but seeing the odd expression on his face, Elizabeth wondered whether she had spoken aloud.

"Lady Courtenay, you seem unwell." He took her arm and led her to a seat.

"I am indisposed," she announced with as much dignity as she could muster. "I have a headache."

"Forgive me, I should not have come. I wanted to speak to you about…but no, now is not the time."

Elizabeth wondered whether something was amiss with the contents of that flask. What had she been thinking to partake of something that had lain in a desk for two years, maybe longer? Without thought, she blurted, "Pray, speak sir. I am not so ill that I cannot hear you."

He gazed upon her with great fervour, and unabashed, she returned his look, thinking of how lovely his eyes were, so deep and dark. It had been an age since Elizabeth found herself so close to a man unrelated to her. How difficult it was to be a widow sometimes! To have known the comfort of a gentleman's embrace and the pleasing intimacies of marriage and then have it taken away. At least a maiden had no notion of what she missed.

What she wished for, sometimes more than anything, was merely to be held just as Darcy had held her in Kent—to enjoy the security felt within his arms, particularly in a week such as this one when all the sorrows of her past years seemed to be crashing down upon her, making her feel afraid, alone, and desperate.

She recalled the strong warmth of Mr Darcy's arms and how very good and right it had felt to be there. Her longing to experience that again was almost unbearable.

"I must tell you something. I…I have partaken of some rather strong spirits this night. There was a flask…I know not how much it held, but I had a good portion of it."

Now he looked a bit amused. "Yes, I had come upon that notion myself, having retrieved your flask—which, by the by, was empty—from the floor. You need not worry, I—"

"Shhh." She held her finger to his lips. "I must tell you something."

Her finger remained pressed to his lips as he said, "Yes?"

"How much do you suppose George Wickham was paid to kill my husband?"

"George Wickham! George Wickham is your husband's assassin?"

She nodded. "I learned it from Colonel Fitzwilliam today…his name, that is. You know him, I think."

"I do." Darcy was clearly stunned. "George was the son of my father's steward. I could not have imagined him to be involved in something of this nature. Debts and other schemes for monetary gain are more to his credit."

"Monetary gain," Elizabeth scoffed with an inelegant huff that became a hiccup. "How much to you suppose they gave him? He was not part of the plot, so he cannot even claim the dignity of supporting a cause, treasonous as it was. He was a hired killer, nothing more, and how much do you think they gave him?"

"I am sure I do not know."

A sound bubbled up from her chest—something between a sob and another hiccup. She edged closer to Darcy, hoping he might put his arms around her. "Twenty-five pounds. Can you account for it? What sort of person ends the life of another for twenty-five pounds?"

She began to cry, and Darcy obligingly pulled her into his arms, just where she yearned to be. He gently pressed his handkerchief into her hands. She took it gratefully, using it to cover as much of her face as she could as she wept.

"That is dreadful." He spoke softly into her hair.

"Twenty-five pounds!" She hiccuped another sob, mortified by her lack of elegance and manners, but she could not stop herself.

He hushed her, one arm holding her while the other lightly caressed her back. She closed her eyes and rested her head on his shoulder as she regained her equanimity. After a few moments, she tilted her face and met his eyes, which were trained on her. "Pray, forgive me, sir, for this disgraceful behaviour. I am not myself, and I am humiliated that you are witness to it."

"No matter what you do, I find I adore you all the more for it."

He was so warm and comforting, and she was so lonely and sad, that she could not help herself. She began it, placing her hand on his cheek and pulling his face down to hers. He resisted but a moment before she softly caressed his lips with hers, both succumbing to what they knew they wanted, but for different reasons.

IN THE MORNING, ELIZABETH FELT EVERY BIT OF THE REWARD THAT comes from a night of indulgence in spirits. The sun coming through her windows was painfully bright, causing her to wince as a headache roared to life.

Oh, Elizabeth, what did you do? She was mortified by her indiscretion and could only console herself with the fact that she had managed to escape detection by nearly all of her servants and her son. *Just Mr Darcy and Burney and, thankfully, both of them are inclined towards silence.*

She reviewed the events on the settee in her mind. Mr Darcy had resisted her efforts for a few minutes, but he eventually returned her kiss. It was a relatively chaste business at first; Mr Darcy had permitted himself no more than to caress her back lightly. She could boast no such restraint. One hand had roamed his chest while the other had rested on his thigh, supporting her as she leaned into him. *It was his thigh, was it not? Please, God, it was only his thigh!*

She was not entirely certain how it had gone on from there. After some time, he had laid her back on the settee—*Perhaps, I pulled him on top of me? I cannot bear to recall it!*—allowing some of his weight to rest on her. And their kisses! Remembering those kisses made her smile through the mortification. Her skirts were mostly between them, but she could not deny that her leg had encircled one of his. He must have discarded his coat and waistcoat, she believed, for she recalled the searing, hard heat of him pressed against her chest and legs. Her hair had escaped its pins, and he had combed his hands through it over and over, telling her it was beautiful and that she was beautiful.

Yet it became worse. She had briefly entertained the notion of taking Mr Darcy to her bed and prayed she had not voiced the idea. How utterly humiliating to be drunk and as wanton as a harlot, begging Mr Darcy to join her in her bed! She had only wished for the particular consolation that comes with the intimate knowledge of a man and to feel the sense of belonging and dear regard of that state.

Such a gentleman. No matter what I did, he pulled away and apologised. Did I even see him out? Did I wander around with my hair wild about me, looking so obviously lustful?

Her maid had left her a glass of water along with a packet containing some powders. Elizabeth blessed her for her foresight, pouring the contents into the water and drinking down the bitter liquid with no hesitation.

Her morning ablutions proceeded slowly. Burney persuaded her to eat some breakfast though her stomach could not enjoy the idea. As she finished dressing, her housekeeper came to her with a card. "Mr Darcy, madam. Will you receive him?"

"Ohh," she moaned, putting her head into her hand. Then, with a quick shake and a rally of her spirits, she said, "Yes, I shall."

Minutes later, she entered the parlour where he stood, looking over her garden. Although it was small, she had managed to commission something of a floral paradise. It was early in the season, but the space was sheltered and the sunshine plentiful, so things were beginning to flourish.

He turned as she entered. "I should almost think this a garden from Hertfordshire."

She smiled. "Most of the seeds came from my mother's storehouse, so in some manner of speaking, it is. Shall we go sit out there?"

"Perhaps, or would you prefer a walk?"

"Always." There was a brief delay as the maid fetched Elizabeth's bonnet and gloves, and then they were off.

It was a lovely day, the sort of day that just begged for people to fall in love within it. The air was fresh and smelled of new grass and blooming flowers, and baby birds hopped about on the paths around them. It was a day formed for happiness and renewal, and Elizabeth felt it, despite her shame.

She waited to speak until they had walked for a time. "Mr Darcy, I am exceedingly ashamed of my vulgar behaviour last night."

"You were rather amusing, actually."

"My head was not amused this morning," she told him ruefully.

"I should think not. Fitzwilliam told me a bit more of the news you had received yesterday. How shocking it is—I could scarce believe it myself, particularly the role of George Wickham."

"Have you known him a long time?"

"Nearly my entire life. My father even supported him at school. I am glad he is not alive to see what Wickham has become. What misfortune it was for George to meet up with his oldest boyhood friend while using an assumed name."

"How frightening to think he was so near." She paused a moment, lost in thought. "I cannot say why the price on Henry's head distressed me so. It somehow made things worse, that his assassin had done his deed for such a small payment. I could not bear it, and then I found Henry's flask and sipped it as I went through some of his papers. Not the behaviour of a lady, is it?"

Darcy offered a kind smile and patted the hand that rested in the crook of his arm. "You have managed so well for so long. Many others in your position would have turned frequently to such comforts."

"I do not know why you do that."

"Do what?"

"You take the most glaring examples of my faults and follies and somehow make them a source of admiration."

"When you love someone, you love them for their imperfections, not in spite of them."

A queer fluttery feeling came into her stomach. She turned her face away from him until the moment had passed. When she looked at him again, he held out a letter.

"You had this last night, and it fell from your hands. I picked it up and then forgot about it."

She took it, seeing it was one of Henry's letters, an unimportant one addressed to a school friend in Kent. She opened it and glanced over the words. "Henry was so disorderly; his papers were a scandalous mess. This letter was a note to a friend. It must have been a draft, or else he neglected to send it for some reason.

"He had been at the friend's estate, and the pair of them were doing a bit of fencing with some old swords they found. The friend's sword slipped, and made a deep gouge across Henry's chest. From Henry's account, the wound bled impressively, and his friend was worried about him. This letter was merely to reassure his friend that he was well."

She sighed. "He had quite the scar from it, nearly the whole way across his chest. I saw it once, and it looked rather mean. Would you be so good as to hold this for me? I did not bring a reticule." She returned the letter to his hands.

"Of course." He replaced it in his coat pocket.

There was an awkward silence until she offered, "I hope you will forgive me for kissing you as I did."

His countenance unexpectedly became teasing. "Having taken such liberties, madam, I am anticipating your offer for my hand."

She laughed, relieved. "I suppose if I refuse to do the honourable thing, you will have Miss Darcy call me out?"

"I might have Georgiana call you out anyway, just to see how you might settle it." He grinned at her.

"If ladies were to duel, we would need a retinue of friends and acquaintances to attend. The pair would face off and begin hurling veiled insults at one another, or perhaps, contrive rumours and gossip to spread to those around them." Elizabeth giggled at the notion. "In any case, the idea of it is certainly awful enough, so perhaps I should just offer for you—or rather, agree to your offer if it still stands—and avoid Georgiana's wrath entirely."

She had caught Darcy short, and he gave her a wary look. "Do you mean that?"

Astonishingly, she found she did. She hardly knew she had been considering it, but having given voice to the idea, she felt peace. It seemed right.

She nodded but added immediately, "I do not wish to hurt you, but neither would I mislead you."

"Very well." His countenance became grave and he stared intently at her.

"We are rather well matched. There is a similarity in the turn of our minds that would serve us well, I think, and moreover, I enjoy your company very much. You are a good and honourable man, and I was a fool not to have seen it before. Our friendship is so very dear to me, one of the dearest I have."

He shook his head slightly when she called herself a fool but said nothing.

"My greatest hesitation is that you tell me you love me."

"That troubles you?"

"I just do not know that I could ever offer you the same. It is unfair." She hated the look of disappointment that came into his eyes. "I gave my heart in full to Henry, and with all that has happened, I cannot imagine I shall ever recover from it. I can offer you my friendship and my affection, but as for more…I just do not know whether I can."

With an inhale she continued, "If you, too, would enter into this marriage for practical reasons, I would be more easy with the notion. Then we would give to each other only what was received."

He smiled faintly. "Alas, my desire to marry you is formed by the wishes of my heart, not my head, so I cannot oblige you."

"If I did feel myself forming a more romantic attachment, I would welcome it. I just want you to understand that I do not know whether it will occur. It must be yours to decide whether or not you can be in an unequal marriage."

"I have considered it," he admitted after a thoughtful pause. "I see how you loved your husband, and I did not expect to supplant that. I shall readily admit that I am a jealous man, and to know that your heart belongs to him is difficult for me to accept. However, my choice is for an unequal marriage no matter what we decide. Either I can be with you—the one I love—or I can marry another and, thus, be with one who might love me but whom I do not love. You see, just as your heart is for Henry, mine is for you. That will not change.

"So, fully apprehending your hesitation, I say yes, I do agree to a practical marriage with you, accepting whatever amount of affection you give to me because I cannot live without you."

Their eyes met and his words—*I cannot live without you*—gave her an inexplicable thrill. She felt her heart swelling under the power of his gaze; it was almost too painful to bear.

"I would be far happier with half of your heart than the whole of anyone else's," he added softly.

She was finally able to tear her eyes from his, lowering them as a light blush heated her cheeks. "I believe we have an understanding."

He took her hand in his and stopped where they stood on the park's tree-lined path. "So, you will marry me?"

"Yes, it will be my honour, sir."

He bowed over her hand, kissing it tenderly. "I hope you know how happy you have made me."

She felt herself blush even hotter and murmured, "I hope to always make you happy."

He put his finger under her chin and made her look up at him. His eyes were unrelenting in their emotion, and she knew, just then, how deeply he felt for her. She could see it written in his eyes, and she felt a momentary pang of fear, hoping she would never disappoint him or make that light grow dim.

She tugged his hand, hoping to induce him to begin walking again and stop looking at her with such passion.

"I long to kiss you right now," he said.

"As I have already behaved exceedingly poorly this week, I must refrain from any more." She laughed uncomfortably. To her great relief, they resumed their walk, speaking of insignificant matters on the way.

As they entered Elizabeth's house, Darcy said, "May I...?"

"May you what?"

"May I meet your son?"

"My son!" She stopped short on the threshold of the drawing room, and Darcy nearly collided with her. She had expected he might wish for more kisses or an embrace or something of that nature. "Oh! I…I am surprised you wish to see him." She continued into the room and took a seat on the nearest settee where Darcy joined her.

"Surprised? If I am to be the boy's father, should I not at least meet him first?"

She laughed lightly at her own stupidity. "Of course you should. I shall call his nursemaid to bring him to us."

"I believe I might prefer to see him in his nursery."

"You wish to visit his nursery? Why?"

Darcy shrugged. "When I was young, and my father sent for me, it always seemed that I was to be scolded. I do not wish for young Henry to feel so when we meet. I believe I should do better to meet him in his own place."

Elizabeth had a strange tight feeling in her throat brought about by Darcy's consideration and with the thought of her son, at long last, having a father to care for him. She agreed to take Darcy to the nursery.

They had barely reached the door of the drawing room when Darcy spoke her name. She looked at him and saw a tender light had come into his eyes as he reached for her hand. Her heart began to pound as he pulled her into his embrace.

He pressed her hand to his chest as his other hand stole around her waist. He was gentle, as if she were a fragile and precious object, and he pressed lightly on her back to draw her close. His heart pounded too, she discovered, feeling it against her chest.

"Tell me this is not a dream," he murmured as he bent his head to kiss her, and she met him easily. His kiss grew more urgent, and she felt the door against her back as he pressed her into it, dropping her hand and using both of his to cup her face as he kissed her deeply.

Licentious, wanton thoughts flooded her almost immediately, causing her to pull away, certain Mr Darcy would not wish to know he had just become betrothed to some harlot. *I must control myself. Is my long time of loneliness making me wish to abandon all restraint with him?* His body felt so hard and muscled against her, so manly and strong. It was almost irresistible.

She was breathless when he pulled back. "You tempt me too well, Mr Darcy."

"No more Mr Darcy, my Elizabeth."

She smiled playfully at him. "Very well, Fitzwilliam."

He smiled and then grew more serious, placing gentle kisses on the side of her face and neck. "I did have one question regarding this marriage of friendship between us."

"What is that?"

He hesitated. "You do know that I require an heir."

She laughed as a hot blush rose on her cheeks. "It will be a unique friendship, I suppose. I did not anticipate a celibate relationship with you, sir, I assure you."

"Good." He kissed her again. "Because that, madam, I do not think I could manage."

YOUNG HENRY WAS SEATED AT A TABLE, A MEAL BEFORE HIM, WHEN they arrived in the nursery. He was as disinclined towards food as ever, and the appearance of his mother and a new friend made him still more uninterested.

He ran to them immediately, arms outstretched, but it was Darcy, not Elizabeth, he reached for. Darcy knelt scooping him into his arms. "Good day there, sir. I wonder whether I might have your permission to marry your mother."

Henry laughed and indicated that he wished to be down. Darcy placed him on the floor, noticing immediately that Elizabeth was fretting over her son's plate.

She saw him look at her. "I sometimes think he must survive on air. I worry too much over it, I know. His nurse assures me that children do not starve themselves. She assures me that, when he is hungry he will eat."

Henry was back, holding a ball that he tried to toss into the air. Alas, his skill at throwing meant that the ball, instead of going towards Darcy, went behind Henry, but he was happy regardless, whirling and chasing it down before trying again.

Elizabeth called to him. "Henry, would you like a bite of this beef?"

"No!"

"Look at this nice bread! Nurse Jenny has put loads of jam on it!"

"No jam!" Henry announced cheerfully, tossing the ball behind himself again.

Darcy went to Henry's small table. "Excellent. I fancy some jam. I think I shall eat it all."

Henry stopped chasing the ball and watched as Darcy took a piece of the bread and pretended to put it in his mouth. With another giggle, Henry came over and, just as the bread neared Darcy's mouth, leaned in and took a bite.

"Shocking manners!" Darcy exclaimed, feigning offence. "Have you ever seen such a thing? I shall have this bite then…"

They continued to play, Henry snatching bites away from Darcy until a reasonable amount of food had been consumed. Elizabeth smiled, surprised by Darcy's ease and playfulness with Henry.

When the bread had been mostly eaten, the ball was tossed around a bit. Henry then decided to show Darcy his most important possessions: a book that he particularly favoured, a rag doll made to look like a dog, and an old, well-used blanket with which he slept. His nap was soon upon them, and Jenny returned to attend to him while Darcy and Elizabeth departed.

Darcy was required to leave soon after, and Elizabeth watched him go with regret and no small amount of wonder at the events of the day. Her heart was full, and her mind rested on the vision of the little family they would have together. She was surprised by how eager she was to see it become true.

SIXTEEN

Elizabeth became Mrs Fitzwilliam Darcy on June 25 1812. The day itself seemed designed to promote their felicity: birds sang, flowers gave off a sweet fragrance, and the sun bathed them gently in its rays.

At the appointed hour, Darcy stood at the altar of St George's and watched her approach on the arm of her father. He took deep breaths that did nothing to assuage his breathlessness nor calm the pounding of his heart. *Is this true? Will she truly be mine?* It was too much felicity to be borne. His mind would not make sense of it.

Then she looked up, catching his eye, and for a moment, only the two of them were present. He hoped she could see the emotion in his eyes for, poor, stupid man that he was, he knew he could never explain it to her. The words "I love you" seemed woefully inadequate. Nevertheless, he could not stop his lips from forming the words, soundlessly mouthing his declaration to her, unsure whether she could even understand what he said.

And she smiled.

It was a delicious, private smile, her eyes locked on his, and it told him she was glad to be his and happy to make these vows to him. He felt the heavens open as a tear came to his eye, and he had to blink, hating the need to remove his eyes from her for even a fraction of a second.

She joined him at the altar, and the vicar began the service.

DEARLY beloved, we are gathered together here in the sight of God...

She is so beautiful, and I love her very much. Mrs Elizabeth Darcy. I wish to say it over and over again.

...therefore is not by any to be enterprised, nor taken in hand, unadvisedly, lightly, or wantonly...

Elizabeth gave him a faint smile. *Is she truly happy? Will she find contentment as my wife?*

The vicar droned on, pronouncing the words with painstaking solemnity, seeming to linger forever in the beginning part of the service. Darcy mentally hastened him along, wishing for the point where he would hold her hand.

...if either of you know any impediment, why ye may not be lawfully joined together in Matrimony, ye do now confess it. For be ye well assured, that so many as are coupled together otherwise than God's Word doth allow are not joined together by God; neither is their Matrimony lawful...

At last, it was upon them. Their hands joined and they made their promises, one to another.

Their vows seemed so meagre to Darcy. He wished to say much more, to tell her he would protect her and make her happy and ensure that she felt loved every single day of her life. He wished to tell her that she was a part of him in a way no one else could ever be.

Her ring was from his mother, a Fitzwilliam family heirloom intended for his bride. He placed it on her delicate hand with great reverence, and it fit as if it were made for her. Then they knelt in prayer, shoulder to shoulder, as their marriage was sanctified.

- *...Those whom God hath joined together let no man put asunder...*

It was finished. They signed the register and walked as man and wife out of the doors and into the waiting carriage.

As soon as they were in the carriage, Elizabeth surprised him by moving into his embrace and tilting her head up to receive his kiss. They were still kissing when they realised that the horses had stopped.

"So soon?"

"The house is regrettably close to the church." He looked at her lovingly. "I have a splendid idea."

"What is it?"

"Let us run off. With so many at the breakfast, they will never notice us gone."

Elizabeth giggled. "Where shall we go? Somewhere disreputable and seedy, perhaps?"

"Only an unfashionable sort of place would do." He pulled her hand to his lips and sighed. "It cannot last so long, can it? And then we may have peace, together."

Elizabeth smiled and kissed him once again. "I do like the sound of that."

HOURS LATER, ELIZABETH PACED, FEELING ONLY A LITTLE NERVOUS AS she awaited her new husband's appearance in her bedchamber. She was surprised that she was not more nervous. In truth, she was a bit impatient, wanting this first time to be finished so the anxious anticipation within her would be gone.

It did reassure her to remember how pleasant her marital relations were with Henry. Henry was a gentle man, and even their first time had not been unduly uncomfortable. After that first night, she thought they had gone on rather well. Henry was generally quick, and afterwards, they would lie together and kiss and embrace in an enjoyable manner. She certainly could not complain, and she had nothing to dread or fear.

When the knock came, she nearly jumped out of her skin. "Come in," she said, sounding a bit breathless. She schooled herself to appear confident and welcoming as Darcy entered.

He was so handsome. It was both disconcerting and enticing to see him in so intimate a setting, clad in only a dressing gown and, presumably, a nightshirt. A fit of stupidity struck her—she knew not what to do with herself—so she moved immediately to the bed.

"Should I…let us…"

"Will you join me by the fire for a moment?"

"Of course."

They sat in silence by the hearth. She stole a glance at him and, seeing his pulse throb in his neck, knew he was nervous too.

"Are you well?" he asked. "A second wedding night, such as it is, must seem—"

"Does that bother you?" she asked quickly and a bit too loudly. "It bothers me a little. I worry that it is unfair to you."

"I feel like the most fortunate of men to be here with you as my wife." He lifted her hand to his lips. "Pray do not be uneasy. If you would like to wait until—"

"Oh no, not at all. There is always going to be some uncertainty the first time no matter the circumstances, but a delay will not help."

He kissed her hand again and waited until she met his gaze. "Promise me, if you become distressed in any way, you will stop me. This need not occur tonight."

Something in his tone struck Elizabeth as very dear. She looked at him, realising how fortunate she was. Gathering her courage, she kissed his lips. He immediately brought his hand up behind her head, holding her to him as he responded. Their kisses grew increasingly ardent until he pulled away and stood, holding his hand out to her.

When they reached the bed, Elizabeth removed her dressing gown and laid it on the chaise at its foot. She turned to see him standing motionless, watching her. She smiled shyly.

"My beautiful wife," he murmured as he assisted her into the bed and then joined her. "May I ask you something?"

She nodded.

"Is there something you would especially wish me to…I want to please you, but not knowing what you like…" he trailed off, looking discomfited.

Elizabeth was unsure what he meant, but he appeared so uncomfortable that she felt it was incumbent on her to say something. "Nothing particular. I do like to be held and ah…talk…afterwards."

"Held?" He laughed, looking relieved. "I shall hold you all night long if you wish."

"All night? Truly?" She was surprised; Henry had never stayed the night with her.

"I shall gladly stay."

She did want him to. In fact, she wanted it very much. "Yes, please."

He began to kiss and touch her. Her first shock, which she thought she managed to conceal, occurred when he pulled off his dressing gown, revealing that he was naked underneath it. Henry had never been naked, and they had always been under the bedclothes, so in truth, she had seen very little of him or he of her. Darcy not only threw off his dressing gown, but all the blankets and bed linens were somehow lost off the side of the bed, leaving his nudity on display.

She felt she was on more familiar ground when his hand reached down and eased her night shift up her legs, but that too was a surprise as he pulled it over her head. To make matters worse, when she was naked, he gazed upon her for a moment that felt like it lasted an eternity until she blushed and turned her face away. He bent to kiss her neck, saying, "You are the most beautiful creature I have ever seen. Forgive me—you stunned me with your beauty."

Elizabeth believed she knew what would occur next, but things did not proceed as she had anticipated. She could see he was erect and wondered that he did not get on with things. Was it not time that he should?

Instead, he kissed and caressed her everywhere: her neck, her breasts, her stomach. As his hands slid down her body, he commenced touching her intimately. Her breathing quickened, and several times, she gasped at a particularly pleasurable touch or sensation.

It was both pleasurable and distressing as nothing of the sort had ever happened to her before. There had been a bit of a ritual to Henry's sort of intimacy. He would come to her, kiss her for a little while, and caress her breasts over her night shift. While he did that, he would generally put her hand on him through his nightshirt, then ask whether she was ready, raise her gown and his, and it would be short work from there. *In six months of marriage, I do not think Henry ever saw my breasts.* She glanced down at Darcy as he kissed her bosom.

As her pleasure mounted, so too did her panic. These sensations were taking her beyond the bounds of her control, making her feel a fire in her blood, and were as upsetting as they were pleasurable. She was in uncharted waters. This was nothing she expected, and she felt as though she might scream or cry or…she knew not what.

Her anxiety increased as the sensations Darcy produced in her grew more maddening. She felt herself shiver at some points and forced herself to remain calm, biting her lip to remain quiet even as it became increasingly difficult to do so.

She was losing control, and she could not like it, no matter how good it felt. *I cannot do this.* A fine sheen of sweat broke out over her skin, as much due to pleasure as fear.

"Please stop!"

Darcy stilled immediately, moving his hand to rest against her hip. "Have I hurt you?"

"No." Her breath came quickly as she tried to calm herself, hoping he did not notice her peculiar state, which was a combination of arousal, fear, and a need to scream.

"What is it?"

She could not answer, could not even look at him, and at last managed to choke out, "I am not well. I feel ill." *Oh, the look on his face! I have disappointed him.*

In a low tone, he said, "Forgive me."

"No, no." She turned her face into the pillow feeling as though she might weep with her stupidity, her anxiety, and her embarrassment at being such a poor wife, and on the first night of their marriage, no less. Her disappointment in herself was acute, but she did not know what else to do. She was too afraid to abandon herself to him. She knew not where it might lead if she did.

Finally, he quietly asked, "Shall I go?"

Still facing away from him, she nodded, and within moments, she heard the click of the door as he left her. Her tears began soon after.

IT WAS A LONG AND WEEPY NIGHT FOR ELIZABETH. *I RUINED OUR wedding night.* The refrain circled endlessly through her mind, and by the time dawn came, she knew she must speak with him about what had occurred.

She knocked on his door, but he did not answer. His man said he had awoken early. Marshalling her courage, she went to find him and met with success in the breakfast room. He was grave and quiet as he rose and helped her to sit, and they remained quiet until the footman departed, leaving them alone.

"Are you well?"

His solicitude caused tears to threaten immediately, but she tried to smile. "I am so sorry."

"Please do not apologise." He spoke in low but earnest tones. "I cannot know how this affects your spirits, but I am glad to give you time to become accustomed to being a wife again."

Her face flushed red with embarrassment. "It was not that."

"What, then?"

She hesitated, her mortification looming large. "I believed I under-stood…it was so different than…some of the places…when you would…I felt such odd feelings, almost an illness or a fever, and…"

"Did I hurt you?" His expression had moved from concern to alarm.

"No, it did not hurt. In truth, it was pleasant—almost too much so, if you understand me."

Darcy continued to appear confused.

She sighed and dropped her face into her hands. "I do not wish to be vulgar or uncouth, but I cannot explain it otherwise."

"Shall we go to your private sitting room?" he asked in a voice that showed his trepidation.

She stood, and their breakfast was forgotten. He followed her on what seemed an interminable walk until they were at last within their chambers and assured of privacy.

With a sombre countenance, he said, "May I say one thing first?" On her nod, he continued, "I apologise, quite heartily. I believe I was so determined to bring you to pleasure that I was overeager and too zealous, and I did not realise you had grown uneasy."

"You need have no regrets. This is entirely my fault. I am sorry I ruined our wedding night." Her words were full of emotion, and he touched her hand gently.

"You ruined nothing."

"I was anxious because I thought I understood what to expect, but it was different—vastly different—and I just did not…I tried to calm myself, but I did not know what I should do."

He gave her a rueful smile. "I assumed far too much. I anticipated some hesitation with regard to your feelings but not for the physical act itself. I went too quickly."

Elizabeth laid her hand gently against his face and shook her head as he once again offered, "We shall wait until you are more comfort-able with me and our marriage."

"No, we need not—"

"I think we should." She understood his view of the matter. Last night had been dreadful for him, and the last thing he could want was to repeat it.

Some words he had spoken earlier were echoing in her mind as she considered the unusual manner in which he had phrased them. She was determined not to fail him again, and she gathered her courage to ask. "Will you clarify something for me? Something you mentioned before?"

"Of course."

She blushed hotly but remained determined. "To bring me to pleasure." Determination failed her at the last, and she looked away quickly.

When her gaze returned to him, she saw he was confused. "It has been my teaching and my experience that a lady's pleasure lies in pleasing her husband and in the possible creation of a child." If it were possible, her face grew even hotter. "It would seem that nothing of last night had to do with either of those things."

Something shifted a bit in Darcy's eyes. She could not quite make him out, but she was glad to see less disappointment and something like relief in its stead.

"You do not mean...you do know a lady may have the same pleasure as a man."

She had no response to that.

"The feelings of pleasure and release occur for both man and wife." He paused and then asked, "Has that not been your experience?"

Elizabeth opened her mouth but did not know how to answer the question. "Henry was a very good, very traditional sort of gentleman."

Darcy stared at her blankly.

"Things...transpired as my mother explained they would: mostly clothed, under blankets, and in darkness. It was generally brief, and I felt..." She paused, all of the awkwardness of their boldly honest discussion coming upon her. She put her hands over her face, unable to look at Darcy.

He leaned closer to her. "Please tell me."

Her voice was small. "Everything was agreeable. Sometimes there was a pleasant, warm feeling but not like last night."

"I see." Darcy pulled her hands from her face, forcing her to look at him, and gently kissed them. They sat there for a moment, hearing the sounds of the household around them.

After a short pause, he said, "It need not be so. I love you, and I wish you to have every manner of pleasure in this as in all aspects of our marriage. However, I will not make you anxious or afraid over it. If you wish it to be for us as it was for you before, so it will be, but first, give me a chance to show you how enjoyable it can be."

"I...I do not know if—" She stopped.

"I can think of no better method to show my deep and abiding love for you. Why would I wish you to be denied of something so wonderful when it is within my power to give to you?"

I cannot disappoint him; or rather, I cannot disappoint him again.

"In any case, once you realise what enjoyment we might have together, you will scarcely be able to keep yourself from me."

It was a little tease, but in the anxiety of the moment, it made her giggle wildly. "I fear I might become rather...discomposed."

"I would count it an absolute success if I might see to your discomposure. In fact, I wish for nothing more than to discompose you completely—several times, perhaps."

She giggled again, anxiety making her sound somewhat maniacal. "Oh, I do not know about that."

"I do know. Will you permit me to show you?"

"Well...what if...I do not...what if I cannot bear it?" She giggled again, hating her nervousness.

"I shall stop whenever you wish. Just forget about whatever you knew previously. We shall make our own way in this."

She laughed again, hardly able to look at him. He awaited a response, and she nodded.

"Excellent." She peeped at him, and he gave her a broad, pleased smile. On impulse, she quickly kissed him, causing his grin to grow even more. *He is so handsome when he smiles.*

He kissed her back and then became aloof. "Do you require your maid? I can assist you if you would like."

"Require my...do you mean now?"

"Are you otherwise engaged?"

"No." She giggled. "Are you?"

"What could be more agreeable than to spend the day delighting my wife?" He then stood, taking her hand and leading her into her bedroom.

THE RUMBLING OF HER STOMACH WOKE HER. ELIZABETH CAME INTO consciousness gradually, seeing by the light that it was already late afternoon, possibly early evening.

It astonished her to realise how little she knew of the marriage bed. *I am fortunate Fitzwilliam has shown himself an able tutor.*

She had decided that she must approach intimacy as any other accomplishment in which she wished to become proficient. Rather than allow her mind to worry or feel unsure, or think of Henry and what was past, she dove into her present circumstance with as much enthusiasm and willingness to learn as she could muster.

Thus, when Darcy had undressed her, she followed his lead and undressed him as well. She had needed his assistance with his cravat, but otherwise, she had managed well, save for accidentally tearing a button from his trousers. He made a little joke about telling the gentlemen at his club that she had literally torn his clothing off—which, in truth, she knew he would never do—causing them both to laugh, and that too relaxed her.

The day had been spent in rapturous, unrestrained amour. Much of what Darcy suggested had shocked her initially, but he had seemed so happy with her pleasure that she could not deny him. Although Darcy had more than amply proven his assertion that a lady could experience the same heights of pleasure as a man, he had also shown her that, in his capable hands, she might experience it far more frequently than he could.

"Good afternoon, Mrs Darcy." He rolled over, coming awake as slowly as she had and reaching for her even before his eyes were fully opened.

She grinned like a fool. "Good afternoon, Mr Darcy."

"You are hungry, I think." He smiled lazily.

"Oh, did you hear that? How mortifying!"

He had rolled towards her and began kissing her neck. "We have eaten very little these two days past."

"And exerted ourselves much," she teased. "At least these"—she leaned to see the clock on the mantle—"eight hours past."

"Eight hours!" He was mockingly horrified. "I did not realise we had been here so long. I am afraid I am woefully behind."

"You are?" She quickly sat up, swinging her legs around and reaching for her dressing gown. "I would not take you from your duties."

Sitting up behind her, he wound his hand around her waist and slid it up to caress her breast. "Perhaps I had better explain the nature of my obligations before you leave me with such haste."

"Very well…" She felt an immediate response to his touch.

"You will recall, I think, when we were first in here this morning. I believe I had pleased you a bit, and you gratified me by saying my name in a way that I enjoyed immensely. It was rather less speaking my name than moaning it."

She was close to moaning again, but instead, she breathily whispered, "Yes."

"If you recall, I vowed I would cause you to do that at least once an hour, and now we have slept for over two hours, causing me to be three short of where I must be to remain on course."

"Three!" Elizabeth half laughed and half moaned. "I shall not prevent you from tending to your duties, sir."

He laughed, gently tugging her back onto the pillows.

THEY LEFT THE BED AS DARKNESS WAS FALLING, RINGING FOR FOOD TO be brought to their sitting room. Elizabeth felt embarrassed when the servants were outside of the door arranging things, but quickly discarded the feeling, not wishing any awkwardness to mar what had been a wonderful day.

She clandestinely studied Darcy as they ate. She had told him she was capable of offering him nothing more than friendship, but now she wondered whether that were true. She already felt the ties that moored her heart giving way, and it was only the second day of their marriage.

The pleasures of the marital bed have confused your mind. Who could not feel kindly towards a man who had…exerted himself so nicely on your behalf?

She smiled as he put aside his plate. He took hers from her hands, setting it with his. For a moment, he did nothing more than simply look at her. She blushed under his intense gaze. "You discompose me, sir."

"Not yet, but soon," he responded with a mischievous grin. He stood and swept her into his arms, carrying her towards the bed, kissing her all the while. She gave a little, shrieking giggle and pressed her lips to his neck just before he tossed her onto the bed, jumping in after her.

At once, he was serious, his face inches from hers as he tenderly kissed her cheeks. "Do you know how much I love you? All I wish for, from now until eternity, is to have you in my arms, just this way. All else may come and go from me, and I shall be happy so long as I have you."

"You are too good to me," she whispered.

"Impossible."

AFTER THE COUPLE ENJOYED A WEEK OF SECLUSION, DUTY INTRUDED upon them. Elizabeth had calls to receive and her child to attend, and Darcy had his affairs to manage, including meeting his cousins and uncle at his club.

After Colonel Fitzwilliam and Lord Matlock departed, he remained with Saye for some time, both with their papers and tea.

"I beg your pardon, sir. Mr Darcy, is it?"

A man stood there, remarkable only in that he appeared so wholly unremarkable. Every one of his features was of the middling variety—his height and build were average, his hair was light brown, and his eyes were brown too. His clothing was neither unfashionable nor fashionable, and his voice was well modulated, being neither deep nor high, neither exceptionally loud nor soft. He was a man made to blend into walls. Darcy knew they had been introduced, though he could not recall the man's name. Embarrassed, Darcy searched his mind as Saye looked on with a dispassionate air.

"I am Hanley. Mr James Hanley. We met at a card party earlier in the spring."

"Oh yes." Darcy recalled that he was a boyhood friend of the late Lord Courtenay and second son of the Baron of Walsingham. "How do you do, sir?"

"Very well, I thank you. I wish to congratulate you on your recent nuptials. Lady Courtenay—rather, Mrs Darcy—is a fine lady. My sincerest wishes for your joy."

"Thank you." Darcy motioned for him to be seated.

Saye leaned forwards. "You were at Brower's the other night. We shared a table, I think."

"We did, Lord Saye." The two gentlemen shared a brief discussion on shared acquaintances and a fondness for cards. Darcy was not interested in the conversation and hoped it might conclude shortly so he could leave for home and his wife.

Wishing to move the conversation onwards, Darcy spoke. "You were an intimate of the late Lord Courtenay, yes?"

"Yes, I am; rather, I was. I still cannot believe he is dead. I knew him from when I was only eight years old."

"A loss deeply felt, then."

"It is," Hanley agreed. "I was with him when he met Mrs Darcy in Bath."

"Yes, she gave me an account."

"It was a happy time for Henry, and although his life was cut short, I am glad he shared the last of it with one whom he loved and who loved him in return."

Darcy leaned back, taking the measure of Hanley and trying to gauge his purpose. Quietly and confidently, he replied, "Yes, she did, and still does, love him. I would not take that from her."

"You have a reputation as a good man," Hanley replied. "I am pleased for her to have married a gentleman such as yourself. Neither Henry nor I would wish her to languish in suffering."

Darcy pursed his lips, considering. "She suffered a great deal for nearly three years. No one could accuse her of marrying hastily."

"Of course not." Hanley gave him a bland, expressionless smile. "How is our young earl? Adjusting well to his new family circle?"

Darcy nodded slowly. "He is a fine boy."

Hanley stood. "I shall not importune you further, sir, but please accept my best wishes, and give my regards to your wife."

"I shall."

When Hanley had gone, Darcy turned to his cousin, who had ostensibly paid no heed to the conversation after the talk of cards and gambling had ended. "That was odd. I felt there was something he wished to say, but I cannot tell if he said it."

Saye lowered his paper. "He is a rather dull gentleman, so quiet and placid I would almost forget he was there as we played the other night. What do you know of him?"

"Nothing at all."

"He was a good friend of Elizabeth's late husband?"

"As you heard."

Saye pursed his lips.

"What do you know? If Elizabeth remains in danger, she must know for the protection of—"

"No, nothing like that," Saye assured him quickly. "I cannot recall what it was that I heard. He comes from a good family with a large and prosperous estate. It was nothing I am sure, some tale perhaps of trifling with this debutante or that, or a rout of some sort. Nothing of consequence."

Darcy looked at him doubtfully. The bland pudding of a man he just saw hardly seemed the rakish sort, but then again, if his fortune was good, there were ladies who would pursue him. Miss Bingley came to mind as an immediate example.

"Are you certain?"

"Fairly so," Saye replied, no longer interested. "I shall tell you whether I hear more, but I am sure it was nothing."

SEVENTEEN

PEMBERLEY, JULY 1812

The newly wed Mr and Mrs Darcy travelled to Pemberley in the middle of July. Henry was along, but as often as not, he rode with his nurse in the servant's carriage. He was a great favourite, and they would often vie for his favour, playing little games or showing him little tricks to amuse him. Henry, even at his tender age, enjoyed giving them all their turn.

The Darcys' carriage was far more sedate, though as they rode, their discussion would inevitably veer towards the beginning of their acquaintance and the situations in Hertfordshire that had come between them. It could not be denied that Darcy had made his share of errors, but Elizabeth came to see that she bore a significant responsibility for having seen his every action in the worst possible light.

"You were flirting with me?"

"Of course. I believed you saw my admiration and that my efforts to control my outward expression of emotion could not deceive you."

Elizabeth determinedly closed her gaping mouth. "What, then, was the purpose of tossing ink on your letter?"

"To say you were correct. I *was* filled with all manner of riotous emotion whenever I was in your presence."

Elizabeth laughed. "I thought it a rebuke."

"A rebuke! How might ruining my own letter rebuke you?"

"I cannot remember." She laughed. "Another example of how a

prejudice, when held to the critical light, can rarely hold to its supposed truth."

"Prejudice?" Darcy asked.

Elizabeth's smile was a bit rueful. "From the moment I heard your insult, my sketch of your character was made, and anything you did could only verify what I supposed." She leaned over to kiss him. "Will you ever forgive me?"

"No," he replied.

"No?"

He shook his head. "One kiss to forgive so much prejudice? Who can know what other manner of evil you have ascribed to me? Certainly one kiss cannot answer for all."

Elizabeth laughed. "I must admit that my dislike of you—which I thought at the time to be rather immovable—was based on more than merely that."

"You should confess it all that I might determine precisely how many kisses are required to ease my soul."

"Very well, then." She settled herself in her seat. "I noticed your gaze would linger on me a bit too long, and I believed you were finding fault."

"I was admiring you."

"You once scowled while I played and sang at Lucas Lodge. I considered it a criticism of my performance."

Darcy laughed. "That was certainly no criticism. My scowl was directed at myself for imagining you at Pemberley."

"A scowl for imagining me at Pemberley?"

"Some evening, I shall demonstrate my thoughts for you, and you will see that I did indeed deserve that scowl for thinking such things in company and of a lady for whom I had no claim."

Elizabeth blushed red. "Oh." For a moment, she was discomposed that he had thought of her so even back then.

"There was another time I saw such a frown: when you and Colonel Fitzwilliam were riding on Oakham Mount. You looked as though you might have liked to turn about without speaking to me but then realised I had caught you."

"That was a jealous frown. I wanted to greet you, but I did not want you to meet Fitzwilliam."

"Why?"

"He is so easy with ladies, always the gallant. I could not bear to see you fall to his charms." He offered her a smile, but she detected a bit of insecurity therein.

She kissed him gently. "Instead, I fell to yours."

He smiled against her mouth. "I did prevail, it is true, and I must wonder why."

She pulled back to look at him and saw still the light of vulnerability in his eyes. *This cannot be easy for him. He freely professes his love, knowing he will not have a return.*

Elizabeth removed her glove and caressed his cheek. "I suppose I might say something of the goodness of your character, your charity, or your honour. I could also say something of your intelligence, your loyalty, or your diligence. All of that would be true, yet it was much simpler than that.

"After we returned from Kent, where I had grown accustomed to seeing you each and every day, I realised that I wanted to be with you more than anyone I knew or had ever known. Just be with you and talk to you…it was unimaginable to think I should forgo such pleasures."

Elizabeth kissed him once again. "I am happy to be married to you. Please never doubt my affection."

As they entered the grounds of Pemberley, Darcy could scarcely contain his enthusiasm. This was the moment he had dreamt of, longed for, and many times doubted would ever come to fruition: bringing Elizabeth to his home as his bride.

Her thoughts must have tended towards the same for she looked over at him with the mischievous sparkle in her eyes that he was coming to know so well. "When we were at Rosings and I invited myself to Pemberley, neither you nor I would have imagined I would be coming as Mrs Darcy."

"Being that I had already proposed to you twice, I would have to disagree. I had imagined it many times by then."

Pemberley had a lovely approach through a pristine woodland, and Elizabeth appeared to be lost in admiring the trees and the landscape, which were different from any she had known before. He enjoyed watching her admire his land and almost missed her teasing him.

"Shall we reach the house itself before nightfall? These woods are beautiful, but I am not of a mind to spend the night in them."

Darcy laughed and caressed her hand with his finger. "Yes, teasing miss, we shall reach the house soon and, before that, a place from which to see it before we arrive."

He watched her again for a moment before commenting, "I love that you tease me. No one else does, and I rather enjoy it. It is a surprise to me. I once imagined you were rather timid."

"Timid? Me?" Elizabeth laughed. "I have been known as many things but never timid."

"You were so quiet when we met, and at times, a look of trepidation would be on your countenance." He shrugged. "I could not comprehend you, so I believed you timid."

"I have you to thank for it."

"Me?"

"In my younger years, I was known for my vivacity. However, that part was swallowed up by everything that happened to me, and I became more serious and restrained. When I met you, I wished to tease you. So I did."

She shrugged. "I once told Jane that if I did not begin by being impertinent, I would undoubtedly grow afraid of you. So you see, I am much in your debt. You found a part of me that I believed had been lost."

Darcy's heart pounded with her sentiments, but he could say no more as the carriage had ceased moving. He smiled. "The men have stopped the horses so I believe we can now see the house."

He assisted her out of the carriage, leading her to where the house could be seen, and he watched with great enjoyment as she saw her new home for the first time. He pulled her back to his chest and put his arms around her as she exclaimed over the house. "Will you be happy here, my love?"

She tilted her head, looking at him as best she could with the restriction of her bonnet. "I shall be nearly mad with felicity, and I shall make certain you are too."

"Let us go then. Let us get you to your new home."

THEIR FIRST DAYS PASSED QUICKLY AS ELIZABETH BUSIED HERSELF IN coming to know the household while Darcy tended to matters requiring his attention. They also began receiving callers from among the local gentry, including Mr and Mrs Graham Russell.

Mr Russell was the son of a local baronet and nearest to Darcy in consequence among those in Derbyshire, though not as wealthy. He was in his early thirties, and his wife, Sarah, was in her mid-twenties and increasing with their first child.

Mrs Russell was pleasant enough, if a little too determined to impress. She spoke of any titled person among her acquaintance with a too-familiar air and had a vulgar habit of discussing the cost of things such as gowns and jewels. As Elizabeth was accustomed to her mother doing the very same thing, she could not hold it against Mrs Russell and reasoned she would stop once she knew Elizabeth better.

Darcy had told her that he liked Mr Russell a great deal, and Elizabeth's first meeting with them confirmed that she would as well. Mr Russell was not the most talkative of men, but when he did speak, he proved learned and interesting.

"I was at university with Lord Courtenay and his brother, Mrs Darcy," Mr Russell told her. "I once visited Warrington Castle. An enjoyable time, indeed."

"I have been there but little," Elizabeth confessed. "I am fortunate the land steward and the housekeeper are both excellent."

The evening passed enjoyably, and when it had concluded, both Darcy and Elizabeth agreed they would not mind spending more time with the couple. After preparing for bed, Darcy joined Elizabeth in her bedchamber.

Although Elizabeth had never slept in the same bed as Henry, Darcy made it plain from the beginning that he wished to stay with her. She liked having him there even when more amorous activities were not included, though they generally were.

"I must offer my compliments," he said as he slid into bed.

"For what?"

"I am impressed by how well you have overseen the Courtenay estates and fortune."

"Both my uncle and yours have been of great assistance."

"They could not have done everything."

She shrugged slightly. "It is my son's inheritance. I wish to ensure the estate prospers for him and his future."

"Well, perhaps I shall hand over the books of Pemberley to you," he teased, "and see how you do with those."

"I thank you for the compliment," she teased in return, "but I think I have more than enough of that at the present."

He chuckled lightly, settling down into the blankets and drawing her near.

"Warrington Castle has been much on my mind of late," she continued. "I was last there in September, above nine months ago. I had only just returned to Hertfordshire when Mr Bingley took possession of Netherfield. I cannot imagine that I shall be there more often."

"I am always willing to go with you. We should go before our visitors arrive. It is but fifty miles from here, an easy enough distance."

"You think fifty miles an easy distance?"

He smiled teasingly. "It is fifty miles of good road. At this time of year, we would need but two days for travel and some days in between to tend to whatever needs to be done."

Darcy's scheme for a visit to Warrington Castle met with Elizabeth's approval, and they soon found themselves in the carriage once more, headed towards Lancashire.

WARRINGTON CASTLE HAD BEEN IN ITS PLACE OVERLOOKING THE River Mersey in some form or another for nearly seven hundred years. When its services as a fortress were no longer necessary, it had fallen into ruin. But in the early part of the eighteenth century, Henry's ancestor had built a 165-room country house using some of the original features of the castle. It was a striking building—rather Gothic looking but grand nevertheless.

The housekeeper was a woman named Mrs Inwood. She was a cheerful, bustling soul who kept up a running monologue as she efficiently moved them through the reception hall and into their rooms all the while directing orders to the other servants who had gathered and the boys who were bringing the trunks. She was delighted to see the young earl with them; she had not yet made his acquaintance.

They were quickly settled into their bedchamber. Darcy was surprised to see they had been given a guest suite—a lovely, large guest suite, but nevertheless a guest suite.

Elizabeth blushed at his look. "This is where I resided when I came before, and as we stay together, I supposed you would not mind."

"Why did you never use the mistress's bedchamber?"

"Henry had never moved into the master's chambers," she explained. "He was still in the rooms he inhabited as a young man before his father's death. It seemed silly to have rooms opened for me that had been closed for so long. This room was recently redone, and in any case, I am told it is warmer."

Darcy soon learned that far more of the house was closed than was open. After settling in, they went on a tour, with Elizabeth telling him as much as she knew given her limited tenure as Lady Courtenay.

As they strolled down one long, dark hall, Elizabeth remarked, "As any proper castle should, Warrington has its own mystery—a supposed buried treasure."

"Oh?" Darcy smiled. "Shall we find it while we are here?"

Elizabeth laughed. "It is not as easy as that! There is an excessively complicated cipher that leads the way. My father and I spent many long nights trying to break the code, which was something along the lines of the Babington cipher."

"And did you?"

She nodded. "Aye, but alas, when I searched for the fortune, there was nothing to show for it. I fear the whole thing is simply some old wives' tale or else grossly exaggerated. If someone were to bury a great fortune in a castle, they would certainly return for it later."

"You are correct, I am sure," he agreed. "Or possibly someone found it before you. It has been two centuries after all."

Darcy was pleased to see that nothing had been left to decay or disrepair. The open rooms were clean and well appointed. There were many fine works of art, paintings, and sculptures, and as at Pemberley, there was a Great Hall containing portraits of the Courtenay ancestors going back to the fifteen hundreds. Darcy studied Elizabeth as they came to a portrait of Henry and Francis painted shortly before they left for university. While a more recent portrait of the new earl had been spoken of after his ascension to his title, it had never been commissioned.

Elizabeth looked at the portrait, her expression unreadable. At last, she sighed and turned to Darcy, giving him a small smile. Darcy did not know what to say and offered a benign observation. "I was not aware they were identical. I had heard they were twins, of course, but they were each the exact likeness of the other, were they not?"

"When I first met Francis, it was easy to see the differences."

"Oh?"

"Henry was smaller and Francis was more athletic—he boxed, fenced, and rode so he had a larger, more muscular shape. Although he seemed taller, I do not think he actually was. Francis was also vain about his hair and wore it in long curls. Henry's hair was clipped tightly to his head. Their manner of dressing was also quite different. Francis was exceedingly fashionable—almost a coxcomb—but Henry was conservative."

"I see."

"Were you ever acquainted with them?"

"I knew of them, but I believe they were at different schools than I attended."

"Henry and Francis went to Eton and Oxford."

"Ah, well, I did go to Eton, but I attended Cambridge for university so our paths did not cross. Were they older as well?"

"Henry would be three and thirty now," Elizabeth confirmed. "Five years older than you."

"I might have come to know them if not for my father's death. I was seldom in society for several years after university. I was far too occupied with Georgiana and Pemberley."

She offered him an abstracted smile, clearly lost in thought as she turned her attention back to the portrait. When she wandered away minutes later, he quietly followed. They left the hall soon after, going into the nearest gardens, which were rather spare but well tended.

By the time dinner was called, Elizabeth had recovered her usual spirits and said no more of the portraits or Henry. Darcy wished to know what she was thinking, but she did not say, and he did not think he should ask.

FOR ELIZABETH, THE TIME SPENT AT WARRINGTON WAS ODD. SHE could not name the sensation, but her lack of ease at Warrington was striking, especially following the effortless comfort of Pemberley. After Henry's death, she had spent hours labouring over the care of Warrington, involving herself in everything she could, shirking no duty when she easily could have done so. She had managed the books, concerned herself with servants' cares, and reviewed planting plans. Yet, she felt no connexion to the place. It was simply her son's legacy but nothing to her heart or soul.

In contrast, from the first time she looked at Pemberley, she felt she was home. She knew scarcely anything of it—she had gotten hopelessly lost on her way to the pinery just the day before their departure —nevertheless, she felt a comfort and a sense of belonging. The position of mistress of Pemberley was her own in a manner that mistress of Warrington had never been.

They remained just a couple of days after that, seeing all was in order as Elizabeth had expected it to be. As the carriage left the castle grounds, Elizabeth looked out the window thinking of her prior visit. That had been a painful reminder of what would never be and led to a worsening of her loneliness and her anxiety. She vividly recalled how it had then felt to stand beneath the portrait of her husband and his killer. She had visited daily, sometimes a few times a day, weeping tears of sorrow and anger mixed with sobs of longing and despair.

This time was different. When she looked at his image, she felt regret and sorrow but without the sense of futility and hopelessness that had marked her before. *I am moving on. I am ready to enjoy another life, one that is not dominated by this tragedy.*

She looked over at her husband and son. Having been awoken and pulled from his bed far earlier than he wished, Henry had cried and fussed a bit. Neither Elizabeth nor Nurse Jenny could console him, but Darcy, it would seem, had his measure. Now Henry was asleep on his back using Darcy's lap as a pillow, one hand curled into Darcy's waistcoat and the other flung into space.

Darcy too had drifted off, his handsome face softened and made younger by the early morning light. He had been busy viewing the estate with her and riding out for hours with the steward to ensure things were in order, and he was no doubt exhausted. *You, Elizabeth Darcy, are the most fortunate of women.* A sweet warmth stole into her chest as she gazed upon her little family.

They were passing through the village, and Elizabeth turned to the window to watch the people beginning their day with industry.

I am happy, truly happy. No guilt, no regret—only joy.

She was sorry that Henry had died, but she did not regret the opportunity to become Darcy's wife. *I cannot feel guilt or shame in this. The old life is gone, and the new life is begun. I would not wish otherwise than to be mistress of Pemberley and wife of Fitzwilliam Darcy.*

EIGHTEEN

Shortly after the Darcys returned to Pemberley from Warrington, they were joined by Jane and Bingley. Since her sister's marriage, Elizabeth had seen little of her, and she longed for a time of girlish laughter and conversation. Likewise, Darcy was eager to spend time with his friend in gentlemanly pursuits and discussions. Jane and Bingley also brought Georgiana and her companion with them. She had been residing with Lord and Lady Matlock to give the Darcys and their son time to settle into their own domestic circle.

Several days after their arrival, the Bingleys departed on a day trip, the purpose of which was held secret. Darcy left on a matter of business in a nearby town while Georgiana and Mrs Younge were devoted to some studies. Elizabeth and Mrs Reynolds met shortly after Darcy's departure, and by the middle of the morning, the household had its orders, and Elizabeth was left to her own devices. She immediately went to her chambers, seeking a small trunk that had been retrieved from Warrington.

Elizabeth found Henry's journals, which she had learned about from his old school friends. Although a poor scribe, Henry was a prolific writer, and his journals numbered seventeen in all. She supposed he must have begun them at an early age, and she found that the first began with his entry into school when he was only eight years old.

She did not intend to read them thoroughly; instead, she thought they might be a nice surprise for her son when he was older and wished to know something of his father. However, as she perused them, she found herself drawn to the man—the boy rather—she had not known.

Henry had been as disorganised in boyhood as he was as a man, with loose pages stuffed into the journals every which way. Some had markings on them that looked like ancient Greek, and Elizabeth thought it might be some schoolwork forever lost from his language master.

She giggled reading stories of the various escapades on which he and Francis had embarked, such as the time at age twelve when they decided to each sit for half of their examinations. Henry excelled in mathematics, science, navigation, and geography, while Francis chose to take the examinations in history, literature, and classical languages.

Elizabeth was fascinated by an account of a woman who was hired by several of the boys of the upper form, including Henry and Francis, to rid them of the odious burden of virginity in one grand night of fornication when they were sixteen. She found herself morbidly curious, poring over the disappointingly scanty details and questioning what desperate straits would lead a woman to undertake such a thing. She wondered for a moment whether she were jealous or distressed by such things but then realised it would be absurd to feel so. The liaison of a deceased schoolboy that occurred more than a decade prior to their meeting could have no bearing on her whatsoever. In any case, it was possible Darcy had done something similar. She briefly entertained the idea of asking him but decided against it. Certain things are better left unknown.

Moving into the university years, Henry became more like the man she had known. He was no scholar, but he did enjoy the social aspects of university life to the fullest extent.

Elizabeth was still reading when she heard a quiet knock on the door. Looking up, she was surprised to see her husband leaning on the door frame.

"Fitzwilliam!" She quickly replaced the journals in the box and went to greet him. "I lost track of time, and there was no word of your return!"

He smiled, looking very handsome albeit with an odd lump under his coat. "I concluded my business a bit more rapidly than expected though with much success."

Elizabeth's attention was drawn to the lump that was writhing and squirming. "I am glad to hear it." She rose up on her toes to kiss him and then returned her notice to his coat. "What is that?"

"What?" he teased in an innocent tone.

"Either there is a misshapen portion of your abdomen moving around or you have something under your coat."

"You caught me." Reaching under his coat, he pulled out a small puppy—a precious little creature with a white coat and tan spots.

Elizabeth was immediately enchanted by the little pup, which was small enough to be nearly encased in Darcy's large hands. "Oh!" She reached for it, and the puppy went to her eagerly, wriggling and frantically attempting to nip and lick her fingers. "Welcome home, my little sweet! Oh, she is dear! Wherever did you find her?"

"Mr Russell has a cousin near Quorn in Staffordshire who breeds these excellent little foxhounds. Astonishingly quick little creatures and intelligent too. The man had business in Derby and brought her along so I could see her."

"Why did he wish to part with her?" Elizabeth laughed as the dog took hold of her sleeve with its teeth, fighting the lace at Elizabeth's wrists with great vigour and a comical, babyish growl.

"She did not seem a promising hunter," Darcy explained. "Mr Meynell is exceedingly particular in which dogs he keeps for his own pack, and Annie did not suit him."

Elizabeth sank into a seated position on the floor, and Darcy joined her. Annie pawed at her skirts, rolling and tumbling in her lap, and Elizabeth laughed at the pup's antics.

"Will you hunt with her?"

"I am not in need of another hunting dog, but with her sweet disposition and playful manner, Annie was thought ideal for a pet."

"I have never kept a dog as a pet; however, I have always wished for it!" Elizabeth exclaimed happily. She lifted the dog to her face, giggling again as it licked her nose.

"Alas, my love, this gift is not for you. I thought she would be a good companion for Henry."

"For Henry!" Elizabeth ceased laughing immediately, her heart growing soft at the thought of Darcy seeking a playmate for her son.

"So much has changed in the little lad's life," Darcy explained. "Leaving the Gardiner's home, our marriage, coming to Pemberley. How well he has borne it all! I only wished to do something for him, to make this a happy time." He paused a moment, then added hesitantly, "Something a father might do for his son."

Elizabeth's throat tightened and tears blurred her eyes. She reached for her husband, laying a hand on his shoulder. "How perfect," she said softly.

In her lap, the puppy, exhausted by her exertions, curled into a little ball and dozed. "Henry will be delighted. He always points at the dogs in the park or in the fields." She kissed her husband. "You are a wonderful husband and an excellent father."

"I have done very little for that praise," he murmured, his face close to hers. "Though I am proud to claim any right to either."

"Being thoughtful and loving is the best part of it," she whispered in reply. "And in that, you have proven expert."

Darcy captured her lips in a brief kiss. "Have you any notion how much I adore you?"

She pulled back just enough to look at his face. Her heart pounded with feeling, and she felt as if she might either laugh or cry with the painful sweetness of her regard for him. *Regard! This cannot be mere regard. I am falling...I love him!*

"What I do have is a notion of my good fortune to be married to you." Her voice was soft but, she hoped, filled with meaning. "How could I have refused you! It frightens me to think I might have missed such felicity."

"Let us not think of that. I can no longer imagine my life without you." He kissed her again gently. "Come, let us go find our son."

They went to the nursery to find that Henry had been late for his nap and was still asleep. They returned to the sitting room, put a sleepy Annie into her crate, and waited for what seemed an eternity. Jane and Bingley came back just as Nurse Jenny entered the room to announce that Henry was awake and ready for a visit.

Bingley looked over at the crate with curiosity. "What is that, Darcy?"

"A little gift for my son," Darcy told him as Elizabeth lifted up the little pup. As the two couples entered the nursery, Annie rapidly became alert, her ears pricked and her eyes bright with anticipation. Before entering the room, Elizabeth hid the dog in her shawl.

Henry was excited by the appearance of his parents and his aunt and uncle. Darcy knelt beside him at a small table where a snack had been laid.

"Henry, I have something special for you. Close your eyes and stretch out your arms just so," Darcy arranged the boy in a suitable position and took the puppy from its hiding place in Elizabeth's shawl.

The boy was obedient, tightly screwing his eyes shut and not moving his arms from where Darcy had placed them. Elizabeth bit her lips to keep from giggling like a child as Darcy carefully placed Annie in Henry's arms, leaving one hand beneath the puppy to ensure Henry did not accidentally drop it in surprise.

"There you go, my boy. Open your eyes now."

Tentatively, Henry opened one eye; then both eyes flew wide as a shriek of delight escaped his lips. He almost crushed the dog to his chest, screaming and laughing as the puppy was overcome with happiness and began to wriggle and play, mouthing the hem of Henry's garment and running about the nursery madly.

Georgiana was drawn to the sounds of commotion and gaiety from down the hall. She entered in time to witness the puppy with her funny puppy growl attack Darcy's boot as everyone laughed.

What followed was a happy thirty minutes. Henry was thrilled with his new pet. Bingley was enthralled almost as much, promising Jane that he would ride to Staffordshire and obtain such an animal for their household.

DURING THE FIRST WEEK OF JANE AND BINGLEY'S VISIT, THE PARTY made a picnic in a lovely, shady spot. Darcy and Bingley took Henry to play with a ball, intending to teach him the rudiments of cricket. Elizabeth and Jane sat and gossiped on the bank nearby, and Georgiana watched the puppy as Annie rolled around the grass with a stick, chased butterflies, and barked at clouds moving in the sky.

The men were far enough away that Jane felt comfortable in sharing confidences with her sister.

"Nothing is certain yet, Lizzy, but I think it probable that I am with child."

"Already! How marvellous!"

"Well, as much as has been…attempted, I should worry if there were not at least some signs of success." Jane blushed at her own daring intimations.

Elizabeth's mouth dropped a bit in surprise. "Oh! So Mr Bingley is ardent then."

Jane giggled. "You might have noticed, dear sister, that my husband is a man of much enthusiasm, and in this, there is no exception."

Elizabeth laughed. "Jane! You naughty girl! Soon you and I shall sound just like Mama and Aunt Philips."

"Oh, please do not mention Mama. I cannot stand to imagine her and our father in such activity."

"With five daughters born within seven years, Papa must have had a great deal of enthusiasm at one time."

Both ladies dissolved into giggles even as Jane chastised, "Oh, Lizzy, how can you even say such a thing!"

"'Tis nothing but the truth!"

When they had settled, Jane asked, "Has it been strange to have a second husband?"

"Darcy is wonderful to me—a wonderful, perfect husband in all ways, including that one. In fact"—Elizabeth cast her husband a sly glance, ensuring he was well occupied—"he has taught me that I knew much less about marital intimacy than I had supposed."

"Really?"

"Oh, I had no complaints with Henry, but evidently, I had no idea what I was missing." She laughed, feeling a blush heat her cheeks.

It was now Jane who cast a sly look at Darcy. "Who would have thought the haughty man we saw in Meryton had such hidden reserves of passion?"

Elizabeth watched her husband, Bingley, and Henry playing their little game, oblivious to the discussion of the ladies. "He is a good man, and he owns my heart in a way I had not believed possible."

Jane gave her sister a fond smile. "Your heart was made to love. It could not remain so hard."

"My heart was indeed made to love," Elizabeth agreed. "There will always be a part of me that loves Henry, but it is different with Darcy."

"How so?"

For a moment there was nothing but the sound of the men playing, shouting encouragement to one another.

She continued, beginning to understand it even as she told her sister, "Henry was a first love. It was romantic and exciting and wonderful. I thought he was entirely perfect, and he thought the same of me, and neither of us had any cause to challenge that notion. We were swept away in each other, doused in the excitement of betrothal and marriage and travel to the Continent. It was wonderful although unreal."

"Are you saying it was not true?" Jane looked worried.

"No, no," Elizabeth assured her. "I do not mean to undervalue it. It was true, and it was a delight in all ways, but it was the blush of first love, and I was so very young. Henry and I had not the opportunity to grow a deeper love together."

She looked again to where her husband capered about with her son. "It is different with Darcy. We have fought passionately. He has seen what is bad in me, and I know what is lacking in him, and somehow it has made our attachment to one another stronger.

"I used to think myself so sure." Elizabeth laughed lightly. "So right, so quick witted. I thought that my cleverness in disliking him was a sure tribute to my own intelligence and discernment. Now, I realise that I am as disposed to vanity as anyone. I was determined to hate him forever when he slighted me at the assembly, but I cannot imagine how much I might have missed had I not permitted myself to truly know him.

"He has chosen to love me, knowing full well that another man is in my heart. It must hurt him—I know it hurts him—yet he loves me still. He is an ideal husband and father, and he truly wants what is best for me, even to his own detriment." She shook her head, eyes trained on the blanket beneath them. "I do not deserve him."

Jane reached over and squeezed her hand.

"I used to think if I admitted I loved him it would mean I was glad Henry was dead, but Henry is dead regardless. I shall always cherish my memories of Henry, even as I love Darcy. Does that make any sense?"

"Perfect sense," Jane said with a kind smile. "You must count yourself fortunate to have called two such extraordinary men your husband."

Elizabeth nodded with a smile, even as tears came to her eyes.

"Does he know you love him?"

Elizabeth shook her head, and Jane advised, "Tell him as soon as you can. If nothing else, the loss of Henry must have taught you that much. Do not waste a day without telling your loved ones what they mean to you."

"I HAVE MARVELLOUS NEWS TO SHARE WITH YOU BOTH," BINGLEY announced that night at dinner, a blushing Jane by his side.

Is this it? Is the possibility of a child certain? Elizabeth smiled in eager anticipation, giving Darcy a quick glance.

"There is an estate for sale not fifteen miles from here. The price, the income from it, and the size all suit us well, so unless serious problems present themselves, in December it will be ours!" Bingley beamed, rocking on his heels.

"You are not retaining Netherfield?" Darcy was surprised that Bingley's thoughts tended in such a direction.

"Netherfield has been good to us," Jane replied demurely, "and a part of me will always feel that Hertfordshire is my home. However, my dear husband and I have come to realise that it is possible for a lady to be settled too near her family."

"Jane!" Elizabeth exclaimed. "How boldly you speak!"

"I apologise, Lizzy, but you cannot imagine—"

"No, no!" Elizabeth laughed. "I do not censure you. Indeed, I am quite happy with you, only shocked that you have gained the ability to speak as you find. I would certainly not wish to settle three miles from Mama."

"Tell me the particulars, Bingley," Darcy requested, and Bingley recounted as much detail as he could on this marvel of land ownership. His excitement was clear, and Elizabeth and Darcy were exceedingly pleased on behalf of the Bingleys and for their own reasons.

They spoke of it that night as they lay together in bed.

"The place was formerly in the family of a friend of my father's. There was no heir, and the report was that some of the family went to America: to New York."

Elizabeth absently drew her fingers across Darcy's chest. "Is it a good situation for them?"

"I believe it will prove to be perfect. Before Bingley leased Netherfield, I had considered it, but it was not yet for purchase, and I did not think Bingley would settle so far from town."

"But now you do?

"He is a happily married man now. He looks at things differently than he did as a young buck going back and forth between friends and amusements and with a demanding sister to satisfy as well. In fact, the greatest attraction for this place might be Miss Bingley's disinclination to stay there. So many miles to go for the shops and balls will not satisfy her."

"An excellent point, and one I am sure Jane appreciates as well." Elizabeth laughed.

She shifted closer to him. "I believed they would announce a child when he stood."

"The thought occurred to me too." Darcy moved closer to her. "Soon, I am sure."

Elizabeth kissed him lightly and continued her task of caressing his chest with her fingers. "And what about us? Do you hope we shall have such an announcement soon?"

"I value this time we have now—time to enjoy each other and Henry—but yes, I shall be well pleased when it occurs."

"As shall I."

"You are eager for another child?"

"I am eager for *your* child."

It was a statement fraught with meaning, and he knew it. His face grew soft, and a slight smile appeared. "I wonder whether you realise what it means to me when you speak so."

"I do not say it to appease you. I mean it with all my heart. I am eager to have your child, and I am so very happy we are married."

"I am as well." He kissed her lightly on her forehead.

He turned onto his side and drew her close, preparing for slumber. She settled into what had become her usual position, her head resting partly on his chest. He kissed the top of her hair and murmured sleepily, "I love you."

Moments later, he was asleep. She lay there, her eyes wide open, watching the rise and fall of his chest until she had gained sufficient courage to tell him in the smallest, quietest hint of a whisper, "I love you too."

JANE AND BINGLEY SPENT MANY DAYS AT WHAT WOULD SOON BE THEIR estate, and on one such day, Darcy and Elizabeth took advantage of the fine weather to take a long ride out to one of the farther vistas overlooking some of the rocky crags that defined Derbyshire.

They were rather indolent, resting next to a charming little stream that bubbled obligingly. The air was a nearly perfect temperature, the sky was brightly blue, and the sun warmed them into a state of superb laziness. Darcy lay on his side, reading to her from a book of poetry, but she scarcely heard him as she was lost in thought.

She was disappointed in herself. Since her confession to his sleeping form, she had not yet acquired sufficient courage to admit the truth to his conscious person. She wanted to badly, and she often woke in the morning telling herself she would do it that day. Various things would happen to prevent her: a servant or sister would enter the room, Henry would require their attention, dinner would be called, or Darcy would fall asleep. There was always some excuse though she suspected that the true culprit was fear. It seemed silly to lack the courage to tell a man she loved him, particularly as that man was so free in his expression of love for her.

Earlier that day, she went to look at Darcy's portrait. Unlike Henry's, Darcy's was completed after he became of age, and although young, one could already see in his bearing the man he would become: honourable and dutiful with a capacity for deep attachment and love. Her heart had pounded as she looked at it, thinking, *this is the man who loves me, who chose me and pledged himself to me.* It astonished her and gave her a queer sense of unworthiness. Something in her could not apprehend how she had inspired ardent emotion in such a man.

The same queer sense stole over her now as she watched him read aloud. He paused, glancing up to catch her gaze with just the barest lift of the side of his mouth. "You are miles away."

"You are making me fall in love with you," she said quietly, running her fingers across the side of his face.

He made a little joke of it. "Truly? This is an extraordinary book then."

She smiled and shook her head slightly. "No, it is not the book."

He grew serious. "You need not dissemble, Elizabeth. I am happy; I am content with what I have."

"I mean it with all my heart." His face did not change, but she saw the warmth of true joy come into his eyes. She stretched out alongside him, propped on one elbow as he was. "Promise me you will not die. I could not bear to lose you."

"You have my word," he whispered, deeply moved. He pulled her close, kissing her cheek tenderly. "Do you have any notion of how very much I love you?"

"Yes, I have known for some time," she whispered back. "But I am ashamed it has taken me so long to tell you that I love you." She then kissed him deeply, pouring her heart and soul into showing him the depth of her feeling.

They kissed and caressed until it could be withstood no more, and they beat a hasty retreat back to the house.

They arrived in their chambers breathless, warm, and eager to resume their activities. They enjoyed removing one another's clothing, kissing and caressing as they went, and then Darcy, as was his custom, insisted on freeing her hair.

When her tresses had fallen about her, he lifted her, taking her to the bed and laying her down gently on the mattress. He took his place next to her and leaned to kiss her, but she stopped him. Looking into his eyes, she said, "I love you, Fitzwilliam. I do, truly I do. I love you."

He kissed her tenderly, promising, "I shall love you forever."

She whispered, "I am glad, so very glad, to have the opportunity to love you. I realised at Warrington Castle that, for the first time, I did not wish to go back. Although I still feel some guilt for it, I know it is this life and this love I was meant for. I love you with my whole heart."

Darcy said nothing in response to her declaration, but his eyes did not leave hers. They were lost in a gaze for several moments until he pulled her down against his chest. She cuddled into him, feeling the powerful beat of his heart against her and wished the moment would last for an eternity.

As September reached its end, the Darcys made arrangements to travel to London. Viscount Saye had proposed to Miss Redgrave in May, and their wedding date was set for early October.

Darcy asked Elizabeth whether she wished to remain in town for some weeks to visit the theatre and shops. She agreed, planning to see her family as well. They would return to Pemberley at the beginning of December, the same time Jane and Bingley would take possession of their new home.

Georgiana considered remaining at Pemberley with Mrs Younge, but in the end, decided to go to town with her brother and sister. "After all," she told her companion, "it might be nice to see a play or two and do a bit of shopping."

Mrs Younge smiled knowingly. "And perhaps see an old friend?"

She frowned. Witnessing the good manners and behaviour of Elizabeth and her sister had made Georgiana wish to be more like them. It could not be denied that both Mr Bingley and her brother were utterly enraptured by their wives. She hoped that someday she too would have a man who would hold her in such esteem, and she knew that such sentiment could not be easily won.

She also realised George Wickham was not that man. Certainly, George was charming and handsome, but to have any sort of relationship with him would mean to cast off her family and friends. She did not want that—not for George Wickham, not for any man.

"Mr Wickham is an amiable gentleman, but I...my brother and sister would not approve if they knew. I should, perhaps, tell them, but it might be better to simply end the acquaintance."

Mrs Younge did not reply for a moment, her attention ostensibly on the table in front of her where she organised Georgiana's lessons.

"I want them to trust me," Georgiana added. "If I make them unhappy, they will be angry and disappointed, and I shall be a child again, alone in my room while they enjoy themselves. I do not want that."

She closed the case she had been packing, which contained her books for the carriage ride. With resolve, she said, "If George Wickham should call again, pray tell him he should not come around."

"That seems a bit unfair, my dear." Mrs Younge looked up from her papers, her lips pursed into a prim frown. "Do you not think you should see him and explain your wishes? It seems rather unkind to cut the connexion with no explanation whatsoever."

Georgiana thought about it. "Very well. If he calls again, I shall see him just once more."

The trip to London was uneventful, and on the first day of their return, Mrs Younge hurried towards a much-needed meeting.

The tavern was in the worst section of town but Mrs Younge scarcely noticed. She hurried through the crowded, dirty streets with nary a look about her, her thoughts and fears on only one subject. She found Wickham where he usually was: at a game table in the back of the public house with a loser's scowl on his face and a publican at his shoulder holding an unpaid bill in his hand.

She gave the publican enough coins to satisfy him and then leaned in to George. "We must talk—now." Wickham immediately made his excuses to his fellow gamblers and followed her out of the tavern and into a deserted alley where they could speak freely.

"I thought you were in Derbyshire."

"Mr Darcy needed to return to town for a short time, and this is your chance. Do not waste it."

"I shall call on her tomorrow." Wickham was casual—too casual and too confident—leaning back against a wall with great ease.

"She intends to turn you away." Mrs Younge began to pace. "You are running out of time, and I begin to doubt your commitment to this plan."

"Doubt my commitment?" Wickham laughed mirthlessly. "Need I remind you which of us has a death warrant over his head?"

"Then enough of your stupid plan of seduction," Mrs Younge spat. "Finish it, now, before she stops seeing you—and then where shall we be?"

"Darcy is always around these days," Wickham complained. "It is difficult to sneak in when he and that wife of his are about."

"Mrs Darcy has devoted herself to her new sister and encourages her husband to do likewise. If the servants are to be believed, he dotes on Miss Darcy more than ever."

"I need to know when they will be out: an evening engagement, preferably one with late hours. I shall visit her and—"

"And what? Flirt some more? You have accomplished nothing with that."

Wickham flushed. "I had hoped she would think herself in love."

"Listen to me," Mrs Younge hissed. "I shall get you in and then you will do whatever is necessary. Take what you need to make this marriage an undeniable thing. Mr Darcy will only grant you her hand if he believes he must."

"Give me the date, and it will be done."

NINTEEN

LONDON, AUTUMN 1812

The wedding day of Viscount Saye was much as expected: the bride was pretty and seemed nervous, Saye was affectedly apathetic, and the parents all appeared pleased. The breakfast was well attended by all of the most prominent people, and soon enough, Lord and Lady Saye were off to spend a month in Brighton to enjoy the seaside and each other.

Georgiana had behaved poorly at her cousin's wedding breakfast. Lady Matlock saw it and later spoke to Elizabeth about it. The result had been many long hours of discussion on the proper behaviour for a young lady. Although Georgiana had at first chafed at the restrictions imposed upon her, she soon realised they were for the best.

Several mornings later, as she strolled in the park with Mrs Younge, they happened to come across Mr Wickham looking exceedingly handsome in a blue coat and a new hat.

"Ladies, may I join you?" He smiled as Georgiana looked quickly to Mrs Younge who nodded.

"Of course, Mr Wickham. I am pleased to have your company." He offered his arm, and they began to stroll. Despite the sedate nature of their pace, Mrs Younge walked slower and soon dropped well behind.

"I believed you were lost to me." Wickham's voice was a low murmur, thrilling and seductive. Despite her intentions, Georgiana warmed to it.

"We were in Derbyshire. Not lost at all." She smiled up at him with just a hint of a flirtation.

"Ah, Pemberley." There was evident wistfulness in his tone. "How I long to see it again! I think particularly of a certain spot where your brother and I used to ride. A rather high rise that overlooked nearly all of the land, including that one very rocky area—"

"I know just where you mean," Georgiana replied with eager fondness. "It is a lovely prospect."

They strolled in silence for a few minutes until Wickham said, "I hoped I might call on you soon."

"Oh? Why is that?" She gave him a sidelong glance.

He appeared bashful. "Georgiana, I do not deny that what I feel for you is not entirely proper, and yet—"

"Mr Wickham"—Georgiana was stern, pronouncing his name with precision—"I should not see you. I am not yet out, and it is not proper for me to form any attachment to a gentleman."

"When I am with you…I feel so…so…I can hardly express it. I only know it is nothing I have ever felt before." He looked at her beseechingly.

Various emotions warred within Georgiana as she looked upon Mr Wickham's handsome face. He was so clearly enraptured by her. It was a heady sensation to see this man so desperate for her.

But it was not right. It could not be.

"I am sorry, Mr Wickham, but I must insist that you do not call on me again." She drew a deep breath, relieved to have come to a decision.

Mr Wickham swallowed and then removed a letter from his pocket. "Will you do me the honour, then, of reading this?" She accepted it, and her would-be suitor bowed, turned on his heel, and departed. Mrs Younge was beside her in a trice.

"What is that, Miss Darcy?"

"I should not have accepted it, I know." Georgiana stared after his retreating form, looking so dignified and handsome. "I could not turn him away."

"He cares for you deeply." Mrs Younge spoke with great gravity. "It marks his every feature. Even his bearing is changed when he is with you."

Georgiana did not reply, but her soul thrilled. To imagine having such power was intoxicating—the first bloom of her feminine wiles at play. She looked down the path, seeing his figure growing ever more distant, and then looked again at the letter in her hand.

"If you need his direction," said Mrs Younge, helpfully, "I have it."

"I BELIEVE I HAVE A HEADACHE." DARCY STOOD IN THE DOORWAY OF his wife's bedchamber, looking at her. She had just bathed and was in front of the fire, combing through her wet hair in hopes that it would dry sufficiently for her maid to dress it.

"Come here." She smiled, and he went obligingly, sitting in front of her and leaning back as she rubbed his temples and ran her fingers through his hair. She murmured in his ear, "Do you want to know what I think is the cause of your headache?"

"What?"

"I believe you do not wish to go tonight and will take any thought of pain to give us cause to remain at home."

He laughed. "How well you know me! But no, I did not invent this ache. It is real, I assure you. I believe the lamp in my study was smoking."

"Undoubtedly, it was though I do suspect you are not fond of the Ellises," Elizabeth replied, naming their hosts for the evening.

"There are few people I know whose society I would prefer to an evening spent alone with my beautiful wife." He tilted his face back to her.

She kissed the top of his head. "Shall we plan to return early then?"

Darcy closed his eyes for a moment. He knew that to stay home was unlikely, but he wished for it nevertheless. To leave early would have to suffice. "Yes, love, we shall come home early."

IT WAS A SMALL PARTY—ONLY EIGHT COUPLES—AND DARCY FOUND most of them tedious. However, Elizabeth was fond of several of the wives and had accepted the invitation. He did enjoy seeing her take pleasure in the evening. She laughed, smiled, and enchanted the room, and he thought, not for the first time, how privileged he was to have her as his wife. For a moment, he closed his eyes and relived the day she first said she loved him. She said it to him often now, and he to her, yet nothing could dim the glow of that first time.

When dinner had ended, the gentlemen had their requisite time of cigar smoking and port drinking before joining their ladies in the drawing room where a small musical party had been planned. It was pleasant, but Darcy found himself itching to be home. Later, he would wonder whether some sense of foreboding had heightened his anxiety that night.

The Darcys were not the first to depart but left soon thereafter. It was a short ride, and they were anticipating nothing more than to retire and be together.

When they entered the house, the first thing seen was a toppled chair in the middle of the hall. Overhead, a great many footsteps were heard moving quickly, and in the distance, a man was shouting. Elizabeth turned to Darcy. "What is the meaning—?"

Mrs Hobbs interrupted, her voice revealing her fright, "Jervis has stopped an intruder in the house, madam. A thief!"

Elizabeth took the older woman by the hand and proceeded to the servant's wing to comfort and reassure the help. Darcy was off like a shot after learning from his butler that Jervis and the intruder were in the library, and his sister and son were both well and in their respective bedchambers.

He was at the library in a trice, tearing open the door. As soon as he entered, he came to an immediate and abrupt halt, stunned to see Jervis and Samuel, another of Elizabeth's footmen, standing over none other than George Wickham.

Darcy would be forever grateful to Jervis for protecting Georgiana's reputation as he learned that George Wickham had been found attempting to seduce his sister in her sitting room. Thus, he was not a true intruder but an invited guest—though it was not a distinction that would ever matter.

The quick-thinking Jervis had brought Wickham down to the library and made the scene appear as though an attempted robbery had occurred. He pulled books down from the shelves and tossed things about as Wickham watched helplessly from the chair in which Jervis had bound and gagged him.

Moments after Darcy entered his study, Colonel Fitzwilliam arrived, clapping both Jervis and Samuel on their shoulders. "Well done, men! This will mean a nice promotion for you both."

He roughly jerked the gag from Wickham's mouth then sat on a chair across from where he was bound, silent and sullen, and did nothing more than regard him for a moment. "Wickham, I must say, you proved far more cunning than I ever believed possible."

Wickham said nothing, turning his face away from the colonel's merciless stare.

Fitzwilliam continued, "You led us on a merry chase, but your next dance will be the Newgate hornpipe."

Wickham jerked his eyes to Fitzwilliam, and for the first time, Darcy saw a flash of fear run through his eyes. He could almost pity him. There was no doubt that George went into this with no more than the chance of quick, easy money on his mind. He surely never imagined it would end with being hanged for treason for the gain of a mere twenty-five pounds.

The door opened once again, and the butler ushered in the constable and a man called Harris who had led the investigation. Harris was a large, beefy man in his forties who walked, talked, and breathed loudly. "There he is!" Harris exclaimed as if Wickham were some long lost relation he was delighted to see. "Thought we had lost you for sure! Well, off we go now. We have the finest accommodation arranged for you."

Wickham, seeing his fate at hand, began to speak. "See here, it was not I who did this; there was another. I just—"

"Save your breath, fellow. You will need it for the gallows," Harris remarked then laughed uproariously. Darcy found it rather cold-hearted, but he supposed in such an occupation that a morbid sense of humour might develop.

"Wait! He did not die!" Wickham exclaimed in desperation. "I swear to it! His lordship might yet live!"

Harris gave Jervis a quick nod, and Jervis pulled Wickham to a standing position. "That's enough. Time to move along."

Wickham became frantic and struggled against Jervis's hold. "No, no you must hear me. It...things did not go as planned...there might be..."

"Samuel, his other arm if you please." Samuel was quick to assist, seeming to take pleasure from wrenching Wickham's arm tightly behind his back.

"I speak the truth!" Wickham was in a full panic, sweat rolling from his brow as he stupidly and ineffectively fought against the restraint of the two soldiers. "You must not do this! I am the only one who knows where Lord Courtenay is at present. He is yet alive!"

With a violent jerk, Samuel and Jervis forced Wickham to move towards the door, which at that moment, opened to reveal Elizabeth standing there and looking shocked. Lord Matlock was by her side, having evidently been in the process of dissuading her from entering.

Samuel and Jervis came to an immediate halt with their hapless prisoner stuck between them, his toes just barely touching the ground. Darcy went to his wife immediately, but she did not remove her eyes from Wickham.

Her voice was small and quiet. "What did you say?"

Wickham apparently found a glimmer of hope. "I did not kill him! He was alive when I left him, and when I returned, there was only one body where there had been two."

The room erupted in commotion. Fitzwilliam, Harris, and Lord Matlock were all speaking, telling Wickham to be silent and Elizabeth to discount his nonsense. For Darcy, a cold finger of dread traced his spine even as an inner voice whispered, *I knew it. I knew such felicity could not last.*

Elizabeth's eyes never left Wickham's countenance. She spoke in a voice that was calm and exquisitely controlled. "Put him back in the chair. I shall hear him."

Lord Matlock tried to intervene. "Elizabeth, my dear, this man is a criminal, we cannot—"

Elizabeth gave Lord Matlock a brief glance, her eyes nearly shooting fire. "Since the day this all began, I have done everything I was told to do, and I have caused no problem to anyone. Now I demand my compensation for that obedience in the form of hearing the tale of my husband's killer."

Abashed, Lord Matlock fell silent as did the others in the room.

"Sit him down," Elizabeth ordered sharply.

Samuel and Jervis were not gentle, shoving Wickham back into a chair like a foot shoved into a boot that was too small. Through his restraints, Wickham did his best to become comfortable, shifting himself awkwardly about.

"Speak, Mr Wickham."

"He was not dead when I left."

Elizabeth advanced on him until her feet nearly touched Wickham's shoes. There was an air of fragile determination to her. She looked so very small, yet Darcy knew rage was rising within her.

"The details, Mr Wickham. Where you stood, where he stood, how close you were when you shot him, the way he looked when he fell, and why you believe he might not have died. Tell me this instant, and spare me nothing." Her voice was frightening in its quiet ferocity, and even Darcy dared not attempt to dissuade her.

"Ah, well…" Wickham swallowed nervously, looking at Harris who glanced away refusing to either support or deny him. Realising there was nothing left to lose, Wickham began to speak.

"We had determined a likely place ahead of time—"

"Who is 'we'?"

"Mr Francis Warren and I."

There was a brief pause. "Go on."

A bead of sweat rolled down Wickham's face, and he moved again, tugging at the restraints on his arms. "There was a copse of trees to conceal me, and I dug a ditch, hidden within the road's heavy ruts, to cause the carriage wheel to break. It did as we expected, and the coachman and outriders alighted to see to it. The coachman, along with one of the outriders, went off directly for assistance. The other man remained behind—as guard, I suppose."

"Where was Mr Francis Warren at this time?"

"After supplying me with a double-barreled pistol, he met his brother's party in Crewe, and they travelled together from there. When the accident happened, he remained in the carriage as planned with his brother and his lordship's valet." Wickham paused, waiting to see whether more questions would be posed. When there were none, he continued to speak. "I shot the outrider first. I was within close range, and there was no doubt he died quickly. The three men then came out of the carriage with their own pistols drawn. Sir Francis dealt with the valet, and Lord Courtenay was my…my job."

"How did you do it?"

Wickham looked uncertain, surely unnerved by the manner in which Elizabeth's eyes bored into him.

Harris spoke quickly, "Madam, these sorts of things can be distressing for a lady. We would not wish—"

Elizabeth acted as if she had not heard him. "Where exactly did you shoot him? In the head? The chest? How many shots did you fire, and how many met their mark?"

"One." Wickham licked his lips. "I had but one shot left after the outrider. I fired at his chest. He fell and…there was a great deal of blood."

"Was he conscious?"

Wickham did not answer her, his eyes lowered to his boots.

"Mr Wickham?" Through sheer force of will, Elizabeth compelled Wickham to meet her eyes. "Was he conscious?"

Wickham was visibly struggling within himself. Softly, he admitted, "He was."

"Did he say anything?"

Wickham was silent, locked into Elizabeth's frightening, hard gaze.

"What did he say?"

"He begged me to help him—otherwise, to finish what I had begun."

Darcy could scarcely breathe as he fixed on Elizabeth's eyes. He had never seen them so cold and inscrutable. Nor had he seen her as dispassionate as she was at this moment. There was a tension in the air, like the gathering of a storm before the first crack of thunder. All those gathered in the room seemed to feel it as they waited with bated breath to see what would transpire.

Her voice quiet and steady, Elizabeth asked, "What did you do after that?"

Wickham's breath came faster and harder.

Elizabeth leaned over him. "What did you do after that?"

Wickham's eyes remained locked on hers. His voice small, he admitted, "I left."

She darted forward, her fist connecting firmly with George Wickham's face. She split his lip and broke his nose with a crunch that was audible to the room, and he was covered in blood almost instantly. Elizabeth shouted, "Coward! How could you leave him there to suffer!" She slapped him hard, imprinting her hand upon his cheek and causing his head to jerk violently to the side. Then she burst into tears and ran from the room with Darcy hard on her heels.

ELIZABETH CRIED UNTIL THERE WAS NOTHING LEFT IN HER. IT WAS A heaving, torturous sort of cry, with her sobs ripping from her chest, her nose running, her eyes aching, and her stomach boiling with nausea that eventually culminated in her losing her dinner to the chamber pot. When she could form coherent thoughts, she thought it was dear of Darcy to stay with her, cradling her gently on the floor and wetting handkerchiefs in cool water to wipe her face and relieve her aching eyes.

Once her tears subsided, she remained pressed into his shoulder for some time, inhaling his soothing scent and listening to the beat of his heart until she was able to sit up and try to put herself to rights. Darcy still did not speak, running his hand gently over her hair.

Finally, he asked, "Where did you learn to punch like that?" She had managed to do it with scarcely any damage to her hand, as was usually the case.

Somehow, she laughed, her voice hoarse. "Jervis made me learn when he started to watch over me, and he showed me the best places on a man where a lady can inflict the most damage with the least harm to herself. As Mr Wickham was seated, the place under his nose was my best target, and I did not strike him with my knuckles but rather the lower part of my palm."

"I am all astonishment."

"I can fire a pistol fairly well too, but with a blade, I have no chance."

"Yes, well, it takes a good bit of strength in one's arms and chest to run someone through." He drew her into him again, careful to put her face somewhere other than the spots already soaked with her tears. "I am deeply sorry," he murmured.

She felt dangerously close to more tears. "It has been awful imagining him shot down in cold blood. I have often wondered about his last moments: whether he suffered and his thoughts as he knew he was dying. To know that he lay there in agony for an untold amount of time pains me."

She raised her face to look into Darcy's eyes. "Why would Wickham do that? Why would he not finish what he had been commissioned to do?"

"For exactly the reason you said," Darcy replied, still gently caressing her hair. "He is a coward. He shot the others in the back of their heads and Henry as he ran. When Henry had fallen, and Wickham needed to look him in the eye and do it in cold blood, it was a different matter entirely."

Elizabeth inhaled a deep, shuddering breath. "I wish I did not know but...I had to."

Darcy nodded, understanding her need. A few moments passed as Elizabeth just rested within his arms. At last, Darcy said, "It is nearly one in the morning. Perhaps I should have Mrs Hobbs bring you a sleeping draught?"

Elizabeth agreed. In a short time, both were ready for slumber, and the sleeping draught had been drunk. He climbed into her bed, pulling her into his arms while she succumbed to sleep, knowing well that slumber would not come easily to him.

Wickham's words echoed through his mind. *He was alive when I left him...one body where there had been two.*

Could Henry have survived? Could he be out there somewhere even now, thinking longingly of his wife?

He looked down at her beloved face, her eyelashes so dark against her cheek, which remained flushed from crying, and he had but one thought in his mind.

Henry's wife.

HE AWOKE IN THE NIGHT, FINDING HIMSELF ALONE IN THE BED. SHE was sitting on the floor by the fireplace, her shoulders shaking with the effort of silencing her anguish.

He rose, taking a blanket and going to her. Sitting behind her, he pulled her into his embrace, wrapping them both in the blanket. She did not speak for a moment, and he felt his shoulder become wet with her tears.

Finally, she said, "What if...?"

He kissed her head, glad that the darkness hid his wince. There was no need for her to finish her question; he knew exactly what she meant.

Her face was hidden by the glimmering firelight that cast looming shadows on the walls. She whispered—as if speaking it aloud would make it that much more likely—"What happens if he is alive?"

"He is not." He sounded more certain than he was.

"How can you say so?"

He shrugged. "I do not know, only that—he cannot be alive. Not after such a long time."

"The thought of losing you terrifies me."

"You will never lose me. You own my heart."

Her tears began again. "But what if—?"

He hushed her, not wanting her to give voice to fears that he could not truthfully deny. "One step at a time. I love you, Elizabeth Darcy, and you are mine." He kissed her, at first softly but quickly becoming possessive.

She pulled him tight, with kisses equally possessive and greedy. "And you, Fitzwilliam Darcy, are mine, now and always, and I love you with all that I am."

He gently pushed her to the rug, laying her back, desiring the comfort and security of loving her. "Always, Elizabeth. Forever and always."

FITZWILLIAM ARRIVED EARLY THE NEXT DAY, AND DARCY WONDERED whether he had slept at all. His face was grim and tired, but he brightened when Mrs Hobbs arrived bearing strong, hot coffee and a heavily laden breakfast plate.

Darcy sat playing with his coffee cup as he watched his cousin eat. Fitzwilliam did not make his customary banter, leading Darcy to suppose there was bad news ahead.

When his plate was empty, Fitzwilliam leaned back and quietly told Darcy, "The plan was, according to Wickham, to have the brothers meet in Crewe, which they did. I know not from whence Francis came, but he was there to see that his brother was properly eliminated.

"Wickham's story changes every time he tells it. He now claims he did not fire the shot that killed Lord Courtenay. He insists that Lord Courtenay was ready with his own pistol and pulled his pistol on his brother. His brother also had a gun and did his own shooting—everyone shot everyone else according to Wickham."

"In the smoke and confusion it may have been hard to know."

Fitzwilliam shrugged. "Details were changed and interchanged so many times, it is difficult to know what is true and Wickham is always a liar in my experience. In any event, at the end of it all, Francis took one of the horses and rode off, leaving his brother on the ground—presumed dead—and his brother's servants most definitely dead.

"It was left to Wickham to deal with the rest. He disposed of the outrider, or what remained of him, in the woods, leaving Lord Courtenay and the valet on the ground. When he returned, only the body of the valet remained. According to Wickham, Lord Courtenay's body was not found although he searched the area diligently."

"Wickham has never been diligent a day in his life," Darcy shot back with disgust. After a moment's consideration, he asked, "What of the other two men? The coachmen and the outrider who went for assistance?"

"Wickham said he took care of them too."

"What was buried then?"

Fitzwilliam shrugged. "Elizabeth was in London, which is four days' travel from where Courtenay was shot and five or more days' travel from the family plot. In the heat of August, a quick burial was not questioned. No one knows exactly who or what was buried save Mr Francis Warren, and he took his secrets with him to hell."

"No one attended Lord Courtenay's body save his brother? It seems rather odd."

Fitzwilliam shrugged again. "No one knows who was there. It would be a matter for investigation if one were inclined to do so."

Darcy pushed back from the table, rising to look out the window. "How do we know that Mr Francis Warren did not return to the scene and take care of his brother's body from there?"

"That is possible," Fitzwilliam opined. "Or his lordship might have tried to go get help in his weakened state and collapsed somewhere. There are a thousand different possibilities that I can conjure, and none of them have Lord Courtenay remaining alive at the conclusion."

Darcy's worries congealed like a heavy mass within his gut. "Will the investigation be re-opened?"

Fitzwilliam shook his head. "No one sees any need. Wickham's words are the desperate rambles of a man who knows he will be hanged—or worse. A man in that situation will say anything he thinks might spare him. I would not be surprised to learn it was all Wickham's imagining, first to last."

Darcy paced and said nothing.

"The investigation was thorough; I can attest to that. Nothing, not one thing, has ever suggested that Lord Courtenay lived."

"Evidence was not found because it was not looked for," Darcy shot back. "The death of Lord Courtenay was assumed."

"Lord Courtenay is dead. Where would he have gone and why? He had no reason to run. He would have returned long ago for his wife and heir."

"Unless he was ill or suffered some sort of debilitation."

"In which case, whoever cared for him would have attempted to find his people or, at the least, put out word. Darcy, Lord Courtenay is gone."

Darcy turned and looked into his cousin's eyes. "I wish I could take your assurance."

AFTER A NEARLY SLEEPLESS NIGHT FILLED WITH DISTRESS, WORRY, AND despair, Darcy hardly wished to deal with his sister, but he knew it must be done. He went to Georgiana's room, knocking and then entering when bidden. Georgiana quickly dismissed her maid, who had been finishing her hair. She was wide eyed and pale as she watched her brother sit.

Darcy did not immediately speak, looking around and clenching his jaw in anger. Finally, he said, "Would you care to offer me an explanation for George Wickham's presence here last night?"

"I should have told you...Mrs Younge said it was not improper..."

"You are not out!" Darcy roared. "What would make you think it was permissible to entertain gentlemen callers? Callers who are *not* gentlemen, I should say!"

Georgiana looked down at her hands on her lap. "We...George and I are...he cares for me...and—"

Darcy laughed harshly. "Foolish girl. George Wickham loves no one. He is a murderer, Georgiana—a thief, a liar, and a murderer—and he is going to hang for it.

"My patience with you has reached its end. You have gone well beyond being 'spirited' or 'difficult'—you are a disgrace. Now, tell me immediately, is there a possibility that you are with child?"

Georgiana gasped. "No! I...it did not go so far as that. Brother, please, I am so very, very sorry. I did not mean to disappoint—"

"Just how far did it go?"

"He has been calling since last autumn. He came to ask for a sponsor for his commission."

"Last autumn!"

"When you were in Hertfordshire...I...he said our father wished him to be in the military."

Darcy's laugh was short and without humour. "So you paid for his one day in the militia."

"I suppose I did. He visited every now and again after that. He was always proper—"

"Proper? I assure you, there is nothing proper in the behaviour of a man who sneaks into someone's house to seduce a child of fifteen or sixteen, much less one with the sense of a twelve-year-old."

Georgiana looked hurt.

"I am disappointed in you and in myself, Georgiana. Elizabeth and I expected better of you."

Georgiana began to cry. "I know. I did not permit him liberties. He did try, just last night, he tried, but Jervis…Jervis came in and grabbed him."

"Thank God for Jervis, else you would be ruined." Darcy shook his head. "Needless to say, given the night's events, we have not yet decided on the consequences of your actions, but I can assure you, you will feel them deeply."

Georgiana continued to cry and stutter out apologies. "I told Mrs Younge I did not wish to see him but then he wrote me a note. He said he might die without me—"

"He will die regardless," Darcy replied darkly. "Do you understand that? He committed treason. He killed Elizabeth's late husband in a plot to overthrow the government. Does that seem like an honourable gentleman?"

Georgiana was now sobbing, apologising, vowing to change, and begging for forgiveness, but Darcy heard nothing. He walked out the door.

TWENTY

The day after the discovery of George Wickham in Darcy's home was spent in careful silence. Elizabeth had the pleasure of dismissing Mrs Younge, having learned of her complicity in Georgiana's actions. She and Darcy had determined that to publicly disgrace the woman would bring unwelcome consequences to their family and thus could only admonish her and send her away without a written character.

After that, Elizabeth had little to do but think. Thoughts of Henry and Crewe and what was to come turned and twisted in her mind.

Dinner was sober and perfunctory with neither Elizabeth nor Darcy interested in their meal. Georgiana merely pushed her food around her plate until she was dismissed to return to her bedchamber. They went to the drawing room, and Elizabeth decided she must make Darcy speak.

"Fitzwilliam?" Apparently lost in thought, her voice startled him. He offered a forced smile.

"Could he live?"

Darcy sighed and rubbed his hand across his mouth. "George Wickham does not know the meaning of the word honesty. He would say anything to save himself from the scaffold."

"True."

"Colonel Fitzwilliam says the investigation will not be opened again. No one sees cause for it, not on the testimony of a murderer."

Elizabeth felt an odd contrariety of emotions: guilt, relief, anger, and indignation. "Is it not worth asking a few questions?"

Darcy looked at her, his expression inscrutable.

Heedlessly, she forged on. "Someone would have had to assist in the burial at Warrington, the grounds keepers—Oh! What of the person who made the coffin? Surely, someone must have made a coffin."

Her words and thoughts gained momentum. "The road is not populated, but it is fairly well travelled. A man who had been shot could not have simply run off. Someone must have helped him or at least seen him. Do you not think so? Some enquiries could be made to determine—"

Darcy stood hastily. "Excuse me; I must attend to business in my study." Without further word, he quit the room, the door closing loudly behind him. Elizabeth sat in shock, staring at the closed door for several moments until she rose and went after him.

She entered the study to find him leaning on the mantel, staring into the fireplace. As soon as he heard her, he raised his head, and Elizabeth was shocked by the anger she saw on his countenance.

"You are my wife." His voice began in a low tone. "My wife! Do you understand that? Mine! Henry died, and I cannot…I shall not…" He stopped, his jaw clenching and unclenching furiously.

"You never did forget your love for him, did you? I am second best, and it likely relieves you to know—"

"That is not fair," Elizabeth cried out. "I love you—you know I do."

"You do not love me!" he spat. "There is a mere suggestion that Henry might live, and you wish to run to him!"

"You are being foolish and jealous! This has nothing to do with my feelings for you!"

"Then what?" he demanded. "What would make you wish for him to live? You still love him!"

"I love you too!"

"Argh!" He made a noise of intense frustration, kicking at a log in the fire with the toe of his boot.

Elizabeth felt her heart pounding even as it was breaking. Her eyes begged for the relief of tears. She went to her husband, understanding that his unkind words were borne of his fear of losing her. She laid her hand gently against his back. "Fitzwilliam, I—"

With a violent wrench, he jerked away from her, turning to stride out of the room. He paused at the door, his eyes seeking her and burning a hole into her heart. "You said you loved me, and I believed you. I despise myself for both my weakness and my stupidity."

He stormed from the room, leaving her once again. This time, she did not follow him.

"Idiot," Darcy chastised himself. "Stupid, jealous brute. She is as frightened as you are, and you behave like a fool." He tripped over the front stoop of his house, his vision in the pitch black of the night not aided in the least by the gin he had consumed.

The vision of her face when he had left haunted him. She looked so sad and bereft, and he could scarcely imagine what had moved him to behave as he had. He would not blame her for wishing him gone. No doubt, Henry never would have lost his temper in such a way.

It had never been easy for Darcy—the business of Elizabeth's dead husband. By sheer virtue of being dead, he was a sainted spectre. His every thought, word, and deed had taken on a benevolent, rosy hue. Darcy had told himself repeatedly that it was ridiculous to be jealous of a man whose brother had betrayed him and whose wife and son were lost to him. Yet, it would not do. Darcy knew he shared Elizabeth with Henry, and it could never sit well with him, no matter how well he performed to the contrary.

"I share her with Henry," he slurred, going down the hall to his bedchamber, "but I do not fool myself into thinking Henry would do likewise."

He opened his door to see Elizabeth in his bed, a number of damp handkerchiefs crumpled around her. A dagger of painful remorse rent his heart as he settled next to her. Sleepily, she opened her eyes.

Darcy gathered her into his arms, relieved that she came willingly. His voice hoarse and low, he said, "Forgive me, I beg you."

He felt the movement of her nod against his chest. "I know I share your love, and that I always have, but to know that when faced with a choice—"

"You misunderstand me." She sat up. "I love you deeply, and it is not a contest. My love for you has nothing to do with what I once shared with Henry. It is a separate entity, residing in a wholly different sphere.

"I explained it once to my sister: although I loved Henry, it was a different sort of love—a heady, infatuated, giddy sort of love. It would have been more in time, but we were not granted that time.

"With you, it was different from the beginning. We had argued and angered one another, and we had spoken of sad and difficult things. Our love is proven and sure: a fine stout sort of love. Some might consider that time of heady infatuation to be the best part of love. For myself, I take comfort in having gained the latter."

Darcy considered her words. It was true: their love was tried and tested. He squeezed her gently. "I cannot deny that there is nothing that could turn me from you."

"When you left me tonight," she said, turning in his arms to look at him, "I knew you would return, and I understood your mind even if I did not like it."

"I am sorry I left you." He paused a moment, his throat feeling tight. "The thought of losing you devastates me, but that should not have been my first concern. I should have considered your feelings above my own."

She caressed his face. "I do not want him. He is gone—I know that. What I want, what I need, is to know what happened.

"I have known for a long time that he was gone. You cannot love someone without knowing when that love leaves this earth. If, perchance, he survived beyond that day in Crewe, surely he would not have stayed away so long. He would have found us or found a way to get word to us."

"Unless he was ill or hiding from his brother's companions."

"He still could have sent word to us," she replied, her voice just slightly too determined. She was afraid too, he knew that, but he chose to put the idea aside for a moment, choosing instead to be solaced by her reassurances.

"I love you," he whispered. "Being with you is a happiness unlike anything I have ever known."

"For me also," Elizabeth said, and he knew she meant it with her whole heart.

"But I must know," she continued. "I cannot have a cloud hanging over our life together. I do not want to wonder or fear that it will all collapse somewhere down the road. I do not long for him, nor do I pine for the life I knew with him. I just need to know."

"I understand." Darcy held onto her tightly. "But do know that I cannot relinquish you."

"It will never come to that."

COLONEL FITZWILLIAM ACCOMPANIED DARCY TO THE GAOL TO MEET with Wickham. When he appeared, Darcy inhaled sharply, shocked by his bruised and bloodied face.

Fitzwilliam chuckled. "Darcy, remind me never to anger your wife."

Wickham scowled. "What do you want? You kept me all night with your questions, Fitzwilliam. What more would you have me say?"

"The truth perhaps?" Darcy asked, taking a seat on a hard, rough-hewn wooden bench. "Your story was far too mutable from the recounting I heard."

Wickham shrugged and seated himself on a similar bench. "I shall hang, Darcy. High treason is my charge, and nothing you can say or do will alter it."

"Lie down with dogs and you wake with fleas. Take that lesson with you into the afterlife." Fitzwilliam was still far too amused by the entire situation, and Darcy sent him a censuring frown.

"If you did not kill the earl, there might be a means by which your sentence could be altered."

"To what? Years spent in this miserable place? I think I might rather hang."

"Transportation," Darcy replied, and saw the brief glimmer of hope enter Wickham's eyes before he quickly looked away.

"Impossible. A peer is dead, and the gun is in my hand."

"Unless that peer is found alive."

Wickham said nothing, but a muscle in his eye twitched.

"If he is dead, truly dead, then you are no worse than you are now; but I am willing to fund the search for him."

"Why?" Wickham shot Darcy a rebellious look. "You cannot want to find him. Lord Courtenay will surely be unwilling to share his delectable wife with you. From what I see, I did you a favour."

Darcy looked at Wickham, so stupid with his false bravado. He made an elaborate shrug towards his cousin. "Fitzwilliam, you had the right of it. Let us go and leave old George to his fate." The two cousins rose, Darcy making a show of dusting off his clothing.

They had reached the door when Wickham cried out, "A moment, gentlemen!"

Darcy turned back, but Fitzwilliam did not. "Darcy, he is lying. Come."

"I am not lying," Wickham protested. "I am not."

Darcy sat down slowly. "It is improbable that he lives. I shall demand your honesty in this. If I find you lied to me, the search is off at once. If you send me on a fool's errand, I will entreat the hangman to allow me to assist."

"I shall tell you all I know, Darcy, and as to the truth of it—I assure you of its validity on the grave of my father."

Two hours later, Darcy and Fitzwilliam were in the carriage, despising the stench of the gaol that clung to them and pondering the events of Lord Courtenay's ostensible death.

Darcy was first to speak. "Was he lying?"

Fitzwilliam was careful in his answer. "He has every cause to lie, of course. You need his assistance while he considers himself beyond help."

"Deceiving me does him no good. There is nothing to be gained by sending me off on a fruitless search for a man dead and buried in the woods around Crewe."

"If Henry was somehow able to drag himself from the scene of his shooting—if he lived beyond that day—it is to Wickham's advantage that you discover it."

"So?"

"So, from that, I would conclude that he likely told the truth." Fitzwilliam looked at his cousin with great trepidation.

Darcy frowned pensively. "Wickham is the master of disguise, but even he must realise there is no good reason to have me needlessly searching."

"Save for the fact he cannot admit outright that he killed Lord Courtenay. That would be tantamount to a confession."

"True." Darcy rubbed his eyes. "There are no answers, just more questions."

Fitzwilliam nodded his agreement.

"What now?" Darcy asked.

"We should first investigate some of Wickham's claims. Hire some men to determine whether a man bearing the description of the late Lord Courtenay was put in a grave in Warrington. Someone—a servant or a merchant—must know something."

Darcy continued the thought. "If there is nothing in that grave, then we begin a search in earnest. However, even if there is something there, a right sort of something..." Darcy rubbed his hand over his face. "I shall hire someone to investigate, and we shall go on from there."

FITZWILLIAM WAS LET OFF AT MATLOCK HOUSE, AND DARCY, AFTER A moment's consideration, departed on another errand.

Darcy's great uncle—the younger brother of Darcy's grandfather—was a judge, and his son Robert had become a barrister. Darcy did not maintain the close ties with his father's family that he did with his mother's branch. Nevertheless, he did not doubt his cousin's willingness to be of assistance nor his understanding of the need for discretion at this early stage of events.

Robert Darcy was nearly seventy, tall, and distinguished. As a barrister, he had a comfortable income. He and his wife had not been blessed with children, and they had spent much of their time travelling or in the country until her death at about the same time as Darcy's father. Since that time, Robert had mostly resided in town, whiling his days away quietly in reading, politics, and his duty to the law.

He greeted his cousin cordially. "How do you do, sir! It has been some time since we have met, just the pair of us." Robert had attended his young cousin's wedding breakfast, but their interaction there had been understandably limited.

Darcy bowed. "That it has." After a short time spent discussing news of family and recent items of interest in society, Darcy came to the heart of the matter.

"I would like your opinion on a situation of some delicacy. An opinion, nothing more, save for your customary discretion."

Robert nodded. "Very well."

Darcy hesitated a moment, drumming his fingers against his cousin's table. "You know my wife is the widow of the late Earl of Courtenay, Henry Warren. His death had a number of unusual circumstances to it. Do you know the particulars, or would you have me repeat them to you?"

As it turned out, Robert did know the details rather well, having been involved in the trials of several of the radicals involved. Moreover, the latest events with Wickham had been brought to his attention.

"I do not suppose that your concerns rest on Mr Wickham's behalf? If they do, I must tell you, he will almost certainly hang. Only something extraordinary could alter his fate."

"I am here because of some information Wickham has given me—information that might lead to the discovery that Lord Courtenay is still alive."

"Ah," said Robert, tenting his fingers and looking thoughtful. "And you believe him?"

"I do not know," Darcy replied quickly. "However, given what he has said, I am interested enough to look into matters. My question for you is this." Darcy leaned forward. "Should Lord Courtenay be found alive, what becomes of my marriage? Shall we be required to annul it?"

Robert sighed heavily. "Annulments are a complicated business and not easy to come by. There are, in truth, two kinds of dissolution of a sanctified union. One, considered voidable through the ecclesiastical court, can be granted for legitimate marriages in which conditions exist that are grounds for annulment of the union: insanity or incompetence of one of the spouses, consanguinity, or affinity.

"However, for a marriage in which one of the parties was found to be already married to another at the time of the wedding, the second marriage is not dissolved, it is void. It simply never was because one of the parties was not eligible to be wed in the first place. The person—in your case, Mrs Darcy—who had undertaken the marriage while being wed to another would be guilty of bigamy and potentially subject to criminal charges. Any financial matters or other arrangements would be matters for the civil court."

Darcy leaned back with a heavy sigh of his own and rubbed his hand over his face.

Robert hastened to console him. "I cannot see that such a thing would occur, or if it did, it would be only in the most cursory manner. Lord Courtenay died in 1809 I believe?"

"August 1809, and we married in June of this year, almost three years since his death. No one could accuse her of mourning him in haste."

"Not at all. Moreover, she acted in the interests of the monarchy, first to last. Her fealty and her morality cannot be in question."

"That is not my worry. I am more distressed over the potential dissolution of my marriage. Would there be any recourse for me?"

Robert chose not to directly answer him. "It is highly unlikely that a peer of the realm would hide himself away all this time. The key conspirators were apprehended some time ago. He has been safe since then, and he could have sent word to her. Mark my words: this is nothing worthy of fear or even concern."

"But thinking of worst possibilities—would there be anything at all that I could do to save my marriage?"

His cousin tilted his head back, studying the ceiling. After several long minutes, he looked kindly at the younger man and admitted, "I think not."

THE HIRED INVESTIGATORS MADE SHORT WORK OF ONE OF THEIR TASKS: it was a simple matter to learn that Henry's grave in the family plot at Warrington was empty. The groundskeepers exhumed the coffin and opened it to find a bag stuffed with grasses and hay.

The task of finding out what had become of Henry, or Henry's body, was more difficult. October passed and moved into November and then December with still no word.

The months proved to be busy ones regardless. Jane Bingley was approaching her confinement, expecting a January birth if the midwife's predictions were accurate. They were enjoying their new home in Derbyshire and impatient for the Darcys to return for Christmastide.

Elizabeth received word from Mrs Bennet that an unexpected match had occurred. Miss Mary Bennet had caught the attention of the man who would take Netherfield Park. He was an older gentleman who had once been a parson until a distant relation passed and left him a fortune. He desired to join the landed gentry and had visited Hertfordshire in the autumn. He was drawn to Mary for her morals and prudent interests, and he proposed within a month's acquaintance. Mary would be wed in February, and Netherfield would become the couple's permanent home.

Reading the letter to Darcy, Elizabeth laughed. "Kitty writes that Mama is incensed that there will be three of us married to untitled men.

But she says that Mary is as happy as her husband is old. Evidently, the man claims to be in his fourth decade, but Kitty believes him of an age with my father."

"I hope they will be very happy."

As the weeks passed, Darcy alternately hoped and feared for news to come. He persuaded himself that Henry must be dead and then believed just as strongly that he lived, still in hiding. He would decide each morning that they could safely claim to be devoid of fear, and then he would be resolved to yet another day of waiting.

The reports that came were varied: a man who had been shot, one who had left on a ship bound for the colonies, another who had been ill with fever for several weeks in Crewe before giving up the ghost. There were so many possibilities in the world for a man who did not wish to be found that Darcy despaired of ever learning the truth.

He broached the subject with Elizabeth one night after they had dined.

"I received a letter from the investigators today."

She looked up from her needlework. "Any news?"

He shook his head. "There are, unfortunately, many ways for a man to vanish. If he has gone overseas, I fear we might never know the truth."

"Shall we call off the search?"

"Not yet. There are still possible clues to follow that might prove promising."

"I shall rest easy as long as I know we have been diligent."

SOMEWHERE IN BOTH OF THEIR MINDS, THEY HAD DETERMINED THAT, IF nothing of import was learned by the end of the year, they would abandon the search. The investigators, even though continuing to search for answers, had already concluded that Henry had left the scene of his shooting either on his own power or with the aid of another, and he had succumbed to his injuries shortly thereafter. Elizabeth and Darcy were increasingly satisfied with that conclusion, particularly as it answered their own interests.

George Wickham remained in the gaol and grew increasingly desperate for his chances. Darcy was doing all he could for him though there was little to be done. He was seen, thus far, to be of use to the men who searched for the earl, but if nothing was found, he would be branded a traitor and hanged.

On the third day of January 1813, all of them experienced a reversal of fortune.

Darcy and Elizabeth had decided to remain in London for Christmas, and the investigators paid them a visit.

"We have found a man working in one of the mines in Kidsgrove. He was shot and injured grievously somewhere in the latter part of the summer in 1809. The owner of the mine found him and nursed him to good health, and the man then chose to take work in the mine. His name is Henry Sumner."

"His mother's name," Elizabeth whispered, looking faint.

The investigator nodded. "When he first recovered from his injuries, there were some issues with memory, and he believed that to be his name."

Darcy replied gravely, "I see."

"I have seen Mr Sumner," the investigator told them. "If you have a miniature or portrait, I might be able to make a determination."

Elizabeth went to retrieve a miniature of Henry done in Italy. She returned with it and wordlessly handed it to the man, who studied it for an excruciatingly long time.

At last, he nodded. "Yes, I believe it is the same man."

ELIZABETH PREPARED TO RETIRE THAT NIGHT WHILE HEARING DARCY IN his bedchamber undergoing his own nightly ablutions. She was eager to be in his arms and desperate for the solace she found in him, her mind a tumult of the meaning of all they had learned.

They had spoken little so far. Darcy had been silent and reserved, and she had been confused and distressed. Both of them had gone through the remainder of the day with little feeling or expression, operating by rote. She had presumed they would speak when they were alone in their chambers for the night, and she was ready to give way to all of the thoughts that surely must haunt them.

He did not come to her.

She lay there, the minutes ticking by, wondering what he was doing and why it was requiring so much time for him to do it. Then she went to the connecting door and knocked gently.

"Come."

The room was completely dark save for a low-burning fire. "Fitzwilliam?"

"I am in bed."

"What…why did you not come to me?" She was shocked that he had retired to his own bed. They had not slept apart once since their first night married.

She perched beside him on the edge of the mattress.

He would not look at her, rubbing his face with his hands roughly. "Elizabeth, I love you deeply, but I cannot make you my mistress."

"Your mistress!" She was shocked, hurt by what he suggested. "I am your wife!"

Softly, he asked, "Are you?"

"Of course, I am!" Elizabeth felt a tear of anger and sadness roll down her cheek. "Am I to pretend I am not your wife? Am I to sleep alone and be denied your love?"

"I do not know what to do." His tone was quietly frustrated. "I have tried to persuade myself that all is well using a multitude of reasons and imaginings, yet I am faced with the probability that Henry lives. If so, you are *his* wife, not mine. I cannot take you, knowing you might well belong to another."

Elizabeth raised her hand to her face, allowing a sob to come through.

"What if we were to conceive a child?" he asked "A son? This situation is complicated, and a child would make it more so. The risk of a child that I could not rightly claim as my heir is too great."

Elizabeth began to cry in earnest, the truth of his fears cutting her like a knife. She could understand his feelings all too well, for he did nothing more than give voice to her own fears. How she hated them and hated the unfairness of the entire situation in which they were suddenly mired.

With her face covered by her hands, she felt his arm encircle her waist as a gentle kiss was placed on her hair. "Please try to understand," he whispered. "I do not know what to do."

Elizabeth jerked away from Darcy's grasp. "Then sleep alone!" she cried, rising quickly and nearly running into her bedchamber. She tossed herself onto her bed and wept violently until she could weep no more.

Darcy did not come to her for the entirety of the night.

TWENTY-ONE

WINTER 1813

I t was not a restful night for Darcy.

He could feel a cloak of reserve coming over him. It was too painful to contemplate that his love and his felicity were being taken from him in this way, so he withdrew. *You are indeed a selfish, disdainful man. She needs you. She is pained as well as you are—more than you are—yet you hide yourself from her.*

It was his nature, and as such, it was nearly impossible to deny. He had learned it through the loss of his mother and perfected it during the long illness and death of his father. To appear stoic and inscrutable, to show pain to no one, and to go about his business, tending to the needs of others and disregarding his own—this was the way he survived then and the way he would survive now.

He was angry with her too. It was perhaps irrational, but she had insisted on knowing the truth about George Wickham's rambles when everyone else was inclined to dismiss him. She wanted the truth, and this was where it had brought them.

Avoiding the truth does not change the truth. If Henry is alive, he would have come to our notice eventually.

Darcy entered the breakfast room the next morning, seeing his wife already at the table. Sadness marked her every feature, and she looked away from him. Her sadness pierced his cloak of reserve. He waited until the servants had gone then went to kneel by her chair.

He took her hands in his and rested his forehead on them. After several moments of silence, he said, "Please know how deeply I love you."

She pulled her hands away, wrapping them around her teacup and taking a sip. "You love me so much that you turn your back on me?" Her voice was cool, but he heard a tiny quaver in it.

"I do not wish to turn my back on you."

"Can you possibly understand…" She stopped and drew a deep breath. "I am terrified. You are upset, and I am too, but I wish for us to go through this together, not alone."

Rising, he sat in the chair next to hers. He stared at the tablecloth a moment before saying, "Yet we cannot do that. You will leave me."

"I shall not leave you!"

"You will have no choice!" His voice had risen, and he stopped himself. The entire house need not know that he and Elizabeth were shouting at each other in the breakfast room.

He took a deep, calming breath. "Elizabeth, do you not see? We have opened Pandora's Box, and now everything is beyond our control."

Elizabeth lowered her face into her hands. "Like Pandora, my curiosity has ruined me."

"It is not mere curiosity," he owned. "I know you needed to find the truth just as I would have wished to do. It was right to find him—if indeed it is him—but it does not mean it is easy."

They sat in silence for several moments until Elizabeth offered, weakly and without conviction, "It is not Henry in Kidsgrove."

"It is likely," Darcy replied gently. "We both know that. A man named Henry found in the right place, at the right time, and bearing the surname of Henry's mother? Mere coincidence is improbable."

Elizabeth pressed her lips together tightly, turning her head away from him. "So by your estimation, we are, even now, not truly married."

Darcy looked at her, his heart sinking anew as he struggled to remain strong. He could not say it though. He could not utter what he knew in his heart to be true: that she was already lost to him. Weakly, he said, "We must go see this man before we can rightly carry on as we were."

Elizabeth was on her feet and out of the room before anything else could be said.

ELIZABETH THOUGHT SHE MIGHT RETURN TO HER ROOM AND HAVE A good cry but found she could not. Instead, she went to her sitting room window, staring out on a January day that was deceptive in its prettiness and sunshine. She knew that if she were to walk outside, the bite of the wind and the chill of the air would drive her right back in.

When she allowed herself to consider what might happen, she could feel nothing but confusion and misery. She deeply regretted that she had undertaken these actions; yet, she knew she could not have done differently. Mostly, what she wished was that George Wickham had never uttered the fateful words that had led them on their quest.

At dinner, the two of them pushed the food around their plates in a dispirited and quiet manner until it was a suitable time to withdraw. Then they sat in the drawing room, Darcy engaged in reading and Elizabeth tending to her correspondence. She considered telling her family what had occurred but reasoned against it and wrote a lighthearted note filled with a generous number of inconsequential topics.

At long last, it was time to retire. When her maid had prepared her for sleep, Elizabeth went to the connecting door between their chambers and leaned against it, closing her eyes and resting her cheek against the wood. She heard the sounds associated with her husband's nighttime rituals.

As she stood there, she felt compelled to confess the truth to Darcy though he likely would not hear it. Indeed, she did not want him to hear it, for it marked her as the cruel creature she was.

"I wish he would remain gone. I do not want him. I want you."

She stayed for several minutes more, the hard wood cool against her face, listening to him and praying he would come to her.

He did not. She eventually heard him settle into his bed and blow out the candle. She listened for a long time—knowing not what she waited for—then she finally went to bed and stared blankly at the canopy above her until dawn.

ON THE FIRST DAY OF THEIR TRAVEL, THEY WERE AS TWO STRANGERS, careful and pleasant with one another until they arrived at the inn where they would break their journey. It was not yet the hour they preferred to dine, and Elizabeth decided she would like to walk.

The village wherein they stayed was a lively market town, its populace thronging the streets even at a time close to the dinner hour and in
such cold weather. Elizabeth was soothed by the bustle, her observation of these strangers diverting her mind. She walked slowly, and
when she heard someone call out the time, she was surprised that well
over an hour had passed.

She hurried back to the inn, rushing to her chamber where she
encountered Darcy in the process of ordering his man to gather up
some of the inn's workers to search for her. "I am here," she announced
as she entered the room.

Darcy's face was white with rage, but he remained calm as he
dismissed the servants and requested dinner trays in their sitting room
for an hour hence. As the door clicked shut behind the servants, he
pulled her to him, kissing her gently on the top of her head. "Are you
well?"

"Perfectly so," she answered.

Then, pushing her back, he bellowed, "Where on earth did you
go? What were you thinking to vanish in such a way? Jervis had no
idea... I had no idea... Do you have any notion of how frantic I have
been?"

It was too much. The days of worry, the sleepless nights, and the
feeling—unreasonable though it might be—that he had abandoned her,
all coalesced into powerful anger.

"I beg your pardon, sir, but your speech strongly resembles
husbandly concern."

"No one knew where you were, darkness was nigh, there are
villagers all about the streets—"

"What do you care!" she cried out. "Now you choose to be a
husband? You have scarcely said two words to me, and now you wish
for an accounting of my whereabouts?"

"Do not dare suppose you know how I feel. I am being torn in
two—"

"You are cold and silent, and I am in agony! You make me feel like
Netherfield Park!"

She began to weep, and Darcy looked at her in utter bewilderment.
"Like Netherfield? What does that signify?"

Elizabeth cried with increasing vigour, and she felt Darcy's hand
upon her back, guiding her over to a small sofa by the fire. She slowly
gained her control as he sat close by.

"I am a leased property, and now the owner wants to return, and you will walk off without a look back."

Darcy sighed and reached over to caress her face. "Of course not."

"It certainly seems so to me. I am discarded."

For several moments he said nothing, and when he finally spoke, his voice was hoarse with the effort of suppressing his emotion. "This is difficult, but I do not know a different way. I do not wish to hurt you or abandon you, but you...you will abandon me. You will return to your former life with a man and a son you love, and I shall be left with nothing and no one. If I think about it, it will destroy me, so I do not think of it."

He inhaled deeply with a small shudder. "I want you to be happy, even if it is not with me. If it transpires as I believe it will, you will walk away, and I hope—truly I do—that you will go gladly."

"How can you speak so?" She was weeping again, the tears rolling down her cheeks.

"Because it will occur. Every part of me wishes to scream and rage against it, but that will not help. It will only make this more difficult for you. So I am frozen in my silence, just hoping I do not make it worse."

She pressed her wet eyes to his shoulder. "Do not be silent with me. It is not yet done, it might...it might..." She stopped, feeling the futility of her words.

His lips pressed into her hair. "Just know that I love you with all that I am, and I shall love you forever. Even if you can no longer be my wife, I promise you that I shall remain your husband, always."

ELIZABETH WATCHED DARCY AS THE CARRIAGE ROLLED ON IN THE MID-afternoon of their second day of travel. Her eyes gently traced his handsome features in repose. Both of them had slept poorly for several days, and particularly after their argument the previous evening, so it could be no surprise that he had fallen asleep.

She thought of the sentiments he had expressed the night before, and in them, she understood the trueness of his love. He wished her to be happy—this man, the best man she had ever known. Never could she love a man more, and never had she understood it better than now when all love must be in vain.

For so long, for so many months, she had done little more than bemoan the loss of Henry. She had longed for him, felt the unfairness of her widowhood, and cried bitter tears of love and yearning for her dead husband. So why, when it seemed she would now have everything she had wished for, was she so despondent?

She whispered quietly to Darcy's slumbering form. "Loving you is like nothing I ever knew could be possible."

Had she ever even loved Henry? She had, she knew she had, with all the ardour of a seventeen-year-old girl who had known nothing of men or of life.

While not so many years had passed since then, a world of experience had marked and changed her. She had come to understand loss and deceit, duty and responsibility. She had become a mother. She had changed from a vivacious and, at times, impertinent country girl to a woman who had to run an estate, honour a title for her country, and care for a family. Neither Lady Courtenay nor Mrs Elizabeth Darcy was the same as the girl, Miss Elizabeth Bennet, who had given herself so freely to Henry.

Although prudence would dictate that it was fortunate she had not borne Darcy a child, particularly a son, how she wished that she might have. She longed to have that connexion to him: a bind to Darcy that could not be untied. She wished to have a son or daughter at whom she might look and think, *oh she has her father's eyes*, or *he is tall like his father*. That would be yet another complication to this tangle though, so she supposed it was for the best that it was not to be.

THE INN WHERE THEY STAYED AT THE END OF THE THIRD DAY OF TRAVEL was of superior quality, and the proprietor quickly had them installed in his best rooms, promising hot baths and a hearty dinner to be served shortly. He held true to his word, and soon enough, they met to dine in the sitting room adjoining their bedchambers. The food was excellent though neither Darcy nor Elizabeth could do the meal justice, both of them picking disinterestedly at what lay before them. By unspoken agreement, after they had dined, they remained in the sitting area, both attempting to read books whose pages did not compel them until an acceptable hour came to retire.

Sleep would provide no relief, failing to find either of them. Elizabeth tossed and turned for several hours, sleepless, restless, and sad. The feeling of foreboding upon her was unbearable, especially as the very one she needed to relieve her was the one she felt so certain she would lose.

She rose from her bed, going to a window to stare at the town beneath her. It was a neat little town, prosperous due to the colliery, and all below her looked well ordered and nicely kept. The cold caress of moonlight fell upon the streets, making all appear unreal and ghostly, and she shivered with the ominous feel of it.

It was shortly after midnight when Elizabeth finally succumbed to her wishes. She knocked softly at Darcy's door and pushed it open, seeing him sitting in a chair by the fire, a book closed on his lap.

He did not speak, regarding her in silence as she crossed the room towards him. He held out his arms, inviting her into his embrace, but she knelt instead and laid her head on his lap. He entangled his hand in her hair, caressing the back of her neck gently with his fingers. They sat in this manner for some time until she spoke, her voice hoarse. "Take me home."

"Home?"

"Pemberley, London…wherever."

He did not reply.

"Or…or perhaps we can…can you take me away? Take me away, please."

His fingers stilled for a moment. "Away?"

"Ireland, America, the colonies, the Indies…wherever you would like. A place where no one has ever heard of the Earl of Courtenay or the Darcys."

"Would you truly wish for that?" His tone was gentle. "This man could be Henry, whom you love and for whom you have yearned these past years. The father of your son."

She tilted her head up to look at him. "Fitzwilliam, I want you. I want our life together. I loved him once, but he left me, and I left him, and I do not want to go back."

She thought she saw a tear glint in his eye. "You cannot choose. If it is he, then you are still married to him, and he will be your husband. You are his by law and by God."

"And so, I beg you," she whispered hoarsely, "leave with me now before the choice, or lack thereof, finds me."

A long silence enshrouded them. At last, he said, "I cannot. Heaven help me, I cannot."

As dawn broke upon the town, Darcy and Elizabeth strolled together slowly towards a pretty little wilderness not far from the inn. He offered his arm and she took it, winding hers around his and pressing the side of her body against him, her head resting against his shoulder.

By unspoken agreement, they indulged in their happier memories as they walked. They laughed about their time in Hertfordshire, reminiscing on the assemblies and the Netherfield ball. They spoke of their wedding and of the days following when they scandalised Darcy's household by remaining in his bedchamber with no respite. They did not speak of her son, the son he had called his own for an all too brief time. It was too painful and unfair to mention this reminder that Darcy would not only lose his marriage but his fatherhood as well.

They returned to the inn for breakfast hours later, both picking uselessly at an assortment of breads and meats until their purpose could be denied no more.

The miners lived in a barracks within the colliery, so the owner of the mines invited Darcy to use a small sitting room in his home, Clough Hall, to meet the man who might be Lord Courtenay.

Darcy's eyes roamed over the room, an extraordinary nervousness nigh on engulfing him. His heart pounded and his hands sweated as he paced, awaiting the man. He could not think of what might happen if it were Lord Courtenay.

From the look of Elizabeth, she felt much the same. He saw her hands shake as she sat quietly, her head bowed and her fingers wound with a handkerchief that she twisted and untwisted in her lap.

The man had been told by his foreman to arrive at half past ten, but by Darcy's timepiece, it was only twenty minutes past the hour when footsteps were heard in the hall.

Elizabeth raised her head, looking at the door just as it was opened by a servant.

A man appeared in the doorway. He was short in stature and of a slight build, with fair hair and blue eyes that settled on Elizabeth with an indefinable expression. Darcy had his eyes trained on Elizabeth's face and saw the colour drain from her cheeks as her mouth dropped open wordlessly.

For a moment, the three of them were caught in a moment unbound by time. No one spoke. The momentousness of the occasion was too deeply felt to be marred by words.

The man's face broke into a wide, delighted smile, and he crossed the room in a trice. With a whoop, he pulled Elizabeth to her feet and into his arms, where he spun her around in a circle before kissing her soundly on the lips. "Elizabeth! My darling wife! You found me!"

THERE WAS MUCH TO DO AFTER THE STARTLING REUNION WITH HENRY. Plans needed to be made, the owner and the foreman of the mine were met with, and arrangements for the funds and personal effects Henry had accumulated were settled. Elizabeth returned to the inn with the intent of sending letters to their relations, informing them of the shocking news, but she found herself unequal to the task. She penned one short note to Lady Matlock and another to the housekeeper at Towton Hall and then sat in her chair, staring at the most hideous wall covering she had ever seen. It soothed her, this ugly paper of jonquil and fawn. It suited her mood completely.

Henry came to her once everything was settled. Seeing him enter, she smiled, but it must not have appeared genuine, for he gave her a look of concern. He sat next to her on the settee in front of the fire.

"I cannot believe you are alive," she told him. "It is almost too much to be comprehended. You must tell me everything that has happened to you these three years past."

"Elizabeth," he said kindly, "please know that I do not expect things between us to be exactly as they were."

His gentleness brought a tear to her eye. "Henry, I am overjoyed that you are alive. I never even imagined it possible. It is shocking."

"I know." He smiled gently and caressed her cheek with the backs of his fingers. "We shall take our time with this. We must be reacquainted. I am happy that we are reunited, but I do know you have made a new life. You mourned me, and you fell in love with another."

She felt her cheeks becoming wet. "It is unfair. I grieved for you, I longed for you for years. It seems I am not pleased, but I assure you, I am, truly I am."

He embraced her, putting his lips briefly to the top of her head. "One step at a time, dearest girl. We shall find our way again."

And she smiled at him in response but with traitorous thoughts in her mind. *One step with you is a step away from Fitzwilliam. How can I withstand such pain, much less inflict it upon myself?*

THE DAYS FOLLOWING THE DISCOVERY OF HENRY WARREN, EARL OF Courtenay, among the miners in Kidsgrove were nothing short of agony.

Darcy wondered that neither he nor Elizabeth had given any thought to how awkward and discomfiting travel arrangements could be when a woman is thought to be married to two men. It was the first step of separation: returning to the inn to find that his man had already altered the accommodations by putting him in a room best suited for an unmarried man travelling alone while the rooms he had occupied with his wife were given over to Lord and Lady Courtenay.

The first night was the worst. Darcy lay in his bed torturing himself by wondering whether Courtenay was even then exercising his rights as a husband with Elizabeth. He cursed himself for having been so foolish as to end his own relations with her. He should have lain with her every hour of every day, and any consequence be damned.

The past days had taught him that he could not bear to sleep without her, and this night only heightened the effect. He missed the sound of her breathing and the feel of her feet, always cold, burrowing beneath his legs. He longed to wake to the caress of a strand of her hair across his face, her scent in his nose.

Darcy supposed he must be in some sort of shocked state for he was entirely unable to cry or rage or do anything at all but move slug-gishly about his routine, succumbing to his valet's hands in order to complete his morning ablutions. He stared into the mirror after he had been shaved, seeing nothing but the hollows of his pale face and the dark emptiness in his eyes.

How stupid that he had never imagined what must follow if Henry was found alive. Was there nothing more to do, no ceremony, no rite or ritual involved in the loss of a beloved wife to another? Elizabeth was transferred to Henry as any piece of property might be. She was correct in calling herself Netherfield Park, for it was just that easy: one minute, Darcy's; and the next, sole property of Lord Courtenay.

A breakfast spread had been made in a private sitting room of the inn, and Darcy went to it, not knowing whether he could bear seeing Courtenay and Elizabeth together. In his mind's eye, she would be laughing and happy, filled with delight after a night of loving reunion, though the more rational being in him knew it could not be this way for her. For her, as for him, there was devastation.

No matter the misery associated with seeing her on the arm of another man, he could not deny it. He considered making arrangements to return home by post or hiring a private chaise—but he could not. He was not yet ready to surrender; he needed the pain of this defeat. She belonged to another man, not to him, and there was nothing for it but heartrending acceptance.

Lord Courtenay sat at his breakfast, still wearing his labourer's raiment. Darcy took a seat at the table across from him.

"Sir, I cannot think your apparel is to your liking. May I loan you some clothing until we have returned to London?"

Courtenay's smile appeared forced as he shrugged. "It does not bother me, and the clothing of a labourer is far more easy than a gentleman's apparel. It will do until we are home."

Darcy nodded.

For a few moments, the only sound was that of forks hitting plates and cups clattering on saucers.

Darcy broke the silence. "May I say something?"

"Yes, of course."

Darcy dismissed the footman who attended them, bidding him to close the door. Darcy put his fork down and leaned back in his seat, inhaling deeply. Speaking quietly, he said, "If you divorce her, I shall marry her in a trice. She will not suffer in shame."

"You would marry a woman so disgraced?" Courtenay raised his eyebrows in surprise.

"My name is important to me, as is my heritage, but neither of them can have any claim on my heart as she does. She is the most important thing in the world to me, and I would have her at any cost."

A sad expression crossed his lordship's face. "You love her. This was not, for you, about her fortune."

"I love her with all of my heart and soul and with every fibre of my being. Her fortune is nothing to me; take every farthing of it back. I loved her when I knew her as nothing more than Miss Elizabeth Bennet, a girl of little consequence from an entailed country estate. I am not in need of money; it is my heart that I truly want."

Courtenay was silent, absently playing with his fork. His eyes were trained on the cloth covering the table, and his mouth was turned down. "You love her, so you will understand me when I say this to you. Three years—three long years—I have been without her. I despaired of seeing her again. I longed for her, and I dreamt of her. There were nights when the hope that I might one day see her again was all that kept me from ending my life.

"I have never felt such pity and remorse for a man as I do you. I have lived this heartbreak and would wish it on no one. As you do, I too love her. I have waited to be with her for three exceedingly long, horrible years." He gave Darcy a compassionate, pitying look. "I am so very sorry."

Darcy released a breath of anguish, closing his eyes for a moment as he gained his composure. With a hard, painful swallow, he said roughly, "Please be certain to make her happy. I beseech you to adore her. You have reclaimed your treasure—cherish it every day."

"I shall," Courtenay agreed softly. "You have my word."

TWENTY-TWO

There are a thousand little intimacies of a marriage, small actions that when summed together describe the belonging of one person to another. For Darcy, the loss of these intimacies proved excruciatingly painful, and over the days during their return to London, it was a loss felt many times over.

It began that morning in the breakfast room when Courtenay rose and said nonchalantly, "I shall see whether Elizabeth is prepared to be off." It required great restraint on Darcy's part to refrain from saying that it was his duty, not Courtenay's, to determine Elizabeth's readiness.

There were further examples as the first day of their travel wore on. It was Courtenay who handed her into the carriage and reached over to adjust the rug on her lap. It was Courtenay who complimented her gown and leaned into her to point out some item of interest in the passing landscape. Darcy watched it all silently and miserably, feeling acutely the pain of separation from his wife.

Elizabeth appeared to be in a stupor. She said little and scarcely looked at either man as the carriage moved on.

Courtenay did all he could to ease the awkwardness of their journey. He regaled them with stories of the places he had been and the things he had done in the past three years, and he asked question after question about his son though Elizabeth did not respond with much vigour.

The second day of travel was no better than the first, and soon Darcy could do nothing but yearn for the interminable journey to end. When they stopped at another indescribable inn within the confines of some little village Darcy would hate forever, Elizabeth sent word that she must see him, asking him to meet her in a sitting room designated for their party. He went to her at once.

She stood by a window with her back to the door, looking frail and despondent. She turned as he entered and rushed into his arms. He felt her tears immediately soak his chest as the sobs ripped out of her.

"I cannot..." she gasped, "I simply cannot...I am no longer married to him. Please think of something, some way—"

"Shhh." Darcy pressed his lips together tightly, his eyes screwed shut to prevent the escape of emotion welling within him. They had both put on an excellent face these two days, as polite and amiable as anyone could be, but their pretence was now cracked wide open, spewing out the truth indiscriminately.

"Do something!" Her voice sounded scared and wildly sad. "Challenge him or...or...we can run away, now, we will go...somewhere, anywhere, please."

He swallowed hard as she sobbed into his waistcoat. "Just remember that you love him and he loves you. You, him, your son... you are a family. You will learn to love him again."

"Never!" She shook her head violently. "I do not want to. I cannot do it!" She raised her tear-stained face, painfully beseeching, entreating him, "Please—is there not some way?"

He traced the path of a tear on her cheek. "I begged him to divorce you so that I might marry you, but he loves you, and he could not do it. In any case, that would not do; he would get Henry."

She inhaled, a deep shuddering breath.

"He does love you, Elizabeth, and I know somewhere in you is your love for him."

"I am married to you," she insisted. "My heart, my mind, and my soul are entwined in yours. To untangle that will kill me."

He cupped her face in his hands. "This pain is unlike anything I ever have known, but there is no escape. You are married to him, not to me."

Her breaths came quickly as she shut her eyes, an expression of pain furrowing her brow. "How selfish I am to think only of my own unhappiness," she choked. "You suffer as much as I! Oh, how you must hate the day you ever came into Hertfordshire and saw me!"

"I would not trade it for anything. The time I have had with you is worth any pain I must bear."

"For me too," she whispered and clung to him. He relinquished the appearance of stoicism and let his tears fall into her hair as they stood together, pained and desolate.

They remained for some time until, gingerly, they pulled apart, allowing only their hands to touch. Elizabeth raised her eyes to his, her futility and desperation readily evident.

"Tell me in all truth: have we any hope? Any at all?"

Darcy had spent enough hours twisting and turning their dilemma to know for certain that there was no recourse, nothing that would immediately release them. He slowly shook his head. "You are Lady Courtenay, and I cannot save you from that."

They sat for several minutes until Elizabeth had regained her equanimity and he was confident that he, too, appeared as he ought. With a faint smile, she asked him, "If he would divorce me, would you truly marry me?"

"Lord, yes," he answered quickly. "That scarcely requires even a moment's contemplation."

"How different you are." She looked at him with fondness and admiration in her eyes. "Your character is not much like the man who left Hertfordshire determined not to see me again because I lacked consequence."

"That man did not know what it was to love you. That man did not understand that he needed you as much as he needed water to drink and air to breathe, and that man did not understand—" He choked, the feeling of their words affecting him too deeply to remain calm.

This is real—it is going to occur. For all of his purported understanding of the situation, now he knew it in full. This journey would end, and with it, Mrs Elizabeth Darcy would be no more. He would surrender all claims to her. He would watch her walk away, knowing he was nothing to her and never could be anything to her, and he would spend the remaining days of his life watching as she carried on as Lady Courtenay. His breath came quickly, jaggedly, as the heinous reality of it set upon him, and he could not contain his grief.

"Oh, Elizabeth!" He clutched her, pulling her tight. "I do not think

I can do this." He gasped out the words and buried his face in her hair, feeling a large, painful lump of agony caught in his throat. "I cannot let you go, I just cannot. Heaven help me."

He fought his emotion, not wanting to hurt her further. He knew not how long he suppressed his anguish, but he could bear no more and rose quickly, pulling away and turning his back to her, unable to endure the agony of seeing her.

His voice thick, he said, "I shall hire a carriage to return to London. I cannot...I am sorry." He moved quickly to depart the room but stopped in the doorway, his back to her.

"I love you. I love you so much. Forgive me."

ELIZABETH KNEW THAT WHAT HAD OCCURRED IN THE SITTING ROOM had been their goodbye, and the following morning, she was not surprised to learn that he had departed the inn before dawn, leaving her a letter. She contemplated it for several minutes before gaining sufficient courage to open it.

> *My Dearest, Loveliest Elizabeth:*
>
> *I take the liberty of addressing you as such for this one last time, though I shall always think of you this way. For when we meet, and I say your proper name as I must, in my mind you will always be this: my Elizabeth, my own, and my love. Although our marriage was far too brief, you have given me more felicity than I should have ever dared to imagine, and I shall treasure that bit of you for always.*
>
> *My mind cannot begin to understand the contrariety of emotion within you now, but I do hope—truly I do—that therein resides some happy feeling for a reunion with the man who holds the exalted title of your first love, as well as the father of your dear son. I beseech you to feel that happiness, to stir up your joy so that your regret for our life can be overcome. I wish for you to enjoy nothing less than exquisite felicity. I beg you to do all in your power to reach that state.*
>
> *I know not how your husband will permit you to meet me in the future, but should we be allowed to call ourselves friends, let it always be with a fond remembrance for what was. I shall never cease loving you, nor shall I ever forget the joys we have shared. I can never, in truth, be your husband, but despite that, the vows I made to you on that blessed day will be forever upheld.*

I do not pretend to be anything short of devastated, nor would I wish to show you a disguise. I would do anything in my power to make this different, but as I cannot, I shall do my best to console myself and carry on as I must. I dearly hope you will do the same, finding all the happiness that you so richly deserve.

Someday, when he is old enough to understand, please tell little Henry that I have loved him, and I shall always love him as much as any father could love their child.

I shall only add, God bless you. Fitzwilliam

She admired him for his fortitude in making the break between them. He would go on and so must she, and if her happiness could be nothing more than a disguise, then so be it. She would practise joy as she had practised riding, speaking French, and playing the pianoforte, and in time, it would become easier. She and Henry would discover each other once again.

So resolved, Elizabeth swallowed the tears that threatened, raised her chin, and went forth to meet her husband.

IN RETROSPECT, ELIZABETH COULD NOT SAY CLEARLY WHAT transpired throughout the remainder of their journey back to London. Part of her mind occupied itself in presenting an appropriate face to Henry. She related more about their son and her time in Hertfordshire, and he told of his illness, his recovery, and his constant fear for Elizabeth's safety.

"I had so little understanding of what had occurred outside of Kidsgrove," he explained. "News from London was scarce, and I knew not whether the situation there had quieted."

He did not, Elizabeth discovered, realise that his brother had been hanged. Fortunately, Henry readily apprehended what his brother's end had been and did not require much explanation. Nevertheless, the telling of it cast an additional shadow of sorrow over the carriage. "It is strange. No matter what he has done to me and to his country, he is, yet, my brother—my twin brother; we are halves of a whole. His passing must affect me."

Entering Towton Hall on her husband's arm was eerily and disquietingly reminiscent of coming there as his bride. It was evidently so for Henry too as his homecoming recovered his spirits a bit.

The servants were pleased to see him, having received an express from Elizabeth informing them of the extraordinary series of events that had happened and would alter the household as they knew it. They had all done their best to ready the house, but given the short notice, it could not be perfect. Henry was delighted, however, pronouncing that it looked as though he had left but a day ago and congratulating them on their industry.

Elizabeth was thrilled with an express that had arrived just that day, proclaiming her an aunt. Her sister had given birth to Mr Bingley's son. All were healthy and well and enjoying the company of Mrs Bennet, who had arrived in December and had no imminent plans for departure.

She showed it to Henry, remarking lightly, "I suppose it was one of the happy circumstances of my situation while increasing that my mother was unable to attend me for Henry's birth."

"Would she not have been of use to you?" Henry asked her.

Elizabeth raised an eyebrow, certain he was making a joke. "My mother?"

Henry looked oddly confused. "No, I beg your pardon...I do not... you were happy she was not there?"

Elizabeth forced a light laugh. "My dear, you must have lost the part of your memory that concerns my mother! No, I assure you, she would not have been of any use at all. She would have made us all nervous but require assistance for her nerves. Once she had recovered, she would have found any number of things that I did incorrectly, both in delivering your son and in all of my actions thereafter. You will see when you meet her again, and you will wonder that you could have forgotten."

Henry joined her in her laughter and no more was said of the matter.

As she prepared for bed not more than an hour later, she wondered whether she should expect his visit.

Henry had shown no inclination to come to her in the brief time they had been reunited, a forbearance in which she took great relief. She did not know how she could honour her marital obligations with a man with whom she felt so unattached. At this juncture, she knew she must love him far more than she felt. She was prepared to bear her wifely duty with equanimity, but she hoped her resolve would not be tested this particular night.

Rather than wondering, she decided to speak to him about it. Raising her courage, she knocked gently upon his door. He opened it quickly. "Elizabeth?"

"Would you join me for a moment in the sitting room?" He nodded and followed her.

They sat, and she folded her hands carefully on her lap, not meeting his eyes. "I wanted to discuss your expectations."

"My expectations?" He looked bewildered.

"It is difficult for me to know how we must go on. I am ever fearful that I offend you by my reserve, yet I feel singularly incapable of offering more to you, especially in the...more particular aspects of marriage."

He looked relieved. "Pray, do not make yourself uneasy. I do not expect us to act as though nothing has transpired. As for our conjugal relationship"—he paused, looking awkward—"be assured that I am content to take our time. In fact, I think it might be rather prudent if we abstained for several months."

"Several months?" It sounded agreeable, but she could not deny that she was surprised by his preference for it.

He spoke carefully, his eyes averted. "We should wait until we are certain you do not carry Darcy's child. I should not like to look at a child and wonder whether it was mine."

"Oh!" Elizabeth blushed. "Of course."

"I believe you loved him, did you not?"

Elizabeth averted her eyes quickly, unable to meet his gaze. "Yes, I...I did. I do, still."

"I believe you will for some time."

Elizabeth felt a sob within her throat and could not answer him. *How can I admit that I had forsaken him for another man? It will break his heart.*

"Do not be ashamed," he said gently. "I wished, oh, how I wished that you were happy, wherever you were and whatever you did."

A tear rolled down her cheek. "I mourned you, Henry, I did. I was afraid and scared and sad. My life was cold and grey, and he made it full of life again. He brought back parts of me I had not truly realised were missing."

Henry spoke woodenly. "I am glad to hear it." After a short pause, he added, "Darcy is a good man. I am grieved for him. I see how he loved you, and I know he must suffer."

Elizabeth felt a pain cross her chest at the mention of Darcy's grief.

Henry picked up her hand, and kissed it. "I do not anticipate that things will be immediately as they were. You will take your time to become accustomed to me again, and I shall learn to be a husband and an estate master again, as well as how to be a father. We shall find our way, my dear."

"Thank you," Elizabeth replied, feeling the tears threatening once again. Henry bowed before going back to his bedchamber, and she fled, tossing herself onto her bed and allowing the tears to flow while being careful not to sob too loudly.

I do not want to. I have no wish to stop loving Darcy. The refrain repeated itself all night long.

LADY MATLOCK ARRIVED WITH YOUNG HENRY AND HIS NURSEMAID early the next morning. It moved Elizabeth to see how deeply affected Henry was by the appearance of his son, reaching for him and cuddling him close, pronouncing him as fine a boy as ever there was and beaming broadly at him. Little Henry was good tempered as always, young enough to readily accept a new person in his life whom he must call Father.

Lady Matlock was reserved as they related the miracle of Henry's return, his time in Kidsgrove, and the journey back to London. When the story was finished, Henry excused himself, leaving the ladies to chat.

When the door closed behind him, Lady Matlock showed her true feeling to Elizabeth, a tear hovering in her eye. "Lady Courtenay, Mrs Darcy, Niece…I scarcely even know what to call you much less what to say to you."

"I shall set a new fashion." Elizabeth smiled wanly, addressing only the first point, "I shall ask whosoever I meet—man, woman, child, servant, or peer—to call me Elizabeth. It is the only name I can be certain to always claim as my own."

Lady Matlock sighed. "I am pleased to see your humour is at least somewhat present."

"If I do not laugh, I should cry all day. That I do not wish for. After all, how distressing it must be to my husband to have the joy of our reunion entirely eclipsed by my sorrow in parting from another man."

"He seems to bear it well."

"His forbearance is astonishing," Elizabeth admitted. "He has been patient and kind. He has told me I must take my time to become accustomed to being his wife again; he makes no demands of me."

Lady Matlock touched her finger to the edge of her eyes to remove a tear. "This is extraordinary. I am so grieved for you and for Darcy."

"How is he?"

Lady Matlock shrugged, replying, "I shall call upon him after this if he will see me, but I do not anticipate seeing him well. I suppose, for both of you, there will be nothing but time to answer for this."

Elizabeth went to the window, gazing out on a light snow that had begun to fall. "I suppose you are correct. In any case, what can be done? I am married to Henry and was never, despite all evidence to the contrary, married to Darcy." She slowly returned to the settee. "But married to him or not, I love him, and that love will always be a part of me."

Quietly, in a voice that was almost too low for Lady Matlock to hear, she added, "What if I cannot do this? I do not, in truth, want to do it, yet I must."

"Do what, my dear?"

Elizabeth looked at the piece of cake on a small plate before her, taking her fork and mashing it into pieces. "The love Henry and I had before was so...it was like a novel, all pounding hearts and pretty words. What if there is nothing else? What if that fades and we are left with nothing?"

"Marriage always requires effort, even in the usual circumstances."

Elizabeth nodded, not looking at the woman she still wished to call her aunt. "I am afraid I do not love him enough—particularly now with a heart divided."

"You must try to love him, and even if you do not, you must put on a good face. He is your husband. Love him or not, he is yours, but it will be best if you can love him again."

"I know," Elizabeth said despondently. "I shall do my best. How tired I am of forcing my sensibilities to align with my duty!"

"One day at a time, my dear girl. It will get easier." Elizabeth only heaved a sigh in response.

When Lady Matlock had departed, Elizabeth undertook a task she had been avoiding: notifying her parents and sisters of all that transpired. They had known of Wickham's accusations, but Elizabeth had been careful to understate the possibility that Lord Courtenay remained alive. Their shock would surely be great, and she was relieved she would not witness it.

Her message to them all, including Jane, was simple: Henry had been found alive, and she had returned to her duty as his wife and the mother of the future earl. She made no mention of the devastation that resided within her, or the daily thoughts she had of begging Darcy to permit her to be his mistress. She despised the necessity of sending such a note to Jane and could only hope Mrs Bennet would have the sense to consider Jane's delicate state as a new mother in relaying the news.

HENRY CAME TO HER A SHORT WHILE LATER, AND SHE SUMMONED HER best effort to appear kindly to him. "My dear, would you walk with me?"

Elizabeth glanced dubiously at the window. "Did it not snow earlier?"

"Now, that is a change indeed! The Elizabeth I know would not shy away from a walk in any weather! In fact, I do recall a certain drenching rain in Bath…"

Elizabeth forced herself to laugh. "Oh, of all memories that should preferably have been lost! No, my character is not so much changed. I still enjoy a walk above all else. Let me send for my things."

Suitably clothed, they were in the park minutes later, the snow around them lending a wintry hush to the brisk air. Henry offered Elizabeth his arm, and she took it, walking with him in silence for several minutes.

She glanced over to see him watching her and offered a smile. "An excellent idea. I am glad you suggested it."

He smiled at her. "I want to make you happy, Elizabeth. This is but a small way that I can do so."

"Thank you." She turned her gaze to the path in front of her for a moment. They were near the area where she and Darcy had decided to marry. She determinedly did not look that way.

He cleared his throat gently. "I think we might expect a good bit of talk about all of this. It is quite a sensation."

"Mm," she agreed absently.

"I must admit, my inclination is to shy away from it."

"You have always met parties with such eager anticipation."

"Oh, the parties, certainly. The gossip..." He sighed. "I dread having to speak of it over and over again, yet I fear we must. I have thought much on this, and I think the best way for us to overcome it is to meet it head on."

"What do you mean?"

"We shall attend as many parties and engagements as we reasonably can. Let everyone see that we are together and happy, tell our story to all who wish to hear it—let them have their fill, so to speak."

It sounded exhausting. "If you think it best."

Henry stopped, taking her hands in his. "The story is too extraordinary to avoid notice, and if the facts are not made plain, I fear the conjecture could go on for months. If we tell the tale ourselves, there can be nothing left to debate or discuss, and after a period of conversation—which, I do not fool myself, will certainly be fatiguing—it will die."

"I see your reasoning." Elizabeth thought she would well like it when her life was no longer a subject of interest to the *ton*.

"Instead of a full Season, perhaps we could have an extended Easter. We shall remain in town until mid-April and then go back to Warrington. Maybe we shall stay in Warrington thereafter. Will that suit you?"

Warrington. Not Pemberley, not Derbyshire, and not Darcy—which is, of course, how it must be. The thought gave her a deep pang of loss. She did not see him now, but it was some comfort to think they were in the same town. "Yes, that suits me very well."

WITHIN THE NEXT DAYS, THE POST BECAME AN UNWELCOME EVENT AS letters from family, friends, and those who fancied themselves as such poured in.

She was unsurprised when her aunt and uncle Gardiner called immediately after receiving her note.

Her intimacy with the Gardiners had suffered a bit during the first months of her marriage to Darcy. It was a neglect in which they delighted, however, for it portended the return of their beloved niece to happiness in marriage. A new bride in love should forget her relations, no matter how dear, for her every thought and moment should be dedicated to her new husband.

Understandable as it was, it left them rather rudely shocked by the announcement that Lord Courtenay had returned. Elizabeth had not seen fit to tell them that such a thing was a possibility.

Henry received them with Elizabeth, and there was much exclaiming and well wishing. Afterwards, he excused himself to attend to some business in his study. When the door closed behind him, the Gardiners looked at Elizabeth in shock.

Sir Edward spoke first. "Elizabeth, I have never been so stunned in all of my life. I had to read your note four times to be sure it was not some joke."

She gave him a weak smile in an attempt to stave off tears. "No, it is certainly not a joke."

She explained the entire situation: that George Wickham, in gaol for treason (she saw no reason to blacken Georgiana's reputation), had denied killing Lord Courtenay with enough credibility to warrant investigation. They had investigated, and they had found, at the end of their searches, Henry.

"So shocking," said Lady Gardiner. "But, what of Darcy? Surely, you cannot simply resume your marriage with one man when you had married another?"

"A married person cannot be lawfully wed," Elizabeth explained wearily. "My marriage to Darcy was never lawful. I am a bigamist, I suppose, though it will be pardoned due to the circumstances, or so my husband assures me."

Her eyes were drawn to her handkerchief twisting in her hands. "I am delighted to find Henry alive and well," she said listlessly. "I must accustom myself to the change."

"So you will," Lady Gardiner reassured her, her own eyes worried and sad. "I have no doubt of it. But I am grieved for poor Mr Darcy. How he must suffer, particularly as—"

"Pray, excuse me." Elizabeth found herself suddenly standing, her voice high and shrill even in her own ears. "I find myself…a headache.

I have a headache, excuse me." She quit the room, and the Gardiners were left to see themselves out.

THE COURTENAYS QUICKLY AMASSED A LARGE PILE OF REQUESTS TO drink tea, dine, dance, and play cards. Elizabeth grew tired just looking at them and used Henry's secretary, a newly hired man, to sort through them.

The talk, as they had expected, was rampant. Everywhere they went, they were a subject of interest with whispers abounding and people of all ranks jostling for position within their circle. Inevitably, there were those who wished to be scandalised and speculate on her marriage and marital relations with Darcy, but for the most part, people had an extraordinary degree of pity for them all.

Elizabeth tried her best to be accepting of the situation, maintaining her dignity at all costs. But throughout, all she could think of was Darcy.

Thinking back to their time at Pemberley, she almost wondered whether it had truly happened. Such an idyll! Was it real? Or was it all some dream—some magical, fantastic dream—of a man whom I once believed I hated?

It was challenging to think of Darcy nearly incessantly yet to act for all the world as though her mind and her attention were focused solely on Henry. She became a proficient, however, with one part of her thoughts greedily caressing her memories of Darcy while the other asked Henry, "Is the tea to your liking, dear? Shall we go to the Millers' dinner? What did Lord Bourne say of Lady Bourne's health—is she at last recovered?"

Her only hope, her dearest wish, was that it would become easier with time, but as January was replaced by the mizzling rain and fog of February, that hope grew increasingly distant, and she contemplated the reality that she would forever mourn Darcy.

"My dear, you are stunning."

Elizabeth startled, having fallen into one of her trance-like stupors, sitting and staring into the mirror over her vanity. She saw Henry in the reflection, quite well in looks himself, which prompted the ideal response. "As do you, my husband. Is that a new suit?"

Henry wore a finely made suit of the latest fashion, and his cravat had been tied with exquisite care into a complicated knot. Seeing it brought to mind the time she and Darcy had been in such haste that she attempted to undo his cravat herself, somehow managing to make it tighter. Darcy pretended he was strangling, gasping for air, and she was so alarmed until he laughed...

She giggled thinking of it, and Henry's voice recalled her to the present. "Is something amusing, my dear?" He was looking over his attire as if something would be found amiss, and she blushed guiltily.

"No, I only was thinking of...of...oh, just an amusing little on dit I heard of Mrs Miller once."

"Oh?" Henry assisted her in rising from her vanity, and they went to the front of the house where their carriage awaited them.

Elizabeth frantically searched her mind for something amusing about Mrs Miller. "It is a dull thing really. Just that she..." Her mind went blank, and she could not recall so much as one even faintly amusing story about Mrs Miller or anyone else.

Henry was staring at her in confusion, so she explained, "It is...in truth, I just recalled, it was not about Mrs Miller but someone else entirely."

"I see." Henry gave her an odd look.

Nothing else was said as they entered the carriage and settled themselves. As he always had, Henry awaited the motion of the carriage to move beside her, tucking the blanket around them, his actions familiar and soothing. As he could not see her face, Elizabeth felt compelled to confess.

"I was thinking of my...time with Mr Darcy. I saw how nicely your cravat was arranged and it brought to my mind a time that I had tried to help him remove his cravat and made a right mess of it. He pretended he was choking and scared me out of my wits. It made me laugh to recall it."

There was a prolonged pause.

"Forgive me," she ventured after a time. "I am trying to forget these things—"

Henry shook his head, a pained look on his face. "I am glad you have fond memories of him and that he made you happy. I could not wish less for you, but I shall not deny that it is difficult knowing your heart is divided."

Elizabeth did not know what to say. She could not contradict what they both knew was true. She turned to find him staring at her intently.

"I can only hope that one day you will once again be mine and mine alone," he said.

She smiled uncertainly as he took her chin in his hand. The kiss began gently but grew more passionate as he pulled her to him, deepening the kiss and caressing her. A sense of panic grew even as her mind counselled her to remain calm. This was as it must be, and she was his wife and could not rightly deny him the physical expression of her love.

When the carriage stopped, Elizabeth nearly fainted with relief, hurriedly righting her clothing as Henry whispered, "I love you," and kissed her cheek once more.

The door opened, and Henry hopped out, turning to Elizabeth to assist her down. "By the by," he said, his voice cheerful, "I do believe Darcy will be here tonight."

TWENTY-THREE

LONDON, FEBRUARY 1813

S ince his return to London, Darcy congratulated himself on managing to maintain some semblance of dignity, despite the fact that he felt very much as if he had been eviscerated.

On the day of his arrival, he found an express awaiting him; Mrs Bingley had given her husband a son, and they called him William. The note joyously proclaimed that he had a nephew, and he morosely reflected that it was one more thing that he had lost in all of this: the right to claim a family tie to the Bingleys.

All of his household were naturally curious as to why Mrs Darcy had not returned with him and why he floated around the house like a darkened spectre. He called Mr and Mrs Hobbs into his study on the second day of his return to tell them the news.

They stood before him nervously as he cleared his throat. "Mr Hobbs, Mrs Hobbs, there has been some…unfortunate…news. Mrs Darcy is not… she is not Mrs Darcy. As you know, she was believed to be a widow since August of 1809. Her hus—" His voice broke on the word. "Lord Courtenay was found alive in Kidsgrove, and he has returned to his former life, which includes Mrs…Eliz…her."

His two most senior servants stood before him in shocked silence, completely still with their mouths agape.

After gaining his composure, Darcy added, "Our marriage is thus to be annulled. That is to say, it is annulled. It never was, after all, a legal marriage."

Mrs Hobbs's shock caused her to behave out of turn though Darcy would never censure her for it. Faintly, she questioned, "But...little Henry...what about..."

"Henry is not my son. He belongs to his father. Please see that his things are sent to Towton Hall at once." These words caused him to feel his emotions were dangerously close to overcoming him, and he hurriedly said, "That is all. You may go."

They did not move.

"Please go," he whispered fiercely, certain he would lose his composure. They hastily bowed and left but not before he saw Mrs Hobbs dabbing a tear from her eye. It would not be the last time he witnessed a servant mourning the loss of not only Mrs Darcy but little Henry, who had captivated the entire household during his short time in residence.

On Darcy's third day back, an excessively remorseful and obsequious retinue of servants accompanied Elizabeth's maid to Darcy's house, where they efficiently removed her personal effects, and Henry's, from her chambers and the nursery. Darcy knew they had come, of course, and despite the pain it caused him, he could not stay away.

He entered Elizabeth's bedchamber, and all the servants immediately stopped, looking at him uncertainly. "Please carry on," he told them, and hesitantly, they did. Gowns were packed into trunks, books were boxed, and items from her vanity were carefully wrapped. He sat on her bed and watched in silent agony as all trace of her was removed from the room.

A manservant named Redmond came to him to tell him they were finished. Darcy stopped him.

"Lady Courtenay, is she...she is well?"

Redmond froze in confusion, not wishing to act beyond his station, yet utterly undone by the expression on Darcy's face. He replied tentatively, "As well as can be expected, sir."

Darcy did not know what he had imagined he might hear but was relieved to know even that small bit.

There is nothing quite as desolate as a room abandoned by its owner. The hollow ache of it matched the one in Darcy's gut as he entered her dressing room where her scent still lingered. He opened the empty closet with its bare shelves, and he sat at the vanity whereupon no perfumes, powder, or jewellery remained, only a blank surface.

Mrs Hobbs and a young chambermaid entered unexpectedly, both surprised to see him. "Oh! I beg your pardon, sir."

He nodded, and they turned to depart. In a low voice, Mrs Hobbs said, "When the master has left, remove the bed linens—"

"No," he called after them. "Pray, do not."

Mrs Hobbs paused, her face again surprised. "Sir?"

"Leave this room just as it is—no alteration. In fact, no one is to enter it without my permission."

Mrs Hobbs stared at him, her countenance blank, and then curtseyed. "As you wish, sir."

THE REMAINING DAYS OF THE FIRST FORTNIGHT WITHOUT HER WERE passed in a dark despair. Darcy drank often and much. Thinking of how he might kill himself became his most diverting occupation, followed closely by reliving his memories of their short time together. He knew not how he might go on with the gaping wound of loneliness in his chest.

The essence of the problem was that there was simply nothing he could do for the situation. He had never before been faced with a challenge for which some action could not be taken. He could neither buy anything nor persuade anyone, work at something nor study a topic, take himself away from his pain nor have the pain removed. He did not even have the comfort of despising someone. There was no one to despise, not even himself, for all had acted with honour and integrity and done the best they could with the hand they had been dealt. It was nothing more than a circumstance beyond anyone's control, and that made it completely insupportable.

After leaving him to wallow about in his despair for a fortnight, his cousins came for him as he had suspected they eventually would.

"Have you left your house at all, Darcy?" Fitzwilliam's face bore a look of vexing kindliness.

"What do you think—that I sit here all day pining for her?" he snapped.

"That is precisely what I think," Saye replied, tousling Darcy's hair as he walked by and then further compounding his sin by not even looking to see the angry scowl Darcy gave him. "Let us go have exercise—a visit to Jackson's perhaps?"

The idea of punching something was enormously appealing to Darcy, and he agreed at once.

Jackson's was crowded with young gentlemen who were feeling the effects of too much time indoors, resulting from the poor weather in London of late. After changing into the appropriate attire, Darcy sparred with Saye while Fitzwilliam partnered with another colonel from a different regiment.

It was relieving to engage in sweat and exertion, to punch and be punched, and to feel oneself grow weary from the task. Darcy thought he might frequent Jackson's parlour daily to enjoy the respite from thoughts of Elizabeth and the all-too-brief time he was able to call her his own. Sweat poured from him, and he wished it might cleanse away all his troubles and cares.

When they had finished, he accompanied his cousins to their club where they sat over tea, speaking of future engagements and the like. Darcy decided he would attend the theatre soon. There was a play he wished to see, and he was beginning to recognise that his days would pass more quickly if he kept himself busy.

As they rose to return to their homes, Saye remarked, "I question why Courtenay did not come back sooner."

"I have wondered that too," Fitzwilliam agreed.

"He likely wished to see his killer put to death before he appeared," Darcy replied, tiredly. "Wickham was a bit player, but Courtenay did not know that. He did not know who his brother's friends were."

"Wickham might have gone on for several months before being apprehended, though, or perhaps even indefinitely. Would he have remained a miner?"

Darcy shrugged. "I suppose you will have to ask him that."

In the late autumn, Darcy had sent Georgiana to Rosings to spend time with Lady Catherine while they sorted out the mess to which she had lent her hand. He wrote to her now to bid her return. The house was far too empty and desolate without someone to talk to, and he desired her company even as much as he did not wish to punish her by requiring her to linger with Lady Catherine longer than necessary.

The Georgiana who returned was a far different Georgiana than he had sent to Kent.

Her time at Rosings had been pleasant enough. Lady Catherine, although tending to be overbearing and officious with a never-ending stream of commentary and advice, had good intentions. Her daughter had been absent for almost a year, and she was pleased to devote herself to restoring her niece's good character. She had done so surprisingly judiciously and with the assistance of Mrs Collins who, having a sister in her teens, understood the sensibilities of a young girl.

Georgiana felt her errors keenly and was appalled by what her introduction of George Wickham into their lives had ultimately wrought. She believed her brother must despise her, and she was sure Elizabeth hoped never to see her face again. As such, she was timid and respectful, speaking and eating little in her first days back in her brother's home.

A week after her return, Darcy went to her in the music room.

"Georgiana, I am glad you are home."

"Thank you, Brother."

He sat next to her and took her hand in his. "I have spoken harshly to you on this subject. I was angry and wished for someone to be held accountable, but I do realise that the truth would have become known at some time. In some manner, you might have done us a bit of a favour by bringing it to light before there were children or other further complications."

"Do you truly think this was inevitable?"

"I do," he acknowledged. "What man would not wish to reclaim his wife and family? I would in a trice. If there was anything that could bring her back to me, I would not hesitate."

Taking advantage of his uncharacteristically talkative mood, Georgiana asked, "Is there anything to be done to that end?"

"Nothing." He shook his head. "Only a divorce, I suppose, and Lord Courtenay does not want that." He sighed. "He loves her, and she loves him."

"She loves you," Georgiana told him quietly.

"She does," he agreed. "Unfortunately, it does her no good. She cannot leave him. Her heart was always divided, but legally, she is his. It will be a reality I shall know myself one day. I shall have to marry another, knowing I love Elizabeth."

"That sounds very bleak."

He shrugged. "It is my duty. I must produce an heir. I had my solicitor examine the entail to see whether your son might inherit, but alas, it must be mine."

"Will you seek to marry again soon?"

"I will not." Darcy spoke definitively, disgust rising in him. "Someday, but not soon, I assure you."

I<small>T WAS REMINISCENT OF THE PREVIOUS</small> F<small>EBRUARY WHEN</small> D<small>ARCY HAD</small> first learned of Elizabeth's identity as Lady Courtenay. The opera house was filled to overflowing with nearly everyone who had a claim to be there.

Colonel Fitzwilliam was resolute in attending with him even though the rest of the family had gone to Matlock. Although the gossip was neither unkind nor had a poor reflection on the Fitzwilliams, the infamy coupled with seeing their nephew's sorrow was a bit much to bear, so they left town.

Darcy was early and made his way quickly to his box, Fitzwilliam remaining close behind. The Courtenays would be in their box directly across from his. He and his cousin sat silently, watching the opera house buzz with gossip and anticipation of seeing Lord and Lady Courtenay. He was also the object of much attention. He saw their glances and even some pointing in his direction, but he did not care.

When at last they entered, he almost cried with the relief of beholding her. She looked beautiful but pale; she surely had not been sleeping well. She wore a necklace he had not seen before, something elaborate and expensive looking. A recent gift, he supposed, from her husband. He watched enviously as Lord Courtenay removed the wrap from his wife's shoulders and handed it to a waiting manservant while saying something in her ear. She smiled at him a bit wanly.

They sat, and Elizabeth did not hazard so much as a glance in his direction. She stared resolutely at the empty stage, an audience of one, for nearly all others in the place looked at her, at Courtenay, and at Darcy.

The opening aria brought no change to matters. Everyone murmured and whispered as Elizabeth watched the stage and Darcy watched Elizabeth. Courtenay was kind to her, he observed. He spoke to her, held her hand, and even kissed her hand once. She looked at him gratefully when he did and said something that made him smile.

Darcy was surprised to find he was not more pained by seeing Courtenay's affection for Elizabeth or hers for him. He wanted her to be happy and to feel loved. He would never wish it otherwise.

He did not remove his eyes from her for a moment and would

have refrained from blinking if he could have managed it. Fitzwilliam spoke to him on occasion but Darcy was too lost to acknowledge him.

It happened in the second act, at about the midpoint. Elizabeth must have lost her determination, and her eyes moved from the stage to Darcy. Their eyes met across the crowd.

Time ceased to pass, and the sounds of the crowd died away as he found himself within her thrall. Did he breathe? He knew not, but he believed it likely that his body had suspended its physical needs so that his spirit might commune with hers. He knew her thoughts and hoped she understood his: he loved her so dearly and so deeply and could never love another. In her look, she told him the same.

The right corner of his lips lifted a fraction of an inch, and that seemed to recall her to her situation. She jerked her gaze back to the stage and then allowed it to drift down to her lap as she appeared to struggle with her emotion.

Courtenay had been insensible to the whole exchange but noticed his wife's downcast eyes. He leaned in to speak to her, and she responded. Moments later, Courtenay went to the entry to the box, summoning Elizabeth's wrap. He assisted her in placing it over her shoulders and then offered his arm as they departed.

When they had gone, Darcy heaved a great sigh that mixed relief with disappointment and sorrow.

"Do you want to leave?" Fitzwilliam whispered. Darcy nodded.

They went to the front of the house to call for Darcy's carriage, just in time to see the Courtenay carriage pull away. Darcy stared at the empty street where it had travelled until Fitzwilliam's hand on his arm meant his own carriage had arrived.

"DO YOU KNOW WHAT YOU NEED?" FITZWILLIAM ASKED, AS THEY later sat in Darcy's study, glasses of port in hand.

Darcy responded by raising his eyebrows.

"Pemberley, just you and me. We shall go for wild rides over the worst terrain we can find, and when we tire of that, we shall take out the guns and shoot anything that moves. We shall fence, play billiards and card games, and we shall drink brandy by the gallon. It will be splendid."

"It sounds horrid," Darcy replied, but he appreciated that his cousin sought to cheer him. "It is amusing, really, these suggestions you have all made to me."

"What suggestions?"

He smiled faintly. "Well, Bingley wrote to beg me to return to Derbyshire, insisting that the best thing would be to return myself to the marriage mart immediately. He already has a lady in mind. Saye recommended that he and I should spend at least a month setting ourselves upon the town in whatever ribaldry engages us: routs, brawls, and naturally, as many brothels as possible."

"Not something you wish to hear from a newly married man."

"No," Darcy smiled ruefully. "Evidently, the bloom has gone off that rose rather hastily."

Fitzwilliam winced but was not entirely surprised. "So none of our grand plans will suit you. We are worried about you. Your heart is broken in a way that is cruel and unjust. It is as if she has died but with the added pain of seeing her live and love another."

"Something in me requires anguish," Darcy remarked as he swirled the liquid in his glass. "I derive no pleasure from it, but it is all that is left to me. The pain tells me our love was real. I am afraid that when the pain is gone, I might wonder whether our love ever existed."

"You do not yet wish to go on," Fitzwilliam observed.

"I know I must." He shrugged. "I simply cannot. Everything she touched in me was changed for the better, and I am afraid that, without her, it will all go back to the way it was."

"Your life was not so trying before her."

"No, of course not," he agreed quickly. "I am a blessed man in many, many ways, and I cannot bemoan my lot, but I was a better man with her. My life was not only good but splendid and marvellous. It now seems stale and colourless."

Fitzwilliam sighed, bemused. "You know I shall do anything you require. I see your misery, but I have no notion what to do for you."

WITHIN SEVERAL DAYS OF SEEING ELIZABETH AT THE OPERA, DARCY was surprised by a call from Lord Courtenay.

Courtenay smiled affably as Darcy entered the drawing room, offering a correct bow that Darcy mirrored. While Mrs Hobbs poured coffee, Darcy watched him, assuming the man had something to say, and prepared himself for further distress.

When Mrs Hobbs had gone, Darcy remained silent. Although, at times, he disliked his taciturn nature, at other times, he found it quite useful, and this was one of the latter. He calmly studied Courtenay, hoping the silence would induce his lordship to speak his mind.

"How are you faring?"

"How am I faring?" Darcy echoed.

Courtenay cleared his throat. "This cannot be easy for you. Of us all, you have been the most wronged in this."

Darcy shrugged and said nothing.

"My purpose is to thank you for all you have done for my wife. I could easily see that you cared well for her and my son, and I am deeply grateful."

Darcy kept his eyes averted, lifting his coffee cup and taking a sip.

"This is all dreadfully inconvenient for you, I know, and I hope to assure you that there will be no unpleasantness in the courts or the scandal sheets because of it. I have spoken with the editors and have their words. If only I might silence the gossips!" He chuckled. "In the event you were concerned for any sort of repercussion for either yourself or Elizabeth, you may rest assured there will be none. You have my word."

Darcy afforded him a look and a silent nod.

"In fact, I have heard some rumblings about a barony for you. Nothing official yet, of course, but do know that I shall be your most ardent supporter. Not that I think you should require my assistance, but you will have it, nevertheless."

Darcy looked at him blankly before relenting. After all, this man was not his enemy despite the fact that he held what was dearest to Darcy in the world. *For what do you fault him? Remaining alive? Surviving his brother's treachery?* "I thank you for your assurances. This is a difficult situation, and I feel it keenly."

Courtenay leaned forward, sympathy and regret in his eyes. "I wish to offer some sort of amends to you."

"Amends?"

Courtenay spoke with great delicacy. "A wife can be a costly object. New clothes are a constant requirement, and perhaps your home was altered in some way? May I offer some recompense?"

Darcy now believed he understood the true meaning of this visit. "I see your purpose. You wish to pay me, and in return, I shall forget all of this occurred and stay away from her."

Courtenay looked surprised. "Certainly not."

"No?"

"Mr Darcy, please believe me when I say that this is exceedingly difficult and strange for us all, especially my dear wife. She is depressed, and I would do anything within my power to ease her suffering. If that means she must spend time in your company, I shall never deny it. By all means, call on her. It would ease her spirits considerably."

Darcy was puzzled as this was the last thing he might have expected from this call. "That is good of you, sir."

"Please, do not mistake my intentions. I have no ulterior motive and no desire to influence you or her. These are strange days for us all, and I came here today to see what I might do to make them easier for Elizabeth, for you, and for me."

"Very well then, sir, I thank you. Your position is unexpected and not one most men would take."

"Anyone with any claim to compassion and charity must feel this much. You have been put into the middle of an intrigue that had nothing to do with you, yet you have been wounded."

"Thank you," Darcy replied, still feeling unsettled.

Courtenay remained in Darcy's home just a few moments longer. As soon as he had donned his hat and greatcoat, he turned to Darcy and offered his hand. "Call on her, please. I love my wife, and she is unhappy. If seeing you will make her happy, I would never wish to deny her that."

Darcy studied him a moment, seeing a bit of tension and a suggestion of sleeplessness beneath the affable air. Gravely, he said, "Very well, I shall."

Courtenay inclined his head in thanks and took his leave. Darcy was left puzzled and slightly suspicious of the entire affair. No matter how he viewed it, it appeared that Courtenay's motive was wholly altruistic, and that made Darcy uneasy.

A sign of your innate scepticism. You see a gift horse and immediately check its mouth.

It was very odd. Were he in Lord Courtenay's place, he would take his wife up to his castle where no one would disturb them. Lord Courtenay's inclination appeared to be the opposite. He was promoting the relationship of his wife to her former—former what? Darcy did not know what to call himself, but he knew if he were in Courtenay's place, he would take Elizabeth as far away as possible from other romantic entanglements.

Perhaps he truly wishes for her to be happy regardless of the distress to himself.

THE FOLLOWING DAY, DARCY STARED UP AT THE IMPRESSIVE EDIFICE OF Towton Hall. *Am I going to go in there to see her and pretend we are nothing? That nothing of romance and love has ever existed between us? It will take a far better actor than I to affect the countenance of a man who has never tasted the sweetness of her lips or breathed in the scent of her hair as it lay across his face in the morning. Whose fingers do not know the softness of her skin, and whose ears have not heard her speak words of love—Stop this! Go in and see her. A simple call so that we, all of us, can exist together and begin to put this behind us.*

He was shown in to where she sat with Lord Courtenay.

It was evident that the month since Kidsgrove had not healed her wounds. She was depressive and carried the anxious air that he recognised from Hertfordshire. He could not comprehend it then, but he understood it now and felt a sort of appreciation that such sentiment would be on his behalf.

Courtenay was first to speak. "Mr Darcy, it is good to see you."

Darcy bowed. "And you as well." To Elizabeth, he said softly, "Lady Courtenay."

"Mr Darcy."

Mrs Baynes served them tea, looking as if she wished to toss the tea on the table and escape. When she had gone, an awkward discussion ensued.

Elizabeth spoke first, raising her chin and inhaling deeply. "How is Georgiana?"

"I thank you, she is well. She is recently returned from visiting Lady Catherine in Kent."

"Was it a nice visit?"

"Yes. She says Mrs Collins is increasing and expects the child in the summer."

"How nice. I had heard as much in a letter from my mother, but it is good to have the news confirmed."

"Yes."

Elizabeth turned to Courtenay. "Do you remember my girlhood

friend, Charlotte? She married my distant cousin, a Mr Collins who, by coincidence, is the parson of Mr Darcy's aunt Lady Catherine de Bourgh."

"I do not believe I remember her." Courtenay looked embarrassed and explained to Darcy. "I suffered some damage to my memory from my illness. My doctor thinks it might have been due to the fevers."

"I see," Darcy replied.

The conversation languished for a moment until Darcy dared to ask, "How is Henry?"

Elizabeth's face softened, and she replied, "He is doing well. Annie is—"

"My son is very well," Courtenay interrupted. "Very happy and in excellent health. He is a fine boy."

It was an oddly vehement response, and Darcy and Elizabeth both looked at him in surprise. Courtenay looked away.

Darcy cleared his throat, searching for a different topic. "Bingley wrote to me that he and his family will come to town in March. You must have heard it as well."

"I am a bit behind on my correspondence," Elizabeth admitted.

Darcy nodded, understanding that she might wish to avoid seeing her family's responses to the change in her situation. Courtenay appeared not to apprehend and said cheerfully, "I am looking forward to meeting Mr Bingley. I understand he is a great friend of yours, Mr Darcy."

"He is," Darcy agreed. "One of my dearest friends. He is an amiable man, and I can hardly think of a soul who does not esteem him, save for those who are offended by the source of his fortune."

"Ah yes, trade was it not?" Courtenay shrugged. "Soon enough such distinctions will hardly matter."

"I would like to believe that we might one day live in a world where character is valued over heritage," Darcy agreed as Courtenay gave him an odd smile.

Courtenay rose soon thereafter. "I beg you would excuse me, Mr Darcy. I must meet with someone at my club, but please stay as long as you are able."

"Thank you." Darcy stood as Lord Courtenay departed, and then sat again, pleased to have a few moments alone with Elizabeth but curious that Courtenay would permit him to remain.

Elizabeth appeared ill at ease. "I had heard you might be present at a dinner we attended recently at the Millers."

"I had planned to go," Darcy replied. "But at the end, I could not manage it and sent my regrets. Had I known you were present, it would have changed my mind."

She raised her eyes to meet his. "I did not know how I could meet you with equanimity in any case, so I suppose it must have been for the best."

"Both of us are, I think, in a good bit of turmoil and unrest," he replied sympathetically. "And I expect we shall be for some time."

Her eyes looked pained as she regarded him, and she appeared to struggle with her emotion. "I know you are suffering, and I am sorry, so very sorry that all of this has—"

"It is not your fault. I was angry—I admit it. I do have times when I feel rage, but it is at the unfairness of it all, not with you. Never with you."

"I do not deserve your regard." She returned her eyes to her lap. With a sigh, she reached to the table next to her, finding a small parcel that he had not noticed previously. She handed it to him.

"What is this?"

Without looking at him, she murmured, "Your ring."

His mouth dropped as a lance of pain shot through him. "Oh...oh, I did not...you should..." He was stammering, staggered, and most of all, not wishing for this—this final step. He had not thought of it, that she still held his family ring, this last tie to her time as Mrs Darcy, but he did not wish to have it back. It was a finality he could not abide. He took it unwillingly, unwrapped it, and looked at it, feeling dull and nerveless, entirely unable to respond.

"Your future wife will have it," she said quietly, her eyes still affixed to her lap, but he saw a tear slide down her cheek.

The ring had been in his family for at least four generations, but he decided at once that it would stop here. "No, no it...she will not."

"She will."

He thought of that day—that blessed day—when he had placed it on her hand and beheld it sparkling in the morning light, looking for all the world as though it had found its home. He shook his head slowly. "It was meant for you, and it belongs on your hand. If it cannot be there, it will languish in a box somewhere."

Elizabeth moved next to him on the settee, and he determinedly kept his gaze fixed on the ring. She seated herself far too close, and it required all of his resolve to stop himself from pulling her to him and kissing her until all of this was nothing but a distant dream.

She entwined her fingers with his. "You will feel better in time. I hope you do. I wish for nothing more than your happiness, just as you have so generously seen to mine."

"I shall never be happy so long as I do not have you."

"I love you, and I want you to have a happy life, even if it is not with me."

"I cannot be happy without you. In truth, I do not even wish to attempt it."

She smiled ruefully and whispered, "I do love you, so very much."

For a long moment, they stared at one another. She moved first, coming closer, tilting her face towards his. Their lips almost touched, but did not.

Knowing it went against everything he had ever been taught and everything he believed about himself, he slowly raised his hand, placing it behind her head, and permitted his thumb the pleasure of caressing the nape of her neck.

They were thus suspended, almost kissing, yet not. He could feel her breath against his mouth, as he knew she could feel his against hers. The side of one of her breasts brushed against his arm as it rose and fell with her respiration.

They were suspended in a moment of combined agony and bliss. Darcy longed to close the half an inch that separated them, to join his lips with hers and kiss her just as he wished to. He debated violently within himself: the gentleman telling him to back away while the lover, Elizabeth's lover, said to kiss her as she clearly wished to be kissed.

He knew which voice he should obey, and it warred violently against the voice that he wanted to heed. The two could arrive at no good solution, leaving Darcy to remain motionless, with Elizabeth following suit.

TWENTY-FOUR

A blustery wind threatened to remove the hats of the two gentlemen who strode with purpose along one of London's less fashionable streets. They glanced about them as they approached a plain wooden door, but naturally, there were none of their acquaintance about to observe them. Habit did not end easily.

Entering a modest apartment, they requested drinks from a serving girl who appeared dull and uncomprehending. She nodded and departed as they made themselves comfortable in front of the fire, tossing their outer garments on a side chair. When the girl returned, they thanked her, and the slighter man gave her a coin, causing her moon-like face to split into a wide grin. She made an awkward, unpractised curtsey and left them.

The taller man asked, "How are you doing?"

"Perfectly well," the other man answered querulously, "if a bit impatient."

"We have all been impatient."

"From the sounds of it, no one has done a thing but drink and vent his spleen."

"It is easy to see errors from afar."

The slighter man shrugged, taking a generous drink of his ale.

"How is your wife?"

"She is well, but you did not request this meeting to ask about her."

"No," the taller man agreed, shaking his head. "I only wished to speak to you and see if...well, to see whether you are as you had been."

The slighter man looked quizzical. "As I had been? I do not take your meaning."

"It has been some years now; things have changed."

The other man's jaw dropped. "Do you dare suggest—"

"No, no," the taller man replied hastily. "I suggest nothing but enquire about everything. No one knows what to think when so much has been lost...you have suffered..."

"Nothing has changed, and I shall thank you to remember that." The slighter man finished his ale, setting his glass down on the table with a sharp rap matched by his tone. "Yes, I have suffered—suffered and sacrificed—and you dare question me?"

The taller man held up both hands. "I do not accuse you. You are perfectly right: with all you have done and the distances you have travelled, to question you is ungenerous. Pray, forgive me."

The slighter man smiled begrudgingly. "I could do no less. I must go now as my wife expected me to return directly. When is the next gathering?"

"Tomorrow."

"Same place?"

"Of course."

"I shall meet you there then." The slighter gentleman donned his overcoat, hat, and gloves and departed, his step betraying his anger.

The other man sat for some time enjoying the fire. After twenty minutes, he went to select a book from the amply supplied library. He returned to the fire and read for about half an hour more until he heard a bell announcing the arrival of another visitor.

A tall, stout man entered. "Hanley."

"Good day to you, sir."

The large man asked without ceremony, "Did you speak to him?"

"I did. He became angry."

The large man sat. "He always did tend to get a hot head. We need to be sure of these things."

"He assured me of his dedication to the cause."

"I remain...unconvinced," the large man replied. "He is not as he was. I have seen it myself."

Hanley shrugged. "We have little choice but to believe in him."

They spoke on matters pertaining to their business. Plans were made and ideas put forth. When they had finished, the two men stood.

"Will you return to Mayfair now?" The large man sounded a bit derisive in his query, but Hanley disregarded it.

"I shall. May I drop you somewhere?"

The large man laughed. "Do you not fear the likes of me might soil the seats of your carriage?"

Hanley disregarded that too. "Well?"

"No, thank you."

SLOWLY, WISHING TO DO THE OPPOSITE, DARCY DROPPED HIS HAND from Elizabeth's head, sitting back and breathing deeply to release himself from the thrall in which he had been.

"I am sorry. So very sorry. This is not the behaviour of a gentleman."

"Nor a lady." She once again lowered her eyes to her lap; then she rose and moved to a chair. "Pray, forgive me. It was I who began."

He shook his head. "Do not trouble yourself."

"Please understand, it is not some wanton urge causing me to act so. I can only say that I just do not feel married to him. I feel married to you. It seems so wrong when he touches me and so right and natural to be here with you."

Darcy smiled tightly. "It will improve. It must, after all."

"I pray it does, yet I hope it does not." She shook her head. "I am a creature of contradictory and warring spirits."

"I believe I should depart. I do not think Lord Courtenay would prefer to see me still here when he returns."

"He is not apt to return for several hours," she replied, seeming unconcerned.

"He has much business to transact then?"

She shrugged. "With both his illness and prolonged absence, I would imagine much of it pertains to reacquainting himself with the workings of the estate."

"I am sure you are correct." Darcy hated to take his leave and hated even more the cloak of despondency that had fallen onto her.

She seemed to rally her spirits as he moved to the door. "Please tell Georgiana I would love to receive her call. I miss her."

Darcy gave her a fond smile. "That is very good of you. She will be relieved as she is certain you despise her."

"I do not," Elizabeth replied as she saw him out. "Please assure her I do not. What occurred was likely inevitable."

Darcy bowed and took the liberty of tenderly kissing Elizabeth's hand. When he rose, they locked gazes for a moment until he mouthed, "I love you," and departed.

JANE AND BINGLEY ARRIVED WITH LITTLE WILLIAM DURING THE FIRST week of March. Elizabeth was delighted to meet him; however, as she saw his little round face and flailing arms and legs, she could not keep herself from again wishing she had borne Darcy's child—*What a comfort that might have been!*—even though she knew a child of an annulled union would have faced innumerable difficulties.

"Jane, are you certain it was safe to travel with him? After all, he is but two months old."

Jane was impatient. "It did him no harm. We must talk about your situation though."

Elizabeth looked down and shrugged. "What is there to say?"

Jane studied her. "Are you happy?"

Elizabeth shrugged again. "I suppose so. I miss him, but Henry has been generous in promoting my friendship with him. It is not easy for any of us."

"Henry is permitting you to remain friends with Darcy?"

"He encourages it. I applaud him; few men could do the same. He is genuinely concerned for my well-being, but then, that should not astonish me. He was always kind."

Unsurprisingly, given the gregarious nature of both men, Bingley and Henry got along famously. As the weeks of March passed by, they made an almost happy foursome, frequently together in company and in the homes of one another.

Little Henry was enchanted by his young cousin and asked his aunt almost daily whether William could play with him yet. He could not apprehend that the baby was too young to run about or see his puppy, and he soon made up his mind that he required his own brother, one who would play and caper immediately upon his entry into the world.

"Mama will gets me a bwother," he informed his father one morning when they visited.

"Will she!" Henry had looked at Elizabeth with a teasing expression in his eye. "What if she gets you a sister? That would be nice too, would it not?"

Little Henry looked unsure. "No, a bwother," he insisted. "To play bwocks!"

Looking away from her husband's eyes, which bore a look she could not yet encourage, Elizabeth said, "Oh, I think a sister would play blocks if you asked her. But you must remember what I told you: sisters and brothers come along when they are ready to, and they will not be hurried, no matter how much we wish for them."

Little Henry gave her an odd look, and Elizabeth nearly laughed as his father inadvertently did the same. It was the younger Henry who spoke. "But you pwomised! You have to!"

Elizabeth sighed. *Oh yes, I surely did promise, and I do indeed have to.*

JUDGING BY THE LINE OF CARRIAGES, THE SOIREE AT THE HOME OF SIR James and Lady Thomas-Reese would be an undisputed crush. The notion of it was already fatiguing even though she had not yet set foot in the door. But Henry felt it was important to regain their standing and acceptance as a married couple, so retreat was not an option.

"I am all anticipation of dancing with you." Henry leaned towards her in the carriage, taking her hand and kissing it through her glove.

"And I with you." She smiled at him as he would expect.

Henry spoke cautiously, having learned that his precipitous announcement of Mr Darcy's possible attendance at the Millers' dinner had displeased her. "Sir James mentioned that they received an acceptance from Mr Darcy for tonight."

Elizabeth felt a burst of happy excitement at the thought of seeing him and nearly broke into a broad grin. She disciplined herself to remain serene. "How nice."

"I hoped that having him call at our home would ease the relations between our families." Henry smiled at her sympathetically. "I know this is difficult, but only a few more weeks and we shall go to Lancashire. I am eager to be home with you."

"I am eager to be there as well." She smiled faintly, feeling, as she often did these days, rather removed from it all. Then the time for discussion was ended as the footmen moved to assist them from their carriage.

The public rooms were nearly overflowing, making it difficult to move or breathe, much less dance. A set had nevertheless formed in the ballroom, and in the drawing rooms, there were card tables. In Sir James's study, a group of older men debated politics and other news.

Elizabeth danced with her husband, drank punch, and greeted her acquaintances, but through it all, she had one eye on the door. She made herself laugh and talk just as she was expected to do, and she made inconsequential chatter as was required for such parties. But her thoughts were for him, wondering when he would arrive. Every sense was honed to awaiting the appearance of Darcy, but he did not appear.

When she finally saw him, her heart plunged. She had returned to the ballroom and found Jane and Mr Bingley. They had escorted Miss Bingley, who was dancing with Darcy. Elizabeth felt a stab of the acutest sort of jealousy as she watched them move through the patterns.

They made an attractive pair, both of them elegant and handsome. Miss Bingley laughed at something Darcy said as he drew near, and Elizabeth swallowed hard, forcing away the moisture that had risen to her eyes. She felt an intense urge to stride onto the dance floor and scream invectives at Miss Bingley, tearing her away from Darcy at once.

She wanted to look away, but she could not. *He will marry. Not Miss Bingley, perhaps, but another beautiful, elegant woman, and she will know him as I have, only for a much longer and truer time. How shall I bear that?*

Suddenly, he looked up and saw her. Their eyes locked, and Elizabeth was pained to see the sadness there, knowing it was reflected in her own expression.

"Lizzy?" Jane was at her side, and Elizabeth turned to her, determined to appear sanguine.

Jane looked to where Elizabeth had been staring and frowned. "She forwarded herself to him in a manner most unbecoming. You need not worry about that; he had to dance with her."

"She is a beautiful lady," Elizabeth replied with a tight smile. "They look wonderful together."

"But they are not together. They are only dancing."

Elizabeth sighed deeply. "What does it matter? Her or another lady —it cannot be me, and that is the painful part."

The dance ended, and Darcy escorted Miss Bingley to their group though it appeared to Elizabeth that Miss Bingley was protesting their route. From nowhere, Henry also arrived, placing his arm around his wife's waist.

Darcy bowed as soon as he reached them. "Lord Courtenay, Lady Courtenay." Elizabeth curtseyed, her eyes glued to his face.

"Lady Courtenay, would you do me the honour of dancing the next with me?" Elizabeth's eyes flew to her husband, wondering how he would bear it, but Henry appeared untroubled and calm.

"Oh yes, my love, do go, and while you are at it, I believe I shall see what the lads in the card room have going. Will that suit you?"

"Of course," Elizabeth agreed, pleased to have some time without the burden of his presence, a reminder of her guilt over not loving him well enough—or at all. He excused himself just as Miss Bingley's next partner came to claim her. Bingley and Jane decided to dance as well, and thus, Elizabeth found herself alone with Darcy. She looked up and, seeing his intent gaze upon her, felt that she might burst into tears under the weight of it.

He leaned in closely. "Let us forget about the dance. I shall go out into the gardens using that door." He gestured towards the end of the room. "Go have some punch and follow me by another way. Do not take long. I do not wish to waste even a minute." He was off, striding towards the door he had indicated.

Eyes were upon her, she well knew that. The Courtenay-Darcy triangle was of enormous interest to the *ton*. There could be nothing more that those gathered would like better than to catch a whiff of improper behaviour. Thus, she was superbly cautious, nonchalantly strolling through the crush of people to the refreshment tables with ambling, aimless movements.

After spending five minutes greeting a few people, sipping at punch, and making her way in fits and starts towards a door, she turned, and slipped out into the inky darkness of the garden. The faint sliver of moonlight was barely discernible through the cloud cover and did nothing to light her path, and she hoped Darcy would come forward soon, as she had no notion of how she might find him otherwise.

She expected him yet nearly screamed when she felt his hand grasp hers, pulling her towards a bench in a little secluded spot among the shrubbery. "Shh," he chuckled, his voice low. "Come, Lady Courtenay."

When they reached the bench, she sat as close to him as possible, revelling in the feel of his warmth. "Pray, do not call me that," she whispered. "It must be 'Lizzy' to you."

He tilted his head a moment, a bit quizzical. "I never called you 'Lizzy,' did I? Only Elizabeth."

She reached over to run a light caress over his arm. "You did indeed call me 'Lizzy,' and they were moments I treasure—wonderful, private moments."

"Oh?" He thought for a moment, and then understanding dawned upon him. "Oh yes, I see now."

"I want you to know that I do appreciate how honourably you have behaved in this. I am mortified when I think how much I wish to forget decency and propriety."

"It is an odd thing to go from being married to suddenly being unmarried. The usual strictures surely do not apply," he reassured her. "I admire how well you have comported yourself in this."

"You do it again," she told him tenderly.

"What is that?"

"You take my bad behaviour and somehow turn it to my credit."

He reached over to run his finger lightly along her wrist. "As I have said before, that is what it is to love somebody."

"I am a greedy and selfish creature," she admitted. "I long to hear you say that every time I see you and even on the days I do not, although it is to your detriment to continue to love me."

"Detriment or not, I shall not stop. I believe I once told you that my good opinion, once lost, was lost forever—did I not?"

She nodded.

"Likewise, my love, once earned, is earned forever. You will see."

"You cannot know how very much I long to kiss you. I wish to be on your lap with my hands in your hair, holding you as tightly as I can."

"I would love that," he murmured. "I dream of it."

She paused a moment, considering, and then decided she could not care. What good was it to be so rigorously ladylike when her entire world had collapsed upon her? She lowered her voice, speaking in a seductive tone as she laid her hand on his leg. "What else do you dream of?"

He did not miss her meaning and gave her a low chuckle. "Minx. What you do to me!"

She edged a bit closer to him. "Is your mind still married to me as mine is to you? My thoughts contain a different world, one in which none of this ever happened. A world where Mr Fitzwilliam Darcy met Miss Elizabeth Bennet, free and unencumbered, and they lived happily ever after."

"That might have done very well," he agreed.

"Of course, had I been the lady you thought I was in Hertfordshire, I never would have seen you again," she teased. "You left me without a look back."

"Do not think it for a moment," he responded with earnestness. "I might have been so stupid—indeed, I was so stupid—but even in January, I had already begun to think of a way it might be done. I knew then that I needed you. I was stupid on many accounts, but I was wise enough to realise you were everything I could ever need and wish for."

She blushed. "Then I suppose it would have been for the best, for we might now be married to one another. I think of it often."

"It is always in my mind as well."

"Well then, tell me what we are doing in this marriage in your mind."

He shifted a bit in his seat. "My imagination is poor, but I am fortunate to have had some taste of a beautiful reality to feed it."

She was silent but allowed her fingers to trace his leg.

"Do you recall," he asked, sounding a bit embarrassed, "when we went for a ride on horseback to one of my favourite spots at Pemberley: a rise that overlooks the river?"

She immediately knew the day of which he spoke. "I remember that day well. We kissed a long time."

His voice became husky. "I became rather desperate for you."

She knew where his thoughts had gone, and it made her blush hotly. She had been in that time of the month when to do more than kiss was impossible, yet she had clearly seen his need for her. She had once read a book where a woman had placed her mouth on a man and, not knowing precisely what she was doing, had sought to emulate the act. "I hoped to ease your suffering."

"You did...I had never imagined experiencing such a thing by your ministration."

"The pleasure was as much mine as yours."

"You are a remarkable woman. I had always believed a lady might find such things distasteful. I could never have asked for it but surely thought I was favoured by fortune to have you do so of your own inclination."

"There is nothing of you that I find distasteful, nothing at all. I only wish that I might do it again."

"Ah, Lizzy." He rested his forehead on hers, breathing as heavily as she was. She closed her eyes a moment, enjoying the scent and the nearness of him, even as she attempted to calm herself. She knew, at his slightest hint, that she would go off with him and do anything for him, and she supposed she must be grateful for his greater restraint.

He leaned back with one last deep breath. "It seems you are right. In certain situations, I do call you 'Lizzy.'"

She laughed, lightly and quietly. "Yes, you do." They were silent for several long minutes.

"Will he miss you? I would imagine the time for a dance has long since elapsed."

"My husband is devoted to card playing far more than ever before. Then again, there likely has been little else to amuse him these last three years. I console myself in that he seems to have no idea of the complexity of his father's financial system; therefore, he can do little damage with his wagers."

"What do you mean?"

She shrugged. "Just that his father, the old earl, had a rather elaborate means by which he kept his books. It took me many months to fully learn it, and even so, I do not know that I yet comprehend all his methods."

"But what of the years after Courtenay inherited? He must surely have looked at it then."

"If he did understand, it has been forgotten due to his injuries. The manner of its construction made me wonder whether his father had some suspicion of the traitorous doings in which his younger son was engaged."

"That seems a dangerous game. What if both he and Henry had died? Would the fortune have been lost?"

"No," Elizabeth assured him. "It can be understood. It is just complicated and requires a mind for numbers. Once Henry approaches it with a bit of patience and diligence, he will learn it, but as yet, he has not." She heaved a sigh. "Why do we speak of Henry? I wish to speak of you."

"There is nothing to say about me. I am a man with a broken heart, doing what I can to heal and succeeding not at all." He sighed. "I find solace in knowing that you have a good man, one who loves you and whom you love. I could not bear it otherwise."

It was shocking, the sense of repulsion she felt when he mentioned her loving Henry. Before she could stop herself, she whispered, "I do not."

"You do not what?"

"I do not love him." Her words came almost in spite of her. She was horrified that she had said it yet also liberated as if a burden dropped from her mind upon admitting the truth that lurked in the shadows of her consciousness.

"You do, I know that you do. You are distressed."

"No...no, I am not," she insisted. "I do not love him. You, I love you."

"You cannot. You cannot love me, no matter how I yearn for it." He pulled her hand to his lips and kissed it, lingeringly and tenderly. "But I do assure you, I love you. I ache with how much I love you."

"Lady Courtenay?" A man's voice came into the garden, and Elizabeth started, removing her hand from Darcy's. She wondered whether whoever was there had seen them, even knowing it was impossible in the shadows of the dark garden.

Turning, she saw the form of a man looking off in the opposite direction. By the shape of him, she guessed it was Mr Hanley. *How long has he been there? He surely saw us and now only pretends he does not.*

It was shocking that she felt no wash of guilt, only annoyance that he dared to interrupt her interlude with Darcy.

"Remain here until I have gone." She rose, gliding to where Hanley stood. She dared not look at Darcy as she listened to Mr Hanley explain that Henry had been called away on an urgent matter and asked Hanley to escort her home. Taking his arm, she allowed him to do just that.

Mr Hanley said little in the carriage as they travelled towards Towton Hall. Elizabeth made the polite, expected banter with him for a bit and then lapsed into silence, trying not to wonder what Hanley might have overheard in the garden.

He entered the house with her. "I have a brief matter of business to discuss with his lordship. I shall not detain him over long."

Elizabeth smiled and retired to her chambers. As she surrendered herself to the ministrations of her maid, she wondered—assuming Hanley had heard her with Darcy—what he might tell Henry. She had no wish to pain Henry, and he already knew well that her heart was divided. However, for him to know that she no longer loved him, and had said as much to Darcy, was just too cruel. Surely, Hanley could not be that unkind.

She did not fear what Henry might do. Indeed, were he to divorce her, even for adultery, the scandal could hardly be more than it already was. She was nearly inured to the whispers and conversation about her. If tattle circulated about an intimate relationship between her and Darcy, she doubted anyone would think it odd. There likely were many who already assumed something of that nature still occurred between them.

What she truly feared was hurting Henry. He was a good man, and she despised all that had happened to him. The treachery of a brother now leading to the faithlessness of a wife—it was despicable.

A soft knock came at her door, and Elizabeth inhaled, thinking that her question might well be answered as to what Henry had learned from his friend.

"Come in," she called softly as her heart began to pound, dreading any sort of confrontation.

Henry entered and smiled. She knew immediately that he wore nothing beneath his light silk dressing gown. He came to her where she perched on the side of her bed and sat next to her. He looked into her eyes, and she smelled the brandy on his breath. Gently, he said, "Elizabeth, you know I love you very much, yes?"

"I do." She nodded, swallowing, and felt her anxiety grow. "And I wish you to know that I appreciate your patience with me. This situation has been a trial to us all—you most of all—yet your kindness has been indefatigable. I...I would not wish you to think..."

He laid his fingers on the side of her cheek, caressing her with great tenderness. "I adore you. I would do anything to take back these years and begin again where we left off: newly married with all that was good in life before us."

A slight smile was her only response—the only response she could make through her trepidation.

"I must admit, my patience this night has been sorely tried." He pressed soft but ardent kisses to her cheek that left her in no doubt of his wishes.

"Has it?" she whispered, her heart pounding wildly. Is this, then, to be my penance? Henry finally coming to assert his rights? "I am sorry, I know…"

"Your beauty has enticed me to the point of madness. My desire for you is overwhelming." He reached for his waist and loosened the ties of his gown, which fell partly open, revealing him to her eyes.

She blushed, looking away quickly, even as he reached for her hand and pulled it to his half-covered chest. She could scarcely look at him, unnerved by the thought of seeing those parts of him that were previously hidden.

"Please, my love." He was sweetly entreating. "I am filled with an almost wretched desire for my wife. I would not have anything from you that you did not give in willingness and in love, but my need for you is nigh on killing me." He edged closer to her, leaning in to kiss her lips. She turned slightly, causing him to kiss the corner of her mouth.

"I thought you were worried about a possible conception."

"I am, but there is much to be enjoyed without risk of that, is there not?"

He knew. Elizabeth inadvertently stiffened. Hanley had heard her reminiscing with Darcy of their time in the meadow, and he told Henry. She supposed she deserved as much for speaking so, and for having such licentious wishes for a man who was no longer hers. Her guilt and her shame washed over her, guilt for having spoken of Henry so unkindly and for no longer loving him as she should.

She pulled back, and he released her hand, moving to cover himself. "You are unwilling. I would not wish—"

"It is not that," she said hastily, feeling relieved once he was completely covered by his gown. "I just…my head aches and I…"

He shook his head, giving her a smile that, to her guilty eyes, seemed sad. "If you are not yet ready for further intimacy between us, I understand."

She pressed her hand to her forehead, mortified and ashamed. "I am sorry, so very sorry…"

"You need not be." He moved to leave her. "I understand, truly I do."

"Henry, I—" She stopped, having no notion of what she might say. He turned back, and she offered him a rueful, regretful smile. "I am sorry. I wish I could…I just cannot, not yet. It is too…"

He returned to where she was seated on the bed, and trailed his fingers across her cheek. "Do not fret about it, my angel. I am not upset and would not wish you to be so either."

"Angel?" She laughed a bit. "I had forgotten you often called me that."

"Did you?" He smiled. "I called you that from almost our first meeting, I think. Impertinent of me to claim such a familiarity back then. Does it amuse you to recall it?"

She shook her head. "I did not think of that. I smiled only because our brother Bingley calls Jane that too."

He bent, kissing her cheek. "We must tell him that it was our endearment first, and thus, he must share it." He kissed her lightly once more. "I bid you good night, sweet angel."

She smiled faintly. "Good night, Henry."

Minutes later, Elizabeth lay in her bed, staring up at the canopy over her and considering what had just transpired.

She could not fault her husband for his needs. His forbearance and his patience were exemplary. They had been reunited for two months, and it was not surprising that he should think her accustomed to his presence in her life again by now.

Alas, she was not. Having Henry enter her bedchamber felt like having a stranger enter. She was still Mrs Darcy, not Lady Courtenay, and until that feeling changed—and she doubted it ever would—to willingly accept Henry into her bed was impossible.

Her mind returned to the admission she had made to Darcy earlier that night: *I do not love him.* She did not love Henry any longer; she knew that. At times, she felt that she loved him less and less each day, and at other times—disgraceful times—she hated him.

Loving a man I cannot have is preventing me from caring for the man I do have. There is no escape. Whether I love him or not, I am his wife until death do us part. It cannot go on. I am making myself miserable.

As she drifted off to sleep, she noted that Henry had grown much more muscular in their time apart. Although he was certainly not as attractive as Darcy—*stop thinking of that, Lizzy!*—his figure was appealing now, manly and athletic. Henry had not been so well built before; he was more inclined towards reading and strolls in the country than he was to fencing, boxing, or even riding. It must have been the mines, she concluded. Such work must make a man strong.

TWENTY-FIVE

Darcy had given his word that he would see to Wickham's transportation if Lord Courtenay was found, and he could not say he regretted it. He despised Wickham for his weakness and slothfulness, as well as for what he had attempted to do to Georgiana, yet Darcy's conscience could not allow him to stand by and see the man hanged. Wickham would be sent to a penal colony, and his death at sea was probable, but at least he would be afforded some slim chance at life.

It took a bit of effort—the charge of treason was not so easy to lay aside—and required some doing to show that Wickham was not a conspirator but a hired gun, and a poor one at that. At last it was done, and Wickham's passage was set for Van Diemen's Land on the next convict ship.

Darcy could not trust that Wickham had gone unless he saw the departure with his own eyes. Thus, he found himself on an unseasonably cold day near the end of March by the Wapping docks, watching as Wickham boarded the prison hulk.

Darcy turned to leave soon after. The neighbourhood was rough, and crime was prevalent, so he had no wish to linger. As he met his carriage, however, he saw a surprising sight: Lord Courtenay leaving a small building on a side street.

His curiosity aroused, he followed Courtenay as the man walked around a corner and found a hack chaise. Darcy could see no more without following him so continued on his way towards home.

Wishing to discuss Lord Courtenay's strange behaviour, Darcy diverted to Matlock House where he found his uncle and Fitzwilliam playing billiards.

"Darcy!" his uncle exclaimed. "Will you join us?"

"Continue as you were. I need to speak to you both."

Fitzwilliam lined up his next shot. "About what?"

Darcy sank into a nearby chair. "I saw Wickham board the prison hulk today."

"Why on earth did you go down there?" Lord Matlock demanded.

"Everything has been so irregular in this matter, I suppose a part of me half expected him to escape or otherwise subvert justice." Darcy shrugged, accepting a drink from the footman. "In any case, he is where he should be. But that is not what I wished to discuss. While I was there, I saw Lord Courtenay down by the docks."

There was a crack, and the balls hurled about the table.

"Down by Wapping? A dangerous place for him as well as for you. I do hope you had adequate protection."

"Both his lordship and I were alone, but as you see, I made it out unharmed, as did he. My point is: What was he doing there?"

Fitzwilliam shrugged, watching his father take his shot. "Does it truly matter?"

"He is rather eccentric," Darcy insisted. "Curious behaviour from first to last."

"How so?" Lord Matlock asked.

"He permits Elizabeth to do many things that I could not imagine most men in his situation would, such as dancing with me and leaving us alone when I call. Quite unusual, do you not think? I would not do it were I recently reunited with my wife."

"He wishes for her to be happy," Fitzwilliam said absently. To his father, he commented, "Excellent shot, sir."

"Being happy is one thing; keeping company with a former lover is entirely another," Darcy snapped, frustrated that they did not seem to apprehend the import of his words.

The two men looked at Darcy, Lord Matlock with a sympathetic countenance that immediately annoyed Darcy further. He turned his head to avoid seeing it.

Fitzwilliam said gently, "Perhaps he has a mistress or frequents a brothel down there, and he remained into the morning. Perhaps he has fallen in love with someone else. I thought of it the other day when Saye questioned why Lord Courtenay had not come back sooner. The only explanation that would satisfy was another woman."

"I have considered that myself," Darcy admitted. "Such a travesty! He loves another, she loves me, yet both of them must live out this marriage whether they wish for it or not."

Lord Matlock clapped his nephew on the shoulder. "Darcy, you must put these things from your mind. No matter whether Lord Courtenay has ten lovers, Elizabeth cannot belong to you. Always thinking of what you cannot have will do nothing but keep you in pain and prevent you from finding your own love."

"I know." Darcy felt a wave of fatigue overwhelm him. He rose, losing his balance for a moment.

"Darcy, are you well?" Fitzwilliam asked with alarm.

"Not at all," he admitted. "I am exhausted by the effort of pretending I am accepting of this. I am frustrated and sad, and so very tired of it that I do not wish to awaken in the morning. My only comfort is that, when night draws near, another day is soon done—but it is a cold comfort, for the dawn is sure to follow." He sighed. "I wish something could be found to change this."

"There is nothing," Lord Matlock replied, his tone more gentle than his words. "You must see that, Darcy. This is how it is; everything has fitted up too neatly for it to be otherwise."

Fitzwilliam was studying his next shot and spoke, unthinkingly. "Save for the two plans of course."

"Two plans?" Darcy enquired, even as Lord Matlock made a dismissive snort.

"A contingency plan, Darcy, and nothing more."

"The need for secrecy be hanged! I must know."

Fitzwilliam was chagrined by his slip. "Darcy, believe me, it is nothing. There existed two plans for the murder of Lord Courtenay: one on the road to Crewe, which involved our friend Wickham, and another at Warrington Castle."

Darcy grew excited. "There it is! Strange facts that do not align! It must mean something that—"

"A contingency plan," Fitzwilliam repeated with a firm shake of his head. "They wanted him dead, and despite having planned for it twice, they were foiled. Rather ironic, but so it was."

"But why two plans? Who was the other assassin, and where is he now? Surely, these things —"

Lord Matlock shot his son a vexed look. "Darcy, listen here. Two assassins, one assassin—what does it matter? Francis Warren is dead, and Lord Courtenay is not. Those are the facts, as incontrovertible as the fact that Elizabeth is Lady Courtenay. I am sorry; no one is more sorry than I."

He put his arm on Darcy's shoulders in a fatherly manner. "No matter what we might tease out of all of this, what conspiracies or intrigues come forth, it still cannot change. She is his wife. Would that I could change it, but alas, I cannot."

"It must mean something," Darcy protested weakly. "Was it looked into? Perhaps..." He could not immediately determine any reason for the double plan. He resolved to think on it further later that night. His insomnia might at least be useful in this.

ONE EVENING, HENRY AND ELIZABETH WERE INVITED TO DINE WITH the Bingleys. The small party included Miss Bingley and her potential suitor, a Mr Alistair Neaves, son of Sir Richard Neaves, a baronet from Essex.

Mr Neaves had been at university with Henry, and Elizabeth thought bitterly how eager he must be to renew the acquaintance and thus be armed with fresh gossip to relate to his friends at the club about the *ton's* most delicious scandal.

As the days of March slipped away, Elizabeth found herself less and less inclined towards weeping and sorrow but more predisposed towards vexation and irritation. Everything was a source of aggravation, from the sounds of carriages and people passing by on the streets to the temperature of the air and the tightness of her corset. She was short tempered with everyone—her husband included—and then she would be filled with angry guilt for having acted so. The guilt, alas, vexed her further, which made her even more angry—and around and around she would go. Some days she thought she might go mad, and she wondered whether Henry might wish to return to the mines to escape her.

She resolved that, for this night, she would make every effort to be amiable, and she smiled kindly at Henry when he came in to escort her to the carriage. He leaned in to kiss her, and she turned her head to give him her lips.

It pleased him; his eyes became soft upon her, and he smiled as she stood. "My love, you are very beautiful tonight."

"Must you say that every single time?" Good intentions were thus dispersed in the wake of Elizabeth's irritation.

He looked shocked. "What do I say every time?"

"Nothing. I beg your pardon." *A fine effort towards being amiable, Lizzy.* "Pray, do not regard me. I am not feeling well." She forced a smile.

"Another headache? You are often unwell these days."

"Forgive me, I—"

"If there is something I have done or something I am doing to cause your peevishness, let us discuss it."

You have done nothing worse than remain alive. "I…I am sorry. I know I am uncommonly shrewish right now. I am trying to lift myself from it."

He was hurt; she would have preferred him angry. "I am doing my best to repair this marriage and to break the wall that has been built between us. Your constant ill temper does not make that an easy task."

"Surely, you did not expect any of this to be easy."

"No, I did not, but neither did I expect it to be so damned difficult! I did not expect my wife, for whom I have longed all these endless months and years, to look disappointed whenever she beheld me!"

"That is ungenerous!" she cried, even as she knew the justice in what he said. "I am happy that you returned—"

"Are you? I do not think you can say that with truth. In fact, I think your low spirits are because you do nothing with your days besides sit about bemoaning the loss of your precious Darcy!"

"That is cruel and unjust."

"Is it?" he demanded, his voice raised. "Do you have any idea how this is for me? How it pains me each and every day to know that I might have regained my wife but lost her love?"

His face was now angrily red, and catching sight of himself in the mirror, he gave a jerky bow and stormed into his bedchamber, slamming the door after him.

Elizabeth, horrified, began to cry. She was shocked out of her tears, however, when she heard a loud crash from Henry's bedchamber and the tinkle of broken glass. She rose quickly and went to him.

Opening his door, she saw him in a chair at the side of the room, his head in hands. On the opposite wall was a mark in the paper, and on the carpet beneath, many tiny shards of glass glittered in the light.

"Take care, I broke my urn," he said weakly.

She stepped around it carefully, aghast when she realised it was a hand blown glass urn he had purchased in Murano during his Grand Tour. "Henry! You loved this piece! You brought it all the way back from Italy!"

He had truly loved the urn and had expended no inconsiderable effort in bringing it from Italy, where the art of blowing glass was renowned. She could not imagine what possessed him to throw it, but he clearly did, for it was a great distance from its customary place on the mantel above his fireplace.

He sat back in his chair, affecting calmness. "What does it signify? I was angry and I threw it."

She looked at him uncertainly. She had not known him to have a volatile temper, but the situation they currently faced was very different from the life they had known. She approached him slowly, pausing a moment before sitting on his lap. He leaned back to make way for her but did not put his arms around her. After a slight hesitation, she pressed a kiss onto his cheek.

"I am so sorry for upsetting you. I have been unkind and selfish, but I do care about you."

"I do not want you to care about me. I want you to love me as you did before."

Stricken, she whispered, "I am trying to be what I once was. I shall get there in time. Please be patient with me even though you have borne so much already."

He nodded, still looking glum.

"I am in a particularly bad humour this night. As much as I love my dear sister, I am disinclined to spending the evening with Miss Bingley and Mr Neaves, knowing what gossips they are."

He appeared the tiniest bit mollified, and so she pressed on. "I abhor being the subject of interest. It has gone on for far too long, and I cannot abide it longer."

With a deep breath, Henry replied, "We shall go to Warrington soon. It will be better for us both, I daresay."

"Yes, it will." She kissed his cheek. "I shall summon one of the maids to clean this. Are you ready to depart, or shall I send our regrets?"

"No, no. Let us go. I am ready."

THE EVENING WITH JANE AND BINGLEY PROVED TO BE LESS ANXIETY provoking than Elizabeth thought it would. Mr Neaves was an amiable man, agreeable in company, and if he was storing on dits about Lord and Lady Courtenay to relate to his friends, he hid it well.

Miss Bingley was unexpectedly charming as well, being neither ingratiating nor malicious. It was a side of her Elizabeth had seen but rarely, and she wondered whether the lady was in love with Mr Neaves. Surely, little else could cause her to act in such a pleasant manner.

Elizabeth's guilt was made that much more profound because she had initiated a fight with her husband—in and of itself egregious—based on a supposition that was false. Her error was thus doubled. She shook her head, vowing once again to pull herself from her doldrums.

I am not formed for ill humour. I never have been, and I do not wish to begin. True, I cannot have what I wish for, but that is so for many people. You are no different. Accept this with gratitude, for it might be far worse.

She knew what she needed to do, much as it pained her to do it.

I must take myself, my heart, and my mind away from Darcy. The friendship, the connexion cannot be maintained.

The agony that accompanied such a thought was breathtaking.

If I am ever to be happy and at peace in my life with Henry, Darcy must be set aside. There is no other way.

She looked at Henry and saw that he was listening attentively to a story Bingley was relating while absently eating a dish of peas and pearl onions. Elizabeth's mouth opened with alarm, recalling the fact that he often grew ill to the point of vomiting from onions. Even a food merely touched by an onion might cause him to become sick. She saw it happen to him in Italy.

She cleared her throat gently and caught his attention. "The onions," she whispered. "You are eating the onions."

He looked at her blankly. "Is something wrong with the dish?"

"The onions," Elizabeth gestured to his plate, but he appeared uncomprehending.

"Lizzy?" Jane asked. "Is something wrong?"

Elizabeth was embarrassed, having wished to avoid notice. "Everything is wonderful. You do set a lovely table. However, Henry sometimes becomes ill from eating onions or dishes containing onions."

Jane looked to Henry with wide eyes. "Oh no! I beg your pardon, sir, I did not know they would make you ill!" She gestured to a nearby footman. "Smith, please remove the plate."

"No need, I assure you." Henry waved the man off. "The onions will do me no harm."

Neaves then launched into some tale he had heard wherein onions, like asparagus, could predispose the body to infection. The rest of the table fell silent, not wishing to distress Lord Courtenay. Elizabeth watched her husband closely.

The last time she had seen him eat an onion, it was part of the very dish he had just consumed, and he had developed sharp pains in his stomach within a few minutes. The pains had doubled him over, rendering him almost unable to walk, and had not relented for several days. Moreover, he had developed a rash around his mouth and on his neck.

Yet, he was perfectly well now. The onions did not affect him though he did push them aside, eventually permitting Smith to remove his plate. Nevertheless, he had consumed a good portion before she stopped him.

Elizabeth did not know what to think of it. Was it possible for these sorts of problems to dissipate entirely with age? She supposed it must be so, for throughout the rest of the night and even when they retired, Henry showed no sign of pain or distress. She was glad for it as the only thing that might make the night worse was for him to take ill.

Elizabeth laid awake long into the night, thinking of her marriage. The thoughts begun earlier and resisted had continued to worm their way into her consciousness. She had not seen Darcy often and soon would go into Lancashire where she would see him not at all. Yet, he was constantly in her mind, an ever-present spectre in her dreams. The memory of his face was the siren's song that lured her to him, even knowing she could not have him. He haunted her.

No more Darcy. No more thoughts, no more love, no more memories. I must be wholly Lady Courtenay.

Turning onto her stomach, she cried into her pillow, feeling the deepness of her loss and mourning the true happiness that would never again be her own.

IT WAS NEARLY FOUR IN THE MORNING WHEN THE MAN ENTERED THE brothel, nodding to the proprietor as he followed his usual girl to the room he preferred at the top of the stairs. It was an out of the way room with a separate stairway out the back, ideal for a clandestine removal.

The young courtesan was a delight—winsome and eager to please —but on this night, the man had more pressing concerns than those of his body. He entered the room, closing the door behind him, and the girl smiled prettily as she prepared to leave. "Do you wish me to return later?"

He offered her a kind smile and handed her some pound notes he had earlier secreted in his pocket. "I do not think so, my dearest."

The girl thanked him and left, and the man turned and unlocked the door to the back stairway. Moments later his compatriot entered.

"My lord." The man's friend bowed deeply and affectedly, and the two men both laughed with the irony of it.

"Yes, indeed." They took two chairs that had been put in the room for this purpose and moved them close to the fire, as they had no other means by which to warm their blood.

"So, what have you learned?"

Lord Courtenay knew he had not all of the information that was needed and so chose to prevaricate a bit. "She found the cipher with some journals, my journals."

"Yet, she has done nothing to find the money," the man retorted. "I can only suppose she is too dull to apprehend the meaning of it."

Courtenay shrugged. "She has been to the castle rarely. She was in hiding, in case you had forgotten."

"And a damned nuisance that was! We might have had this settled long ago."

"Well, so it is." Courtenay shrugged. "The pieces are together now."

"Yes, but does she understand the cipher?"

"I cannot be sure."

"Not sure!" The man exclaimed in disbelief. "Ask her, you fool."

Courtenay scowled. "Let us not forget whose fortune this is." He went to the fire and toed it with his boot, permitting his friend to bask in the error of his ways for a moment.

"Forgive me." His friend was properly penitent. "You are correct; this is your fortune. I am only eager for things to happen. The years have drawn long."

Courtenay turned back, magnanimous and amiable in his forgiveness of the breach. "That they have. Do not grow impatient now—all things in due time. I shall take my wife to Warrington in the next fortnight, and then we shall see to the rest. Elizabeth is a witty, curious sort of girl. I do not doubt her ability to unravel the portions in code, if she has not already."

The man nodded. "Of course. What are your plans for her then?"

"My plans?"

"Once all has been settled and the fortune retrieved."

Courtenay shrugged. "I do not know."

"I suppose you could keep her. It would save you a fortune in the brothels."

"Wives are more costly than harlots, I assure you." Courtenay laughed. "Moreover, I have never been so terribly inclined towards matrimony. A wife is one woman, always. For a harlot, you can suit your fancy on a night-by-night basis."

The man knew he had erred earlier and wished to be complaisant. "If you require some assistance, I am pleased to help you."

"Perhaps." Courtenay yawned, the time of the night taking its toll on him. "She is a sweet girl. I would not wish her to suffer. I have grown excessively fond of her, after all."

"What of the boy?"

"Oh, nothing to be done there," Courtenay was quick to insist. "The earldom, in whatever form it remains, must have an heir. If I have not an heir, people will push me to remarry and create one. Young Henry has his purpose in the times to come, but Elizabeth, alas, does not."

"Do you not wish for a second son?"

"Heaven forbid!" Courtenay exclaimed. "A second son is not a fate I would wish on anyone, not with so much still uncertain."

"So you say." Chuckling, the man rose. "I shall leave you now until we meet at Warrington."

FITZWILLIAM HAD PESTERED UNCEASINGLY FOR DARCY TO JOIN HIM AT a ball given by one of Lord Matlock's close friends. Sir Frederick Latymer was an exceedingly wealthy gentleman from Northampton-shire who had three beautiful daughters, and Fitzwilliam was keen to flirt with them.

"Come, Darcy, there are three of them: one each and a spare," Fitzwilliam teased with a leer.

"Do not do that," Darcy replied immediately, a warning clear in his tone.

Fitzwilliam knew immediately that his joke had gone awry. "I apol-ogise. You are correct; such a joke is thoughtless."

Darcy did not reply immediately. From the desk chair in his study, he looked out the window a moment. Softly, he said, "If before, I was a disinterested suitor, I now find the idea abominably repulsive."

"Forgive me; it was not an appropriate jest."

"It occurred in October." Darcy spoke as if to himself. "The thing with Wickham, that is, and then we had to wait and worry until January when we found him."

"I know."

Darcy seemed not to have heard him. "Now it is the beginning of April, three months since the truth was known, and it is not yet easier —not one bit. When will it improve, I wonder?"

"No improvement at all?"

"I still cannot comprehend the fact that she is not my wife and she never was. My heart is married to her, and it cannot be undone." Darcy went to the window. "I hired someone to check into things."

"What?" Fitzwilliam was surprised. "Why would you do that?"

"For my own peace of mind, I imagine."

Fitzwilliam sighed. "Your peace of mind?"

"Something in this is not right. There is deviltry afoot, and I wish to ensure Elizabeth is not caught in the midst of it."

"Is it not her husband's prerogative to see to her safety?"

"Unless her husband is involved," Darcy replied sharply.

"There has never been any suggestion of that."

"No one was looking for it," Darcy insisted, turning to look at his cousin. "Even though she can never be mine, I want to see that she is safe and happy, always."

They were interrupted by a knock at the door and a footman

informing them that the carriage awaited. Darcy rose with a sigh of reluctance.

"I shall go to this ball for a short time, but I shall not promise you more than that."

"That is fair enough," Fitzwilliam agreed.

HE WAS SHOCKED TO SEE HER THERE THOUGH HE DID NOT KNOW WHY. Lord and Lady Courtenay had entered into the social fray with a vengeance, the earl clearly eager to reacquaint himself with all the pleasures of town society. Darcy supposed their design was to meet the gossips unashamedly. If everyone saw them everywhere, there could hardly be as much to say about them, could there?

He did not go to her immediately but watched as she danced, noting that her smile was dull and her manner gracious but restrained. She had a pinched look about her eyes that he knew mirrored his own.

Courtenay had left her by the fourth set, and she stood among other young married ladies who chatted lightly as they watched the dancers. He went to her immediately.

"Lady Courtenay, will you do me the honour of dancing the next with me?"

She turned to him, her eyes filled with an emotion he could not discern. "Mr Darcy. Yes, I would be honoured."

He was aware of the eyes of the ladies upon them as he offered his arm and silently led her to the dance.

The set that had formed was large, which suited Darcy well as it gave them ample time to talk while the others moved through the pattern.

"How are you?"

She gave him a small smile. "Well enough, and you?"

"Dreadful," he whispered. "I think of nothing all day but my longing for you."

"In that we are equal," she replied with a slight lift of her shoulders.

When they spoke again, it was simultaneously.

"I must speak—"

"Where is—"

He smiled at her. "After you, please."

She looked away quickly, and he saw tears fill her eyes. "Will you escort me out for some air? I must speak to you, and I cannot do it here."

He wondered what new pain was nigh upon him as he agreed, indicating she should lead the way and following her with dread.

Her tears fell quickly once they reached the terrace. He offered his handkerchief, but she did not take it. Instead, she pulled a handkerchief embroidered with her husband's initials from her reticule. He disregarded the meaning of that, taking her elbow and guiding her towards a small bench.

"How is young Henry?" He missed the boy dearly and often spent the scant time that he was not dwelling on Elizabeth in thinking of the little boy he had once called his son.

"Wonderful, as always." She wiped her eyes. "We are for Warrington within the next week to be there for Easter. We shall not return for some time—a year perhaps."

He nodded through the pang of sadness that smote him. "I see."

"Fitzwilliam." She sighed more than said it as more tears came to her eyes. "I cannot go on this way. I love you, I love everything about you, and I suspect that I shall never feel that way for anyone ever again."

"Anyone except for Henry."

"No." She shook her head, looking down. "Heaven help me, I just do not love him any longer. As gradually as my love for you came on, so did my love for him wane, and I cannot seem to find it within me again.

"That is why I must…we must sever the ties between us. How I despise it!" Her tears came again. "It is impossible to continue. I am living a double life, wanting that which I cannot have while forced to pretend the one I want is before me. I cannot act; the role I have been assigned is more than I can feign, and I must…I must remove you from my heart and my mind in hopes that I can regain what I have lost for him."

Darcy rose from the bench, putting his back to her. He went to the edge of the terrace and stood against a column, staring out into the inky night.

Quietly, she spoke to his back. "I cannot continue with half a life and half a heart, and the one who owns me wishes for the return."

He was silent for several long moments when he heard her rise and come towards him. Leaning her face against his back, she wound her arms around his middle.

"This is your final goodbye then," he said, his voice rough.

She whispered fervently, "Had I any other choice, I would take it, but I do not. This is killing me. I cannot go on in this divided way. I must do my best to love him once again. He is my husband and the father of my son, and I must make myself love him again."

Darcy could not bear more pain or more sorrow, and thus, the flush of anger spreading over him was welcomed. He removed her hands from his waist and stepped away, turning to face her.

"Very well then." His voice was clipped and cold. "Henry has played his hand well."

She looked puzzled. "What do you mean?"

Darcy shrugged, looking off into the distance of the black night. "I could not understand his liberality with you. He was neither jealous nor possessive. He unlocked your door and let you come to this as you had to, and now he is the ultimate victor. He has won it all. You are his once more and by your own choice. Could anything be more sweet?"

"He was always going to be victor." She, too, sounded angry through her sorrow. "My choice is only to avoid descending into madness, for that is where my love for you is taking me."

"Well, that is the difference between us. I would gladly take madness so long as I had you there."

She stepped closer to him, crossing her arms over her chest. "I have a duty! I have a son to raise and a marriage vow to fulfil, and I cannot do that when my heart, mind, and soul are filled with you!"

"So you come to me this night to tell me you will have no part with me? That is your duty? To tear my heart out?"

"No!" Elizabeth cried out. "That is not—"

"Are we speaking of your marital duties then? You wish me gone from your mind so you can be more engaged in Henry and his tedious intimacy?"

She closed the distance between them in a trice and slapped him soundly. He was glad she struck him for saying such a wretched thing. He knew he was despicable even as he said it.

After she slapped him hard enough that tears came to his eyes, she turned, prepared to run, but he grabbed her hand, pulling her back and into a tight embrace. She was sobbing intensely, and his anger dissolved, leaving a new sort of tear to burn his eyes. "Lizzy, darling, forgive me, forgive me please. You do not deserve such vile words from me."

She said nothing, but neither did she leave his arms, crying into his waistcoat as he stroked her hair and murmured his apologies over and over. "I have already become a bitter and wretched man, so very wretched, and it is no excuse. It does not give me licence...I am appalled and horrified by what my sorrow has made me. We are both victims of this."

When she finished weeping, she stepped back from him, raising Henry's handkerchief to her eyes.

There was a rain barrel nearby, likely used to water the flowers within the courtyard. He took her handkerchief and went over to wet it, bringing it back for her to clean her face and help restore her appearance to some semblance of her usual beauty.

She stood silently, holding the cloth to her eyes with her other hand in Darcy's grasp. At last, she dropped the cloth, turned to him, and kissed him on the lips.

He knew, deep within him, that this was it for them—a final good-bye, a last acknowledgement of what they once were to each other—and thus, he heeded neither honour nor duty but allowed his heart its small claim on him. He ran his hands down her body and across her back as she plunged her hands into his hair, holding him tightly to her. He prayed that somehow they might make this kiss last forever. His need for her was fierce, and he imagined taking her then and there, partly from want but mostly from his desire to own her.

When she pulled away, heaving a sigh, he stopped her for a moment. Gently, he traced the features of her face with his hand, winding his fingers into the softness of her hair, and doing all he could to memorise the sight and feel of her in his arms. It would need to sustain him, he knew, and thus, he wished to burn the sensation into his skin, to press her into him and leave an indelible mark so that he could always know she was once his.

"I must commit you to my memory for the long nights when I am bereft and feel my loneliness even more keenly than I do now."

Tears came to her eyes as she fell back into his embrace, hugging him tightly, much more tightly than she ever had, causing him to gasp for breath.

She released her hold just a bit and rested her head on his chest, her curls tickling his chin. "Will you do something for me?"

"Anything."

"Find someone else to love, someone who loves you too…"

He shook his head firmly.

"Yes, please, for me. I insist. Do not allow your anger and your sadness over this to make you bitter. Find someone who will help you be happy, someone who will love you and help prevent you from becoming, once again, the lonely, sombre man I met at the assembly in Meryton. Forget about me; forget about us. It is the only way either of us will survive this, for you as well as for me."

He could not look at her but nodded once, silently, to give her his word. As soon as he did, she gave him one more soft kiss, barely touching his lips, then she turned away, leaving him standing there as she returned to the ballroom.

TWENTY-SIX

D arcy stood on the terrace of the Latymers home, watching as Elizabeth vanished into the crowded ballroom and out of his life.

The pain assaulting him was so real that he could scarcely breathe. It filled his chest and pierced him, cleaving him in half. He knew he must go, but for some time he had not the strength required to walk, no matter how much he wished to leave the scene of the greatest pain he had ever known.

Eventually, he was able to don the cloak of his characteristic reserve, holding himself stiffly upright as he began the walk home. He gave his leave to no one, caring not that Fitzwilliam would wonder where he was or that his hosts might be offended. He required solitude and could not imagine making any sort of polite conversation, not even for a moment.

There was a decided chill to the night air, which was a relief, particularly after the close heat of the crowded ballroom. He walked along, lost in his thoughts, not knowing or caring where or how he went, just pointing himself towards home and assuming he would get there in due course.

It was finished. Their love was a stinking, bloated corpse that had lain in the viewing room far too long, well past the time it should have, and it was time to bury it. It mattered not whether she loved him or he loved her; she belonged to Courtenay.

For Darcy, there would be nothing. The loneliness he had felt in the summer before he met her was trifling compared to the gaping maw that now opened within his soul. He foresaw a bleak, empty future: he would grow old and embittered in his solitude. He thought longingly of old age. What a comfort it would be if he were sixty or so and knew it was soon over!

A sound came from behind him—footsteps? He glanced over his shoulder and seeing no one, retreated into his thoughts again.

A wife would be necessary at some point, but it would do nothing to ease the hole in his heart and the halving of his soul that had just occurred. *I must marry someone mercenary, someone whose true joy is in fortune and position, someone who will neither notice nor care whether my affections are fixed elsewhere.*

Another sound, this time a sort of scuffle.

He turned again, vexed that the moon had retreated behind a cloud and removed its scant light from the pavement. Shadows and shades abounded; the street appeared empty, but he felt the prickling unease of hidden eyes upon him.

He continued walking, his attention now more attuned to his environs. Then came the faint sound of a throat being cleared. He turned just as a figure vanished into the shadows. With a frown, Darcy knew he must make haste. He was without protection and did not fancy being robbed or worse. His home was near, and he hastened his step, eager to be in his study with a drink.

Another glance over his shoulder as he neared his house revealed a man quite close to him. When the man realised he had been noticed, he approached rapidly and pressed close to Darcy's back. "I must speak with you, sir. Bring me into your house, but we must not be seen."

"What the devil!" Darcy jerked away, glad he did not carry any money. "Blasted pickpockets! I should call—"

"No," the man hissed. "It is Hanley, and I must speak to you about your wife. Inside, and quickly, man!"

Darcy had a rapid succession of thoughts run through his head: punch Hanley, shout out an alarm, and do any number of prudent things that one might do when confronted by an interloper. For some reason, however, he did none of these, but he brought Hanley into his home with an uncharacteristic trust in a man who had done nothing but gall him from the first.

Darcy slipped Hanley past the footman at the front door, and they made it to Darcy's study unnoticed. He poured them both a generous brandy even as he wondered at the wisdom of allowing Hanley to be in his home at a late hour. He could not trust this man, nor would he be easy in his company, despite his rather insipid appearance.

They settled in chairs by the fireplace. "If you wish for some refreshment, Mr Hanley, I am afraid I cannot oblige you without summoning my housekeeper."

"I do not wish for anything but to speak to you."

"You have an odd way of requesting a meeting," Darcy told him severely. "You are lucky I do not carry my pistol."

Hanley shrugged. "You would not be the first to pull a pistol on me —nor the last, I believe."

The man's face was as dull and placid as ever. He had little expression as he removed from the pocket of his frock coat a small paper that bore many scribbled notations. Darcy could not read any of them, but it appeared to be some kind of code.

"You must have been away from town," Darcy began. "For if you had been privy to the gossip, you would know I do not have a wife. As it turns out, I never did."

"In that, I must say you are incorrect," Hanley replied. "You did, and still do, have a wife, at least by my accounting."

His heart leapt hopefully at such a statement, but Darcy was outwardly stern. "Absurd."

"I believe that the man your wife presently lives with is not Henry Warren, but Francis."

Darcy scoffed at Hanley even as a profound sense of joy flooded him. A preposterous notion, fanciful in the extreme, though he could not stop himself from asking, "Do you imagine that Mr Wickham shot the wrong brother? If so, would not Lord Courtenay have returned to his wife and his earldom immediately?"

"Not exactly," Hanley replied. "Before I tell you what I know, however, I must caution you: this story is solely my cause. I have not the proof needed to interest others. The men who investigated the murder of Lord Courtenay do not wish to hear they made a mistake. If Francis Warren was shot by Mr Wickham and lived to tell the tale, then it was the Crown and the men who acted in its stead that executed the earl. It is not an idea they are interested in exploring, particularly your own uncle, Lord Matlock."

"Why has it come to your interest?"

"I have known for some time that Henry was involved," Hanley answered. "So, I quietly sought information to implicate him, but that has been even more difficult since his return. He has proven far more cunning than he was previously, and thus, there is little to implicate him in these schemes. If we can prove he is Francis, then we have a problem solved for both of us. I believe that Francis—or rather, Henry, if I am correct—was hanged before your marriage?"

Our time at Rosings Park. I could never forget that. "Yes."

"Then Lady Courtenay was not married when she married you—if the man hanged was Henry."

Darcy's heart beat with excitement at the notion, but he remained inscrutable, watching as Hanley helped himself to a bit more of Darcy's brandy.

"My father, Mr Darcy, is the Baron Walsingham, and he served in the House of Commons as Lord Chief Justice of Common Pleas as did his father before him, settling debts and so forth. He is a man with a firm belief in king and country and honour above all, and he has always had a keen interest in exposing those who aim to harm our great sovereign state.

"As such, when I reached a certain age, I was asked by some highly placed individuals to do a small service to the Crown. It was a peculiar sort of position and carried with it the idea of danger, but as a young man, that would only entice me. I was uniquely positioned, you see, being an intimate of the Warren family, most particularly the heir, Henry Warren."

"You were not equally intimate in your friendship with his brother?"

"I was friend to both, but Francis was always a bit wild and inclined towards mischief and associations with questionable people." He drank deeply of his brandy. "In any case, in 1807, after the death of Frederick Warren, the old earl, I was asked to join a small group with the two Warren brothers—a group that met for cards and drinking now and again but whose activities and conversation had become suspect to the king."

Comprehension dawned on Darcy. "The treasonous radicals."

Hanley nodded. "Yes, though the king and Parliament did not suspect how far gone they were even from the start. There was talk of beheadings, murders, and the burning of estates—all the usual sorts of rebellious things."

"And you say both Henry and Francis were involved? I am aston-ished. I only knew Francis to be a part of the plot."

Hanley shook his head, a faint smile on his lips. "I was friend to Henry Warren nearly all of my life, and believe me when I say that the roles of the brothers—with Henry appearing the saint and Francis the sinner—were well rehearsed. Henry had become expert by that time at keeping himself untainted while Francis bore the consequence of what-ever mischief had transpired. No, I assure you, they were both in it, but Henry covered himself and his involvement very well."

"But why? Why would Henry involve himself in such a thing? Francis's impetus is more readily understood, but I cannot think why a wealthy, well-positioned man would want to do away with the order that exalted him."

"That, sir, brings us to the heart of the matter. Henry and Francis each took a different view on the group's objectives, and it caused a division. They both wanted to change things but each in his own way.

"The faction that included Francis wanted to establish a new sort of government—a democracy, if you will, with all men being equal or at least having equal opportunities in life no matter the station to which they were born.

"The other faction, Henry and one or two others, wanted to retain the old structure but destroy certain individuals within it, which would yield greater power to him and his allies. This caused great disagree-ment within the group as a whole, especially between the two brothers. The arguments grew vicious, and death threats became almost commonplace. However, in late 1808, Henry began to suspect that Francis's threats had become less talk and more of a true call to action."

"Dreadful," Darcy murmured.

Hanley continued as if he had not heard him, "Henry formed his own schemes, but he was a cunning man and could not content himself with only the killing of his brother. He wanted to ensure that, were he killed, his legacy would live on. He sought immortality the only way a man can."

Darcy inhaled sharply. "An heir."

Hanley nodded. "We were in Bath, the two of us, when he hit upon the notion. Henry had a deceptively gentle demeanour but do not mistake it; he was a determined man when he knew what he wanted, and he would go to great lengths for the pleasure of having his way.

"He knew that his brother had contracted a killer, and thus, he did likewise. He was not afraid to die, but what he did wish for was glory for the Courtenay legacy. He wanted a son, and he wanted to outwit his brother. By this time, the feud between them had grown quite bitter.

"We were walking the streets of Bath and looking in the shops, aimlessly wandering and speaking of his plans, when a lovely young girl from Hertfordshire caught his eye. It was done before I could believe my eyes: a courtship and marriage within mere weeks. He then hied her out of the country, desperate to get her with child."

Darcy's mouth hung slack—this was a shock. Not once had he imagined that Henry's motive in marrying Elizabeth was anything but true love. He grieved for her, for a loss that he hoped she would never know she suffered. "He never loved her?"

Hanley shrugged. "He had some affection for her, but no, theirs was not a romance, not on his part in any case. I believe the money he lavished on her and her family was a sort of apology for the fact that he had used her to this purpose. His design, as he said to me in Bath, was to marry someone beneath him who would be so enraptured by her change in fortune as not to question the rest of it. It had to be a woman unknown among the *ton*. The last thing he needed was someone with their own purpose and connexions. He preferred a country girl because he believed she would fall with child more quickly and more often than a lady of higher society. Elizabeth fit the bill on all accounts. He was happy with her though, and I do like to think he might have loved her, at least a little."

Darcy thought for a moment. "If he knew of the plot against him, why did he respond to his brother's summons to Warrington?"

Hanley smiled. "It was a case of the mouse entrapping the cat. Henry went to Warrington knowing what Francis had planned for him yet planning to have Francis dealt with on the way."

"The double plot!" Darcy exclaimed.

"Correct. What looked like a contingency plan for Henry's death was, in truth, one brother against the other. Mr Wickham believed he was hired to kill Lord Courtenay, but in fact, he was hired by Lord Courtenay to kill his brother. Being an identical twin has its benefits, and Henry likely used it to dupe Mr Wickham into thinking he had killed Henry instead of Francis. There were differences between them —build, length of hair, even style of dress—but Mr Wickham did not know them, and he could have been easily misdirected to one brother over the other.

"I believe Henry intended to remain in hiding until Mr Wickham was dead to avoid any possibility that the truth might be uncovered. He paid Mr Wickham a pittance as a final sort of insult to Francis to show that his life was worth so little. Of course, in the end, he got what he paid for, which was an incompetent assassin."

"How could Francis have known he would survive his brother's attack? Did he know?"

"I think not. I believe Francis, after recovering from his illness, realised he had a unique opportunity to take on the identity of Henry. It was the only way to emerge the victor."

Hanley took a sip of the drink Darcy had set before him. "Francis, you see, would not have wanted Henry killed on the road to Warrington. It was very much in Francis's interest to have Henry arrive, hale and whole, at their family seat."

"Why?"

"Money," Hanley replied simply. "Is that not the reason for everything?"

HAVING COMPLETED HER PREPARATIONS FOR BED, ELIZABETH FOUND herself feeling restive and thought she would not be able to sleep, despite the late hour.

By her appearance, she was all that Lady Courtenay should be. She smiled, she laughed, and she conversed well in society. She showed her love for her husband, and she paid no heed to the silly rumours and gossip that continued to surround them. All was as it should be.

Inside, her mind was quite different. There, she lived in a world where she was still married to Darcy, reliving their old conversations and inventing new ones. They carried on with the happy life they had known all too briefly. It was the colliding of those two worlds that left her feeling odd.

This is why I have relinquished the friendship with him. This will pass once I no longer see him, wish for him, and think of him.

Elizabeth was sitting with a book and a cup of tea when Henry entered. He was looking well, she noted disinterestedly. He had recovered a better complexion after leaving the mines, and he had gained weight as well, appearing more muscular. His hair was longer and curled, and he had ordered many new, fashionable clothes.

Yet she did not want him. The notion of kissing him, holding him, or permitting him to touch her still sickened her. Nevertheless, she knew she would need to permit it, and soon. The night he had requested her service thankfully had not been repeated, but it was a respite and not a cessation, and she did not fool herself into thinking otherwise.

"I hope I do not disappoint you when I say that we shall not go to Warrington by Easter."

"May I enquire why?"

"My business here is taking longer than I had foreseen. There are some people I must meet that I have not yet been able to."

"I am sorry to hear it. I know you are eager to be in the country."

"I am. It is far too long since I have seen my home."

"I do hope the actions taken by my advisers and me in your absence have not caused undue problems."

"No, no," Henry reassured her immediately. "Ah, but my limitation in mathematics and science hinders me! I have never had the mind for the study of investments or the science of plantings and so forth. It is tedious stuff, and being away from it has only confounded me further."

A memory pricked at her mind and without thinking, she said, "I thought that you excelled in mathematics and science."

He smiled. "Those were subjects for my brother. I have always enjoyed history and politics."

He departed, leaving Elizabeth with her thoughts.

She clearly recalled that young Henry had written in his journals that mathematics and science were his favoured subjects while Francis was interested in history and literature. Now he claimed the opposite.

Was it significant? She believed Henry had been only twelve or thirteen when he had written those words, still a schoolboy at Eton. It was entirely possible that a younger Henry believed himself excellent in those subjects only to have later study discourage him.

Gooseflesh rose on her arms and she rubbed them absently. The writings of a young boy in his journal are nothing to what a young man of nearly four and thirty says pertaining to the running of his estate. Sums on a slate have nothing to do with the enormous interests of the Courtenay family or the management of Warrington.

As Henry matured and better understood his responsibilities in

Parliament and the running of his estate, topics such as politics and history had likely become more interesting to him.

Yes, that is surely the explanation.

WITHIN DARCY'S STUDY, THE NIGHT DREW ON AS HANLEY CONTINUED relating his astonishing tale.

"There is a legend of a fortune buried in the underground of Warrington Castle. Who can know whether or not it is true? It dates back to the time of the Civil War when the Earl of Derby used Lancashire as his position."

Hanley drained his drink and set the glass firmly on the side table as Darcy leaned in closer. "Elizabeth told me of this once."

"The good citizens of Warrington, which even then was a thriving market town, were devoted Royalists, first to last, and when Derby thought he might rather burn the town to the ground than surrender it to Charles's enemies, there was no opposition. The rumour is that before Derby did his deed, all of the money from the markets went into the walls of the castle for safekeeping.

"Like most tales of buried treasure, there was a map with a cipher that had been lost. It was said that Henry and Francis's father had found the cipher, but it confounded him, and he knew not where the fortune was hidden. Henry, having succeeded his father, had access to the cipher, and when he was gone, it went to his widow."

Darcy nodded. "She did have it and told me that she and her father had spent many nights puzzling over it. However, when they eventually solved it, it led them to nothing. Surely, whoever hid the treasure must have retrieved it?"

"That is possible, or perhaps someone else managed to find it in the two hundred years since. However, it is notable that, in the time Mrs Darcy has had control over the Courtenay fortune, she has managed to add substantially to the family coffers."

"Has she? How?"

"If what Francis has told me is true, she has done very well in these years past—well enough to raise his suspicion over where the money came from. He has not a head for numbers and believes she found the hidden treasure and diverted it into the household accounts."

Darcy shook his head. "No, Elizabeth would not have lied to me. If she says she did not find it, then she did not."

"I agree." Hanley shifted in his chair. "I think it more probable that her uncle assisted her in making investments that proved successful. I gave it no more than a cursory look, but the origins of the increase seemed to lie in that direction.

"In any case, as of 1809 when the feud was reaching its most bitter point, Francis wanted Henry at the castle to obtain the cipher and codes to find the fortune hidden within the castle."

"And therefore, a Henry dead on the road to Crewe would have done him poorly," Darcy concluded. "There are so many twists and turns to this."

"It was the double plot that has always vexed me, and I have spent many a sleepless night turning it over in my mind. I could not determine any reason for Francis to arrange a murder when that would have buried the cipher forever, and not when another perfectly laid plan was in place at the castle with a far more able—and more costly—assassin than George Wickham."

"Oh?"

"A man called Joseph Richmond Blunt. Frightening man, surrendered to the mean streets of London at the age of seven by his mother. He survived by stealing and, when he was older, doing odd jobs for criminals: a theft here, a beating there, probably even murder when it was needed. He went to gaol for the first time when he was twelve, which was likely more of an education than a punishment. He was not caught again, but his name has turned up on occasion for various evil deeds. Francis Warren paid him three thousand pounds and his passage to the Indies up front, with the promise of another two thousand pounds when the deed was done."

"That is certainly a far cry from the twenty-five pounds George Wickham received," Darcy observed.

"Mr Blunt would have finished his job," Hanley remarked wryly. "It also lends more weight to my belief that it was Mr Blunt who was truly hired to kill Henry. Any able assassin would want passage for killing a peer."

"Truly?" Darcy was curious.

"From what I have learned, Mr Blunt has killed others who were not peers and was paid a thousand pounds or less, and clearly, passage was not provided."

"Mr Blunt wished to leave for good then," Darcy mused.

"And I do believe he did. He either received word or independently concluded that the situation had gone awry. He vanished, and nothing has been seen of him since, either in Lancashire or London.

"Clearly, Henry never had any intention of going to his castle, not until everything was settled. However, Mr Wickham inadvertently foiled the entire plan by failing to be an assiduous assassin. I believe that when Henry, masquerading as Francis, fled the scene of the murder, he knew that Francis was not truly dead.

"What ensued was a hiding game. Henry hid from the Crown and from Francis, Francis hid from the Crown and from Henry. Henry was the first to run out of luck when he was captured by the king's men and tried for treason. He was discovered based on some anonymous information. I have wondered whether Francis was responsible, but I have no proof. Regardless, Francis surely wished for George Wickham to be disposed of before coming out of hiding."

"Would not Henry have made his identity known when he was captured in Francis's stead?"

Hanley shook his head. "The Courtenay legacy was important to Henry. He still wished for his son to have his legacy, and if he died as a traitor, the title would be revoked. So much effort had been expended continuing his line that to have the Crown seize it would have been tragic. Henry wished for power, if not for himself, then for his legacy. Dying as Francis preserved that for him."

"You have put this baffling story together very well," Darcy mused. "But you say no one else supports this. Why?"

"Everyone believed from the start that Henry Warren was dead, and the strength of the supposition was increased by the fact that he did not attempt to contact his wife. It was widely believed that Henry loved his wife and was eager for his child, so if he had nothing to hide, why would he? For a man to come forth three years later claiming to be Henry was absurd. The whole picture fitted together too neatly. The mystery was solved, and with the execution of the man they believed to be Francis, it was a job well done. No one wanted to entertain the idea of another complication.

"Henry did do a good bit of ranting and raving at the gallows, telling all who would hear about his political position: his belief that the House of Lords was filled with the dissolute and the incompetent. He shrieked and cried that a new force must emerge for England to remain a world power, but it was all just entertainment. The crowd appreciated the show—right up until he dangled from the noose.

"The monarchy's men certainly wanted to believe they had their man then, and particularly now. To think that our government put a peer to death? No, they will not consider it. If they admit an earl was hanged without his right to be tried in the House of Lords, well that is a problem our regent takes upon himself. He would have the entirety of the House at him in a trice."

Darcy nodded. "So, what now? How can the man's claim to being Henry Warren, Earl of Courtenay, be disproved?"

Hanley shook his head. "I do not know. I have much evidence that points in this direction but nothing of true proof. What I need is one thing—one unmistakeable bit of evidence—that the man living in Towton Hall right now is not Henry but Francis. That is where you come in."

DARCY HAD ALWAYS ENJOYED THE DISTRACTION OF DRAWING AND painting, especially figures, but as he had matured, it was a pastime that fell by the wayside. Painting was not generally seen as the occupation of a gentleman, and sport and athletic endeavours were equally agreeable to him.

However, since the tragedy of losing his wife and son, Darcy had found some solace in art. There was a particular spot in the mistress's sitting room where the light came through most of the day, and the morning after his meeting with Hanley, he seated himself there at an early hour in an attempt to still his racing mind from the subjects discussed. Hanley had departed after charging him with the task of considering how best to prove the man who lived was Francis Warren, and Darcy was determined to do it.

He had been at it—the painting and the thinking—for some time when his sister entered and looked at his canvas. "You are advancing in your art, Brother."

Darcy put down his brush. "It gives me pleasure though I do not flatter myself that I have any particular degree of talent."

Georgiana was studying the picture he had drawn of himself and Elizabeth walking in a park. "It reminds me of the way you described the day you were betrothed. You were in the park that day, I think."

"We were." He smiled fondly at the remembrance. Naturally, Georgiana had never been told of Elizabeth's inebriated state the night prior. Elizabeth always remembered that night as one of great mortification, but he cherished it. Recalling the first touch of her lips to his could never be a source of shame or censure, despite the fact that those lips had tasted strongly of brandy.

After a moment, Georgiana looked away and spoke of the matter that had driven her to seek him out: whether he wanted to dine with the Matlocks that night. As it was, he did not want to, but since it seemed less a request than an order, he agreed.

After Georgiana left, he tilted his head back and closed his eyes, willing himself to be lost in the memory of that walk and their subsequent engagement.

They had teased one another, speaking of Georgiana calling her out, and then she had spoken the words he had never even permitted himself to dare to dream.

> *"... perhaps I should just offer for you—or rather, agree to your offer if it still stands—and avoid Georgiana's wrath entirely."*
> *"Do you mean that?"*
> *"I do not wish to hurt you, but neither would I mislead you."*

He had listened carefully as she told him she feared she would never return his love, and that she did him a disservice in marrying him. Those words had certainly been disappointing, yet they ultimately had been proven wrong. She had offered him a love unlike anything he ever could have imagined.

She had spoken, he recalled, on the cautions of an unequal marriage, clearly not knowing that he was desperate for her by then. Any scrap, any morsel or crumb of such a paradise was far above anything else he might have found. Unequal? It was only unequal in that she had believed she offered him less when, in truth, she had given him everything in life that truly mattered.

With a sigh, he wrenched himself from his reverie. "I would be happy if I could think of something that would prove you were now with Francis and not Henry."

He picked up his brush, intending to paint again, when another memory from that same day reared up into his consciousness.

His hand trembled as a smile came across his face. He leapt from his seat so quickly that it tumbled over, and he was nearly gone from the room by the time it hit the floor. *There it is! We have it!*

TWENTY-SEVEN

E lizabeth awoke the morning after the Latymers' ball feeling peevish, melancholy, and rather unfit for company. Most unfortunate, particularly as she believed she would have a great deal of it once the hour for callers came. Her aunt would call and beg her company on a visit to Jane. She believed her mother was staying with the Bingleys, and she felt the throb of an incipient headache just imagining it.

The best part of the morning began when she heard the sounds of her maid preparing her bath. Dear girl, she had anticipated her mistress's most ardent desire: a calming, soothing bath to relax her spirit and ease her body.

In twenty minutes, Elizabeth found herself in a heavenly, hot bath. She dismissed her maid and rested her head with a cloth over her eyes against the edge of the tub, attempting to clear her mind of her worries and distresses. It did not work; instead, it settled her melancholy deep within her. After fifteen minutes of time thus wasted, she sighed, sat up, and began to bathe.

She ran the fine-milled, lavender-scented soap over her body, enjoying the soothing scent and silky feel. As she washed her legs, she saw the scar on the lower part of her right one, earned at the age of twelve when, to her mother's mortification, she was climbing a tree. She still remembered going home with her petticoat and skirt torn and blood running down her leg. It was not such a bad wound, but it did bleed quite a bit, and it left her with a scar.

A scar! What has become of Henry's scar?

Elizabeth remembered seeing it on his chest one night soon after they had arrived in Italy on their wedding trip. In general, Henry did not remove his clothing when they were intimate, but he had purposely shown her the scar, admitting to some embarrassment about it. This, he had said, is what happens to men who act like boys while using men's toys.

Elizabeth had laid her hand over it. It had exceeded the length of her hand, though by just a bit. It was slightly raised, angry, and red, though it was nearly a year old by that time.

Was it possible that now, almost four years later, such a scar could be gone?

She looked down at her leg. It had been a much less impressive sort of wound and was received at a younger age when healing was quicker and scarring less permanent. Yet, a line remained, faint but still there after nearly ten years.

Her heart pounded as she thought of the implications of her husband's scar having vanished from his chest, for she had not seen any hint of it the night he came to her room.

Of course, the light had been dim, and Henry's robe had mostly covered him. Mostly. However, the scar ran across his chest; surely, she would have seen something.

She was overwhelmingly anxious that night though, and in truth, she had looked away the instant he exposed himself. Perhaps she had simply missed it.

If it is gone, what does it mean? She wrenched her mind from considering that and concentrated on whether or not she had seen any suggestion of it. She could not determine that she had, but she also could not be certain it was truly gone.

I must look again. Examining his chest for marks when he came to her had not been foremost on her mind. It likely was there, but she had been distracted and did not notice. Perhaps her recollection of that night was faulty.

Just then, Elizabeth heard sounds indicating that her husband was rising. Impetuously, she leapt from her bath, snatched a towel and her dressing gown, and pulled the latter on hastily. Without stopping to think of the implications, she was determined to see his chest. Perhaps she might surprise him while he dressed and see him bare-chested.

Fortune was on her side.

Henry stood looking out a window, clad only in his small clothes with no shirt.

"Oh!" she exclaimed upon seeing him.

"My darling." His voice was low and a bit sultry as he turned and walked towards her.

The bright morning light streamed through the windows, and Elizabeth clearly saw that his chest was smooth and unmarked with not so much as a hint that any wound had ever been there.

Her heart pounding, she fixed on the more immediate problem: her husband—or was he?—was presently approaching her, having seen some sort of invitation by her appearance in his bedchamber and by the fact that she was ogling his shirtless body.

She took a step backwards.

"Henry, I...I beg your pardon, I have interrupted your morning... toilette...and I only just wished...that is, do you...what are you..."

"You may interrupt me any time you wish," he murmured. His delight was rather prominent, and she could not stop herself from noticing it. Her eyes seemed to slide towards his pelvis no matter how she tried to stop them.

He chuckled, noticing her look. "As you see, I have been thinking of you. It seems a gift that you should appear like this."

She laughed nervously and took another step back. "No, I would... you are meeting Mr Hanley today, are you not?"

"Does it seem that I am thinking of Hanley right now?" He took her hand and tried to draw her closer. When she did not budge, he began tugging her towards his bed. She stumbled, and he reached out as if to pick her up.

A knock was heard from his dressing room.

A flash of vexation came over his face, and Henry called out, "I said I would ring when I was ready for you."

The valet responded, "Beg your pardon, sir, but Mr Hanley has arrived and asked me to bid you make haste. There is someone you must see."

Elizabeth stood breathless with relief flooding her senses. Henry pressed his lips together, clearly trying to abstain from a curse. He sighed and pulled her hand to his lips. "Perhaps later we shall begin where we have so unwillingly ended?" His voice was hopeful.

"Perhaps," she agreed, hoping she sounded discouraging.

HANLEY HAD SPOKEN WITH DARCY WELL INTO THE NIGHT, SEEKING some means by which they could prove Lord Courtenay was Francis Warren. Definitive proof would be difficult to find. Twin brothers who had lived most of their lives in one another's pocket could slip into the identity of the other with ease.

Hanley still felt the frustration as he rode with the man he believed was Francis Warren, travelling towards Towton Hall after spending time together at Brooks's.

"You are for Warrington next week?"

"Elizabeth and I shall go and try our fortune, so to speak." He laughed.

"And then?"

Warren shrugged, his eyes on the road ahead of him. "Then we put our plans into motion—at long last, I might add."

Hanley paused a moment then asked, "Do you never fear capture? You saw what happened to your brother."

"My name is attached to nothing implicating me of any wrongdoing. Even this fortune, when it is found, is not Courtenay money but, rather, the money of hardworking townspeople. It is rather fitting, is it not?"

Hanley did not respond, and Warren continued, "Moreover, as a peer, they can hardly treat me as they did those nobodies, can they?"

"Your brother was a nobody?"

Warren looked irritated. "In time of war, sacrifice is made. My brother is a hero, a war hero."

In a contemplative manner, Hanley said, "Ah, so it will be Francis's name attached to all these actions, good and bad. Francis will be a hero then, and you are left to obscurity."

Warren smiled, looking a bit dangerous. "Perhaps posterity will honour us both."

THE LETTER.

A letter written by Henry that Elizabeth had held, crumpled and forgotten in her hand when Darcy had arrived at her home to find her drunk those many months ago. He took the letter from her and then mistakenly brought it with him when he left that night. The next day as they walked in the park, he had attempted to return it. She had explained its contents, knowing he would not have read it.

"…nothing more than a note to a friend…a draft, or he neglected to send it… the pair of them fencing with old swords they had found… deep gouge across Henry's chest…quite the scar…nearly the whole way across his chest…I saw it once. It looked rather mean."

Darcy's heart pounded with excitement at the recollection. If the letter could be produced along with the testimony of the friend and Elizabeth, it would indeed prove conclusive. He remembered he had carried the letter back to her house, as she had no reticule with her.

Had he returned it to her? Had he left it somewhere at Towton Hall? He did not think so. By the time they had returned to the house, his mind had fixed on only one objective and that was to kiss her. He had not given the letter even one moment more of consideration.

But where might he have put it?

He began his search in his bedchamber, looking in the box within his armoire where he kept items of sentimental value. He then went to his study, rifling through his files to see whether it had been placed with his personal correspondence, then to the mistresses' study where he examined everything and anything to find the letter. Hours later, he remained unsuccessful and summoned the assistance of his valet.

Fields had been with Darcy since university. In his fifth decade, he was nearly as tall and quiet a man as his young master. He prided himself on solving any problem, sartorial or otherwise, with as little fuss as possible. He stood before his employer, his face betraying no expression, as Darcy explained the dilemma.

"Perhaps it was in my coat pocket when I returned home? I do not recall removing it, not after she had asked me to hold it."

"This was last April, you say, sir?"

Darcy nodded.

"I believe, had I uncovered such a letter in your coat, that I would have asked you what you wanted done with it."

Darcy sighed. "I would have told you to file it. Alas, I have already checked my files, and it is not among them. Could it still be in the coat? I cannot recall precisely which coat it was."

"I always verify that your pockets are empty. I would not wish something to be ruined in the laundry. Shall I check your coats to be certain?"

"Please do," Darcy acknowledged glumly, dismissing him. For long minutes, he racked his brain, trying to imagine any place where the letter might be and hoping it was not at Towton Hall.

A knock came at his door, and Fields entered when bidden. "I did not find it among your coats, but I had another thought, sir."

"Yes?"

"Oftentimes, I have noticed you will mark your place in a book with whatever correspondence is at hand."

"That is true, I sometimes do that." A bad habit, and it had caused him to misplace more than one letter in the past. He tried to break himself of the custom but still fell into it on occasion.

"Perhaps if this particular letter lay on your desk, it might have been pressed into service as a marker."

"I do not suppose that you would recall what I was reading a year ago?" He spoke lightly, not wishing to alarm Fields, who might think himself required to know such things.

"I do not, sir."

Darcy never could comprehend the neglect of a family library, and thus his libraries in both Pemberley and London were extensive. He sighed, hoping he was not about to demand the impossible. "Then I believe we have a task ahead of us."

All who could be spared from their duties were pressed into service, rifling through each of the books in Darcy's library. Almost three hours later, a young scullery maid named Betsy found a letter folded within the pages of an agricultural treatise that Darcy had once tried to read but found too dull to continue. His hands shook as he took it from her, opening and reading it eagerly.

According to this letter dated September 29 1808 and written to his friend Mr Silas Barnes, in June of that same year, Henry had received a wound from his friend's errant sword as they unwisely fenced after some time of port drinking and cigar smoking. The blade had been old and dull, but unlike practice foils, it boasted a real point at the end. The wound bled impressively for some time, and it became infected, but in the end, it did heal. However, Henry was left with a scar across his chest that, by his own account, was almost seven inches long, purplish red, and slightly raised.

His servants jumped as Darcy let out an exultant whoop, having never heard such a sound come from their usually sombre master. Betsy was awarded twenty pounds and a week's respite from her duties, causing her to cry with happiness. Fields was similarly grati-fied, having thought of the notion in the first place. Darcy went off to see his uncle and cousin, his step quick and a smile on his face for what felt like the first time since he had heard the dreadful words uttered by Wickham.

ELIZABETH ENDURED THE VISIT OF HER BELOVED AUNT AS CIVILLY AS she could. She was preoccupied and knew that Lady Gardiner noticed. Thankfully, her aunt accepted her excuse of being tired and did not press her for more.

When her aunt departed, Elizabeth hurried to her writing desk. One thing she knew for certain was that her wishes could not free her; only reason and rationality could fulfil the office. She must proceed with her wits about her and not allow undue emotion to colour her perceptions.

She drew out a piece of paper and began to write, making a list of all the little inconsistencies she had noted. The largest and most condemning was, of course, the scar. In retrospect, she thought it telling that Mr Wickham also shot Henry's former valet, one of the few people who could have known about the scar.

Would Francis have known about it? She considered that a moment, placing her pen between her teeth. Perhaps not. The estrange-ment between Henry and his brother began in the two years prior to her marriage. Henry had confided that to her along with his wish that they might—How did he put it?—be a part of the same regiment? It was something like that: a military allusion.

She shivered a little. She had not considered it before, but if Henry proved not to be Henry, but Francis, was she in danger? Would Francis suspect that she knew?

Putting those thoughts aside, she continued to write. The onions came to mind immediately, as well as the assertion that he was not of a mind for mathematics but preferred history and politics, which Henry wrote in his journal were Francis's best subjects.

Other things were less condemning but still curious. His anger was more easily raised and volatile, causing him to destroy a beloved memento that "he" had painstakingly carried back from Italy. And all his lapses in memory were oddly confined to her, her family, and their courtship and marriage.

When Elizabeth had finished writing, she sat back and reviewed the list. Mr Wickham shot the wrong brother, and Francis saw in it an opportunity to take the place he had always wished was his.

Now what should I do? It did not escape her understanding that Henry had probably been wrongly put to death by the regent and his men, and they would be reluctant to admit that Francis was alive. *Should I confront him with the truth or play along?*

It was safest to play along. There was no harm in pretending to be his wife, save for the fact that each day she did was another day without Darcy. Moreover, if she did continue in her disguise, or rather, as a part of his, then she could seek the assistance of the appropriate authority figures. Surely, someone among them would see her concerns and assist her in extricating herself from this madman.

Elizabeth glanced at the clock, seeing that Henry, or the man calling himself thus, was due back shortly. She added a few lines to what she had written, folded it quickly, sealed it, and then summoned a footman. She tried to look calm as she instructed him. "Deliver this note to Darcy House straightaway please—to the hands of the master and none other."

When the messenger had gone, she took up Henry's journals. There was information to be gained therein, she was sure of it, and she was determined to look until she found it.

Elizabeth and the man calling himself Henry were alone that night, the two of them at one end of the long table. He was in high spirits. She hoped she appeared similarly vivacious despite her mood, which was nearly violent with anger and fear.

She had, at the last moment, ordered creamed onions for dinner. Henry looked at them for a moment and then asked, "Did you wish to have onions this night, love?"

Elizabeth smiled at him. "I do like them, and it seems they do not affect you now as they once did. Perhaps you have outgrown your aversion."

"I think so," he replied, eating them with enthusiasm. "Gladly too, for I do enjoy them."

"How was Mr Hanley today? In good health, I hope?"

"Excellent health and very good spirits," Henry replied. "He and I were looking at this little map." Reaching into his pocket, he drew out a well-worn page that Elizabeth knew directed its bearer to the hidden, mythical fortune at Warrington Castle. "I cannot tell you how many hours we passed with this as boys."

Both of them laughed lightly, Elizabeth feeling hers tinged with wariness and vexation. She spoke lightly, "A boy's dream come true, I think. A hidden treasure to be discovered in the walls of the castle."

Henry chuckled. "A girl's too, particularly a curious girl. Have you ever studied it?"

"A little. The code is rather difficult." Elizabeth once again felt the prickly sensation on the back of her neck. "It is fun to consider it, like a parlour puzzle. I have always enjoyed those."

"Let us look at it when we have finished our dinner. Would it not be diverting to search for this fortune when we are finally at home?"

"Vastly diverting," Elizabeth replied. Wanting to test him, she said, "You surely do not think the fortune is real."

"Oh, it is undoubtedly real," he replied quickly. "It might not be as plentiful as some have imagined, but it is there."

They spoke little as they finished their meal. Elizabeth contemplated him and wondered, more and more, how she might induce him to admit that he was not who he professed to be.

She felt a bit foolish for having sent a note to Darcy that contained little more than her rambling suspicions. Had she not, only the night prior, told him they must not see each other? And now to send him some incomprehensible missive—it could only be perceived as odd. She might have felt mortified except that she was increasingly desperate for something to be done about her situation. She feared a delay would have undesirable consequences; this morning's interlude reminded her of one possibility.

As they strolled to the drawing room after dinner, Elizabeth impulsively tested her husband again. "My brother wrote to me today. He wishes to come and see us in Lancashire."

"Bingley?"

"No, my brother, um, Thomas."

Henry looked surprised for a moment but covered it smoothly. "I should be glad to see him. When will he come?"

"You remember him. I feared you would not."

"No, I remember him well! I was quite fond of him. Tell him to write me directly when his plans are fixed."

Elizabeth murmured some vague reply to this instruction.

He does not know I have no brother. The entailment, the situation of my father and mother's marriage—these are subjects on which we have spoken long. Rather—not we, but Henry and I—and this man does not know.

They entered the drawing room, and as was her custom, Nurse Jenny came in with their son before he went to his bed.

Henry was in his usual high spirits. "Come, my dear," Elizabeth said. Kiss your fa—Come kiss us good night."

If her slip was noticed, it was not remarked upon. She could not, would not, refer to this man as her son's father. She knew in her heart that this man could not be Henry and recognised that her pretence would be thusly hindered.

Little Henry scampered over and climbed up on his mother's lap for his evening's cuddling and cosseting. Henry next went to the man who called himself her husband, and to his credit, he gave her son every bit of affection that his true father might have. Elizabeth had to resist the temptation to snatch the boy away from him.

When little Henry had gone, her companion spoke. "Will you sing for me, darling? I long for some music tonight."

She smiled, relieved to have something to take up the time while permitting her to continue fretting. As she rose to go to the instrument, she was dismayed to see that Henry...Francis...whomever, intended to go with her.

"Oh, do you not wish to sit here? It is so much more comfortable by the fire." Elizabeth smiled, hoping she did not appear nervous.

"There is no place more comfortable for me than close to you, my love."

"You are full of pretty words this night," she remarked lightly, leading him over to the bench. They sat together, his touch making Elizabeth's skin crawl. "What do you wish to hear? My fingers await your preference."

"Something soft," he murmured. "Something that speaks of love and romance." Gently, he traced his fingers down her arm.

Her heart pounded, and her throat felt suddenly dry. "Very well." She selected a piece she knew well and began to play, but her fingers would not cooperate, fumbling and slurring along. She did her best, but by the end of the piece, she knew it was not well done.

"Forgive me, I am at ends tonight." She tried to give him a loving smile.

He slid even closer, his thigh pressed against hers, and his arm went around her shoulders. "Dare I hope you are as affected by me as I am by you, sweet Eliza?"

Henry never called me "Eliza."

"Yes, your effect on me is profound," Elizabeth dissembled. *That is the truth though not in the manner you might wish it to be.*

"Play another," he ordered and began pressing moist kisses on her neck.

She attempted to play while her mind frantically sought a way to escape. She had been fortunate earlier in the day when Mr Hanley performed the part of unwitting deliverer, but she could not hope for a similar result now.

He was leaving her in no doubt of his intention to seduce her, and her fear was soon replaced by rage, her hands shaking with it. *Have I no choice in the matter? Is it for him to take what he wants? I am tired of being an object, tossed to and fro as I am needed. I am tired of being a marker in a game I despise playing.*

The man—as she had come to think of him—grew more passionate, his fingers tracing a path down her neck and into her dress. His hand dropped to her skirts, raising them up over her knees and allowing his fingers to creep up her legs.

She abruptly ceased playing, turning her head towards him. "He-Henry, the servants might—"

He rapidly caught her in a deep kiss, plundering her mouth and stealing her speech before pulling back and whispering in her ear, "Wait right here."

No! No, no, no! She knew it, she could just feel it, staring into eyes that were so like Henry's and, yet, so very different. She could not do this—but how could she stop it?

He went to the drawing room door, locking it and ensuring it was bolted. As he returned to her, he took off his coat, tossing it to the side. His waistcoat followed and he sank onto the rug before the fire, motioning her to come to him.

"Did you think Henry looked pale? I hope he is not getting ill. I admit I was not pleased yesterday when I learned he had been—"

"Elizabeth." His voice was low as he patted the floor next to him. "Come."

"Perhaps we should retire? We could go upstairs and—"

He shook his head, his voice silky and seductive. "I cannot wait that long, my love. Come here. The rug is soft and the fire is warm."

ACROSS TOWN, A GROUP OF GENTLEMEN HAD ASSEMBLED IN THE Matlock's dining room for the purpose of reviewing the facts as laid out for them by Mr Hanley and Mr Darcy. Some of the men were the same ones who had gathered over the same subject in 1809, but others were new due to various forces, both political and natural.

Most in the room knew the truth of Hanley's involvement as a sort of spy from within, though they believed his efforts had concluded with the hanging of the man they once believed was Francis Warren. Hanley took charge of the discussion, laying out the facts as he knew them, showing that Francis Warren was alive and continued to operate on his mission of sedition.

He spoke with an authority that was astonishing to Darcy, given his prior impression of the man's nature. "It is important to note that there is ample indication that both brothers were involved. I myself attended many meetings with the two present. Francis was more intimately tied to the more radical activities, but both were fully engaged, no doubt about that."

To convince them required a great deal of persuasion, but they had finally come to Hanley's side of things when he delivered the letter written in Henry's hand that attested to his scar.

"It was nearly five years ago," protested Lord Liverpool. "Surely it would not be so—"

Darcy interrupted. "His wife—*my* wife—saw it in 1809, and it remained large and discoloured. It might have faded, but something of it would remain."

Silence ensued as each man considered it. At last, Harris, the man who had led the investigation from the beginning, spoke. "So were we to prove that the man who now claims to be Henry Warren, Lord Courtenay, does not bear any sort of scar on his chest, we would be certain he was Francis?"

"There is more," Darcy stated, extracting from his coat the note he had received from Elizabeth earlier that day. When it had first arrived at his house, he was astonished by the likeness in the turn of their minds, but quickly moved to the more useful value of the note, which he now shared.

Hanley added his own suspicions, mentioning, "Even if the man is Henry, he remains seditious, and there are several who can attest to his activities. Of course, it would be less desirable since he must be tried according to the privilege afforded an earl, but nevertheless, he is not blameless. However, I think such concerns are unwarranted. There is little doubt in my mind that the man currently living with Lady Courtenay—rather, Mrs Darcy—is Francis Warren."

Harris yawned. Lady Matlock's delightful dinner in combination with Lord Matlock's port made him a bit sleepy. "Let us meet with him tomorrow for questions. We shall rely on some word from his valet and the men in the mines as well. Those barracks the miners live in are rather open; no doubt, they all see each other in various stages of dress. If the scar was ever there, one of them was sure to have seen it. And we need is the friend's word on the wound that he inflicted."

Darcy was not pleased with the hesitation. "Tonight we must go—"

"We cannot be hasty," Harris replied firmly. "We must consider how it is best done, and that is not always the quickest way."

"I must protest, for even now Mrs Darcy—"

"Mrs Darcy has been in residence as Lady Courtenay for several months. One more night will not a difference make."

TWENTY-EIGHT

E lizabeth stared at him, disbelieving his meaning. "Here? By the fire?"

Having apparently grown tired of her confusion, he scooped her into his arms, kissed her neck, and carried her towards the fire. "Right here, love. Let us be licentious and wild, tossing propriety to the wind."

She forced herself to kiss him. "Very well, but you must excuse me for just a moment. I shall hasten my return."

He smiled, settling her on her feet. "I shall count the seconds."

Leaving him, she hurried to her bedchamber. Once there, she paused to look at the journals, particularly the latest one containing Henry's thoughts on meeting and marrying her. For a moment, her eyes closed. Considering what he had written and what had become of her life since then caused rage to boil up within her. She ran her hand over the cover, thinking of the words therein, and her hand shook.

How dare he? How dare *he!*

It took her only a moment to find what she sought, and then she hurried back to the drawing room. She grabbed a shawl from the chaise as she passed.

When she re-entered the room, she saw that he had removed his shirt and his shoes. His purpose was quite prominent in his breeches, and she had no doubt she would know the truth of it soon if she did not do something to divert him.

She gave him a queer little smile, laying her shawl down on the settee and joining him in front of the fire. "April has been a bit cold, has it not?"

"I do not mind. I enjoy the fire."

"I do as well."

He smiled at her in what seemed an attempt to look loving. To Elizabeth, it merely looked feral, and it stirred the anger within her. He kissed her, running his hand over her bosom.

"I, uh, I must tell you…something." Elizabeth frantically searched her mind for any topic of discussion that might distract him. *I am angry, violently angry, and angry people are not always wise. There is nothing for it now but to play along.*

The man caressed her breast, using one finger to draw down the material of her bodice as his lips began to kiss her jaw and neck. "Hmm?"

She could think of nothing. All wit, all reason fled in the face of her indignation and anxiety, and she could not think of anything that would delay him, much less terminate his efforts. The thought of permitting him…it repulsed her. But what could be done?

"I shall not undress you, but do allow me to take down your hair."

Her impulses took over, fuelled by desperation. *Very well then. If I must be in the game, let me play my best.*

She pulled away from him as much as she could. "Where is your scar?"

He did not seem to hear her. The fingers of one hand wound into her hair as the other inched up her skirts.

"What became of your scar?" she insisted.

He stopped his explorations to look at her. "What?"

"Your scar. It is gone." She looked at his smooth, unmarked chest. Like Henry, he had little chest hair; thus, the smooth skin of his chest was plainly revealed.

He smiled genially. "I do not have a scar."

"From fencing, yes, you do." Elizabeth saw an odd light appear in his eyes. She was reeling, losing control of the situation, but she plunged in headlong. *This is the game, and it is at last my turn.* "I should say, *Henry* did."

Darcy and Hanley departed from Matlock House. Darcy was deep in thought, forming a plan to retrieve his wife, when Hanley spoke. "He enjoys brothels. He goes to one almost every night."

He looked over at Hanley, confused by his words.

Hanley continued, "I met him many a night to accompany him. I could call on him now and say we had plans."

"Are you suggesting we go to Towton Hall? I shall take any excuse, no matter how unlikely. She is my wife, and she is with another man. It is all I can do to maintain my composure in the matter."

Hanley considered a moment. "Francis will not mind the excuse, but Harris will not like it. I must tell him it was previously arranged that I would call and accompany the earl to Madame Aurelia's. Francis and I shall leave, and you can take Elizabeth away. Francis will never know the difference."

"You are convinced then? You have no doubt of this change in identity?"

Hanley spoke thoughtfully. "There are things that might be explained away—forgotten memories and changes in appetite, fashion, or preference—but the scar cannot be overlooked. It was there, and now it is gone. It must surely mean I am correct, and Harris knows that. He only wishes to exercise caution."

"That is all well and good for him. It is not his wife who is at the mercy of a madman."

They walked down the street. "We cannot go rushing in there like lunatics. Let us form a plan. If he will go with me, that will do well enough for tonight. I shall get him as drunk as I can, and try to pull a confession out of him. If he will not come with me willingly, then we shall need another idea."

"Such as?"

The two men were interrupted by Colonel Fitzwilliam, who had come out of his father's house and jogged towards them. "Darcy, what are you planning?"

"What makes you think I am planning anything?" Darcy hoped his affected look of guilelessness would pass muster.

Fitzwilliam chuckled. "I have known you your entire life. I could see you planned to retrieve Elizabeth even as Harris uttered his pronouncement."

"You should also know that any attempt to stop me is futile."

"Naturally." Fitzwilliam gave Hanley a serious look. "Of course, for me to accompany you is against the order of my superiors, so I shall not. Alas, you have both tricked me into thinking we would visit a public house, and now I find myself tugged along against my will."

"Very well." Darcy smiled, pleased to have his cousin at his side. "Let our tugging commence."

"I do not take your meaning? Henry did? Henry who? I am Henry, and as you can see, I am unblemished." The man smiled, appearing a bit wolfish as Elizabeth moved away from his grasp and reached down to cover her legs with her dress.

Fear suddenly struck her. *Stupid, stupid Lizzy. What am I doing? What if he attempts to harm my son? I am alone with him; even the servants have retired.*

"I do not know," Elizabeth stammered, hoping to buy some time. She placed her hand to her head. "I am...I do not feel well suddenly. I might have a bit of a fever. Did Henry feel warm...oh, I already said that. Perhaps I should go check on him."

She rose to her feet with haste, and in a trice, he was beside her. He caught her hand, still looking amiable. *It is astonishing how malevolent amiability can appear when one suspects the bearer is insincere.*

He pulled her tightly against him, pressing his pelvis against her. "Are you nervous, my beloved? It does not surprise me that you should be."

"Yes." She seized on the idea gratefully. "I am very nervous."

"Do not be." He ran his hands down her back. "It is just me, just us. Have we not, you and I, always shared a certain...passion? Just allow yourself to be easy, and the rest will follow."

A different idea struck her, and she acted on it. Turning to be more fully in his arms, she wrapped her arms tightly around his neck, pressing her body along his and caressing him, trying to pretend he was Darcy although the two could not have been more different.

Just as their kisses had grown impassioned, she pulled back slightly. Putting her mouth close to his ear, in a breathy voice, she said, "I know. I *know*."

"Know? What do you know?"

She moved seductively against him, murmuring, "After all, do I not wish to retain my title too? The rights of a wife to her husband's fortune? I have no desire to upset things."

He laughed awkwardly and tried to move away, but she did not permit it, clinging to him tightly. "I do not understand you."

"You are not Henry."

"Of course I am."

She ran her hands down his body, her fingers brushing his abdomen. "It can be our secret, you know."

She saw a struggle play out in his eyes and decided to press him. "You are so clever to have apprehended the means by which to further your plans. It is all so very complicated, yet you have emerged the victor."

She had judged rightly: she saw it by the pleased look on his face. Her misjudgement was in arousing him rather brazenly. However, she saw the next opportunity for gratifying his vanity, though it required a gamble on her part.

"It is in this that I am made certain of my suspicions," she whispered into his ear. "Henry was a good husband, but alas, not an ardent lover. There was not a shared passion as you have suggested. I foresee a great alteration in my bedchamber in the near future, and I welcome it, *Francis*."

THE LONDON STREETS WERE HUSHED, AND THERE WAS THE FEELING OF a spring storm in the air although it had not, as yet, come to pass.

As the men strolled down the dark streets between Matlock House and Towton Hall, Colonel Fitzwilliam spoke, "I think you should remain back, Darcy. Let Hanley and me speak to Mr Warren."

"No chance of that," Darcy replied immediately.

"I expected you would say that." Fitzwilliam shook his head. "Onward then, but pray, Darcy, do not play the hero."

"I promise nothing where the safety of my wife is concerned except to get her out of there. That much you may be sure of."

They arrived at the door of Towton Hall only moments later, knocking and hoping some servant would hear. After a pause, the butler appeared, looking baffled by the sight of three gentlemen on the step so late at night.

"Yes, sirs?"

Hanley stepped forward, allowing himself to be seen in the candlelight. "Good evening, Baynes. How are you tonight? I suppose his lordship awaits me?"

Mr Baynes looked confused and glanced over at Darcy and Fitzwilliam, both of whom he knew from Elizabeth's time in residence as a widow. "Mr Darcy, Colonel." He bowed, still seeming a bit uncertain.

Hanley's bland, genial countenance was like a shield upon him. "He was supposed to meet us, and when he did not, we realised we must have had the plans confused. No need to show us in. I know the way. Please, return to your bed."

Mr Baynes looked like that notion appealed to him, but duty prevailed. "I could not hear of that. I shall show you—"

"No, no, I insist." Hanley smiled. "Surely, my long tenure as a friend of this house could permit us both some familiarity, Baynes? After all, it was not so long ago that I recall a certain incident involving myself, his lordship, and a particular cake your wife had intended for some guests."

Baynes's face softened a bit, and he wavered, chuckling at the memory Hanley had brought to the fore. "Oh, yes, well…you were the pair of scamps back then. You are certain his lordship expects you?"

"He certainly should!" Hanley exclaimed with a grin. "I do not doubt we shall have him out for the night shortly."

"Very well then," Mr Baynes acquiesced. "I believe he remains in the drawing room with Lady Courtenay." The three men were free.

They watched as the arthritic butler walked slowly towards his quarters. When he was gone from sight, Fitzwilliam murmured, "Excellent work there, Hanley. He did not doubt you for a moment."

"I have been told I have a face that appears unburdened by an excess of quickness or wit. I must take it for the advantage that it sometimes is."

Then Hanley put his finger to his lips and motioned Darcy and Fitzwilliam to follow him towards the drawing room. They heard from within the voices of Francis Warren and Elizabeth. It sounded as though a seduction was taking place, and Darcy's stomach turned.

INSIDE THE DRAWING ROOM, FRANCIS REGARDED ELIZABETH WITH clear doubt marking his features as she attempted to appear seductive and alluring, enticing him into divulging his secrets. What she thought she might do with the information, she knew not, but she stayed her course, nevertheless.

She took a step towards him, putting an extra sway in her hips and a welcoming smile on her lips. "I do not have a brother save for Mr Bingley," she informed him. "My father's estate is entailed on a cousin. Henry knew that well; we discussed it many times."

"I have forgotten much of what—"

"Much of what you have forgotten is oddly specific to me and to us." Still smiling, she ran her hand lightly across his chest, brushing his abdomen. "Yet you have also forgotten that onions make you sick, to visit your tailor irks you, and you like your hair kept short because, when it is on your neck, it reminds you of finding a spider inside your collar when you were young."

Her fingers slowly caressed his abdomen, gently tracing down. She could see his temptation and did all she could to foster it. "Tell me," she whispered. "Tell me everything so that I might rid my mind of these memories of Henry and think only of you."

A faint smile came to his lips, and he brushed her cheeks with his fingers. "Henry told me you were clever."

"Henry." She tried to sound derisive. "Let us say no more of Henry. Let us speak of you: extraordinarily smart, brave *Francis*."

"It can never be known," he spoke warningly. "A man cannot be wed to his brother's wife. I shall be Henry for now and for always. You must not breathe a word of it."

"Naturally," she said, feigning admiration. "But we shall know the truth of it; our secret will bind us. You are Francis—wonderfully clever Francis, who has found the way to take back his birthright."

"I have always thought it unfair that, but for an hour, he should have all and I should have none. I took what was necessary for me to take my place, not just in Courtenay history but in the history of England."

"A radical." Elizabeth smiled.

"In every sense," he replied, returning her smile.

"Your wife is brilliant yet exceedingly foolish. What must she be thinking to endanger herself so?" Fitzwilliam hissed into Darcy's ear. Darcy batted him away with his hand, intent on hearing the words being said on the other side of the drawing room door.

A small voice was suddenly heard from down around Darcy's knee. "Papa?" Darcy startled, looking down to see young Henry staring up at him in delight. The little boy immediately reached up to be held.

Hanley looked alarmed. "Get him out of here, Darcy."

"Of course. Come, my son." He knelt and picked him up, then carried him down the hall. He was charmed that the boy still called him Papa, but then again, how would he apprehend the many changes, the ups and the downs, that had transpired in his young life? To Henry, Darcy was Papa, and Papa he would remain.

He took the boy to his room, from whence he summoned Nurse Jenny who was surprised to see Darcy standing in Henry's bedchamber. "Mr Darcy, sir," she stammered. "I beg your pardon; I did not anticipate seeing you here."

"I would not expect you to." He smiled. "This young man was out of his bed, and I have come to return him, but first, I must ask an odd favour of you."

"Yes, sir?"

He grew more serious. "In truth, it is less a favour than an order. Get yourself and Henry dressed and summon a footman to escort both of you to my house. Make haste, but make as little noise as possible, and do not raise any alarm. Do you understand? You must get away from here with as much speed as you can but as quietly as you can."

Jenny's eyes went wide. She was a sweet girl, young and with a naturally loving disposition. The notion of disobeying his order would never occur to her, nor did she question his right to command her. It made him wonder what the servants of the house suspected or believed regarding the master. "Yes, sir."

"Good girl. Get him settled in his bed at my house. I do not think Mrs Darcy and I shall be long here."

"Mrs Darcy?" Jenny looked confused.

Darcy smiled. "Yes, Mrs Darcy. My wife."

ELIZABETH AND FRANCIS CONTINUED TO TALK IN THE DRAWING ROOM as Francis laid before her much of the information that had been so painstakingly gleaned by Hanley over the months past.

"I was so ill for so very long—I cannot tell you how many days I thought were certainly my last—but then I began to recover. Once my survival was assured, I realised I had been spared for a greater purpose, almost as if the Almighty Himself approved of my mission."

"You were in the mines for such a long time. Were you ill the entire time?"

"Oh no." Francis shook his head. "It was simple, my dear lady. Of the men on the road to Crewe that day, three of us walked away: me, my brother, and the man he hired to kill me. I knew that eventually I would be the last one standing, but I had to bide my time. Alas, the gunman had heard Henry and me argue—we were angry and not discreet. I know not what he understood of it, but I did not choose to find out at the risk of my own neck.

"You see"—Francis gave her a condescending smirk—"one must plan carefully for these things. Mistakes had already been too numerous. I could not be hasty again even if it meant more time in that wretched mine, not with so important a mission before me."

The thought stilled Elizabeth's heart. She imagined how it might have been had they dismissed George Wickham's rambles and this man had come forward of his own volition months, maybe even years, later. She shuddered to think of it, glad that the pain forced upon her and Darcy was not, after all, in vain.

"How...?" She paused a moment. Her voice had emerged in a squeaking croak and she did not wish it to give away her anxiety. Forcing herself to sound calmly interested, she asked, "But how did you know your brother had been hanged? Did you have someone to tell you these things?"

She could see this raised his suspicion. He gave her something of a searching look before saying, "I have many friends, my dear girl. Friends whose loyalty is indisputable. Even at my lowest point, there was always a way to get information although it sometimes took months to learn what had passed."

Realising she needed to distract him, Elizabeth caressed his arm. "Of course," she murmured. "Of course, you did."

"You see, Henry was soft. In the manner of most people who are handed everything and work for nothing, he had no idea how to survive. I did, and that is why it was he who swung from the scaffold and not me. There are too many of his kind in this country—too many who take position and fortune and use it for no good but to further their own selfish—"

He was growing angry, and Elizabeth interrupted, her tone soothing. "But it will not be thus for long. Not once you have what is rightly yours."

"Quite right." Francis relaxed, seeming to enjoy her flattery. "Parliament is filled with the dissolute and the reprehensible. Our regent is a disgrace, and his behaviour makes us all a mockery. There are people dying in the streets of London, starving, desperate for a crumb of bread while he wastes fortune upon fortune."

"So you wish to make it equal for all?"

He smiled at her indulgently. "Equality is a worthy notion but hardly practical, at least not within my lifetime. Leading a revolution, my dear, sweet girl, is about knowing what you can and cannot achieve. No, I simply wish to complete the first step: to remove the reprobates from governance. We shall never win these infernal wars with such vile creatures leading us. We must remove them and bring in new leaders, ones who will make the changes that are needed."

"So your plans were...? Help me understand, dear husband."

He pulled her hand to his lips for a soft kiss. "A war, any war begins with bloodshed. It is a truth, universally acknowledged, that the blood of one person of note is far more effective at raising the hue and cry than is the slaughter of a hundred of those of lower birth. So it must be the regent, but his abettors in Parliament would follow soon after."

Elizabeth tried not to shiver at the cold look that came into his eyes. "I see." She was searching for something else to ask him when she heard a sound at the door.

"Yes?" Francis called out impatiently.

"It's Hanley."

Francis scowled and quietly said to Elizabeth, "Stay as you are. I will see what he wants and get rid of him."

Francis strode to the door and flung it open. Mr Hanley and Colonel Fitzwilliam entered the room.

"Madam." Hanley acknowledged Elizabeth with a bow then smiled genially at Francis.

"What are you doing here?" Francis asked the two men, not hiding his exasperation.

"There is a gathering down on Wolsey Street, and I hoped you would join us."

"Thank you, but no," Francis replied firmly. "As you see, I am hardly attired." He remained half-clothed from his earlier interlude with Elizabeth and did not seem inclined to alter his appearance.

Hanley looked at his chest, as did Fitzwilliam, and Francis understood it almost immediately. His chin rose, and he took on a rather shifty-eyed look although he attempted to appear amiable and relaxed.

"Perhaps I spoke hastily. Allow me to retrieve my coat, and we shall be off. You do not mind, do you, dear?"

Elizabeth, wide-eyed, shook her head.

"Excellent." Francis turned and left the room, grabbing his shirt and waistcoat on the way out.

When the door closed behind him, the room was silent for a moment, all of them suspended in the questions of what was known and unknown.

Colonel Fitzwilliam spoke first, going to Elizabeth's side. "We know—we know about him, and from your conversation, you do as well."

Elizabeth nodded and glanced at Hanley. "Mr Hanley you are—"

"A spy, I guess you could say," he said with a wry chuckle.

He sobered quickly. "You may be in some danger. I do think he suspects something is gone awry, and I believe he is capable of almost anything. You must leave immediately. Go to Darcy's house and await us there."

"I shall," she agreed. "But what will you do?"

"Arrest him," Fitzwilliam replied confidently. "We are government agents, and we heard everything from behind the door, including his wish to kill the regent. People have been hanged for far less, I assure you."

"I shall go, but I do not believe he will return. If he knows, or even thinks he knows, that you have found him out, there are many ways to escape the house. He could be gone before we know it."

THERE WAS A SIDE ENTRANCE OUT OF TOWTON HALL THAT LED INTO the mews. It was dark and away from the main part of the house, making it an ideal escape route.

Darcy saw Jenny and Henry, along with an overgrown footman by the name of Rhodes, off on their way to his house. Although it was a short walk, he worried for them; however, encountering danger on the street was less likely than what they might have met within the house.

He turned to go back inside in the same manner he left, creeping up the back staircase, which was unlit save for the dim lamp he held. He had not gone far when he encountered Francis Warren.

For a moment, both stood motionless on the stairs, neither having expected to meet any other.

Francis reached towards his pocket, and Darcy reacted immediately, punching him forcefully. Francis fell backwards, striking his head, first on the wall, and then hard against the stairs behind him, but he did not go down easily. He grabbed Darcy and pulled him down the steps in a violent tumble.

Darcy held onto Francis just as tightly as Francis held him. Both were intent on injuring or even killing the other. Punches flew fast and furiously, and still they did not speak, silent save for the occasional grunt. For his size, Francis proved an able opponent.

"Give up," Darcy growled, feeling Francis's knee in a particularly vulnerable place. "You have no escape. You might kill me, but Hanley and Fitzwilliam are right behind me."

"I will kill you, and then I shall escape. I have passage, and I shall be long gone when the cry is raised."

"Never," Darcy spat. "All of the world will know what you are and what filth has been eradicated in your passing."

Francis struggled, clearly wishing for something in his coat that Darcy suspected was a pistol, and Darcy doubled his efforts to keep him from it, ramming him brutally into a wall and causing the much smaller man to cry out. In retaliation, Francis brought his fist up underneath Darcy's chin, snapping his head back and causing him to see stars.

The lapse in his attention, though unavoidable, proved dangerous. Francis was quick to pull the weapon from his pocket, pressing it to Darcy's head and spitting. "Well then, all done with you."

Darcy knew he had no more than a moment and summoned a burst of strength from within. Grasping him by his coat, Darcy tossed Francis's body over his so that the other man tumbled down the remaining stairs, with various loud thuds and cracks along the way. He could not rejoice in his victory, however, as the gun fired nevertheless. Although it was nowhere near his head, Darcy felt it in his chest, the searing, hot agony ripping through him. He cried out once and then blackness overtook him.

TWENTY-NINE

Elizabeth went first to her son's nursery, wanting more than anything to see him out of the house as soon as she could. Moments later, fear, which had not as yet touched her during the ordeal, caught fire within her.

Henry was gone, his bed neatly turned down, which reassured her somewhat. The bed was as Nurse Jenny would have left it—not as a three-year-old boy might. Jenny was absent from her room as well.

Before pulling the bell to summon someone who might be able to tell her where they had gone, Elizabeth spied a note on a small table nearby. She found it was from Darcy, and it had obviously been scratched out in haste:

> *Sent Henry and Jenny to my house—our house. I love you,*
> *Mrs Darcy.*
> *— FD*

A burst of happy relief came upon her, and she laughed at the number of blotches and blots Darcy had scattered about his little missive. "You see there, Mr Darcy, from your penmanship, I can readily discern that your spirits are disordered."

The ink was still wet in several places so Elizabeth knew it was recently penned and likely that Darcy remained close. She wondered whether he had accompanied Jenny and little Henry.

As she considered the note and the likelihood that her husband was with her son, she heard a shot. For a moment, she froze—and then she ran. She believed the sound to have come from the back of the house and raced towards it. She heard footsteps running on the floor below and hoped it was Colonel Fitzwilliam and Hanley.

She first checked a back stairway, the one used by the servants, which would provide the most likely means of escaping the house undetected. It was there that her burgeoning happiness was quashed, seeing the lifeless form of Darcy on the stair before her. He had fallen at an odd angle, his blood all around him.

"No," she whispered. "No, Fitzwilliam, no."

Elizabeth knelt beside him and felt the pulse on his neck, relieved that it was strong and sure beneath her fingers. She kissed his neck and then his lips, which were slightly parted. The feel of his breath on her lips was a vast relief.

Fitzwilliam and Hanley found them moments later. Seeing his cousin, Fitzwilliam cursed, and Hanley asked, "Mrs Darcy, was Francis here when you arrived?"

"He may have gone out the back." Fitzwilliam ran off in pursuit of the man who not only was a threat to the country but was now the attacker of his cousin as well.

As Hanley moved to join the colonel, Elizabeth stopped him. "Mr Hanley, take this." He raised his eyebrows when Elizabeth reached into her pocket and then thrust a pistol at him.

"You are armed, Mrs Darcy? Is this your usual way?"

Elizabeth smiled. "Only when I live with a madman."

IN THE NEXT HOURS, ELIZABETH WAS SURPRISED BY HOW WELL SHE managed. She supposed all the events of her recent past must have served her well in some capacity for she was calm and composed as she tended to Darcy. There was a great deal of blood, but she gave it no heed; instead, she kept her gaze affixed on him. She sedately summoned a footman to go for the apothecary and a surgeon, and she directed two footmen to the chamber where Darcy should be placed.

There was a moment, when she was alone with him and awaiting the surgeon, that fear took hold of her. She kissed his lips and his eyelids before whispering fiercely in his ear, "You had better not die, Fitzwilliam Darcy. You gave me your word, and a gentleman honours his promises."

Elizabeth refused to cry, for to cry would be to admit there was something about which to cry. She would hold fast to the idea that he would be well.

The effort of it made her tremble slightly, but that too was determinedly disregarded.

She was by his side as the surgeon did his work upon him and as the servants cleaned him. Darcy's valet was summoned from his house to bring fresh attire. The man was industrious despite the hour. He began by removing the remains of Darcy's shirt and cravat. The surgeon had cut some away but left tatters, and Fields clucked in sartorial distress over the ruin of a fine shirt.

When his chest was bared and cleaned, Fields paused and looked at Elizabeth. "Lady Courtenay, I must remove the rest of his clothing."

Elizabeth did not remove her gaze. "I assure you, Fields, I have seen much more of him than this. Furthermore, I am not Lady Courtenay. I am Mrs Darcy."

If Fields found such a statement baffling, he said nothing of it, giving her a short bow before setting to work.

Elizabeth was still by Darcy's bedside when Colonel Fitzwilliam returned just as dawn was breaking over the town. She started at the sound of his voice. "How is he?"

She shrugged. "He has lost a great deal of blood, but the bullet did not penetrate his body. It tore a strip of skin from across his chest."

"Very good."

"Good for now, but it could lead to an infection."

Fitzwilliam nodded gravely and took a seat on the other side of the bed. "He has a strong constitution. I do not doubt that he will be well."

"Nor do I," she answered firmly. "Dare I ask about Francis Warren?"

"We caught him. He has not been in contact with his old group enough to know that loyalties have shifted. People of this sort are generally willing to turn on each other, particularly if there is a sum to line their pockets."

"Was money given?"

"The credit must go to Hanley. He knew just who to bribe. He is a useful sort of fellow and far more brave than he looks. Had the most absurd little gun on him..."

Despite everything, Elizabeth chuckled. "It is a lady's pistol, Colonel, and it was a gift to me from your father. I thought it a rather pretty little thing."

"A weapon should never be described as a 'pretty little thing,' but it served its office well. Hanley persuaded Mr Warren to give himself over, and now he will remain in the gaol to meet his destiny—a destiny he has cheated for several years now, I might add."

"Does he deny who he is or all that he has done?"

"Of course," Fitzwilliam replied. "I daresay there is no man more ardent in his declarations of allegiance to the king than one who faces the consequences of prior sedition. It cannot hold. Both Hanley and I clearly heard his confession. And let us not forget that the same evidence leading to the first Warren brother's hanging still remains for the right man. It will be a speedy business, I assure you."

"As speedy as any business that has gone on for so many years," Elizabeth agreed ruefully.

They sat through the rest of the early morning hours, watching over Darcy as he slept and saying little. Elizabeth urged Fitzwilliam to rest, but he would not hear of it, not until his eyes were closing on their own. When he left to avail himself of a guest bedchamber, Elizabeth remained, her eyes on Darcy and her mind urging him to be well.

It was the wetness that woke him.

A persistent, snuffling sort of wetness punctuated by sniffing at his head and neck and then shoved unceremoniously into his ear. More sniffing and then a warm, furry body pressing itself alongside him.

He wondered at the sensation even as he came into consciousness, though the comprehension of pain soon caused him to stop wondering about the wetness. His chest, his head, his arm—all were agonisingly painful. He tried to move and almost cried out, restraining himself to a grunt.

Shifting just slightly, he turned his head towards the warm body that shared his pillow, inhaling the unmistakable scent of a dog.

Then he heard the voice, a small boy's voice, prattling away beside him. Darcy was being told a story, it seemed, although the exact nature of it was difficult to discern as the storyteller had his thumb lodged in his mouth as he told it.

Darcy opened his eyes and saw the small figure of Henry beside him. Henry evidently wished to keep an eye on Darcy's face as he was lying with his feet propped on the pillow next to Darcy and his head resting on his bent arm near Darcy's hip. Annie was tucked into the crevice between Darcy's head and her young master's feet. As Henry weaved his tale, he absently traced his fingers in patterns across Darcy's abdomen, and Annie occasionally sniffed and licked Darcy's head and neck.

The dog seemed to sense that Darcy had awoken and rose to her feet, wagging her tail madly. Henry looked up and saw Darcy watching him. "Papa!" he cried out in delight. "My story maked you wake up!"

Darcy laughed but barely any sound emerged. Henry then began a litany of fears and concerns, most of which centred on the facts that he was not permitted to enter Darcy's bedchamber and did not like taking naps. The effort of trying not to laugh caused Darcy to ache, but it was worth it—well worth it—to see his dear boy perched beside him so high spirited and amiable.

Henry edged his way up, positioning himself as close to Darcy as possible. "Mama sayed you will get dead, and she cried."

Darcy swallowed and cleared his throat in hopes of speaking above a croak. "No, I am not going to die, my son. I am going to stay right here with you and your mama. Where is your mama?"

"In her woom." He might have said more, but just then, a loud, sawing buzz cut through the air. It was Fitzwilliam, sleeping in a nearby chair. Henry burst into laughter at the sound while Annie ran over to sniff and investigate its source.

Darcy smiled to see his cousin so near but realised that it must be the middle of the night. *Which night? How long have I been asleep? Where is Francis Warren?*

"Henry, perhaps you will help your papa? I wish to wake Colonel Fitzwilliam."

"I can do it." Henry smiled, his face innocent and cherubic. He scampered off the bed and approached Fitzwilliam.

A quick survey of his body showed Darcy that nothing appeared to have been broken, but nearly everything had been bruised, and a large weeping gash went across his chest and arm where it appeared a bullet had grazed him. Disregarding the pain, he pushed himself into a more upright position on the bed and was just settling back in his pillow when he heard Henry's voice.

In his short tenure as a father, Darcy had noticed that small children could shriek at a particularly ear-splitting frequency. He was sure that no other creature on earth could produce such a mind-shattering sound at such a volume. It was just this sort of shriek that Henry emitted to wake Fitzwilliam.

Fitzwilliam leapt to his feet, clearly ready to engage in combat with whoever had woken him, and he let loose with more than a few words that Henry should not know. It was fortunate that Henry was rolling on the floor with laughter and did not appear to hear him, or so Darcy hoped. The outward expression of Darcy's mirth was more restrained due to the aching within his chest, but he believed he enjoyed the joke just as much as Henry did.

The colonel was not so amused. "Henry! What are you doing, scaring me like that? Do you not know it is the middle of the night?"

"Papa waked up!" Henry affected the look of an absolute angel, and Darcy pressed his lips together to avoid laughing.

"Darcy! How are you feeling?" Fitzwilliam forgot his vexation with Henry and went to the bed. "You look as though you rode atop the stage down Jumblegut Lane."

"As do you, and at least I have this devil of a wound to excuse my appearance." Darcy grinned.

"And you, sir!" Fitzwilliam looked back at young Henry. "What are you doing out and about? It is only just now"—Fitzwilliam squinted at the nearby mantel clock—"half-five in the morning."

Henry raised his chin and looked down his nose. "Papa wanted me to say a story to him."

Fitzwilliam chuckled. "Well, I believe we shall put you to use then. Run along and wake your mama so she might know your papa is awake."

Henry agreed and hied off to do as he was bid.

Darcy enquired, "How long have I been asleep?"

"You have been kept asleep with laudanum for the past four days," Fitzwilliam informed him. "Dr. Abernethy attended you, and it was his recommendation in order to prevent you from disturbing your sutures. You did give us a bit of a scare, running a fever for a day or so, but you managed to overcome it."

"I cannot recall precisely what transpired. I can clearly remember the meeting at your father's house and all we discussed. I recall coming to Towton Hall and listening to Francis's confession, but after that, I have no recollection."

"You surprised Francis as he attempted to leave the house. Damned fool that you are, you decided to rush at him rather than permit him to leave and allow the magistrate's men to capture him. So you attacked him on the stairway, he attacked back, you struggled, he pulled his gun, and you, by what I saw, pushed him down the stairs, breaking his arm in two places. He shot you as he fell, but the bullet did not enter your flesh, it just grazed it."

Darcy glanced down. "I see. Where is Mr Warren now?"

"He is in the gaol, and there he will remain. I daresay he is the most watched man around."

"Let us hope so." Darcy sighed. "I wish ill on no one, but I assure you, on that day when we might at last..." His voice died off as Elizabeth appeared in the doorway.

The look on her face was a combination of joy, exhaustion, and worry. "Excuse us, Fitzwilliam." Accepting his dismissal, the colonel left the room.

She had clearly put her clothing on in haste and tied up her hair in a barely passable manner, but to Darcy, she had never looked more beautiful. For a moment, she did no more than regard him with a broad smile on her lips that matched the one he felt on his. Slowly, she went to his bedside and sat herself close to him.

Darcy wound a hand in her hair and pulled her down for a kiss. "Mrs Darcy, how are you this morning?"

She pushed her face into the crook of his neck, and Darcy soon realised she was crying. Finally, she choked out, "I am very, very happy. I am Mrs Darcy, well and truly, am I not?"

"There will be some questions, but the scar cannot be disputed. Hanley has much evidence amassed against Francis Warren, to be sure."

"Mr Barnes has already been called upon to attest to the fencing and the ensuing wound."

"It would seem, Mrs Darcy, that you are destined to be married to men with large scars across their chests." He glanced down at the wound showing through the gap in his shirt.

"Dr. Abernethy has every hope you will heal well. The wound is closing nicely, and it has not festered. We were worried it might; there was one day you ran a fever, but it resolved quickly. You also have broken ribs and, as you see, a number of bruises and lacerations." Elizabeth gave him a lingering kiss and sat back again, a fond smile on her lips. "You were so brave with Francis—quite the fighter. I would not have imagined it in you."

"Fitzwilliam and I beat on each other regularly when we were young," he assured her. "Any slight, real or imagined, was avenged mercilessly, and the rub of it all was that, when we were through, we would both be punished by our fathers. It did not stop us, though it did teach us to hit where it could not be discovered."

She gave him a faint smile and fell silent, doing nothing more than gaze at him.

"What is it?"

"It is difficult to believe," she whispered. "How much I wished for it, and how much I despaired of it. Can this be real? How shall I survive if it is not?"

Darcy moved his blanket back, encouraging her to join him. She moved into his arms, snuggling into him carefully, not wishing to cause pain.

He held her for some time before being able to murmur, "It is real, my love. Our long ordeal has ended at last, and things are as they were meant to be."

As soon as Darcy had energy enough for the walk, they removed from Towton Hall to Darcy House. It was a short distance and a pleasant enough stroll through the park, but he was nevertheless deeply fatigued by the time they arrived.

Fields and a large footman were on hand to assist him into his house and towards his bedchamber. He resisted for just a moment, turning to Elizabeth.

"I believe I might like to spend my time in your bedchamber, dear. Does that suit you?"

She looked at the ground and blushed. "Of course."

Fields soon had him established in the mistress's bedchamber, and Elizabeth entered to see to his comfort.

"Mr Darcy, you are a surprising man. Why do you wish to stay here rather than in your own bedchamber?"

Darcy smiled, even as a painful remembrance came to him. He

took her hand, pulling her to sit next to him. "I shall never, as long as I live, forget the despair I felt watching as your things were removed from this room, returning you to the man we thought was Lord Courtenay. I never felt so miserable in all my life."

She closed her eyes for a moment and laid her head against his. "Yes, I imagine so. Why did you watch?"

He shook his head. "I thought it would help me understand it...or to accept it somehow. It did not work. I am here now to assure that, when your things are brought back, returning you to my house and to me, I can watch. For I can say with certainty that, as miserable as I was on that day, I am sure to be in raptures this time. I eagerly anticipate seeing your return and could not bear to miss it."

And so it was. Her things were removed from Towton Hall that very day. A retinue of servants bearing boxes and trunks arrived and set about restoring the room to its proper order. Darcy was pleased to witness it and enjoyed every moment, offering his thoughts on where this box had been before, or where that item had lain on her dressing table. The servants might have been amused by it all save for the fact that they too were mightily glad to see Mrs Darcy returned.

DARCY RECOVERED MORE EACH DAY; HIS WOUND HEALED WELL, AND his bruises moved from dark blue-black to a more faded green. Even his ribs were quick to stop aching. He was more tired than usual, but his doctor assured him it was no cause for alarm.

The news of the capture of Francis Warren and the discovered treachery of his brother was the most canvassed subject of the *ton*. There was little else about which to speak, and although a comprehensive article had been published in the broadsheets, there was still a great deal of conjecture and speculation. For as much as was said, popular opinion suggested there was more left unsaid, and the drawing rooms and salons buzzed with talk of it.

Hanley proved rather forward thinking and put forth a story about Elizabeth being part of a scheme to entrap Francis Warren in a web of his own lies. Few believed it, but the effort was appreciated, nevertheless. It was a good sight better than some of the other tales that were circulated, including that she had lived with Darcy as his mistress, she had lived with Francis as his mistress, and Darcy had kidnapped her and killed Henry. The gossip was unrelenting, but rather than make their society less desired, unfortunately it seemed to instil in the *ton* a deep longing to associate with them.

They had Darcy's recovery to excuse them for some time, and it became a rather pleasurable interlude. The world was forgotten as Darcy and Elizabeth, and sometimes young Henry, snuggled up in her bedchamber, reading, talking, and enjoying every manner of indolent pursuit.

It was one such day as they lazed about that Elizabeth, having done a bit of reading, decided to broach a difficult subject. Henry had gone for his nap; thus, Elizabeth thought it was a good time for the discussion.

"Fitzwilliam, I must speak to you about something. It is not pleasant, but it must be said."

Darcy sat up a bit, feeling wary and having some notion of what the topic must be. "Elizabeth, perhaps it is best left unsaid."

His greatest fear was that she was with child, and he had already resolved that the child would be recognised as his own. He was determined in that though he naturally hoped it would not come to pass.

"The night of the Latymers' ball—"

"I pray you would forgive me," he said quickly, wishing to forestall the difficult speech. "I was beastly. My anger was due to the pain of leaving you."

"I know." She smiled at him kindly. "But the remark you made about Henry and his tedious intimacy…"

Darcy gritted his teeth and said nothing, seeing she was determined to speak of it.

"It never occurred. Not once."

"No?"

She shook her head. "I was surprised. I expected him to…well, our friend Hanley was useful in this as well. For the most part though, he was surprisingly forbearing. Knowing as we do now, I surely cannot account for it, but I am profoundly grateful, nevertheless."

Darcy was silent a moment. In the morning's laziness, her hair was not yet put up, and strands of it fell over his arm. He played with a curl as he thought about it.

"I am relieved. I can scarcely credit it."

Anxiously, she asked, "You do believe me when I tell you that there cannot be a child? There is no possibility of it, none at all."

"Of course, I do," he hastened to assure her.

"Do you think perhaps…" She paused, uncertain how to say what she must.

"What, dearest?"

"Whether or not you believe me, if we were to conceive a child, there might be some who would suggest he or she was not yours. There is so much gossip and speculation right now; I would not wish to incite more. Perhaps it would be prudent if you and I were to…"

"If you wish to abstain, then we shall, and in any case, the doctor has advised six weeks of rest. I cannot care for those who would speculate about a child we conceive. I shall not trouble myself over it. You and I know the truth, and that is all that matters."

She curled into his side a bit more tightly. "You always know just what to say."

His sudden, loud laughter startled them both. "Me?" He laughed again. "Your memory must be quite short to even entertain such a notion. I generally say the most wrong thing, and I shall support that assertion by recalling to you the entire first six months of our acquaintance."

THIRTY

Several days after Darcy and his newly reunited family returned home, he awoke from a short nap to find Henry at play on the floor of his bedchamber with Annie beside him. He had noticed the boy doing this since their removal from Towton Hall. Henry was as good-humoured as always, eating and sleeping as well as he ever had, but he was remarkably reluctant to allow Darcy or Elizabeth out of his sight for long. More than once, Darcy caught him peering into a room where he thought his parents might be to verify their presence before returning to the nursery.

So many changes had ensued in his short life. Fortunately, by all accounts, Francis Warren had been good to the boy. He had played with him and had acted as a father ought. *Another thing for which I am grateful but cannot comprehend.*

It seemed Henry must have read his thoughts, for he paused and looked up at Darcy with his usual frank, friendly gaze. "Papa?"

"Yes?"

"Where is Father?"

Darcy inhaled sharply. He and Elizabeth had not discussed this. Somewhere in the back of his mind, he knew questions might arise, and he had hoped Elizabeth would be the one to answer them. Elizabeth, alas, was nowhere in sight.

He attempted to evade the question. "Henry, you are my son, and I am your father. I shall always be here to love you and take care of you. You need not worry about that."

"No, you are Papa," Henry informed him. "Where is Father?"

Darcy's mind was frantic, desperately trying to form a plan of what to tell the boy. In the end, he decided upon a version of the truth, delivered gently.

"Henry, Father is, in truth, your uncle, and he is in gaol. Your real father died a few years ago, before you were born."

"Why?"

"Ah, well." Darcy cleared his throat and listened a moment, hoping to hear Elizabeth's footsteps in the hall. It was disappointingly silent. "He did some bad things, things that were against the law, and when you do things against the law, you go to gaol and sometimes, ah, you die."

"Father is bad?"

Darcy did not know what to say so he just nodded.

Henry turned his attention back to his blocks, clearly contemplating the information Darcy had imparted to him. Darcy watched him play until a minute or so later when Henry looked up and asked, "Where is Uncle Bingley?"

Darcy smiled, relieved. "Uncle Bingley is a very good man, and he is at his house with Aunt Bingley. He is not in gaol."

"And I have a lot of aunts!" Henry said, growing enthusiastic. "I have Aunt Georgie and Aunt Bingley and Aunt Mary and Aunt Kitty and Aunt Lydia." He grew sombre a moment. "Can aunts go to gaol?"

"Not your aunts," Darcy assured him. "Your aunts always follow the law."

"Who is your aunts?"

"Lady Matlock is my aunt," Darcy told him, relieved the conversation seemed to be going off on a more benign tangent. "I have another aunt as well, Lady Catherine de Bourgh. She lives in Kent."

"Did they go to gaol?"

"No." Darcy laughed. "They did not. Come here, sweet boy."

Henry clambered onto the bed next to Darcy, fitting in under his arm and against his side, just as if he were formed to be there. He looked up intently as Darcy gave him the first of what he hoped would be true fatherly wisdom. "It is important, Son, to do what is right. To do your duty to your family, to God, and to your country. Your actions must be guided by your heart and your conscience. When you allow yourself to be blinded by greed for power or money is when you will go astray."

He had seen Henry's brow wrinkle at the word conscience, so he explained further, "Your conscience tells you what is right and wrong. Right now, Mama and I do most of that for you, but eventually, you will have to do it yourself, and if Mama and I have done well, you will make the right decisions—decisions befitting a gentleman of honour."

Henry lost interest as he saw Annie up on a chair back, looking out a window and growling at something below. He rushed over, encouraging his pet in her ferocity while Darcy regarded him with great fondness, eagerly anticipating the years ahead and hoping that some of what he said might remain with the boy.

A LITTLE MORE THAN A FORTNIGHT HAD ELAPSED WHEN COLONEL Fitzwilliam appeared at the house. Darcy was up and in his study when he was shown in.

"Well, sir?" Darcy felt surprisingly jovial. "You have quite the grave countenance."

Fitzwilliam looked uncomfortable. "I am here in a bit of an official way. We should summon Mrs Darcy; I have news of Warren."

Darcy's joviality was dismissed in a moment. He summoned Elizabeth and some tea; then he and Fitzwilliam moved to the fireplace to await her. "Is this...will she be upset? I am not sure her spirits can bear much more. He remains in the gaol, yes? There has not been some escape?"

Fitzwilliam would say nothing. He just shook his head.

Elizabeth joined them minutes later. She sat with her eyes on the colonel, looking fearful. Her hand, when she slid it into Darcy's, was ice cold.

"I have some news of Mr Francis Warren," Fitzwilliam began gently.

"Yes?" She was steady and calm.

"He is dead. He died in the gaol."

Her mouth dropped, and she regarded Fitzwilliam in surprise. Darcy leaned forward. "How?"

"He killed himself," Elizabeth surmised.

Fitzwilliam nodded. "His final act of rebellion, I suppose you could say."

There was a short silence as they all pondered the information before the colonel continued. "He saw, I believe, that there was no mark of sympathy for him. Even his friends turned on him. They were eager to give him up for the promise of saving their own necks, and the government is far more interested in prosecuting the leaders. The followers can always be replaced, but the removal of the leaders sends a message.

"In any case, he took the matter into his own hands. There is always someone about who grieves the plight of those imprisoned and can offer a way out for the right sum. There was an apothecary—or someone who would pass for one—who secured the right things to induce a peaceful, endless sleep. Francis preferred that to the hanging he faced and gladly paid the requested sum of, ironically, five and twenty pounds."

"I see," Elizabeth said calmly, her face inscrutable and her bearing undisturbed.

"You are certain?" Darcy asked. Although he was neither the bloodthirsty sort nor one who found entertainment in a hanging, in this case, he might have wished to be present to see the body of the man and know it was done.

"I saw him myself." There was a pause, and then Fitzwilliam added, "I saw the box sealed."

Darcy nodded.

"At the end, he admitted to the magistrate that he was Francis." There had been some concern for the Darcy's marriage to that end. The letter from Henry Warren to Mr Silas Barnes had been submitted, and Mr Barnes had also written, bearing witness to the injury.

"It will be kept quiet. Our regent does not fancy such an error coming to light, that an earl was hanged without the proper process. Moreover, there is little evidence that Henry did anything treasonous. However, it will be acknowledged privately that Henry Warren, Earl of Courtenay, died in April 1812."

"Thus, our marriage is entirely, indubitably, unquestionably valid." Darcy could not stop the smile that came over his face.

His smile was mirrored on Elizabeth's face. "I am exceedingly happy to be unquestionably Mrs Darcy."

AS DARCY'S HEALTH IMPROVED, THEY BECAME INUNDATED WITH

callers, including many of their relations, all of whom had heard various rumours of what had transpired and sought the truth behind them.

Mrs Bennet wrote to Elizabeth almost every day, telling her of this or that bit of gossip and demanding to know the truth. Unfortunately, the truth did not satisfy her. She thought something more scandalous and salacious must surely be the cause of all the talk.

"What could possibly bring greater scandal?" Elizabeth asked Darcy incredulously. "What more could there be?"

Darcy did not wish to malign the foolish Mrs Bennet and replied cautiously, "Your mother has a unique perspective."

Elizabeth rolled her eyes. "You are too kind."

Weary from telling the same tale over and over again, Elizabeth held a family dinner for all their relations who were in town: Sir Edward and Lady Gardiner, Jane and Bingley, Lord and Lady Matlock, Lord and Lady Saye, and Colonel Fitzwilliam.

Elizabeth did her best to address the questions and concerns about the three months that she was the wife of a man who was not truly Lord Courtenay, but there was much about which she could not, or did not wish to, speak. Moreover, for all that was asked, it was the most tantalising bits she would not disclose, not to anyone save her husband.

The past months had affected her deeply though she spoke of them in the most dispassionate way possible. She could not fool Darcy: he well knew how to read the emotions in her eyes. Nevertheless, he could not think of a way to pull her from it and reasoned that, just as his wounds required time to heal, so did hers.

When their guests had gone, they retired. Darcy joined her in her bedchamber as soon as he had changed, sitting in one of the chairs by the fireplace to watch as she brushed her hair. "Tonight went well. Did you think so?"

"Well enough." She gave a slight shrug. "I despise speaking of it. It was a trial, and speaking of it only stirs up grief."

"It will pass and soon, I would hope."

She finished her brushing and settled herself on his lap, laying her head against his.

He asked quietly, "What are you thinking about?"

"Just how I long to be happy at last. I look at you and recall the days when I thought I would never have you again. Now I do, and I am so glad for it, but I cannot yet truly feel it. A cloud of uncertainty dampens my soul. I cannot help but think something more will happen. Something else will go awry."

He caressed her back. "Anyone who has lived the ordeal that you have could not feel otherwise. You are a brave and strong woman, my love, and you have come through something that would make most people go mad. You will feel it in time. Your cares will go away, and happiness will take their place. You want only for time."

"I suppose," she replied evasively. Turning to him, she asked, "Can we just leave?"

"Leave?"

"Go to Pemberley. Get away from town and the gossips and the family. Just us, and Henry."

Darcy felt idiotic that he had not thought of it before. "Of course we can."

"You are not fit yet for travel, but when you are, let us go. Even knowing we shall go uplifts my spirit."

Darcy laughed. "We shall miss the Season and enjoy spring at Pemberley instead. How stupid I am for not having considered it before."

THE IDEA OF RETURNING TO PEMBERLEY LIFTED BOTH THEIR SPIRITS, and he slowly saw a return to the Elizabeth he had known all too briefly. He watched her one night in the drawing room after dinner. She was indulging him in a private musical exhibition by his request, playing and singing while he admired her from the settee. His thoughts began by considering how wonderfully strong she was to have endured and persevered as she had throughout her ordeal; however, inasmuch as he admired her fortitude, it could not be long before her other charms intruded upon his notice.

He allowed his eyes to trace her figure as she sang, and he reflected on how very long it had been since he had lain with his wife—by this time, several months.

His healing body was an impediment, as were the rules set down by his physician.

"Your ribs are broken, Mr Darcy, and there is little to be done except to coddle them. No jarring activity. Carriage rides must be limited, do not ride your horse, do not run, no fencing, and you must not"—he paused, looking seriously at Darcy over his spectacles—"do anything vigorous."

Darcy did not misunderstand his meaning and was dismayed at the prospect of such a limitation. "For how long?"

"Six to eight weeks, sir, and believe me when I say that to disobey this order is solely to your own detriment."

Elizabeth knew of this restriction as well as the doctor's none-too-veiled suggestion, but she was not as distressed as Darcy. "Six weeks is nothing. We shall manage."

Thus, he surprised her this night by going to her, a mere three weeks after the eventful evening at Towton Hall. He sat behind her on the piano bench, his fingers grazing her bosom while he kissed her neck, but she merely looked at him over her shoulder, a bit scolding. "Have you already forgotten the doctor's orders?"

"The doctor is an old fool," Darcy murmured into her ear then kissed the side of her face.

"He is not!" She laughed.

"He is. Surely, no one who has a wife as beautiful as mine could refrain from sharing her bed for six weeks. The very notion is preposterous."

"You are healing well. I would not wish to imperil that."

"The only thing that imperils me is the fact that I am so desperate for you, I cannot bear it." He kissed her again, doing his best to tantalise and arouse her through her dress. "Your bodice comes up far too high. I must speak to your dressmaker."

She laughed again. "I am setting a good example for our sister."

"Hang Georgiana," he said into the curls at the base of her neck. "She will wear them too low anyway."

His ministrations were having the desired effect. Elizabeth leaned into him, her breath coming more quickly. "I believe I might have an idea," he whispered.

"Yes?"

"The effort will be mostly yours." He gave her a naughty smile when she turned to look at him. "And naturally, I shall insist that you not be too jarring in your movements."

With that, he stood and pulled her to her feet. "Come along now, Mrs Darcy. I can see that you are ready to ravish me."

"YOU ARE SORE." ELIZABETH LOOKED AT HIM IN DISMAY. "I CAN SEE IT on your face. I believe I must have been too jarring."

"A slight ache," he told her. "Nothing of note, and in any case, the ache I had previously was far more pressing. You have cared for it nicely, my dear, and believe me when I say that you jarred everything in just the right way."

She giggled. "You are a naughty man." She kissed his cheek. "I love you."

"I love you, my Lizzy, so very much."

She settled in the bed next to him, lying on her back and staring at the canopy. She did not speak, but through the gathering darkness, he could see she was deep in thought.

"What is it?" he asked quietly.

She turned her face towards him. "What do you mean?

"I can see there is something on your mind."

She demurred, turning away with a slight shrug of her shoulders.

Darcy watched her for another moment. "Do you know what I have sometimes wondered?"

She looked back at him again and shook her head.

"During the autumn when we first met in Hertfordshire, at times, I would see a look of sadness or fear about you, generally in the oddest moments: for example, at the Netherfield ball. I now understand it, but then I did not. I have often wondered what might have happened if I had enquired about your low spirits."

She laughed lightly. "What would you have said to me? 'Miss Bennet, you have an odd, sad look about you that is in direct contrast to the lively music and rampant flirtation ongoing herein. Pray, tell me what ails you.'"

"I might have. Or perhaps I might simply have tried to be a friend to you, and you would have confessed to me unprompted."

She understood his meaning and smiled faintly.

"So now you will understand when I tell you that I am your friend, and there should not be secrets between us." He turned his head on the pillow, his gaze upon her. "Whatever it is that you are feeling, I would wish to serve as your confidante if you would so honour me."

There was a prolonged pause as she considered his request. Finally, she spoke. "You have no doubt wondered about my behaviour the night of…the night when everything occurred."

He reached for her hand. "What I have wondered about most is why you would undertake such a foolish thing as to bait him as you did."

She leaned up on her elbow, a motion he felt rather than saw as the room had grown fully dark. "I did not truly wish to seduce him."

"Of course not."

"I wanted to hear him say what he did—I needed to hear it."

"You played a dangerous game. Even if he had confessed to all, there is little you might have done with the information save for the fact that Fitzwilliam and Hanley were outside the door and heard it."

"I was exceedingly angry, and angry people do not act from reason."

"Why were you so angry?"

She edged closer, laying her head on Darcy's pillow. "I had read the last of Henry's journals that day."

"Oh?" Unexpectedly, Darcy felt a tear fall from her eyes onto his cheek. "Elizabeth, why—"

"It was a scheme, and I was a part of it! Nothing more than a pawn in the game."

He said nothing, knowing very well to what she referred, but hoping against hope she had not learned the truth.

Her voice from the darkness was angry, shaking, and sad, and there was a soft thud as she tossed herself back on her pillow. "It was always a lie. His plan was detailed in his journal: to find a naive young country girl who would bear him a son to thwart his brother. That was all it was. It was not me; it was never me. He did not love me. He loved his heritage and his money and wanted to keep them from his brother. I just happened to be there, a means to an end."

He felt the sadness for her; a long held, cherished notion of a perfect love had been taken away. It would be a loss that would mark her, he knew, and he hoped he might somehow say the right thing to take that sadness from her.

She drew a deep, shuddering breath. "Did you know?"

He reached out blindly, and feeling her hair, he gently moved a curl from her cheek and tucked it behind her ear. "Hanley told me what he knew of Henry's plan."

There was a moment of silence until she spoke again, bitterly. "I was an excellent pawn after all. I went right along with the plan, gave him all that he needed: a wife, a son, and all of my love. Then, when he was gone, I did everything I was ordered to do: I sent my son away, I lived my disguise, and I did as I was told. I held nothing back. I was all they wished me to be."

Her voice grew louder and angrier. "To know it was just a lie! All I went through—the hiding, the disguise, the fear, and the sorrow—I managed because I believed I was doing it to honour his memory. I wished to preserve his legacy for his son and for his family name. For a farce, nothing more than a farce!" She raised the coverlet to her eyes, and he felt her shoulders shaking. "None of it was worth anything."

Darcy pulled her into his embrace, wincing at the slight pain it caused. "That is not wholly true. You preserved the legacy on behalf of your son after all."

She continued, seeming not to have heard him. "To have found the happiness—the short-lived, cruelly aborted happiness that I had with you—only to be tricked again! I did as I was told I must, only to find I was once again the unwitting fool, and for what? Do you know why Francis wanted me?"

"The hidden fortune in Warrington Castle."

She laughed angrily. "A fool's quest, but Francis believed I knew where it was. He thought I had solved the cipher and planned to use me to retrieve the supposed grand fortune buried in the walls of Warrington Castle.

"Used." She inhaled deeply. "Used to make a son, used to find a treasure, just used. I could take no more. I was used up, my heart taken away, and my soul filled with nothing but indignation. So I provoked him. I knew I played a dangerous game, but I could not stop myself. I suppose I thought—"

She broke off, chuckling a bit.

"Thought what?"

"I had my little gun, and I suppose some part of me believed I might be brave enough to shoot him if it came to that."

"You had a gun?"

"A gift from Lord Matlock. It proved useful to Mr Hanley when he and Colonel Fitzwilliam chased Francis into the streets, although your cousin did remark on its girlish character.

"I have always been my mother's least favourite daughter," she continued. "Always. Jane is the favourite for her beauty, and Lydia is next favoured for her liveliness. Kitty and Mary vex her in turns, and then there is me. I have never done a thing to suit her save for the day I came home and told her a wealthy earl wished to marry me.

"It seemed like my vindication. I should not have seen it so. But for all that I was then—an opinionated country girl inclined towards muddy walks and too much reading—it seemed that since Henry found me acceptable, then surely, I was acceptable. With Henry's love I was assured that I must have been, in some way, admirable and worthy of esteem in my own right."

She sighed. "It is silly to allow this to affect me so, but it has. I would like to have known that Elizabeth Bennet was a lady of worth. It does not really matter now as my experiences have made me into something different."

His ribs ached, but his heart ached even more. "Do you recall when first you loved me?"

Elizabeth thought for a moment. "It came on too gradually. I was in the middle before I knew I had begun."

"I know the very moment when first I knew I loved you, but I shall not confess it unless you swear to believe me."

"Very well, I swear to believe you. You are no master of disguise, and I do not think you would begin now simply to appease my wounded vanity."

"True," he admitted. "You will recall my offence at the assembly in Meryton."

"How could I forget it?" She squeezed his hand to remove any reproach from her words. "It was quite infamous in its incivility."

"Do you remember what you did?"

"I do not remember doing anything at all."

It was easy to be lost in the well-worn, beloved recollection. He was almost there: hearing the music and smelling the scent of candle wax and flowers as she brushed by him. Even the feel of his heart pounding and his breath sticking in his chest were recalled with unusual clarity.

"You rose from your seat in a fluid motion. Whenever I think back on it, I am struck by your elegance and grace, but at the time, I could not think so clearly. I was rendered motionless watching you. You strolled towards me. When our eyes met, you raised your brow a little —just enough to assure me that you had heard my rudeness—and you went to your friends. It appeared that you all mocked me though I cannot know whether you truly did. In any case, I did not care, for it was in that very moment that I knew."

"What did you know?"

He replied with great tenderness, "I knew we could not end any way but this one: the two of us, together, forever. I loved you then, knowing nothing about you, and as I grew to know you, I loved you more still."

She leaned up on her elbow. "That is a great deal to glean from just a look."

"It was all I needed. Anything I learned from there only confirmed that it was in you where my happiness must lie. I did struggle against it, I acknowledge it again, but even before I met Lady Courtenay, I knew I needed you. I needed Miss Elizabeth Bennet just as I needed the air I breathed, and I do not doubt for a moment that, had you not turned up in London, a countess in disguise, there would have been another plan for the pair of us to unite. It could be no other way.

"You see, I did not need your fortune, and I did not need your standing in society. What I really, truly needed was Miss Elizabeth Bennet. I needed an impertinent miss with decided tendencies towards laughter and teasing, who would take me as I was, a proud, lonely man, and make me into something far better.

"To know your love has made me wealthier than I ever could have imagined. Even when we were merely friends, when you assured me many times that you would never love me, it was still far better than anything I knew before. The loneliness that was always within me had begun to dissipate because we were united in something—be it friendship or courtship, it was the two of us, together. Of course, when you actually grew to love me, that was vastly better still, but I shall always treasure our friendship."

Softly, Elizabeth said, "I am glad you never gave up, no matter how much I discouraged you."

"I am too." He kissed her tenderly and looked at her for several long moments then added, softly but firmly, "I shall never believe that Henry did not love you. No matter where it began, coming to know you, he must have loved you. I know what it is to have your love, and it cannot be resisted. He loved you, yet how grateful I am that it is I, and not he, who has you."

EPILOGUE

Summer 1813

They resolved to make the trip to Pemberley easy, travelling for just a few hours each day with frequent stops. Although their intentions were good, Darcy found himself instructing the coachmen to carry on such that, in the end, the journey took only a half day more than was usual.

Upon reaching the rise from where the house could be seen, they alit from the carriage. Elizabeth stood within Darcy's embrace, her back to his chest, as they looked out upon it. They stood in silence for a long time until she spoke. "Is it odd that I should feel such a sense of homecoming in a place where I have spent only a few months?"

"I am glad you feel that way."

"There is so much of you in Pemberley, and of Pemberley in you. It feels natural and good to be here, and I feel more at peace now than I have these past months together." She stood on tiptoe to kiss him as the coachmen looked away diligently. "I look forward to putting the past months behind us here."

"As do I. Pemberley is a wonderful place, and I have always loved it, but never more so than the time we spent here last summer. Let us always have as much felicity as we did then."

"We shall," Elizabeth agreed just as Henry poked his head out the window of the carriage where he had been napping with Annie.

"Mama?" he asked. "Are we home?"

Darcy answered, "We are indeed, Henry."

PEMBERLEY WORKED ITS USUAL MAGIC ON ELIZABETH'S SPIRITS. SHE and Darcy indulged themselves in walks, picnics, and long days together in their chambers, interspersed with happy times playing with Henry outside on the lawns and in the gardens. Elizabeth planted a new breed of roses, shocking the gardeners when she herself took up a shovel and became involved in the digging, young Henry right next to her with his own spade.

When they had been at Pemberley just above a fortnight, a package for Darcy arrived in the post, and he soon revealed it was a gift for Elizabeth. He presented it to her later that night in their chambers.

Elizabeth smiled at him. "You do spoil me, love."

She opened the box and removed an unusual, richly bejewelled chain of keys. She laughed when she saw it, turning it about to see it at all angles. "I have never seen one such as this—or with so many keys."

"You do know, Elizabeth, that I would tell you anything. I think both of us have had more than enough of secrets. You have entrusted me with your deepest feelings and fears, and I am always willing to do the same."

"You are unfailingly honest," she assured him. "I have not the least doubt of that."

"Thank you, but I still wished you to have this." He picked up the jewellery. "These are the keys for everything important here and at all my properties. There are keys to all my safes; to my private box where I store mementos, journals, and whatnot; to the room where the estate books are kept; to my box at the bank in London…" He went on, explaining each key and what it would unlock.

Elizabeth was astonished. "I know of no wife who has such access to all of her husband's doings."

"I would tell you anything you wished to know, but with this, you never need ask. The truth is yours to own, and you hold the keys to unlock it as you like."

"You know I do not need this. I trust you with everything that I am."

"I believe that, but you have it, nevertheless, along with my permission to use the keys according to your own desires. Anything you want to see—go see it. I have nothing to hide from you. My correspondence, my diaries, the books to Pemberley, the house in London—they are all open to you with my blessing."

She had no intention of ever using the keys. She believed that she could ask him anything, and he would answer with truth. Darcy had proclaimed that disguise of every sort was his abhorrence, and she believed it to be true; still, the keys were a fine thing to have, and she loved him dearly for giving them to her.

Then she saw his journal.

She had not seen any great tendency in Darcy towards recording his thoughts and activities, but one day, she noticed a journal on his shelf in their sitting room.

She warred within herself—had he not told her she might look at anything? Would it be dishonourable if she took just a peep? Would it indicate a lack of trust on her part? She was just curious, not doubtful of him. She knew he would tell her anything, yet there were things he might not think to tell her or might think were not of interest. But everything about him interested her.

A day or so later, Darcy was off on his horse, Henry was down for his nap, and Elizabeth found herself a bit at ends. After a moment of consideration, she went to the sitting room upstairs.

She found it just where he had left it, and she held it for a moment, staring at the cover and feeling ashamed of her intense, shameless need to know what he had written. He was completely candid with her, so why this insatiable need to look into his journal?

Laying aside her guilt, she opened it and started to read. It began with Darcy going to Hertfordshire in the autumn of 1811. There was a thorough description of seeing her for the first time. Turning the page, she saw where he had drawn two neat and precise columns. One column was titled: "Love at First Sight is Absurd." In this column, he had written seven to eight reasons why this was a foolish and improbable notion. The second column was titled: "Love at First Sight Can Exist." Only one thing was written there: *Miss Elizabeth Bennet— although I have not yet spoken to her, she is mine, and I am hers.*

That made her cry, and much to her chagrin, several of her tears dropped onto the words, making the ink run. *So much for secrecy.*

The journal continued with Darcy mentioning simultaneous hope and dread of seeing her at events that she had not attended, and finally, his pleasure in spending the evening in her company at Lucas Lodge. She was almost amused by his great consternation at falling in love with one he did not believe he could marry. His resistance might have pained her before, but now, with all they had come through, it seemed almost juvenile and so very sweet. She savoured the words as one might a fine wine, allowing her eyes to drink them in.

The journal was not wholly dedicated to his musings of her. There were other things too, such as his impressions of Hertfordshire as a whole—some good, some bad. He did not profess any direct censure of her parents though there was one passage where he wondered how she and Jane could be so different from them.

She felt regret in seeing his preparations for the Netherfield ball. He had anticipated the evening far more than she realised, and she was surprised to learn that she had slighted him for a dance that night and that he had had words with his cousin.

However, what truly shocked her would come in the ensuing pages.

Following the Netherfield ball, there was a large gap in the time between writings—albeit with some intriguing insights on taking a wife, written in January before they met in London—and then he wrote of her again. Attempts at four syllable words were forgotten as Darcy expounded in great detail on the explicit nature of his desire for her.

Elizabeth felt her cheeks burn as she came upon an elaborate sort of daydream involving a cabin on the grounds of Pemberley where no servants, no children, no sisters, and no one else with any claim to them would be within any reasonable distance. Evidently, he required this distance as loud, rapturous cries—from her—were anticipated.

She gasped and laughed a little. "Fitzwilliam Darcy! When did you write these things?" She was in equal measure appalled and excited though as she read on, excitement gained ground.

She had not read to the end of all he evidently wished to do with her—and what he wished she might do to him—when she heard a sound in the hall that made her jump. Quickly, she closed the journal, shoved it under a stack of books on her night table, and stood, hurriedly smoothing her hair and fanning her cheeks, willing herself to calm even as her pulse raced.

It was nothing and no one. She could not think what she had heard, but the hall was still with nary a sound.

Elizabeth looked at the spot where she had hidden the journal.

Leave it alone now. Anything that causes such guilt and alarm can be to no good. That fixed her in her spot for nigh on two minutes before she sat and snatched the book out while telling herself she would just read to the end of it.

Then she found his illustrations.

Of her husband's skill at drawing, she had been ignorant. Part of her admired the precision of his strokes even while another part blushed anew at the pictures he had drawn—*of her! Of them!*—Such a scandalous thing! What had possessed him to make such drawings and leave them for anyone to see?

The truly amazing part was that the likeness of her was quite accurate. She did not know whether to be impressed, embarrassed, flattered, or a combination thereof, seeing the skill with which he had rendered her.

My cheeks must be permanently scarlet! The effect on her spirit was no less pronounced. She was glad he was out for, was he within, she surely would toss herself upon him without restraint. He would not object, but he would wish for an explanation, and she would be fully exposed as having not only read the journals but for relishing the naughty bits.

I must put this down straightaway. Just another page more, and I shall put this back, never to see it again.

With a deep breath, she turned the next page, certain that even more debauchery awaited her.

Instead, there was a note.

Yes, Mrs Darcy, I suspected you might be tempted to examine my journal. I never had the inclination to record my thoughts except for the time I went to Hertfordshire. My uncle suggested it to me, but I found it a tedious business, particularly as I am far too greatly disposed towards inward thoughts even without writing them down.

My words of love for you were written in Hertfordshire. They are true and just as I felt them with no embellishment or amendment. Do you see how you tortured me, my dearest love?

The pages following the recounting of the Netherfield ball were written recently, but the longing contained in them is no less fierce. For while my experience in Hertfordshire taught me to believe in the notion of loving someone at first sight, it was not until I knew you in full that I could apprehend the notion of the best part of love. For only now do I know the sweetness of your lips and the completion I can only feel when we are joined together as man and wife, a pleasure to both body and spirit. Only now do I know that you twist your hands when you are nervous and your eyes light up when you are amused. I know you as a mother, as a wife, as a hostess, and as a mistress to my homes. Each and every part makes up the whole of my love for you. I fell in love at first sight, but it is a love that grows stronger and more stout with every second I spend with you.

Now off to your horse, my sweet, and do not tarry. The stable boys will direct you to the cabin where I await you, eager to make this journal less of a dream and more of a memory. Do not tarry lest I grow cold, for I am attired much as in the second drawing.

Lastly, Happy Anniversary my beloved, dearest wife. The year has not been an easy one for either of us, yet there is no one who is happier than I this day for the very great privilege of calling you my wife. I adore you, my sweet Elizabeth, more so with each day that passes.

Elizabeth gasped and then giggled. Could he be serious? But he was generally serious, and jokes of this sort were decidedly not his wont.

To go to the cabin would be to admit to her prying. She glanced down at the journal now closed on her lap. Nevertheless, the images were engraved upon her mind.

She thought about it for only a moment, and then she was off, deciding it would be imprudent to waste time changing into her riding dress.

August 1813

Darcy entered the house after an early morning ride, greatly anticipating his breakfast. He was surprised to find that his wife was not yet downstairs.

Soon after, Mrs Reynolds entered the room. "Sir, Burney has informed me that Mrs Darcy is not yet risen."

"Not yet risen!" Darcy was shocked. Rarely had he known Elizabeth to sleep beyond half past seven, and here it was nearly ten o'clock. He finished his coffee in a gulp. "I believe I shall go see whether she is unwell."

He took the steps in twos, arriving in Elizabeth's bedchamber in minutes. As he had been told, she was still slumbering peacefully. He sat next to her on the bed and felt her forehead. It was cool.

His touch woke her. "Fitzwilliam," she said sleepily, opening her eyes a crack and allowing them to drift closed again. "Good morning, love."

"Good morning. Are you unwell?"

"No," she replied, her eyes still closed. "I just cannot wake today. I am so tired."

"Well," he said doubtfully, "you have been busy."

At last, she opened her eyes. "Not so much busy as lazy." She smiled. "What time is it?"

"It is just gone ten."

"Ten o'clock!" she exclaimed, sitting upright. "Dear me! How could I sleep so long?" Darcy was relieved to see her languor dissipate as her customary spirit emerged.

He captured her lips, murmuring against them, "Not so hasty, Mrs Darcy. After all, I have you here looking so charmingly dishevelled…" He deepened the kiss and moved over her.

His amorous feeling was quickly quashed by a gagging sound coming from her throat. Pulling back, he saw an odd expression on her face. "What is it?"

"Nothing! Oh, nothing at all, love, come here." She pulled him to her, but at the last, could not manage and turned her head. It looked as though she was trying not to breathe.

"I have been for a ride." He spoke uncertainly. "Perhaps I ought to have freshened myself before coming to you.

"Of course not." She turned red, obviously dismayed to have offended him. "I do not know why, but smells are troubling me this morning. I feel a bit nauseated, that is all, and the smell of the horse… And I believe you had coffee? It does not sit well with me."

"You are ill."

"I assure you, I am well. A bit of a stomach upset. It will pass." She moved to get out of the bed. "I am so sorry. It will be much better later."

He could not deny he was a bit offended. To have his relations with his wife cut short because he smelled of horse and coffee? It was humiliating. Rising he went into his bedchamber straightaway, intending to ring his man for a bath.

Elizabeth could see he was upset when he left her, and who would not be? She felt mortified to have embarrassed him. She had tried to suppress her gagging, but when she smelled the coffee on his breath and the horse on his person, it felt as if someone had reached a hand down into her stomach, clenched it in their fist, and twisted it mercilessly. At one point, the sensation was bad enough that she believed she might vomit.

Should I tell him of my suspicions? It was early, too early. Her courses had been missed twice, but there had not been a quickening, nor could she expect one for another six weeks or so. He had been so hurt. Perhaps she would tell him, emphasising that nothing was certain yet.

He was in a bath when she went to him, causing her greater dismay.

"May I rub your back?" She had come to know in the brief months of their marriage that after a long ride, he enjoyed having his back rubbed vigorously. He looked sulky so she set to work, leaning her body against the tub. "I am so sorry."

"I suppose I smelled dreadful."

"Not really." She paused in her ministrations. "However, I can recall another time when I was excessively affected by smells."

"When?" he asked, still sounding glum.

"When I was increasing."

His offence was forgotten immediately, and he turned in the bath so quickly that water spilled all over her and the floor. "Lizzy!"

"Nothing is certain," she told him quickly. She laughed as he splashed more water on her, rising up over the edge of the tub to capture her in a kiss. "The early signs are there, but we have some weeks until the quickening, and until then, anything can happen."

He kissed her again, spilling more water over the floor while murmuring endearments and exclamations of joy.

"Pray, do not be excited yet. I told you so you might understand that I could be more sensitive than usual to smells or tastes. It will eventually go away."

"I shall be understanding of that." His grin could not be suppressed.

"I am excited too," she replied. "But now, we just must wait."

October 1813

Darcy and Elizabeth sat silently against the headboard of her bed. She wore her lightest nightgown despite the chill in the air, and it was pressed tightly around her form. When one looked at her in a certain way, it was clear to see the small mound at the bottom of her abdomen though in her clothing, she still looked much the same. Her maid had noticed, as had Darcy, but no one else had remarked on it or knew the truth of it.

Darcy had his hands pressed tightly against the small mound as they silently waited for some movement.

"There!" He exclaimed excitedly. "Was that it?"

She shook her head. "I am hungry. That was my stomach growling."

He gave her a quick frown. "Let us ring for a snack for you then. You must eat."

"If I ate as often as I wished it, I would soon be as large around as I am tall. I believe this child must have your appetite, for such a hunger I have never before known." They grinned at each other, and Darcy again concentrated on her abdomen.

When five minutes more had elapsed, Elizabeth said, gently, "The babe is asleep."

Darcy spoke to her stomach. "This is your papa speaking. While I would not take you from your nap, if you could oblige me with a kick, I would be most grateful."

Elizabeth had felt the baby quicken a week or so earlier, and in the time since, it had become Darcy's dearest wish to feel the growing limbs of his child moving about within her. Evidently, this was not the night.

"Shall we meet here at the same time tomorrow?" he teased his wife.

"I believe I can accommodate you, sir," she teased back. Then she said seriously, "How I long for you to feel him!"

"In time, I shall."

They settled into the bed, and both were soon asleep.

Darcy awoke a little after two in the morning. Elizabeth did not move as he left the bed to throw another log on the fire. With only three days until November, the chill of autumn was full upon Derbyshire.

He returned, now feeling fully awake. His wife slumbered on her side facing him, and he beheld her, feeling the now-familiar sensation of peaceful joy that he had finally regained after their long ordeal of the previous winter. The anniversary of Wickham's capture had gone unmentioned, and no other dates significant to those events would be marked. Both he and Elizabeth had resolved to forget it all.

Elizabeth was deep in sleep, and he slid closer to place his palms on her abdomen. He watched her face anxiously, but she did not stir.

"Darling child," he whispered into the darkness. "I am impatient to know you, and it will be an eternity until I shall meet you, so please, let me feel you. Just a little kick or a punch will suffice."

It took several minutes, and Darcy waited patiently in the dark… until, suddenly, he felt it. An unmistakable, firm thump, not once, not twice, but thrice upon his hands. He could not help himself—tears sprang to his eyes, and he laughed aloud, forgetting that Elizabeth slept.

"You did it! You kicked me!" He crowed with happiness, all the while keeping his palms on her abdomen. "How marvellous!"

"Fitzwilliam," Elizabeth spoke sleepily. "Are you shouting?"

"I felt the baby!" He moved his voice to a hush. "I am sorry to wake you. I felt the kick, and I could not restrain myself! Oh my dearest! We shall have a child together!"

Elizabeth gave him a sleepy smile. He moved his hands from her stomach to cup her face, and he kissed her. "I love you, Elizabeth Darcy. You are an amazing woman."

February 1814

Elizabeth was in her bath, and Darcy removed his coat and waistcoat, eagerly imagining joining her. His cravat was tossed onto a nearby chair.

She was staring sullenly at her body when he entered, and he moved behind her and lifted her hair to kiss her neck. His hand slid around to her breasts, which had grown tantalisingly generous in the past days.

"Surely, you are not serious."

"My desirable wife reclines naked before me." He kissed her neck again. "I assure you, I am quite serious."

"Desirable?" She turned to look at him, and he did not miss her incredulous stare as she gestured at her rounded form. "What part of this can you possibly find appealing? I cannot see my toes, Fitzwilliam!"

"You are beautiful," Darcy protested in surprise. He had never seen her distraught over her looks, and he did indeed find her ripe figure enticing.

"I walked in the garden this morning."

"I hope you were warm enough."

"I was plenty warm, I assure you, sweating and heaving like some miserable old farm nag. You know the little fountain, the one that marks the entry to the maze?"

He nodded.

"By the time I reached it, I had scarcely the vigour for one more step. I looked back at the house and could not imagine how I might return to it. The fountain! A scant half a mile from the house! Yet I required a rest before I was able to return." She shook her head in disgust, staring down at her stomach.

"One month more, my beloved. Our child will be here before long."

"What if I die?" She looked up at him. "What if I die and your final memories are of my looking grotesque?"

"Please do not say such things, even in jest."

"I assure you, I do not jest! I could die and these will be your final memories of me, looking as I do now! Please, darling, promise me this…"

"Anything, love." He was growing alarmed by her mood, as well as the reminder of the risks of childbirth.

"Never lose those naughty pictures you drew of me, for if I should die, they are the most flattering to my person. I looked at them just the other day, and I must say, I appeared quite pretty in them. My waist was so small and trim, especially in the one where I am sitting on—"

"Yes, yes," Darcy interrupted her, laughing. "I know the one. It will be a funeral of note as I show my sketches with a solemn explanation that it was your express wish to be remembered as shown."

Elizabeth would not laugh. "I never thought myself any great beauty, but I at least had a nice enough figure with which to console myself."

"My love, I assure you"—He kissed her once more before lending his hand to assist her in rising from the bath. Taking a towel, he wrapped her in it, gently rubbing her dry—"I have long admired your beauty, including your figure, as you well know, yet you are never more beautiful to me than now."

"You are mad," she whispered.

He pulled the towel tightly around her so she would not take a chill. "I am indeed madly in love with you, particularly when I see every part of you marked by the life of my child within. You see a large, rounded stomach that obscures your toes, but I see you love me enough to bear my child."

Her eyes grew soft as he reached for another towel and dried her hair, pausing to inhale its scent. He heard her sniff a little at his ministrations.

"Fitzwilliam…"

"Yes?"

"I love you enough to bear you ten children." She wrapped her arms around him the best she could, and their child kicked frantically between them.

March 1814

"I beg your pardon, sir?" Pemberley's butler stood nervously in the doorway of Darcy's study.

Darcy looked up.

"It is Mrs Darcy, sir…no, no, not that, not yet." He quickly realised Darcy might suppose that his wife was beginning her labour.

"Yes, what is it?"

"Mrs Reynolds asked me to tell you that Mrs Darcy is moving furniture in the music room."

Darcy shrugged. Odd perhaps, but then, much of the time Elizabeth had been increasing was marked by unusual behaviour. "She may rearrange as she wishes."

"Forgive me, sir, but I mean to say she is moving it herself. The footmen are trying to keep apace of her, but as soon as she puts one thing down, she is on to the next. Perhaps you might be better able to stop her?"

Darcy ran to the music room and found his wife lugging a harp to one side as several of the footman scurried around, taking things from her.

"Fitzwilliam!" she exclaimed happily. "I cannot think how I did not notice it before but this room is arranged entirely wrong! You see, I have had the men move the pianoforte over to that corner, which will better allow more room for dancing should we wish for it, and then the harp seemed awkwardly placed, and—"

"Mrs Darcy." Darcy glanced at his footmen, who were admirably courteous and sweating through their labours. Evidently, Elizabeth had been at it for some time. "I do not think you should exert yourself in this way just now."

"Nonsense. I am strong as an ox—nay, stronger than an ox. In any case, I shall have no time to redecorate once the baby has come. I must get these rooms done now."

"Perhaps if you made up some sketches," Darcy said desperately.

"Sketches will not do because, when one item is moved, more changes become evident. I must move a thing before I know best how to do another." She smiled and pushed a damp curl off her face.

Mrs Reynolds entered and motioned to Darcy. He stepped aside with her for a moment. "It is not uncommon for a lady to become unusually energetic and desirous of change to her home as her time approaches. We shall set it to rights later. Perhaps you might turn her mind to a different activity?"

Darcy returned to Elizabeth, who had lifted a heavy footstool to move it towards the window. He took it from her and handed it to a footman. "My dear, it is so nice today that I long for a walk by the gardens. Shall we see whether the roses show any signs of life?"

Thus was Elizabeth diverted, though Darcy had to admit that his effort that day was exhausting as they walked for several hours.

Two days later

At last, the day was upon them. Jane and Bingley were visiting Pemberley so that Jane could be of use to her sister. Mrs Bennet was told that the child was not due until May to avoid her "assistance," but Lady Gardiner knew the truth and joined them as well.

Lord and Lady Saye also arrived with their infant son. They had named him Edward Jonathan Fitzwilliam. He was a fine-looking, healthy boy, and he had weighed nearly ten pounds at birth. Elizabeth went a bit pale when she saw him.

"A strapping lad, is he not?" Darcy observed.

"The size of his head…" she trailed off nervously, then looked at Lady Saye with a bit of relief. "She seems to have recovered nicely."

Elizabeth laboured for some time—through an entire day and an exceedingly long night. It was a night unlike anything Darcy had ever endured as he was plagued by unceasing worry for the lives of his wife and child, and he was impatient to meet, at long last, his son or daughter. He remained with Elizabeth for as long as he could before he was banned to pace his study and snap at his cousin and Bingley, each of whom made various attempts to distract him.

"Perhaps if you have a daughter, Darcy," Saye suggested, "we might arrange a match between her and my son."

"Not if you raise him to act anything like you, we shall not," Darcy retorted.

"What does that mean?"

"You know exactly what I mean, and if you think I shall permit my little girl to be subjected to—"

"The future Earl of Matlock is not good enough for you?" Saye scoffed.

"Now, now," Bingley interrupted nervously. "There is, as yet, no daughter to argue over. Let us await the child and then we may begin to arrange the matches."

"Easy for you to say, you have a son," Darcy muttered to the window.

"And you might too," Bingley consoled him.

It was nearly midnight when Mrs Reynolds came for him. "Mr Darcy, a young gentleman awaits your call in Mrs Darcy's bedchamber." She smiled her assurances at him. "Mrs Darcy has done very well and is in good health."

He stopped for a moment, allowing the idea to settle over him. *I have a son.*

Elizabeth was looking remarkably well when he entered the room, albeit a bit tired. He could not deny the happiness that marked her features and knew it was mirrored in his own silly, enormous grin.

He joined her on the bed, kissing her forehead as she moved the small bundle into his arms. For a moment, he could not speak; the future of Pemberley, of the Darcys, his own child, rested in his arms. It astonished him that such a tiny creature could embody so much. The baby opened his eyes—beautiful dark eyes, just like his mother's—and simply stared.

Father and mother gazed at him in bliss. "Did we settle on Thomas?" Darcy asked, referring to the many conversations they had had about their favoured baby's names.

"I think it suits him," Elizabeth replied.

"Then it is settled. Mr Thomas Darcy, welcome to the family."

They sat admiring his tiny hands and feet and touching the downy curls atop his head. Although exhausted, Elizabeth seemed unable to sleep, and Darcy was content to sit with her, caught up in the elation of the moment.

There was a small knock on the door, and Elizabeth bid the visitor to enter. It was Henry.

"Henry!" Darcy was shocked. "What do you do at this hour, Son? You should be resting."

"I heard my baby was here." He peered at the child in Darcy's arms, climbing onto the bed beside his parents. "Is this my brother?"

Darcy smiled and held the baby so Henry could examine him. "This is Thomas."

Henry stared a moment, none too impressed. "You may play with my things but do not pull Annie's tail and do not rip the pages in my books."

"You must be his protector," Darcy informed him seriously. "That is what big brothers do most of all."

"Yes, Papa. See how dangerous I am?" With that, he leapt from the bed to the largest space in the room and embarked on a series of frantic and poorly executed kicks and punches designed to take down an invisible assailant.

His nightshirt tangled around him, and just as Darcy was about issue a warning, his shirt bound him, causing him to fall face first on the floor with an undignified thump.

Darcy moved to assist, but Henry jumped up in a trice with a big smile on his face. "I am well!" Then he burst into laughter, which made Darcy and Elizabeth laugh. Even little Thomas opened his eyes, peering sleepily at the loud noises.

Darcy handed the baby back to Elizabeth and lifted Henry onto the bed. Henry again looked at his new brother. "You see, Thomas? You have come to a very happy family. We even laugh when we fall down." He kissed the baby's little cheek as Darcy did the same to Elizabeth.

"We are a happy family indeed," said Elizabeth. "And so shall we always be."

Pemberley, 1848

They were a loud and merry group that gathered at Pemberley that year; indeed, when they were all together, even the largest dining table could scarcely contain them all. There were scores of Bingleys and Courtenays and Darcys, along with Ellises and du Champs since the marriages of their daughters. The grandchildren ran mad in the Grand Hall—Elizabeth would often scold them for knocking things about but Darcy never quite had the heart to do so. If a broken statue was the price paid for youthful merriment, so be it. He had long ago decided he would much rather be remembered as the amiable grandfather than the grandfather with the excellent art. In any case, his grandchildren adored him and he would not have it otherwise. He was never more happy than he was in these wonderful times when Pemberley's halls bustled with laughter and noise.

When the ladies withdrew after dinner, Darcy sat with his three sons: Henry, or Lord Courtenay; Thomas Darcy, his heir, and Colonel Edward Darcy. Fine distinguished men, all of them and as dear to one another as any brothers could be.

"I have a bit of interesting news," said Henry. "You will all remember the old cipher?"

"The one which concerned the fortune at Warrington?"

"Yes," Henry said. "I brought it out recently for James." James was Henry's eldest and only son. At only ten years of age, he had shown a remarkable aptitude for mathematics and his parents were always seeking little puzzles and codes to divert him.

"Did he find the fortune?" asked Thomas with a laugh. The fortune which had caused so much trouble to their parents was spoken of often, in the manner of myths and legends.

"He did not," replied Henry. "However he found a mistake made by our mother and grandfather Bennet when they deciphered it."

"Pray do not suggest she made a mistake," Darcy advised. "Call it an alternate solution if you must but not a mistake."

His advice caused the gentlemen to chuckle; their mother was much beloved but rarely inclined to admit she made mistakes.

"In any case," said Henry, "it would seem that there is most certainly a hidden fortune."

For a moment, everyone ceased moving. Darcy had begun to raise a glass to his lips but stopped halfway there. His jaw dropped, and he lowered the drink with a thump on the table. "Can that be so?"

"My son did not find it—but I did." Henry lowered his eyes, shaking his head. "I can hardly credit it myself."

"How much?" Edward was, as always, just slightly too bold, but in this case Darcy did not mind. He was, himself, mad to know.

When Henry named the sum, he did so quietly and the gentlemen around the table immediately gasped and then doubted the veracity of what they had heard. "How could that be!" "From the purses of simple market folk? No, I cannot credit it!"

"The money is there," Henry replied mildly. "It cannot be denied. My guess is that Lord Strange must have secured a bit of his own coin there as well."

"He did raise quite a lot of money for his troops," Darcy acknowledged. As Lord Strange had become the Earl of Derby back then, it had always been a bit of history that interested him. "He did not, perhaps, spend it all."

"Warrington was dear to him," Henry added. "They protected him as best they could. I think my father and uncle must have suspected his lordship's money was in there too, else they should not have been so keen to go after it."

"Well, good for Warrington then," said Thomas. "And good for James. It will be to his benefit after all."

"No," said Henry. "No, I do not think it shall after all."

The gentlemen looked at him with varying degrees of surprise marking their faces. Henry grinned and in that grin Darcy saw the little boy who had once sat at his feet and played, who had been so good natured his life long, and he knew some proud moment was about to transpire.

"That money came from the town," he explained. "Whether from their labours or their loyalty, it was theirs and though they are long gone now, I would like the descendants to obtain some benefit from it."

As his brothers and father looked on, Henry said, "I shall establish a school with a large library for the children in the town to learn to read and write. All of them, such as are able, shall be able to come and learn and the tutors shall be employed by Warrington—none of the families will need to part with a farthing for it."

"A capital idea," said Darcy. "I have always said that I cannot comprehend the neglect of a family library."

"You have indeed, sir," Henry replied with a smile.

And so it was that the legacy in Warrington Castle was used to establish the Bennet School in Lancashire where generations of children thenceforth, from the highest to the low, could learn to read and write and, eventually, learn mathematics and science.

Finis

ABOUT THE AUTHOR

Amy D'Orazio is a long time devotee of Jane Austen and fiction related to her characters. She began writing her own little stories to amuse herself during hours spent at sports practices and the like and soon discovered a passion for it. By far, however, the thing she loves most is the connexions she has made with readers and other writers of Austenesque fiction.

Amy currently lives in Pittsburgh with her husband and daughters, as well as three Jack Russell terriers who often make appearances (in a human form) in her book.

For more information about new releases, sales and promotions on books by Amy and other great authors, please visit www. QuillsAndQuartos.com.

facebook.com/amy.dorazioauthor

twitter.com/AllAbtAusten

ACKNOWLEDGMENTS

I owe an enormous debt of gratitude to all of those who made the publication of this book possible. Gail Warner whose praises are uniformly sung among those fortunate enough to be considered "her" authors—all the praise is well-deserved and then some! Much appreciation to Ellen Pickels who so diligently perfected the revamped work!

My beta readers for the original, unpolished manuscript of the Best Part of Love were Janet Foster, Debra Anne Watson and Caroline Anderson. Each of them made a significant contribution in shaping the story and I am extremely grateful to them for their contributions. Thank you ladies for all your help as well as your friendship!

Particular thanks to Claudine Pepe who urged me to submit my story for publication; I will happily admit that I would never have done so without her encouragement! Thank you Claudine, you are the best!

I would be terribly remiss if I did not acknowledge the support and friendship of those who have read this and other stories on A Happy Assembly. My thanks to you for reading my stories—you keep me striving to improve and to push my own boundaries and for that I am extremely thankful!

Last but surely not least, my deepest thanks to Tom, Allie and Lexi for making it possible for me to do this, and to my parents who taught me to think anything was possible. I love you all very much.

ALSO BY AMY D'ORAZIO

A Lady's Reputation

"Mr. Darcy, I am eager to hear your explanation for the fact that quite a few people believe we are engaged."

It starts with a bit of well-meant advice. Colonel Fitzwilliam suggests to his cousin Darcy that, before he proposes to Elizabeth Bennet in Kent, perhaps he ought to discuss his plans with their families first.

What neither man could have predicted however was that Lord Matlock would write the news to his sister, or that Viscount Saye would overhear and tell his friends, or that his friends might slip a little and let their friends know as well. The news spreads just as quickly through Hertfordshire once Mrs Bennet opens the express Mr Bennet receives from Mr Darcy, and in a matter of days, it seems like everyone knows that Mr Darcy has proposed marriage to Elizabeth Bennet.

Everyone, that is, except Elizabeth herself.

Her refusal is quick and definite—until matters of reputation, hers as well as Jane's, are considered. Then Mr Darcy makes another offer: summer at Pemberley so that Jane can be reunited with Mr Bingley and so that he can prove to Elizabeth he is not what she thinks of him. Falling in love with him is naturally impossible...but once she knows the man he truly is, will she be able to help herself?

A Short Period of Exquisite Felicity

Is not the very meaning of love that it surpasses every objection against it?

Jilted. Never did Mr. Darcy imagine it could happen to him.

But it has, and by Elizabeth Bennet, the woman who first hated and rejected him but then came to love him—he believed—and agree to be his wife. Alas, it is a short-lived, ill-fated romance that ends nearly as soon as it has begun. No reason is given.

More than a year since he last saw her—a year of anger, confusion, and despair—he receives an invitation from the Bingleys to a house party at Netherfield. Darcy is first tempted to refuse, but with the understanding that Elizabeth will not attend, he decides to accept.

When a letter arrives, confirming Elizabeth's intention to join them, Darcy resolves to meet her with indifference. He is determined that he will not demand answers to the questions that plague him. Elizabeth is also resolved to remain silent and hold fast to the secret behind her refusal. Once they are together, however, it proves difficult to deny the intense passion that still exists. Fury, grief, and profound love prove to be a combustible mixture. But will the secrets between them be their undoing?

Manufactured by Amazon.ca
Bolton, ON

33619798R00238